Save Me

Save Me

ELIZA FREED

FOREVER
YOURS

New York Boston

Copyright © 2015 by Eliza Freed

Excerpt from *Forgive Me* © 2014 by Eliza Freed

Cover design by Elizabeth Turner

Cover copyright © 2015 by Hachette Book Group

Forever Yours

Hachette Book Group

1290 Avenue of the Americas

New York, NY 10104

Hachettebookgroup.com

Twitter.com/foreverromance

First ebook and print on demand edition: March 2015

Forever Yours is an imprint of Grand Central Publishing.

The Forever Yours name and logo are trademarks of Hachette Book Group, Inc.

The publisher is not responsible for websites (or their content) that are not owned by the publisher.

The Hachette Speakers Bureau provides a wide range of authors for speaking events. To find out more, go to www.hachettespeakersbureau.com or call (866) 376-6591.

ISBN 978-1-4555-8359-1 (ebook edition)

ISBN 978-1-4555-8360-7 (print on demand edition)

To everyone who's ever said something crazy like,
"I think I'll write a book."

Save Me

Save Me

Prologue

Noble and I carry our boat as we wade into the calm sea. The water is flat with barely a break at the edge. It's more like a lake today than an ocean, and I welcome the peacefulness. Noble's birthday seems fitting to take *Mindless* out for a sail, I think as I pull myself over the side of the boat. We drove down after dinner, avoiding the crowds, and it couldn't be more perfect. Noble and I lie head to feet, rocking over the gentle waves in our boat as Noble sings "Happy Birthday" to himself, and the cloudless blue sky, and the sun hanging low to hear him better. His voice is soft and gentle and floats along the tamed surf.

The sun warms my skin and I throw some water on both of us from over the side.

"Hey! Do you mind? I'm trying to enjoy a relaxing evening on my boat."

"This bathing suit is made to get wet, isn't it?" I ask as I rub the hem of his board shorts. I mentally compare Noble's bathing suit to Jason's cutoff jeans, and it reminds me of Jason's accusation that I'm taking the easy way out. Maybe I am only in love with Noble because it's easy. We've always been more together than we are apart. Does that make it wrong, or just comfortable? I rub the scar on my cheek. Noble applied the SPF 75 he bought for it—twice. Right before he put my hat on my head.

"What are you thinking about?" he asks, interrupting my ridiculous thoughts.

"How much I love you," I answer, forgoing the lack of a conclusion.

Noble rocks the boat as he sits up, but I keep my face toward the sun. "That's perfect," he says, "because I want to know if you'll marry me."

"Again with the begging, Noble?" I smile at our joke and look up at him. His face is void of amusement and on the end of his pinky finger sits a ring. "Noble?" I am breathless.

Jason jumps into my head, and what accepting this ring will do to him, and I silently chastise myself for letting him into *Mindless*. His invasions are still constant, even after the finality of our last meeting. It's not fair to marry Noble and care what someone else will think. He absolutely deserves better.

"Charlotte," Noble says, and I force myself to focus on him. His hair is wet and shaken off his face. His blue eyes are deeper than the ocean yet shallow enough to reach. The sun's warmth is centered on him, only shining on me because I'm near him. He is glorious. "You are the most stubborn, frustrating girl I've ever known. The months between the snowstorm and the Harvest Dance were the longest of my entire life."

I remember the look on his face when I told him I loved him that night.

"I believe you could literally drive me insane," Noble continues confidently. His expression is the one he always has when he laughs at me. "You have a tendency to collect things in need, specifically misbehaving hound dogs and crotchety old men—and you insist on spoiling them both rotten. To my chagrin, you lack a basic understanding of the purpose of undergarments in everyday attire." He raises his eyebrows, tilting his head in the most adorable way. "Your impact on the opposite sex is an enormous burden to manage, and I'll spend the rest of my life fighting men off you."

I listen to him, speechless.

"Your use of whiskey in recipes is questionable, and your driving? Harrowing."

"Does this pick up?" I finally ask. The joking question is out of habit; the uncertainty in my voice is born of consternation.

"Yes, I'm getting there," he says, grinning. "For months, I've watched in awe as you painstakingly reconstructed your life, and unbeknownst to me, each day I fell more in love with you. Charlotte, I always knew I wanted to farm my land. I never thought much further than that"—Noble looks down at the ring and back at me—"until the snowstorm in January."

He smiles his wonderful, carefree smile and my heart warms.

"I don't know what made you come into my room that night, but that one step through my door rearranged every element of my life forever. Since then, I see myself cooking Sunday dinners, and playing cards by the fire, and taking road trips and boat rides, and God help me, going to church."

Noble laughs and I can't take my eyes off him.

"And hauling in Christmas trees, and hiding Easter eggs, and reading bedtime stories." His voice softens. "And, Charlotte, all of it I see with you."

My eyes move from Noble's to the ring around his finger. It's a round diamond surrounded by emeralds, each a half-moon shape. It's like a flower and I've never seen anything like it, and like the man holding it, it's perfect.

With a finger to my chin, Noble tilts my face and my eyes meet his again. "I want to spend every day of my life like this." I look at the ocean around us. It is vast and calm and meets the quiet sky at an unbroken horizon. "With you."

Noble should be giving this ring to someone who loves him, forsaking all others. "You are extraordinary, Charlotte, and you deserve an extraordinary life."

What I deserve is to fall off this boat and drown.

"I love you, and no one's ever going to take better care of you." Noble takes my face in his hand and runs his thumb across the fresh scar on my cheek.

I close my eyes and lean into his hand. A heaviness washes over me and threatens to pull our entire boat to the bottom of the ocean. Why didn't I see this coming? What did I think was going to happen? I know exactly what this will do to Jason because I've lived through it, every day imagining his life with someone else. I can't inflict that kind of pain on him.

And yet, out here on the water, I belong with Noble.

If it weren't for Noble, I wouldn't be here in this boat, maybe not here at all. As inconceivable as my parents' death is in relation to the grand plan for my life, Noble seems to fit it perfectly. He's the only thing that really makes sense. But I learned long ago that life isn't about making sense; it's about survival. Noble kisses me; his lips pressing against mine force the guilt from my mind, reminding me that I deserve to live this life.

"If in your heart…you know this is how you should spend the rest of your life, then say yes and we'll figure the rest out later. Trust in me, Charlotte."

I open my eyes and see on Noble's face what took me months to comprehend.

My lovely Noble cherishes me.

"Yes," I say, and silently pray for Noble and me…and Jason.

Dear God, thank you for this beautiful day,
And this beautiful man in front of me.
Please watch over all three of us,
And protect us from ourselves and each other,
As we embark on a thousand tomorrows.

~ 1 ~

A Second Proposal

I pull my robe tight around my neck and sit at the head of the table. Right in front of the most glorious breakfast I've ever seen…or smelled. I am spoiled. I inhale the warm, sweet syrupy aroma that conjures every perfect memory still left in me and study Noble Sinclair. He might be the human equivalent of syrup—warm, sweet, and perfect.

"So what do you have to get done today?" I ask as he pours himself a cup of coffee. He slides the glass pitcher back in the coffeemaker and takes a sip from the steaming cup. He looks so young, shirtless and in his pajama pants, incapable of running this farm on his own. But he does. Noble can do anything. My eyes linger on his shoulders and I wish he never wore a shirt; it covers my favorite part of him.

"Plowing something? Planting something?" There's an endless list of things to do now.

Noble keeps his back to me as he lingers at the counter. He rubs a ribbon between his fingers and looks out the window at the fields on the side of the house. The ribbon is blue with silver wired edges and is wrapped around five bridal magazines my friend Violet gave me when Noble proposed, almost a year ago. The fabric facing out is dusty and faded now.

Why didn't I ever open them?

"I want you to go to the shore with me." Noble breaks my contemplation. I'm surprised. He's barely had time to sleep lately, let alone take the day off. We've both been busy.

"I would love to." My eyes traipse across Noble's chest. He and the shore are two of my favorite things. "Will you promise to keep your shirt off the whole day?"

"If you do the same," he says. Always so naughty.

Noble sits on the table near the Belgian waffle he made me. He sips his coffee as I cut through the Jersey strawberries and let the syrup waterfall throughout the waffle. It's as close to heaven as possible on a plate. Giving Noble a waffle maker last year for Christmas was a stroke of genius.

He notices the whipped cream and exchanges his coffee for the canister. Noble tilts the whipped cream can at my waffle and raises his eyebrows to me.

"Let me have it."

He forms a perfect whipped cream heart and places the canister down next to my plate. My heart rate spikes as I grab his hand and hold his whip-cream-covered finger in front of my smiling face. I lick the tip and take his finger in my mouth. His whole finger. I slide my teeth down the side before sucking the tip as I run my tongue over it. Noble never takes his eyes off his hand and my mouth.

When I release his finger from my teeth, Noble stands and drops his pajama pants to the floor. He takes the whip cream and sprays some on his now-hard penis with the naughtiest look ever.

"You missed a little," he says, and I wonder how we ever leave this house. The sight of his penis at eye level makes my mouth water.

I take my tongue to the cream and raise my eyes to Noble as I lick the tip and then my lips. I take him in my mouth completely, and he closes his eyes and raises his face to the ceiling. The sight of his pleasure spreads heat through my body and I shift in my seat, wanting him in me.

I hold Noble's balls in one hand as I stroke him with the other. My mouth finds him again and with only a few minutes of attention, I finish my love off.

"Aaah. You have no idea how good that feels."

"Oh, I think I do," I say, trying to ignore the throbbing between my legs.

In one swoop, Noble lifts me to my feet and pulls my shirt over my head. He shamelessly caresses my breasts with his eyes. They rise under his stare, wanting his familiar touch. "Yes, that's exactly how you should ride to the shore with me."

"We'll get arrested."

"It'll be worth it. I'll spend my days rotting in the cell, imagining you topless."

Noble kisses me, gently at first. He's in control, as usual. I, however, am not. I wrap my leg around his waist and grind against the front of him. I pull myself up him and want him inside of me. Immediately.

"What am I going to do with you, Charlotte? You're insatiable," he whispers in my ear as if it's our little secret. I cannot get enough of Noble Sinclair.

He bends slightly and hoists me over his shoulder. He practically runs up the stairs, jolting me with each step, my arms holding on to the back of him, the sound of my giggle echoing along the old staircase. Noble carries me to the bedroom we've been sharing and throws me on the bed. The devotion in his stare, always filled with the same promise—my home is with him—sends heat to every fraction of my body and I acknowledge the depth to which I need him. It's still profound. I rise up to my knees and wrap my arms around his neck and pull him closer to me. I grab him and try to quiet the throbbing between my legs with him in my hand. I kiss him, my tongue telling him I won't wait any longer, and when I'm sure he's gotten the message, I lean back and pull Noble down with me. I want him on top of me. I need the weight of his love to settle me, now and forever.

He wraps each arm under my shoulders as he pulls me toward him. Noble finds me more than ready as he buries his lips on my neck and slowly enters me. He lowers his naked chest to mine and we are one. He is touching me everywhere. I wrap my legs around his waist and hook my ankles behind his back, pulling him closer still. Again, and again, and again I take Noble, wanting more of him. More than I ever knew existed. He is controlled, deliberately driving me to my breaking point. It's his rhythm that is his gift. My fingernails dig into his back as I acknowledge that Noble has many gifts.

I tilt my pelvis and let him stroke me as he comes into me and I try to breathe. I thread my fingers through his hair and bury my face in his shoulder and release every thought from my mind except the touch of Noble Sinclair. My notched breathing conveys my diminishing hold, and I can feel Noble smiling on my neck.

"Come for me, Charlotte," he whispers, and I oblige, crumbling around him. He doesn't stop, though; he's in me again and I close my eyes as he gives himself away and I pull him to me once more.

He anchors me. I hold Noble close, not a chance of something getting between us. Sometimes it feels as if he'll never be close enough.

* * *

By the time we climb into Noble's truck, it's after lunch. Lazy days are few and far between. It reminds me of Rutgers and waking up after a long night with Noble and the rest of our friends passed out around the house. But now it's just Noble and me, and his farm, and my job in New York.

The farm is in full swing this time of year, and work in New York hasn't let up since Bruce promoted me. I apparently thrive on the added responsibility. I work late every day while I wait for Noble to finish in the fields. We eat together, laughing as we share our days. We make love in Noble's bed and fall asleep as if the world could never hurt us.

The sky is clear this afternoon, not a cloud in it. The endless blue bores me and I turn to Noble, who instead of watching the road has his eyes fixed on me. There's something different about him today. A conversation of some kind is coming. Noble turns back toward the road and lays his hand out on the seat between us, palm up, waiting for me to take it in my own. I unbuckle my seat belt and slide across the seat next to him. I rebuckle as a smiling Noble puts his arm around me and I lay my head on his strong shoulder. This *is* my home now. No parents to love me, but I have

Noble Sinclair. And he is enough. He is home personified. My thankfulness travels through my body and I close my eyes, safe and sound with my lovely Noble.

* * *

"Charlotte," he says, and nudges me with his shoulder. I squint my eyes, still not ready to face the blinding light. "Charlotte, wake up. We're here." *The shore...*

"I slept the whole way?"

"The whole way. My arm fell asleep around Tuckahoe, but you wouldn't let go. I think you were holding on for dear life," Noble says, half laughing, and I know he's not mad.

"I'm sorry."

"Why are you so tired?"

"I haven't been sleeping well. I have strange dreams." Noble's face is wrought with concern, and I know he's worried it's Jason Leer I'm dreaming of. "It's probably nothing," I attempt, and kiss his cheek.

"You did kick me last night." My playful Noble returns.

"That wasn't me dreaming, though; that was me getting you back for the deer head you put in the refrigerator last winter," I say, and the memory of the head repulses me again. Noble had closed one of its eyes, like it was winking at me.

Noble parks on the point in Strathmere and we walk to the beach with a few beach towels and a blanket in our arms. Noble travels light; there's little he needs in this world. He needs me and his farm and the rest is all a bonus. We work together to spread out the blanket and when I lie on it, Noble sprays my back with sunscreen. He stops as I arch my back and wince at the frigid invasion. As I exhale, Noble runs his fingers down the center of my back, warming me with his touch.

"It's okay. I'll get you back in a second," I say, and Noble shakes his head. We finish and lie with our faces to the sun, our toes pointing toward the water. Fully rested, my eyes don't want to close. I lean on my elbows and watch the jet skiers race just past the wave break. The heavy breeze blows my hair across my face and I toss my head to clear it. I see Noble out of the corner of my eye watching me. He has a lot on his mind, or maybe it's just me on his mind. God knows that's a lot.

I sit up completely and contemplate how many miles it is to the horizon. I always wonder the same thing. How many miles can a person see to the horizon? A light shining in my eye releases the pending question as sun catches my engagement ring and it sparkles, reminding me again that I'm engaged. I hold out my hand and marvel at how perfect the ring is. Noble sits up next to me and seems pleased with my admiration. It's perfect, like him.

"Noble, what made you pick this ring?"

Noble takes my hand and examines the ring. He turns my hand over and kisses my palm and his warmth spreads through me. My eyes never leave his lips as he kisses my fingertips.

"It wasn't easy. I knew you were only ever going to receive one." Noble turns my hand over again and grins as he studies the ring. "Sam and I shopped around, but none of the rings were you. Well, Sam thought almost all of them were you, but they weren't."

"Poor Sam," I say. There is a limit to how many jewelry stores a guy's best friend can endure.

"I didn't know what I was looking for, but I knew it wasn't any we saw." Noble turns the ring with his finger so the diamond is facing him.

"All the others were common. They were fine for someone else, but I needed something different. When I found this one, I knew it was exactly what I wanted," Noble says, and the look in his eyes makes me question whether we're still talking about the ring. I turn my hand. It is me, but I've never seen anything like it before.

"It's vintage, art deco actually. I thought you'd like something with a history of its own."

I narrow my eyes, questioning his assessment. I've never thought about it, and I've definitely never thought about engagement rings. Do I hold on to the past too long?

"You cherish things others throw away, Charlotte," he says, and shrugs as if it's obvious. "When I saw the emeralds were each the shape of a half-moon, I knew it had to be yours. No one notices the sky as much as you do."

I lean over and kiss him, kindly and sweetly, being careful with my gentle giant.

"It's a one of a kind, like you, Charlotte O'Brien." His voice is that of a man. When did we grow up? Time spent with Noble makes me forget life is moving on.

"I love it when you say my name," I say, and blush at my childhood friend.

"Will your name be Charlotte Sinclair after we're married?" Noble is hesitant with his question. I haven't thought about that either—my name or being married.

"I guess it will be," I say, liking the idea. "I'll be Charlotte Sinclair. Had you told me that in kindergarten, I wouldn't have believed it."

"Had you told me in college, I wouldn't have believed it,"

Noble says, and I fight hard to not let his reference to college damage my mood. He wouldn't have believed it because I was completely in love with Jason Leer, planning to spend the rest of my life with him. "Let's go in the ocean," Noble says hurriedly, and I think I've failed.

We swim, Noble throwing me over his shoulder into the giant waves. On the third throw I hit the water face-first. I surface, coughing up seawater, and he pulls me into his arms, his eyes searching my face for reassurance. I wrap my legs around his waist and my arms around his neck and we float over the waves connected. Someday we'll be connected forever. I kiss Noble to remind him he is the rest of my life now.

I release him and swim butterfly a few yards. It feels good to swim an actual stroke again. My muscle memory engages as I dolphin in and out of the water, but after a short distance I'm tired, unable to keep up with my pace from six years ago. I swim back to Noble and rest on his back.

"Do you think you're ever going to swim again?" he asks. He swims forward, dragging me with him.

"Maybe. Chris Black mentioned training for open-water swims. I like to swim with the fishies," I say, and Noble takes us both underwater. When we surface, I ask, "Why? Do you want to train with me for a race?"

"No. I'm pretty sure you could kick my ass in swimming." Noble stands, keeping me on his back. "It used to make you happy, though."

I stare back out to the horizon.

"That was a lifetime ago." Two lifetimes, in fact. My mother's and my father's.

"Not everything changed, Charlotte," Noble says, and I realize he is one of the constants. We are still more together than we are apart.

* * *

We lie on the soft sand until the sun dips to the west and our bathing suits dry. He rolls over and rests his head on his hand and stares at me.

"Yes, my friend?"

"Shouldn't you call me your lover?" Noble asks.

"Can't my lover be my friend? You are one of my best friends, you know."

"I know," he says, and stands up without warning. "Let's get some dinner."

I lumber to my feet, not wanting to leave the shore. I pull my sundress over my head and discreetly take off my bikini and roll it up in my towel.

"Must be nice," Noble says as he appraises my quick change. I shake out my hair, which is chock-full of sand, and I love the feel. I could live at the shore, possibly right on the beach. It's amazing how close I came to being so far away from it.

I will not think of Jason Leer.

We walk to the back bay and Noble opens the door to Twisties for me. It's filling already, and Noble and I sit at the bar, facing the bay as the bartender puts two menus down in front of us.

"Can I get you something to drink?" the bartender asks, and Noble defers to me.

What do I want? "I'll take a Stella."

"Make that two." Noble appears satisfied with my decision.

He watches me as I read the menu, the same tense stare from this morning. I peer at him over the menu and return my eyes to the selections as our Stellas are delivered and the bartender grabs a tablet for our order.

"I'll have the shrimp tacos." I want everything on the menu. "Will you have one?" I ask Noble, and he nods. "And the mussels in red sauce." I return the menu to the bartender. "Oh, and can I have an order of Strathmere Bay fries?" The bartender writes a note and focuses on Noble.

"I'll have the mussels in white and eat most of her food," he says, and he and the bartender share a knowing grin.

The tide is going out. It's 6:00 p.m. Judging by the depth of the water, low tide is probably sometime around seven, maybe seven-thirty. The bay is full of boats enjoying the last few hours of daylight. Some have stopped, waiting to watch the sunset from the water.

"You know, if we're actually going to get married, we'll need to plan a wedding," Noble says, and I turn to him. This is what has been weighing on him all day. It's now time for the conversation.

"Is that how it works?" I eek out, wishing for any other topic.

"Should I be concerned that you haven't run out to shop for dresses or dragged me to reception halls? Because that's how I remember my sisters' weddings." Noble turns my body so my knees are between his on his barstool and I am squarely facing him. Nowhere to run. He is serious, and I know it's because he's worried. "Are you having second thoughts?" Worried about Jason; it's always about Jason. I take a deep breath.

"No," I say, and look down, wanting to avoid this conversation completely. *Aren't things perfect the way they are?* With a finger to my chin, Noble raises my eyes to his. "It's just...I don't think I want a traditional wedding without my mom and dad here." Noble doesn't take his eyes off me. "No one to go dress shopping with, no one to walk me down the aisle, no father-daughter dance," I say, and the longing pours out of me. I bow my head, but before I'm hidden, Noble's lips are on mine. I'm on the verge of tears, I feel ridiculous, and I'm sure I am blushing.

"I should have thought of that," Noble says, angry with himself but relieved at the same time. "How about you take a few days and think about what you want this wedding to be like and that's exactly how it will be."

"But don't you want a traditional wedding? A big party?"

Noble holds my face in his hands and runs his thumb across my lips. "No." He shakes his head. "I want to marry you. What that day's like is completely up to you. We can do it in the backyard, in a church, at city hall, on an island…whatever will make you happy. I don't care if we're alone or with five hundred people as long as you're standing next to me." He kisses me again, this time slightly inappropriately for our barstools, but I can't deny him.

"I know one thing I want."

"Anything," he says, completely at ease now.

"I want you to wear a suit. No one wears a suit the way you do," I say with every naughty thought I've ever had of him shining through my eyes.

"I can't wait to get you in my truck," he whispers in my ear.

He pulls me into his arms and fills me with the warmth of Noble Sinclair.

~2~

Betrothment

When Noble leaves Tuesday morning, I call the Realtor in Strathmere. I ask her about the mansion on the point, specifically about possibly renting it for a few weeks to host a small wedding. By her reaction, the request is unusual. So is this wedding. She's much more enthused when I also ask about renting any available property in town for guests to use. As I'm talking to her, BJ studies me with his sweet beagle eyes and I remember to make sure at least one of the properties is pet friendly.

"I can't marry Noble without my best friend there, huh, little guy?" I rub behind his ears and take out a notepad to make a list of guests. Rutgers, Salem County, family...yes, it will be small. Sixty maybe. No mom. No dad.

I can do this. I dial Sean's number.

"Hey, how's it going?" he asks, instead of hello.

"I'm going to marry Noble," I announce.

"I know, dummy. That's what that big ring is for."

"No, I mean, I'm going to marry him soon. Maybe the weekend after Labor Day."

"Wow. Finally getting around to making some plans, huh?"

"Yes, and I want you and Michelle to be there. And Lily, too, of course. Do you think she's too young?"

"She's Irish. She'll be fine. Are you going to send out invites or just let Mom haunt you from her grave for the rest of your life?"

"I'm working on all of that."

"Let me know if you need any help."

I hang up with Sean and check him and Michelle off the list. Next up—Jenn and Margo. Two girls I wish had never left Salem County. Well, they're going to have to come back for this. I text them both:

> I'M FLYING YOU HOME LABOR DAY.
> I'M MARRYING NOBLE 9/10/11.

From Margo I receive:

Love

From Jenn I get:

What's the rush?

I text back:

> LIFE IS SHORT

And I believe it. If there's one thing being orphaned at twenty taught me, it's that life is short.

It takes over an hour to compose a letter to Jason. I don't want him to hear about the wedding from someone else. I don't want him to hear about it at all, but I know that's not how Salem County, or the rest of the world, works. Nothing sounds right. It doesn't feel right. It's just not right. The inadequate note is folded and shoved in an envelope before I realize I have no idea what his address is. I stare at the envelope. I'm not sure even Butch knows. I've never seen him mail anything to Jason.

I pick up my cell phone and dial Jason's number from memory. Will I ever forget a single detail about him?

"Hello?" he says, and his voice through the phone makes my stomach flip.

"It's me," I say.

"Are you okay? Is anything wrong?" *Kind of.*

"I'm fine."

"Hold on, Annie. Let me pull over." I wait and listen to him breathe as I stand in Noble's kitchen. It's wrong to talk to Jason in here. I walk out back and lie on the hammock.

"Okay. How are you?" he asks, and it reminds me of all the phone calls when I was at Rutgers and he was at Oklahoma State.

"I wasn't sure if you'd still have this number, or even a phone," I say, and drink in the sound of Jason.

"I don't want either, but I kept it in case you ever needed to get a hold of me. For right now." I close my eyes. I wish this call was for a different reason. I should have called to talk to him months ago. This is savage.

"I have a letter for you, but I don't know where to send it."

"A letter, huh?" Jason's voice has an edge to it. He already knows, but he's going to make me go through the paces. "Read it to me."

"I'd rather just send it."

"There's nothing you can't say to me."

"There's nothing you won't hear. There are some things I can't say."

"Read it, Annie. It's not going to make anything worse." He's right. Things reached hellish last year and we haven't spoken a word to each other since. I take a deep breath and pull the letter out of the envelope.

"Dear Jason,

"I hope you are amazing.

"That's the way I remember you and I want you to still be that way." I pause. He has to be amazing. I realize that's how I function from day to day, knowing Jason is well wherever he is.

"I'm marrying Noble," I read, and hear not one sound from the other end of the line. "I don't want you to hear it from someone else. I'm sorry. I didn't want to tell you. In fact, the thought of it makes me sick, but I wanted you to hear it from me." *Not really, but whatever.*

"If I could figure out a way to live my life without you, without hurting you, I would, but I can't seem to get out of my own way. I'm sure you know what I mean. You always do.

"Love,

"Annie."

I wipe a few tears from my eyes and focus on the sky. Its gray clouds threaten rain, but the sun peeks through, fighting off the storm.

"Annie." Jason's voice is soft, and a chill runs from my ear through my chest bone. "You marrying Sinclair doesn't change the way I feel about you."

A sob catches in my throat and I swallow to not sound like a blubbering idiot.

"Where?" he asks.

"What does it matter?"

"Where?"

"By the water," I say, and Jason says a quiet good-bye before hanging up the phone, leaving me alone and weeping on Noble's hammock and clutching a letter to the only man I ever thought I was going to marry.

* * *

My mother's jewelry box sits in front of me on my mother's kitchen table. I go through it drawer by drawer, remembering every earring, every bracelet. *She was so beautiful.* I lower my head onto the box. I thought this was an actual treasure chest when I was little. I loved the lid that lifted to expose the hundred tiny squares, each designed for its own riches. Today it's empty and old, like my childhood memories without my parents here to share them.

Clint's finishing the remodel on my parents' kitchen and it's awesome. It is a different house and Clint's talents are solely responsible for the results. He transformed this house while Noble transformed me. What's going to become of it now? I pry open the bottom drawer of the jewelry box with a butter knife. Inside are two cardboard boxes, too thick to fit. *So like you, Mom, to force them in there.*

"Clint, do you ever think of moving out of your mom's basement?" I ask.

"Every day. Every single day I think of moving out," Clint says, making me laugh.

"Would you like to move in here?" His eyebrows rise and I realize my mistake. "Rent the place when I move in with Noble."

"Oh. I thought you were making some big offer. You got me all excited for a minute." Clint turns his attention to the trim work he's installing.

"I'd want someone here who's going to take care of the place and you've been working on it so long, it belongs to you, too," I say, and realize I want Clint to live here. He is the perfect tenant.

"I don't have a job lined up after this one. That's why I haven't moved out. I'm never sure of my income."

"Live here for free," I say, as if it's an obvious solution.

"I can't live here for free," Clint dismisses me.

"Look, I can rent the place and I probably won't know the people and they'll be sleeping and eating in my parents' house. That feels wrong. If you rent it, I know it will be taken care of and I'll be able to visit." I look at Clint, pleading with him to accept the offer.

"Okay, I'll move in," he says, and stands up to hug me. "And you can come home anytime you need to."

"Thanks," I say, and take one of the boxes out of the drawer. Inside is an ornate turquoise necklace, completely different from every other item in my mom's jewelry box. She always wore simple jewelry. Her engagement ring and an anniversary band adorned her hands every day of my life. I never saw this on her or anything like it for that matter. *Where did this come from, Mom?*

* * *

On my drive home, Pastor Johnson calls and confirms he can officiate on September 10. It is time to tell Noble. I've hesitated, as if something might come up that will dramatically change things.

There's only one thing that could come up and if he's not here by now, he's not coming.

I park in the L-shed and grab my bag of jewels from my mother's jewelry box, including the turquoise necklace that I still can't believe belonged to her. Noble is lying in the hammock on the side of the house. I walk over to him, wanting to show him my finds.

Noble's asleep. I rock the hammock back and forth, but he still doesn't wake. I go inside and shower and pick out a dress I haven't worn since last summer. It's green and strapless, and it's one of Noble's favorites. I unwrap two frozen strombolis and start chopping vegetables for a salad. There's homemade sauce in a pot and the kitchen is filling with the aromas of home cooking. Setting the date deserves a meal.

The delicate stems of wineglasses dangle from my hand as I maneuver them out of the cabinet in the dining room. I jump as Noble sneaks up behind me and encircles my waist with his arms. He holds me tight as he rests his chin on my shoulder.

"Why do you look so good?" he asks, his voice rough on my neck.

"Excellent DNA," I offer as I turn in his arms.

"Some of the best, I would say." He kisses my neck. "What time's dinner? I need a shower. I fell asleep in the hammock."

"How are we ever going to run this farm if you need a nap every day?"

"I only need a nap because you climb on top of me in the middle of the night and take advantage of me," Noble says, and I remember waking up and needing him. "I'm not sure what you're dreaming about, but I hope you keep doing it—it's working for me."

There's only one dream. It's always the same. It's Jason Leer and me and not another soul in this world.

"You've got at least a half hour. Take your time." Noble raises my face to his and kisses me, reminding me even more of last night. He releases me and runs upstairs to shower.

On the shelf under the wineglasses are stacked shells from our trips to the shore. I take one out and carry it with my glasses back to the kitchen. I pull down a bottle of Good Karma wine from the shelf in the mudroom and remind myself to stop by Auburn Road and pick up some more. The cork makes a low *pop* as I hastily remove it. I pour myself a glass and search for a marker.

Hmm… Good Karma. Bring it.

There's a drawer of odds and ends, mostly odds, that houses several pens and markers. The first two are dried up and I throw them away before finding the red one. I use it to write, "Marry Me, 9/10/ 11" on the inside of the shell with a little heart. I lean the shell against Noble's wineglass and return to my salad making.

Noble comes down smelling fresh and clean and yummy and begins washing the lettuce. The strombolis heat in the oven as I stir the sauce. Candles would be nice, but it's still light out. The days are long.

"Are you trying to seduce me?" Noble asks, surveying the room.

"Would it take this much effort?"

"I'm not easy," he says, and takes a sip of my wine. "You don't mind, do you?" he asks slyly.

"What's mine is yours," I say. "But you have a glass on the table." Noble walks to the table and I continue to clean a pepper with my back to him. The seconds drag like hours and the silence in the room scares me. I glance over my shoulder to see him. He's engrossed with the shell, staring at it and running his hand over it as if it's some type of artifact. I turn and walk to him, uncomfortable without his smile, unsure of what he's thinking.

"This is the date?" he asks, still examining the shell.

"If you still want me?" I say, and press my body against his front. I want to touch him, let his warmth settle me. Noble's lips find mine and his kiss reminds me of one of our first, when we were on Violet's parents' terrace the night of her engagement party. He was confident, sure we should be together, and I thought he was crazy to even want me, let alone take a chance that someday I would be capable of what this shell is announcing.

"You never have to ask that. I will always want you," Noble promises, and kisses me again. "You won't regret this, Charlotte."

"Did you think I ever would?"

"No. I've known for a long time you belong with me. I thought you were unsure and that that was why you waited to plan the wedding."

"Why didn't you say something before?" How long has Noble been suffering in silence while I was walking around completely oblivious to his fears?

"I was hoping one day you'd figure out you couldn't live without me and set the date."

I take the shell from him and hold it up. "Well, here's the date. We're getting married at the shore. On the point in Strathmere. Unless you have any input to the contrary."

"Strathmere sounds perfect."

"It is perfect," I say, and consider *perfect*. It's brilliant at hiding its flaws.

***

I've been working in the city at least once a week. It seems to calm my boss to have me around. "At his beck and call" has an appeal to him. This week I'm taking advantage of happy hour to share my impending nuptials with the Rutgers girls. Violet is taking the train into the city. I'll drive her home tomorrow. Sydney is working here but lives in Hoboken, and Julia is here all the time. We'll all stay at Julia's and my condo, making it a long-overdue reunion. It's been a while since we've had a good night out, just the four of us. Violet's infidelity and wedding last year left us bewildered, and until recently, things have been strained.

"Charlotte!" Julia yells my name as she waves from the barstool she's kneeling on to see me. I maneuver through the crowd and happily accept a beer upon my arrival. "I wasn't sure what you wanted, so I got you a Hoegaarden."

I take a sip. "Summer nights need a beer." Especially when you spend them in Bryant Park. This is my favorite spot in the city. The Bryant Park Hotel dazzles above us.

"I'm glad you suggested happy hour. I haven't seen you in forever, and I always miss you more once the weather warms up."

"I know. Why is that?" I ask.

"I have no idea. What time are Violet and Sydney coming?" I check my watch and it's six o'clock exactly.

"They should be here any minute," I say. Julia turns her inspection on me.

"Why are we here, by the way?" I look at Julia, confused. My eyes wander to the rest of the park. *Where else would we be?* "I mean, why all of a sudden did you want all of us together? I know something's up. Does it have anything to do with J—?"

"No. No." I shake my head violently. "Noble and I set a date. We're getting married September tenth; it's the weekend after Labor Day."

"Wow! I'm impressed. Let's see, that's a little less than three months. Are you going to expect me to be a bridesmaid? More importantly, are you going to cuckoo out like Violet did and have sex with some loser two weeks before the wedding?" Julia's tone turns dark as she reminds us both of the hell that was Violet's bachelorette party.

"My plan is to stay this side of cuckoo," I say, and question whether I can manage sane.

"Are you going to tell Jason?"

"I already did. I called him."

Julia practically spits her beer right out of her mouth. "You did?" She grabs my arm. "What happened? What did he say?"

"He said it doesn't change the way he feels about me."

"Does it change anything for you?" Julia asks, and I kind of hate her for the question.

"I love Noble. I'm sure of it. It's right with him and he makes me happy every minute of the day."

"But…"

I sigh. *But what?*

"You don't have to answer that."

"Thanks." I take a long sip of my beer and signal the bartender that we need another round.

Violet and Sydney arrive at the same time and the mood is immediately lightened. Sydney begs us to come back to Hoboken with her and meet her new entertainment. He's a comedian and a bartender at the Black Bear Bar. More impressive than

Sydney's promise that he's a funny man is the fact that she swears he's hung like a horse. I'm not sure how this is supposed to entice me out of the city, but I love her enough to go meet the well-endowed comedian.

"No way," Violet says, and orders a glass of cranberry juice.

"UTI?" Julia asks, and examines Violet, trying to decipher the affliction that would keep her from ordering a beer on this beautiful night.

"I'm pregnant."

We all stand very still.

"Is it Blake's?" Julia asks, and my eyes dart in her direction. "What? I'm the only one thinking it?" She's not the only one. Anyone who saw the lover Violet invited to her wedding would have some questions about this pregnancy.

"Of course you are," Sydney chastises Julia, and then asks, "It is Blake's, right?"

"Yes. It's Blake's." Violet is doing an excellent job of not losing her patience with us. I sigh, relieved there's no scandal involved in this news. "But if you, my dearest friends, are asking me, then every other person who knows us is going to ask the same thing," she says, and starts to cry.

"Oh, Violet, no. Everyone won't think that. We're terrible. Everyone from outside of Jersey is going to be immediately supportive," Sydney says, and rubs her back.

Violet leans on Sydney but stares straight at me. "Charlotte? What are you thinking?" she asks, and I can't figure out what I'm thinking. In fact, I can't get the image of Violet making out with the bar-back in Key West out of my head. Cheating leaves a mark, at least on me. Violet seems to be moving forward quite well.

"I think if you and Blake are happy, then I'm happy," I say, and Julia's eyes roll back in her head. "Can I ask you something, though?" I know I should shut up. *Shut up, Charlotte! Shut up!* "Why so soon?"

"I don't know. We weren't trying or not trying."

"Then you were trying. Seventh-grade health explained all of this, Violet," Julia spouts, and I give her the calm-down signal. The girl's pregnant after all.

"Anyway, we've been through a lot. It's nice to have something to be excited about. Something that's ours alone," Violet says, and coming from her lips it is romantic, and sweet, and wholly uniting. "What's going on with you, Charlotte? Still farming?"

"Noble and I are getting married September tenth. Down the shore, and I need all of you to be there."

"What's Noble wearing?" Sydney asks with a shameless grin.

"He's wearing a suit."

"I'll be there," she says, and I shake my head at her.

"I wish you luck, Charlotte," Violet says, and toasts my glass. "If you don't invite your lover to the wedding, you'll probably be fine."

"Good advice," I say, nodding. How we can all discuss this so nonchalantly, I don't know.

~ 3 ~

White, Right?

Noble and I walk hand and hand from the Tractor Supply Store to his truck. He's quiet today; there aren't as many jokes as usual. It's unsettling. I climb in and Noble buckles my seat belt as if I'm a child and then leans up and kisses me as if he just returned from battle. He is so good.

The acres pass by as we head out of town. Rows and rows blink as my eyes take them in. There are soybeans, and tomatoes, and peppers, all lined up in the fields. I had a plant once at Rutgers, but it dried up from lack of attention. How fitting I'm in love with a farmer. I realize we're moving as slow as we were in town. Noble's cautious pace is like slow motion on this wide-open road.

"Is there something wrong with the truck?" I ask, and lean over. We're only going twenty-five miles per hour. "You know you're at risk of pissing off a lot of other drivers on the road." Noble checks behind us and nods at the absence of cars.

"I'm just in no rush to get home," he says, and smirks as he leans back in his seat.

"Painting is not that bad. I kind of like it. Julia and I painted our room at Rutgers and it was fun." Noble looks at me as if I'm a horrible liar. "I mean it."

"Come here," he says, and reaches out to me. I slide over to him and rest my head on his shoulder. "Did you figure out what you're doing about a dress yet? Because maybe instead of painting I should take you dress shopping."

"You can't see me in my dress before the wedding," I say, and turn to him.

"I want you to be happy about your dress, and I don't know how to help. No one is going to replace your mom in the process. Maybe we should just do things completely differently and I'll take you." I lean up and kiss Noble on the cheek, resting my arm across his waist.

"I don't want you to take me. I'm already annexing a big traditional wedding from your future. The least I can do is behave like a proper bride and walk down some sort of aisle with a new dress on."

"None of that matters, Charlotte."

"I know. You're good like that. I'll figure it out."

* * *

Noble and I paint the ceiling and tape on Sunday, I finish the first coat on Monday, and today I'm putting on the second coat. I hope to be done then. This navy color might need a third coat, though. It is rich and beautiful. The master bedroom of the farmhouse is big. I can't imagine how big it was before Mrs. Sinclair cut off part of it to create proper closets, but I'm thankful she did. The deep color warms the room and it reminds me of the effect Noble has on me whenever he's nearby. He was skeptical when he first opened the can and spread it across the beige wall, but I think he's coming around.

I'm using the blunt end of a screwdriver to hammer the paint can shut when I finally remember that today is Tuesday and I have a hair appointment with Nadine. I run to the other bedroom searching for the time. My appointment is in twenty minutes and I have paint all over my hands and face.

I begin with the scrubbing as I mentally go through the limited wardrobe I have at Noble's. The only items I'm sure of are yoga pants and a button-down shirt, which should never be worn together, but they're clean. Nadine will probably have me committed if I show up in them. There's a sundress draped across the radiator and I inspect it for stains. *Lovely.* I throw it over my head and grab my bag on the way out the door.

The clock on the Volvo's dash calms me. There's a shot I'm going to make it. I back the Volvo out of the L-shed without looking and hustle down the lane only to be stopped by the train crossing Noble's lane. I wave to the engineer. It's not his fault I don't know what day it is.

I run into Salon Nadine two minutes late for my appointment and out of breath. Jocelyn brings me back to the color room and Nadine meets me there to talk about "our plan" for my hair.

"So, what are we doing?" she asks.

"Well, Noble and I are getting married in September. We should probably keep that in mind."

"That's awesome. What's the date?" she asks as she covers me with a smock.

"September tenth."

"Oh nice. Nine, ten, eleven."

"I want you to come. I have to get invitations made. I'm a little behind on everything."

"I'll be there. Someone is going to need to do your hair."

I nod in agreement.

"Do you want to be blond for your wedding?"

"Yes," I say, and imagine Noble's reaction to me walking down the aisle a brunette for the first time in my life. "Okay, I'll be right back." Nadine leaves to mix something and I hear my phone ding with a text.

> **I'm starting to love the blue.**
>
> I KNEW YOU WOULD.
>
> **Where are you?**
>
> HAIR SALON
>
> **When are you coming home?**

Is that my home?

> I'LL BE THERE IN A FEW HOURS.
> I LOVE YOU.

Nadine returns with two bowls full of some concoction and begins sectioning my hair.

"So let's have it. Give me all the details."

"Well, the ceremony's going to be on the beach in Strathmere. We'll have a small reception in a house there. I've rented a bunch of houses in town for guests to stay, but I'll give you all that information in the invitation."

"If you ever have them made," she says, half joking.

"Exactly."

"What about makeup, hair, headpiece, dress? All the things I have to work with."

"Umm, well…I don't have a dress." Nadine raises her eyebrows. "I haven't gone dress shopping. I can't quite figure out how to do it without my mom." Nadine softens and contemplates my dilemma.

"I have this, though," I say, and pull my mother's turquoise necklace out of my bag. It's kind of a crazy thing to carry around. It has several large turquoise stones; the largest in the center is surrounded by a sunburst of crystals and turquoise. Lining either side are pearls and crystals, and it's like nothing I've ever seen before. It's a heavy and intricate mix of stones, a significant piece, and I can barely hold it as stones hang off my tiny hands.

"Wow," Nadine says, and I can't gauge her reaction. She puts her comb down and takes the necklace from me. "This isn't a necklace, Charlotte; it's an anchor. Where did you get it?"

"I found it a few weeks ago when I was sorting my mother's jewelry. I never saw her wear it, though. I don't even know where she got it."

"Jocelyn, can you bring in my iPad please?" Nadine yells to the front of the shop. "This is going to be easy. Trust me." She refocuses on my hair. When Jocelyn brings in the iPad, Nadine motions for her to hand it to me and directs, "Go to Saksfifthavenue.com."

I'm confused, but I do what she asks.

"Now go to Women's Apparel. Dresses," Nadine says as she watches over my shoulder, and still paints small sections of my hair. "White, right? Unless you're thinking of something less traditional." Nadine's eyes light up at the thought of it. "No. White is fine." I fol-

low Nadine's instructions through the site, and Saks tells me there
are thirty-six white evening gowns. Nadine leans over my shoulder
and scrolls through the gowns until she stops on a strapless white
one with barely a hint of detail. It has a simple twist at the top and
hangs beautifully to the floor. The back has a long train that appears
hooked to the top of the dress and puddles on the floor behind it. It's
graceful and simple and understated, and the perfect complement
to this necklace. "This is the dress," Nadine says. "At least if that is
the necklace, then this is the dress."

I stare at the dress and select all the pictures, viewing it from the
front and back angles. It is the dress. And they have my size. Nadine
hands me my wallet and just like that, I have a wedding gown.

~4~

Life Is All About the View

Noble and Jenn have already texted me asking what time I'm getting to the beach. Today is probably going to be longer than my actual wedding day tomorrow. Now that everyone's finally here, we have a full day of doing nothing on the beach. At six tonight there's a rehearsal of the ceremony, organized by Noble's sister Jackie, of course, followed by a bonfire, organized by Jenn and Margo.

It's good to stay busy. It keeps my mind off the fact that my mom and dad aren't here. And all the rest of the things that enter my mind that I refuse to even name.

The bathing suit I swam in yesterday still hangs in the bathroom, soaking wet and cold. I wrap my robe around my neck, dreading putting the dripping suit on and looking around for the other suits, but Noble packed them for me and I can't find them. I call him, knowing he's probably impatient to get the party started.

"Hello, Lover," he answers, relieving my mind of the ghosts. "What need can I satisfy for you?"

"All of them, I'm sure. But for now I just need to know where my bathing suits are."

"Oh, need to ask your butler where he packed your suits, huh?"

"Yes," I say, admitting he spoils me.

"They're in the side pocket of the suitcase, but I'll come over and help you. Sometimes those things are hard to get on," Noble says, and I hear a door opening as he hangs up.

My dress catches my eye and I carry it to the guest room closet. I've kept it hidden for weeks; I'm not giving up now. I roll the suitcase to the open floor on the side of my bed and search through all the side pockets. This is what happens when you don't pack light.

I pull out a bottom, and the other suits come piling out, all tangled together with a navy blue scarf. I spread it out on the floor. A pattern of lighter flowers runs through it, and I know it isn't mine. It belonged to my mother.

The cool silk reminds me of another scarf from my past. A chill runs across my breast but stops there. It's not strong enough without his presence. *Neither am I.*

I wrap the scarf in a figure eight around both wrists and bury my face in my hands.

Jason.

"Charlotte?"

"I'm over here. On the floor," I say, and Noble comes to the other side of the bed as I free my hands.

"Oh, you found them." Noble goes through the suits, playfully matching each top with its bottom, and realizes he grabbed the scarf by mistake.

"Oops. Sorry. That's not going to work."

"The blue one is my favorite," I jibe as I shove the scarf back into the pocket of the suitcase.

"You can just wear the bottoms." Noble raises his eyebrows. He lies back on the floor, pulling me with him, and we both look out the sliding glass door at a cloudless blue sky.

"I could lie like this forever," Noble says as I listen to his heartbeat, but I can't seem to embrace the peace. The sky usually calms me, but the contents of my suitcase have unsettled me to the point of preoccupation. My fingers trail down to his waist and I kiss his neck, wanting him.

My hand finds him and I stroke him until he's hard.

"Me too," I say, and lean in closer to my fiancé. The scarf ignited something in me. Something I'm having trouble shoving into the pocket of a suitcase.

I straddle Noble and pull his arms above his head. His wrists, held tightly in my grasp, hit the floor hard and I lean forward to hold them there. My chest heaves as I fight for every breath, my body ruling my mind.

I find his neck and kiss him there, his hard-on behind me inciting me. Noble's earlobe is between my teeth and I'm sure I could bite it off from anticipation. There is a throbbing between my legs that will need attention soon. I swallow hard and return to his neck, stopping only to breathe near his ear and listen to the sound of his moan beneath me.

His biceps swell in this position and I lower my mouth to one. I run my lips across it. I bare my teeth and bite it.

"Charlotte." Noble's shock is a glimmer of myself.

I close my eyes and release his skin from my teeth.

I kiss him, my tongue apologizing for losing myself.

Noble rolls over, pinning me beneath him, and slows things down. He wraps my legs around his waist, his hard-on pushing against the still-screaming throbbing, and he holds my face in his hands as he kisses me gently, warmly, and nobly. I wrap my arms around his neck and drink him in. My lovely Noble.

When he's satisfied I'm not going to turn into a werewolf or some other creature—that I am indeed still the girl he proposed to—Noble pulls me up and onto the bed. He sits me down and unties my robe, pushing it off my shoulders.

I can't take my eyes off his bathing suit. It's bulging and I can taste him in my mouth. I look up at Noble, asking permission. I no longer trust myself. Naughty Noble raises his eyebrows, granting me permission.

My tongue skims the top of my mouth, anticipating him, and I bite my lower lip as I untie his suit and lower it to the ground. I stroke him with only my own needs controlling my actions. I'm aware of my heartbeat and the fury that's leading me and I breathe deeply. I don't want to hurt my beautiful Noble. I take him in my mouth and the throbbing quiets a trace.

Noble hangs his head back and savors my lips around him. In and out I move him and squeeze my thighs together. Noble's hand finds the back of my head as he controls the rhythm that could bring him to his knees.

And then he stops me.

He pulls out of my mouth and looks me in the eye. He lays me back with a gentle hand to my shoulder and lifts my legs to his waist.

"Fuck me, Noble." I have no idea what I am capable of.

Noble rams into me and I squeeze the sheets behind me. I grab my breasts in my hands and roughly squeeze them as my fingers find my nipples and pull. Noble watches me and I never take my eyes off of him, not ashamed but aroused by my own greediness. If I could reach them with my mouth, they'd be between my teeth. Noble looks down as he continues to enter me and the sight of him watching sets me off. I moan until my breath catches and sound is no longer possible. I release my breasts and balance myself on the bed, and Noble comes inside me. I squeeze him inside of me and can only think of how much I want to do this again.

Noble pulls out and leans over me on the bed. His breathing is jagged and his heart is racing opposite my own. I wrap my arms around his neck and kiss the side of his face.

When his heart slows, Noble pulls back and searches my eyes. I want to lower them, but it's a statement I can't make. Instead I smile at him and hope he stops thinking. *That's how I get through this.*

* * *

Jackie runs the rehearsal like a strategic military operation. She should be a wedding planner, or a prison guard. Noble and I stay behind to make sure there's nothing she needs help with. I'm hoping she'll relax some before she drives her husband, Travis, crazy. They were high school sweethearts. He's used to her, but still I hate to think of someone suffering because of our wedding.

Noble and I are hurried out of the house and to the bonfire. Jackie takes Travis's beer out of his hand and replaces it with a guest book and pen and pushes him toward the table in the front foyer. I try and convey sympathy with my eyes, but I'm afraid all I've achieved is fear because he gives me a knowing glance back.

"Save yourself, kid," he says as he walks by.

Noble grabs my hand and pulls me out the door. "She's crazy," he says when we're safely at the curb.

A yawn surprises me and takes over my face as we step into the street.

"Attacking me this morning must have exhausted you."

"I don't know what to say. I couldn't help myself," I say, thankful for Noble bringing it up and not making a big deal out of our near-violent encounter. "Stop being so hot."

I grab the skirt of my navy blue maxi and hold Noble's hand as we ascend the dune. I can smell the smoke of the bonfire before we reach the top. Everyone's brought out beach chairs to surround the fire and Sydney's date is preparing to play his guitar for the group. There are hot dogs and hamburgers on a portable table next to different types of salads. A keg rests in a large plastic bucket and Sam is manning the tap.

Violet comes over and moves different groups into position for pictures, and at the end of everyone's patience, she finally relents and focuses on candids for a while. She is barely showing but completely glowing. Blake is wholly attentive to her and she is basking in his recognition. Maybe a baby is what they needed all along. The idea defies logic, though. That can't be right.

Julia, Jenn, and Margo are smoking a joint down by the water and I join them as soon as I get wind of it, literally. They pass the joint as we all watch the water lap against the horizon and I deeply inhale all of it. The best friends a girl could ever ask for, an adorable dog, the incredible weather, a great husband-to-be. As if on cue, Noble walks up and wraps his arms around me and admires the horizon, too. And this view…

"Life is all about the view," I say, unable to take my eyes off the pink-hued sky. The sun is setting to our west and the sky is soft with its departure.

"From where I stand, it's perfect." I turn my head to the admiring stare of Noble Sinclair. I kiss his cheek and pull his arms tighter around me. He always sees things so beautifully.

"Be careful with perfect, Noble," I say, and Jenn flashes me a knowing glance as she hands me the joint. I suspect she'll never get married. She believes promises are always broken. Why does that seem logical and Violet and Blake's baby is not? I'll bet if I asked Noble, he'd see things completely differently.

* * *

The quiet of the house settles me. I take a deep breath, thankful to be done with today's festivities. I open the door from the hallway, and my room is lit without turning on a single light. The wall of windows beckons the full moon's reflection off the ocean. I walk to the windows and behold it. The moon is absolutely brilliant. It is this year's harvest moon, almost completely full, and its orange face is illuminating the entire eastern seaboard. It's hard to believe a nor'easter will hit tomorrow. The timing is important. We practiced the ceremony on the beach, but it might have to be inside. It'll be close. Noble's mom said she'll be leading the prayers for sunshine until after the "I dos."

"How can such a beautiful moon give way to a storm?" I ask the ominous night.

I have Julia and Margo here with me. It's only Jason to wonder about with this moon. Does he see it tonight? Does he know it's the eve of my wedding? Over the last two years, I've thought of what a horrible person I've become, but when I say "I do" tomorrow, it will be the pinnacle of cruelty I'm able to inflict on another person, especially one that I love. Jason thinks it doesn't change a thing, but it changes everything.

The waves crash on the beach and come to a whimper at the end before crawling out to sea. Such a violent ocean commanded by such a beautiful moon. I take off the dress I've had on too long and slip into my robe. I write "Gone for a swim" on the notepad by the television. There are beach towels piled on the floor next to my dresser and I grab one on the way out.

The wind whips my hair around my face as soon as I clear the point and head due east toward the water, and the moon. The crashing of the waves causes me to pause, contemplating the safety of a swim right now, but the incredible moon promises nothing bad could ever happen to me. Not on a night like tonight. I leave my robe and towel on the sand and wander into the ocean. The breakers almost knock me off my feet, but I run with lifted knees past them and dive into the final wave right before it crests and crashes to the ground.

The ocean's warmth surrounds me. This will be my last swim of the year most likely, definitely my last swim as Charlotte O'Brien. I let the water dance over the top of me as I float on my back with my toes pointed to the moon.

"I wish you were here, Mom," I whisper. "I know you're listening because you guys are probably pissed I'm out here swimming alone at night." I swim fifteen feet farther into the ocean and move south again, the strong current pulling me north with every set of waves. "I'm moving on, Mom. I've given up on understanding why and how things work. I'm just going to live." I shut my eyes tight in defiance, the ocean alive beneath me.

"Don't think I don't know you sent Noble to me. Oh, I know, he was part of a plan that was in place before I was born, but the mere existence of Noble Sinclair, and him loving me, reeks of your hand."

I flip in the water and come up facing the sky as a wave crushes me. I fight to the surface in time for another to descend upon me, forcing me to the bottom. My toes grip the wet sand of the ocean floor and I dive into the next wave and move past the breakers to catch my breath.

Here I rest. I lie on my back, floating over the waves, and focus on the bright orange moon. It has little to hide tonight.

Something catches my eye on the shore and I begrudgingly leave the moon behind. Someone is standing by my towel on the beach and I hope it's Noble, because whoever it is, is about to see me naked.

I fight my way out of the ocean and walk to Noble with tired legs. He wraps me in my towel and holds me at arm's length with a foreign, solemn expression on his face.

"What's wrong?" I ask. "Are you second-guessing marrying me?" I search his beautiful eyes for the reason he's wandering the beach at midnight.

"I'm marrying my best friend," Noble says, and kisses me on the lips.

"Are you second-guessing your choice of friends?" He looks right through me, lost in his own thoughts.

"What are you doing out here alone?" Noble asks, and pulls me close to his body. "If something happened to you, I'd have spent the rest of my life searching for you."

"I left a note in my room that I went for a swim."

Noble takes my towel off and holds out my robe for me to step into. He takes the towel and veils my head with it. I am warm, and safe, and a testament to the love of Noble Sinclair.

"As soon as I saw the moonlight, I knew you were out here. I was certain of it before I took one step toward the window. And sure enough, you're in the ocean risking your life and my future," Noble says, not a hint of anger in his voice.

"What time is it?" I ask, having lost track of time a few days ago. "It's bad luck for you to see me on our wedding day." Noble pulls the corners of the towel covering my head and moves my face closer to him. He kisses me in the way he does that makes me forget what we're talking about.

"Charlotte, I need you tonight." He kisses me again.

"I need you every night," I say, and lose myself in the gentle giant who, as of tomorrow, will be mine forever.

* * *

I open my eyes and Noble's arm is under my own, and his hand's up near my face. What time did we fall asleep? The curtains are open; the dark night is gone. The sky on fire, blazing with the sunrise. *Red sky at morning, sailors take warning.*

It's our wedding day.

"Noble! Noble." He rolls onto his back, a tranquil peace exuding from him. "Noble, wake up. You have to get out of here," I say, and jump out of bed and step into the closet. I watch him stir and reach out for me before fully waking and sitting up.

"Where are you?" he asks.

"I'm in the closet," I say without peeking out.

"This is the time you've chosen to tell me you're gay?" *Noble, Noble, Noble.* He does make me laugh.

"You can't see me on our wedding day. You'll curse our union and we'll have bad luck forever."

"You sound insane," he says. He searches for his clothes, putting them on as he finds them.

"Your mother will kill us both. Didn't you hear her talking to your sisters yesterday about keeping an eye on you?"

I glance up and Noble is standing in front of the closet door looking directly at me, without an ounce of fear in his eyes.

"I love you, Charlotte Sinclair," he says with a naughty grin.

"Oh, you are *so* playing with fire. We may as well call this whole thing off right now," I spout at him playfully. "This is going to be a long, wretched marriage."

"I'm looking forward to it," Noble says, and kisses me in the closet. "I'll see you at six. Call me if you need me." He walks out, leaving me in the closet. I hear the door to my room close and out the window I see Noble sneaking into the house next door. His mother is going to kill him.

~5~

Something Old, Something New

Nadine puts the final coat of mascara on and sprays the final spritz of hair spray with a sigh. She's satisfied with her work. She's fast, too. I have time to grab a quick bite to eat. Wouldn't want to pass out at the altar. I stop and study my reflection in the hall mirror. She brought a special foundation primer and concealer for my scar, and I can barely see the half-inch reminder of a tragic good-bye. It's been a year since the last time I saw Jason, since the day of the accident that left a scar on my face and a hole in my heart. If only there was something that could cover the rest. I reach up to touch it but hear Nadine screaming in my head and my arm snaps back to my side.

Nadine leaves and I sit at the kitchen island and eat my cheesesteak sub as I watch through the side window the mansion on the point. It's buzzing with activity. Chairs are delivered by a team of men all dressed in white, caterers walk in and out with coolers and trays of food on rolling carts, and decorators double-park their cars and carry flowers and baskets and God knows what else down the street.

Noble and his family are staying at the main house. I hope all the activity isn't overwhelming. His sister seemed thrilled to be in charge of the venue operation. I was thrilled to have only my hair and makeup to worry about, and Nadine made sure I didn't have to think more than ten minutes about either one. I told her I wanted it to be soft and wavy and pulled loosely back from my face. Something told me Noble would not want it tied up in a tight bun of some kind. He's gentle; I could be more like him.

And now I find myself alone. Kind of strange everyone else is with their dates and the bride is alone. The bridal party is dispersed in houses throughout the surrounding blocks so Noble and I will have this one to ourselves tonight. I walk up the stairs to my room with no particular purpose other than to not sit and think of how alone I am.

I slip into my dress and shoes. My eyes follow the wind as it blows down the shoreline. It blows through the windows and into my bedroom and over my bare shoulders in my gown. The storm is coming. The ocean's too rough to enter, and the rain will be here soon. *How soon?* I check the Doppler on my phone. The storm is already threatening the coast. What does a violent storm on your wedding day mean?

My grandmother would say the rain washes the past away and cleanses for the new day.

"Let it rain," I say.

I turn toward the bed and gasp at the sight of him.

Jason Leer stands before me, paralyzed as well. I wait for my instincts to kick in, but they've long been rendered useless when it

comes to this cowboy. I just stand, captured in his stare and forgetting every other thing that is happening around us. His cowboy
hat is missing. I run my thumb over the pads of my fingers, remembering what his jet-black hair felt like in my hands. He gray eyes
dip down to my hands, noticing everything. His button-down shirt
sprawls across his chest and I can feel the buttons sliding through
their holes. I stop at the belt buckle I gave him that is covering the
top of his jeans. Any farther would be cruel, and there's been enough
pain already.

The wind blows the bedroom door shut behind him and we both
turn our eyes toward the door. The door that will open soon, the one
I will walk through to my groom, Noble Sinclair. I watch the door
and contemplate just walking out and never looking back.

"I was hoping you'd marry me," he says, and I fight to find my
voice.

"No, you weren't. You know the answer is no." Jason is completely
unhurt, which does nothing to put me at ease.

"Did Sinclair kill dinner for the festivities?" he asks with his smug
grin splattered across his face. Jason nods toward the window as
more food is carried into the mansion. My reception hall. I turn
back to him, my eyes wanting more.

"He is a barbarian," I agree. "Unlike you, who chases animals,
dives on them, and wrestles them for money," I say, satisfied with the
contrast.

"It's never for the money." He steps closer to me. A familiar chill
lands in my breastbone and my lip quivers.

"It's never for the food," I manage to get out. I turn and shut the
window as rain begins driving against the east side of the house and
the wind howls, announcing the storm's arrival.

"Did you come to ruin my wedding day?"

"I'm not here to ruin anything. It's all been ruined before," he says, and moves even closer. "I wanted to see you in your dress."

The lights flicker and I defy the sadness settling under my skin.

"You're like a witch. You wave your arms and the thunder responds. You're evil."

Jason's gray eyes dance in the light that flickers again, threatening to exit the party.

"Charlotte, I came to get you before the storm ge—" Margo says as she swings the door open. She freezes in disbelief. *What's so hard to believe? Are there any two people more fucked up than Charlotte and Jason Leer? Of course he's in my bedroom just minutes before I'm supposed to walk down the aisle to another man.*

"Okay…," Margo says slowly, trying to decipher everything she's seeing. "I'm going to stand outside this door and guard it," she says, and turns toward Jason. "Because if Jenn finds out you're in here, she is going to rip you a new asshole." Jason practically laughs at his childhood friend's threat. "I mean literally. You'll be walking around with two holes in your ass." He's still unmoved. "And the little one from Rutgers—Julia." She points a finger at him as she speaks. "She'll take you out and they'll never find the body. Not to mention what Nadine'll do if you mess up her hair."

"Margo," I say, and she takes a deep breath. "It's okay." Margo walks over and stands between me and Jason. She puts both hands on my shoulders and stares up at me, trying to decipher where I am in this situation.

Is this a situation?

"No matter what happens in the next few minutes, no matter what direction you walk in, I'll be one step behind you. Got it?" she says, and tips her head. I nod slowly, not sure of exactly what she considers a possibility for my future. "I'll be right outside."

Margo walks to the door with evil eyes fixed on Jason until she closes it behind her. I turn to him and although he's not angry, I'm vulnerable. He could crush me at any moment.

"I know you'll go through with it. You're too loyal not to. But I figure you're probably feeling guilty about me," he says, and I can't take my eyes off him. I could lean into him, sit next to him, climb on top of him…I could have all of him. "Trapped in your loyalty, tied by your mercy, but still stubborn enough to see this through." I stay silent, unsure what to say. "You're beautiful, Annie."

I can tell by the way you look at me.

"But you know that."

"Are you planning on being here for the ceremony?" I ask, knowing his presence is the one thing that can stop this wedding.

"Would you like me to be?"

"I would like nothing less than to have you watching as I say my vows to someone else."

"Why is that, Annie? Because you wish it was me?" he asks, and takes my face in his hands.

"I thought you said you weren't here to ruin anything," I eek out, barely above a whisper. The touch of his hand on my face is making my stomach clench.

"It's been two long years since you left and not a day has gone by I haven't wanted you."

I close my eyes and lean into his hand. The lights flicker for the last time and we stand together in the darkness. "You need to go," I say, and open my eyes, begging for him to listen. "We had our day. Plenty of them and we squandered them. Took us for granted." I swallow hard, acknowledging my role in our demise. "I'm not going to make that mistake again." I take his hand from my face. "Not even with you." The touch of his rough skin tears at me and I run my fingers across his palm. "Promise you'll leave."

"I will. This is the one and only time I don't want to see you." Jason runs his lips across my cheek and whispers in my ear, "I love you, Annie." A chill runs across my breasts and down my legs.

I step back and take a deep breath.

I think of Noble and our families waiting for my arrival. Jason's right. I'm too loyal to do anything but marry Noble Sinclair today. Lucky for me, he is perfect.

"Be careful with perfect, Annie," Jason says, and I hate him…

And want him…

And love him.

"I'm ready," I say as I open the door to an anxious Margo.

* * *

Margo drives me next door, from one garage to the other. I am delivered in perfect condition, at least on the outside. The mansion is magnificent, and it's loud. It's a hive of bees swarming, creating a colony fit for a queen. Two caterers stop and nod my way, but otherwise I move about completely undetected. I take a deep breath and center myself. I'm well versed in separating Jason's emotions from my life. I learned to ignore his anger at Rutgers. I kept him just between the two of us, and now I'm leaving him alone.

Sean locks me away in my castle right before Nadine shows up to put on my veil. She's pleased with the results as I stand in front of her, displaying the finishing touches.

"Charlotte, you're beautiful," she says, and I beam.

"Do you think Noble will like the dress?" Nadine's expression calls me ridiculous without her having to say a word.

"He is going to love the dress. The way he looks at you, you could wear sweatpants today and he would love it." Nadine slides the small silver comb hooked to my veil into the back of my head and fluffs out the netting. She watches me in the mirror as she finishes her work.

"Are you okay?" she asks. I must not seem okay. I turn to the window and scan the house Jason and I just stood in. It's calm, painted the color of summer's perfect sky. I was just next door with Jason, and now Nadine is asking if I'm okay. "You look a little…I don't know." She steps in front of me and examines my face again. I smile, but it's fake. I'm guessing it's not fooling Nadine at all. "You seem agitated since I last saw you."

Oh, that's a great term for what he does to me.

"I'm fine." I try the smile again. "Just feeling a little haunted."

"Maybe it's the necklace."

Or my mother's hands choking me for wasting even one emotion on Jason Leer today.

"I'll see you outside," she says, and the wind whistles at the windows. Nadine winks at me reassuringly before closing the bedroom door behind her.

I survey the room and it's obvious someone's prepared it for my arrival. There are flowers on two tables in the room, candles lit on both sides of the bed, and shells leaning against the mirror on the dresser. Each shell has a different letter spelling out "I Love You," and I realize who's been here. The same person who will always be here.

Sitting in front of the shells is a wide silver bangle. I examine it closer and realize it has my monogram, my new monogram, in script letters on the front of it. I will soon be Charlotte Anne Sinclair. I lift the bangle and right before I slip it on my arm, I realize 9/10/11 is engraved inside with the verse, "Noble and Charlotte sitting in a tree," the childhood rhyme we all used to tease each other with.

My hand lingers over the seashells. I pick up my phone and text Noble:

I'M BLESSED.

Yes, you are.

He texts back and makes me laugh.

Send me a picture of you in your dress.

WHAT DRESS?

Even better

He is always so naughty.

Are you lonely?

YES

Do you want me to come to your room?

NO. I WOULD LIKE IT TO BE SIX O'CLOCK SO I CAN BE WITH YOU "LEGALLY"

Not long now. Wait until you see me. You, Charlotte, have made a very good decision.

I put the bangle on my wrist, the rhyme ringing in my head, as the door opens and Lily toddles into the room, followed by Michelle.

"Well, hello, Lily," I say, and beam at the sight of her. She has brought more joy to my family in her short year of life than anything else on this planet. We are utterly enchanted by every sound, giggle, word, and step of Lily Charlotte O'Brien.

"Aunt Shar piddy," she says as she inspects me from the top of my head to my shoes. Her eyes then fix on the turquoise necklace around my neck. Lily touches it, at first with only a finger, and then she takes the whole thing in her fist and pulls it to her.

"No no!" Michelle says as she pries Lily's hand off my jewelry.

"Someday," I say to Lily. "Will you take a picture with Aunt Charlotte?" I ask, and Lily nods. Michelle takes my phone and snaps a picture of Lily and me. Probably my last picture as Charlotte O'Brien. The memory of my wedding will fade for Lily by next week but will forever guide me.

A horrible crashing sound fills the house, and Michelle and I just look at each other.

"I think I'd better go downstairs and help set some things up."

"Please don't go to any trouble. It'll be fine. Really, Noble and I could be married in the back of his truck and neither of us would care."

"That's what I love about you guys." Michelle beams as she picks up Lily and walks out of my room.

I open the door to my balcony and the wind blows my dress behind me. The ocean is gray, the violent surf welcoming the storm as it crashes onto the shore. I breathe in the salty air. *Even a girl who worships the sun loves a storm once in a while.*

"Get away from the balcony," Sean says, and closes the door in front of me. I didn't hear him come in. I was lost in the storm. "You're going to get soaking wet." Sean studies me, trying to gauge if I've lost my mind.

"I'm ready," I say.

"He's waiting for you. We had to switch things around a little. Jackie might have a heart attack, but it'll be fine."

"I'm sure it'll be perfect," I say, and step into the hall, shutting my bedroom door behind me.

I can hear people shuffling around below me as I approach the landing. BJ catches wind of me and barrels up the stairs. I lean over and kiss his head while I rub behind his ears. Sean grabs my arm and keeps me out of sight of the guests. He moves me to the far wall, completely out of view.

"Mom and Dad would have loved Nick," he says, and straightens my veil.

"I know," I say, feeling as if I'm living my mother's grand plan and not my own life. What if her plan is my life? It could be a coincidence. My eyes dart to the dark corners of the hallway. I hope Jason has left town.

That is the last time I am going to think of him today.

This is Noble's day. Every day now is Noble's day.

"I'm glad you're with him, too," Sean says, without a hint of the worry I've burdened him with the last two years. I think Noble has taken one of his greatest responsibilities off his shoulders. "Do you see how happy he makes you?" Sean asks, questioning my expression that must diminish Noble in some way. "I know you've been through a lot, but you are never near him without smiling. It's like you two crack each other up." We do crack each other up. We always have. "You frolic," he says as if we are two silly children.

"Don't fall down and embarrass me," Sean warns, and wraps my hand around his arm.

"I'll try not to." A promise for a lifetime, not just today.

"Not yet." Sean halts me with a hand at my waist. He puts a finger to his lips to silence any response, and we hear the crowd at the bottom of the stairs humming the wedding march.

"It's brilliant," I say as we walk toward the top of the staircase. The three floors of the beach house all commence at the foyer. It's a gigantic room with two levels of balconies overlooking it. The grand staircase is lined with candles dimly lighting the room, and every loved one I still have is lining the railings or pooled at the bottom waiting for Noble and me to be married.

I tighten my grip on Sean's arm as we wait at the top of the stairs, and my eyes meet Noble's. I blush under his stare and the warmth travels through me. If I could, I would fly down to him, but first I have to survive this staircase practically in the dark. Noble is probably thinking the same thing.

Noble, as promised, is wearing his navy suit. The jacket spans from one side to the next with just a hint of how incredible his shoulders are beneath it. He's tall and muscular but still lean. He has the perfect body to carry a suit...or me naked.

Sean and I descend as the lightning strikes and the thunder threatens to drown out our guests' music, but they persevere and I am delivered to Noble as the crowd's hum dies off. I stand facing him on the bottom step of the staircase. Through my veil, I quickly scan the room and find Julia and Violet and Sydney hanging over the railing above me. Margo and Jenn are on the other side, and the sight of all of them fills me with love. Jenn lifts her glass slightly in toast to me and winks.

Butch and Marie are seated in chairs closer to the front door and my aunt Diane stands next to them. Marie's hand is on Butch's shoulder. There's love there. I'm not sure in what form, but it's good.

Clint has his arms around Jocelyn, but his gaze rests on Renee's boobs beside him. They're standing next to Nadine and Derrick, who are embracing as they look down at me. I take a minute to let the sight of them all fill me. We're in the eye of a storm and ready to celebrate a promise of a lifetime.

Pastor Johnson nods at Sean, who takes my hand and places it in Noble's waiting palm. Noble raises it to his lips and kisses it. I'm lost in the sight of my fingers near his lips. Noble's blue eyes, always the color of the clear sky, catch mine before he lowers my hand and covers it with his own. It takes me a minute to remember we're not alone here.

"Dearly beloved, we are gathered here today, in this beautiful place, during this tremendous weather, in the presence of God, to join Charlotte and Noble in holy matrimony. This simple ceremony, a few moments in time, is the celebration of a sacred love, created by and nurtured by you, dear Lord.

"Let us pray. Loving God, we thank you for the ability to love. We thank you for Charlotte and Noble finding each other and loving each other with your love as the ultimate example. They stand before you, their family and friends, and today affirm the love that has brought them to this place. Amen."

"Amen," we all repeat as the rain continues its assault on the house. Noble squeezes my hands, and the edge of my veil brushes across my skin. Sean was supposed to lift it before he handed me over. I roll my eyes at it and turn to Noble for help. He lets go of my hands and raises my veil over my head and back over my shoulders. His closeness moves me, and when he lowers his arms, I lean up and kiss him on the lips. Our "congregation" finds our inability to follow the traditional order endearing and laughs at us as Noble kisses me again.

Pastor Johnson clears his throat and we both turn our attention back to the ceremony at hand.

"Noble and Charlotte have chosen to memorize the traditional vows. I'll turn it over to them and hope we get through this without any awkward moments." Pastor Johnson laughs at us, too.

Sean hands me Noble's ring and I place it on his finger. I take a deep breath and Noble's eyes hold me.

I belong right here, right now, with Noble.

"I, Charlotte O'Brien, take you, Noble, to be my lawfully wedded husband, my treasured friend, my faithful partner, and my love from this day forward." I smile at Noble and sigh, overwhelmed by him. "I vow to be faithful in sickness and in health, in good times and in bad, and for richer or poorer. I promise to honor you and respect you…and laugh with you." It is Noble's finest gift. "And to love you as long as we both shall live."

I exhale and warm under the loving stare of Noble Sinclair. He is, and has been for two years now, my everything. Noble takes my ring from Sam and places it on my finger. I stare at it on my hand, held by his own.

"I, Noble Sinclair, take you, Charlotte, to be my lawfully wedded wife, my stubborn friend, my faithful partner, and my love from this day forward." Noble squeezes my hand and the look in his eyes, the ever-present evidence of how much he cherishes me, makes me tear up.

"No crying," he whispers. "I vow to be faithful in sickness and in health, in good times and in bad, and for richer or poorer. I promise to love you, to honor and respect you, to laugh with you—and at you—and to cherish you as long as we both shall live and forever thereafter."

He is the safest place I've ever known. He is my father and my mother and my life, and he loves me, forsaking all others. I wrap my arms around Noble's neck and lean into him. I kiss him with every ounce of love in my body pouring from my lips. He lifts me off the ground and doesn't return me until Pastor Johnson clears his throat again.

"Well, now, by the power vested in me, and in the name of the Father, the Son, and the Holy Spirit, I now pronounce you husband and wife."

I am beaming. Noble pulls me to him again. He is a promise, and an answer. And I love him. Sam and Rob are howling, and Jenn is doing a Jersey yell as the rest of our guests clap and cheer. The thunder roars outside as Noble takes my hand and leads me to the back of the house and into the library tucked away from the chaos. BJ nudges the door open as Noble takes a candle off the table in the hallway and sets it down on the desk, filling the room with the slightest light. I tap the chair and BJ jumps up as I wrap my arms around my new husband's waist and bury my head in his chest.

Noble takes my face in his hands and tenderly kisses me. I close my eyes and cherish the moment when my best friend became my husband.

"Hey," he says, and I open my eyes. "I'm sorry about the storm. You deserve a sunny wedding day."

I shake my head but never take my eyes from his. "It's exactly what I deserve and I love it. It reminds me of the first night we were together. The night of the snowstorm." Noble kisses me again and I savor the touch of his lips.

"I know my sisters are already stalking us, but before we go back out there, I want to tell you something."

I raise my eyebrows at Noble. "Is this when you're choosing to tell me you're gay?"

"Charlotte." Noble shakes his head. "You're beautiful." He looks me over again and I get a chill.

"Thank you," I say, humbled by his admiration.

"I am the luckiest man alive and I will never take you for granted."

I think I might cry. Even before he loved me, Noble never took me for granted.

"Do you know that?"

I nod, sensing he's not done.

He takes my face in his hands and caresses my cheeks with his thumbs. "And, Charlotte, I don't know what the future holds, but I know we are always going to be together. You'll never be without me."

"I know, Noble," I say, and kiss him. "You are my home."

With that, Jackie bangs on the door and threatens to barge in if we don't open it immediately. She's screaming what she'll do to Noble if he messes me up "in that dress" before our pictures are taken.

* * *

The thunder and lightning die down, but the rain persists. We still have no power, but we have the sound of the rain on the roof, and the road, and the ocean. It's a constant murmur as it cleanses our pasts and prepares us for the future.

We eat the food and drink the wine. Most is either cold when it should be hot or vice versa, but no one seems to notice. The sixty people here make up the perfect gathering. I wallow in the love and support of each of them as lots of flash photos are taken, and I let myself forget those who are gone forever. Noble is never more than a few feet from me and if our backs are to each other, he is pinching my ass. It is the perfect celebration of us.

* * *

I go back to the bedroom upstairs and enter it slowly, carrying my candle, focusing on every corner. I'm not willing to admit what I'm searching for. *Just get changed, Charlotte.* I take off my dress and veil and put them on the hanger over the closet door. I leave my shoes under it and slip on my flip-flops and sundress. I glance once more out the window, but there's only darkness, only the rain.

I grab my phone and step into the hall to find Noble waiting for me, leaning against the wall. He's wearing shorts, a long-sleeve shirt, and a rain jacket, which seems smart considering the short walk next door is going to soak us.

"Why didn't you come in?" I ask, and Noble spins me around and pins me against the wall. I lean into him as the heat spreads through me. I put a hand on each side of his waist and look up naughtily at him.

"I was afraid I would attack you," he says, slightly breathless, and I know it's time to go. I kiss him, a tiny, gentle kiss. Being careful with my giant.

Noble takes my hand and we descend the stairs. I say good-bye to every loved one I have left and pause at the door as BJ cries at my feet. I rub behind his ears. He wants to come with us. I look up at Noble and he leans down and scoops BJ up into his arms, covering him with his rain jacket. I take a picture of my two favorite guys and stow my phone away in the folds of my dress.

It doesn't get better than this.

~6~

Wedlock

"It's strange to have a wedding without music," I say as I put my phone on the table next to the bed. "Don't you think?" I look up at Noble, who's staring out the window, watching the storm conquer the ocean, for now.

"No first dance," he says as he turns to me. I tilt my head and take him in. Noble comes to me and pulls my dress over my head. He kisses me, hungry from our day apart. A day of watching each other, confined by an audience. Noble stops and takes the hairpins from the back of my head and lets my hair fall to my bare shoulders.

I pull Noble's shirt off and caress his biceps. I shiver and he pulls me close to him, warming me from the inside out. His wavy hair is wet from the rain. Noble carried BJ and held the umbrella for the two of us, bearing the brunt of the storm.

"You got wet," I say as I run my hands through his hair.

"Small price to get you out of there." He kisses me again.

I unbutton his shorts and lower his zipper. He drops them to the floor and his giant hard-on falls out as he does. Noble offers me his hand. It reminds me of my date nights at Rutgers when I could steal him for a dance. I place my hand in his and he pulls me toward him, his dick resting on my stomach, and we dance. Noble sings in my ear and we rock back and forth, my hand flat on his chest, his covering mine. I close my eyes and inhale deeply, breathing in the air that surrounds my husband and me on our first dance.

"I think you are making me sentimental," I say.

"I think you've always been sentimental. You've just been missing something of value," Noble says, and I am again struck by the way he sees things. Life is beautiful to Noble Sinclair, and I am beautiful. Lightning strikes and I freeze in his arms, waiting for the thunder. It roars and BJ's snoring pauses, but he rolls over and goes back to sleep on our bed.

"Do you think if we'd hired a videographer for the wedding that they would have filmed this?" Noble gives me a peck as he pulls away and takes his phone out of his shorts pocket. He wraps his arm around me and pulls me close. I rest my head on his shoulder as we both smile at the camera he's holding above us. Noble turns the camera for us to view the photo, my face next to his, resting on his naked shoulder.

"It will be my favorite wedding picture," Noble says, and kisses me again.

His lips part mine and his tongue finishes our dance as I practically climb up his beautiful body. I curl one leg around him and hang off his neck until he lifts me up and I can wrap the second behind him as well. Noble holds me as he kisses me, my heart beating against his chest. I pull back, our chests still touching.

"Can you feel my heart beating?" I ask.

"Always," he says, and sits on the chair in the corner of the room with me straddling him. "Always, Charlotte Sinclair."

* * *

I open my eyes to the sound of BJ snoring and the rain hitting the street. How can it still be raining? How can BJ still be snoring? I guess the wedding was a big day for him. My dog can't party.

I roll out from under Noble's grasp and tiptoe out of the room. In the kitchen, I find a tray and plates. I search for items not affected by the lack of electricity. I place four different bagels and two bananas on the tray. I add glasses and a pitcher of water. Anything else in the house I'm unsure of. I pull a few flowers from my bouquet and place them in a juice glass with some water and carry the whole thing upstairs. Noble's still asleep. I place the tray on the table next to my side of the bed and climb in next to him. I lie still, trying to comprehend that my lovely Noble is now my husband.

When he rolls over and his eyes flit, I kiss him. I can't wait any longer for him to be with me. "Morning, Hubby," I say.

"Good morning, Mrs. Sinclair." Noble rolls toward me. "I'm glad you're here," he says, and I'm confused.

"Where else would I be?"

"I had a dream two nights ago that you left me at the altar." Noble's face is grim, as if I would ever leave him. Ever leave him at the altar.

"That's terrible. I would never do that to you."

"I know. You're too loyal. I don't think you could live with yourself if you hurt me like that."

I hug Noble tight, hoping to rid us of this conversation. I don't want to consider what injury I'm capable of living with.

"Too honest, too."

"Actually, I need to tell you something."

Noble leans up and grabs a bagel from the tray. "What do you need to tell me?" he jibes. "There's nothing you can say that's going to get you out of this."

I chew on my bottom lip, trying to remember how I've kept this from him. Surely it wasn't intentional.

"I have a lot of money. Well, now we have a lot of money," I blurt out.

"What?" Noble is confused. Not confused enough to stop eating his bagel, but confused.

"When my parents died in the car accident, there was insurance…and inheritance…and a liability settlement," I say, listing the horrible papers that had to be signed in the business of my parents' demise.

"I know. That's how you and Julia bought the place in New York City."

"Yes, but there's still some left."

Noble continues eating, thinking this whole conversation is trivial. "How much could be left? Your place in Manhattan is great."

"Almost five million dollars."

Noble freezes midbite. He lowers his bagel to the plate resting on the bed. "What?" Shock has erased his humor.

"*We* have five million dollars. Not all liquid. The majority is invested, but it's ours."

"Why didn't you tell me before?" he asks, completely confused. "Your parents have been gone for four years."

"I know. I just don't talk about it. The money isn't a happy thing for me. It's blood money. I wouldn't have it if it weren't for some company's attempt to cover a scandal. Their death, silenced by a check."

"Why didn't you at least tell me after we were engaged?" Noble's beginning to realize he's married to an idiot.

"I almost did, but I was afraid you'd be uncomfortable with it."

"Shows what you know. I always wanted a rich wife," he says, and runs his thumb down the side of my face. "I would have insisted on a prenup. That's your money, from your parents."

"I think that's why I didn't tell you. There is some happiness attached to it, if it belongs to you, too. But that can be said for me or the money," I say, and kiss Noble's lips. *He makes me whole.*

"So now we have a lot of land and a lot of money. We need to see an attorney."

"Among other things." I move his plate to the side as I climb on top of Noble Sinclair.

* * *

The rain finally stops and we drive home in my Volvo holding hands. BJ is curled up on my lap, his head resting on the console, and my dress is hanging in the back. We did it. We really did it.

I'm married.

When Noble pulls into his—our—driveway, it's different. This is where I live now and even though I've spent hundreds of nights here, something is very different now that I have this thin platinum band around my finger. This will forever be my home. Noble squeezes my hand as he parks the car. Oh my God, this is where my car gets parked now. I think it's going to take some getting used to.

"Leave the stuff in the car. I'll come out and get it in a little while," Noble says, and I climb out without asking any questions. I grab the card I wrote him this morning out of my bag and carry it silently to the door.

Noble stops at the entry, grinning from ear to ear.

"What?" I ask. Not sure what the problem is. Noble lifts me up into his arms, and instinctively I wrap my arms around his neck.

"You can't walk over the threshold."

"Oh right, I can't walk over the threshold, but you can see me the morning of the wedding. Keeping up with which superstitions you take seriously is going to be difficult," I say, and lean my head on his shoulder. "I could get used to you carrying me around, though."

Noble carries me into the house and once BJ follows us in, he kicks the door closed. Instead of putting me down, he carries me straight to our newly painted bedroom and places me on the floor as the painting I hung right before we left for the wedding catches his eye. Noble walks to the painting and studies it.

"It's the farm?" he asks as he examines the house at the end of the waves of fields. It's the house we're standing in now.

"It's our home. Do you like it?"

"I love it," he says, and turns to me. "Almost as much as I love you." Noble takes my face in his hands and kisses me.

"I have a card to go with it." I hand him the card.

"Read it to me." *Can no one read their own letters anymore?* I open the card and sigh.

"Noble,

"If I can find a way for you to experience what I feel when you look at me, I will.

"It's as if everything good, and pure, and fun in this world is all wrapped up inside of you and unbelievably, you're mine.

"I should have married you the day after you asked, but I couldn't imagine I would be as happy as I was this weekend.

"You somehow fill me and instead of remembering those I have lost, I'm enamored with the one person I now have forever.

"Thank you for choosing me,

"Charlotte Sinclair."

The words are barely out of my mouth before Noble has me pinned beneath him on the bed. He kisses my neck while I giggle. His lips slide to my ear and his breath there stops the laughter. It's replaced by a heat dancing under my skin.

~7~

Prayers

Noble opens the back door just as I pull the blueberry bread out of the oven. I laugh at him, unable to contain myself, and he stops walking and gapes at me indignantly.

"What? Something funny?" he asks. He's covered in camouflage. His knit hat is camouflage, his jacket and overalls are camouflage, and his face is painted with black and green camouflage paint. How could I not laugh at him?

"No." I shake my head and turn on the coffeepot. It's only 8:30 a.m. and he already looks like this. "Please tell me you were hunting, though, and this isn't your new style."

"I was not only out hunting, but I was also successful. I got a doe," he says, and kisses me with his ridiculous face paint all over him.

"Poor doe. I'm sure she was no match for you." Noble watches me quietly, lost in his own thoughts. I've never seen a second of remorse from him when it comes to hunting. "Are you feeling guilty about your murder?"

He shakes his head and ends his solemn moment. "I was sitting in my stand—well, really I was thinking about getting down and coming in—when a buck walked right by me."

"Did you shoot him?"

"No. The season has a bag limit of one antlered deer and unlimited antlerless." I can't hide my confusion. "Bag limits" are new for me. "The first deer must be antlerless."

"Oh." *Oh sure, kill off the women first.*

"I was just watching this buck. I took my camera off the end of my bow and started filming him. Next thing I knew, a doe walked right up to him."

I pour Noble a cup of coffee and hand it to him, still listening. "And…?"

"And I shot her with the first arrow. She fell over twitching."

"She's not in the house, is she?" I really am scarred by the deer head in the refrigerator.

"No. She's in the back of the truck right now." Noble pauses as if that's not the end of the story.

"What?"

Noble shakes his head, thinking. "The buck came back around and just stood over her, watching her die." A chill runs down my back. "He knew exactly where I was and he just stood there for twenty minutes."

"Why didn't you shoot him?"

"He was a six-pointer. I want something bigger and I can only bag one antlered."

"Right."

"He wouldn't go away, though." Noble's perplexed.

I wrap my arms around his neck and kiss my clueless hunter. "He wanted you to take him, too." Noble kisses me again, but the look of confusion on his face does not dissipate. "He didn't want to live without her," I say, and remember a time when I wanted to die. I was hanging on a railing in Kansas, watching Jason being rolled onto a stretcher.

"You're quite the romantic, Charlotte," Noble says.

"It makes sense, doesn't it? Next time you see him, put him out of his misery." I cut the blueberry bread. *We were very lucky in Kansas.*

* * *

"You should come to church with me every week. I think you'd like it," I tell Noble as I find my black heels in the bottom of my closet.

"I think I'd like spending every Sunday morning with you. Some weeks it's not possible, though. Do you still sit in the same place? I like to sit in the back." Naughty. Always so naughty.

"Why am I not surprised? I actually sit with Butch now, and Marie if she comes, which is often. It's nice."

"Why don't you ever go to the contemporary service?"

"I don't know," I say, but I do know. This one feels like church. It reminds me of my mother. "Oh, and it's Communion today."

"Good, I'm hungry."

I shake my head.

* * *

We are a little late. Apparently even church is not a significant enough commitment to keep my husband's hands off me. Pastor Johnson is going through the announcements and he nods, smiling at me and the sight of Noble by my side. We enter Butch's pew from the outside. Marie is on the aisle, then Butch, me, and Noble—one big, happy family. Noble puts his arm around me and my wedding ring catches my eye. I still cannot believe we're married. Noble is my husband.

I lean my head on Noble's shoulder and get lost in Pastor Johnson's words. We stand as the congregation prays for the forgiveness of our sins and we silently confess.

Dear Lord, please forgive me for loving Jason as I married Noble. Not to make excuses, but it wasn't as bad as it seems. Jason and I are never going to be together again, and I love Noble tremendously. I took my vows after walking out of a room that held my first love. I promised to love Noble, forsaking all others. I'm okay with it, but I suspect you'd like it to be a much cleaner severance prior to the marriage ceremony.

I am rambling in my head. Trying to talk myself out of the emotions I know are wrong. Pastor Johnson absolves us.

"I needed more time," Noble whispers in my ear, making me forget about my sins and reminding me I've married my playmate. The congregation sings and I glance up at my naughty Noble. His is wearing the look that usually makes me tear his clothes off him. Maybe it's not a good idea for him to come with me every week.

Pastor Johnson's sermon focuses on the power of prayer. It's the most important thing we can do as a congregation. I haven't prayed since my wedding day. According to the pastor, I should be doing it every day, alone and with Noble. I look up at him again and he's watching me. I lay my head back on his shoulder. It's a very lucky head.

The service ends and I am finally able to laugh out loud at Noble.

"You are Presbyterian, right? This is your church? You seemed like you had no idea what was going on."

"I don't remember all this. After Sunday school I stopped coming except for Christmas Eve."

"Perhaps if you weren't so naughty all the time you could fit your confessions into one time period."

"I blame you," he says, and I turn to him, wounded. "You bring out the best and the worst in me, Charlotte. Without you I'm actually a very boring guy."

I roll my eyes. Noble has never been boring a day in his life.

We file out of the church. Marie walks next to Butch, ready to lend a hand if he stumbles. She's good to him. I turn from her to Noble and realize he is walking in the exact position next to me.

Pastor Johnson gives me a generous hug and shakes Noble's hand vigorously. We are the youth contingency in the 10:30 service. The earlier generations seem pleased with our company. I say hello to Mrs. Battaglia. I think she's related to Jenn, but I can't remember how. She pulls my head down to her lips and whispers in my ear, "Your new husband is very handsome." She releases my neck and winks at me, all of which makes me blush. My eye catches Noble's and I see he's confused.

"I know. He's perfect," I say, and the words float off my lips as the content of the conversation registers with Noble. He winks at me and gives Mrs. Battaglia his noblest "good morning." She is enchanted and I can't blame her.

"Will we see you both next week?" she asks.

"I hope so," I say, and walk to Noble, who takes my hand as we exit the front door of the church. I rest my other hand on the inside of his elbow and my head on his shoulder. Noble kisses the top of my head and I know God is smiling down upon us. Surely my mother is by his side, poking him, saying, "See? See? I told you he is perfect for her. He's wonderful and safe."

~ 8 ~

Nice Bed

Noble takes me to brunch at Washington Street Ale House in Wilmington before hitting the furniture stores on Route 202. We're lucky both of our houses are furnished. We can take our time updating each room with things we choose together.

"What kind of bed do you want?" I ask, flipping through the pages of some catalogs I brought with me.

"One with you naked in it," he says, and switches lanes.

"I think they all come with that." I thread my fingers in his hair. Noble leans over, instinctively knowing what piece of him I want, and I kiss his cheek. He stops at a red light and turns his head toward me. He reaches over and grabs my chin, pulling me to him again. His lips part mine and I think we should have just stayed home, in the bed we already have. A horn beeps behind us and Noble waves as he accelerates through the green light.

"Do you want a king-size mattress?"

"Is that the biggest? Because I want the smallest. What is that, a twin? I want you to actually lie on top of me every night."

"You say that now, but after a month of waking up with dead arm you'll likely want more room."

"You still don't get it, do you?" Noble says as he pulls into the furniture store's parking lot. He parks and hops out of the car without a care in the world. I wait in the passenger seat, already accustomed to the fact that he always opens the door for me. Noble opens my door and leans into the car. "I cannot, and will not, ever get enough of you, Mrs. Sinclair," he says, and kisses me. I rest my forearms on his shoulders and forget where we are and why we're here. In this moment, I'm here to be with Noble.

"It doesn't matter how big a bed you get—I am going to be touching you every night of your life. You can't avoid me," he says, and steps back for me to get out of the car.

"I'm counting on it," I say, and slip my hand into his.

We meander through the bed section and tell several salespeople we're just looking. There are different colored iron beds to choose from, a few wooden platform beds, and some ornate carved headboards. I immediately rule out the upholstered ones, unable to reconcile Noble's naked body near an upholstered bed. Something about the hunter and the metro style not meshing.

Noble dives onto an iron bed with large curves of iron intersecting with floral knobs. The bed shakes from the weight of his landing. He lies flat on his back and then rolls over, resting his head on his hand.

"Are you coming in?" he asks, and I just stand next to the bed laughing at him.

"No." I glance around to see if anyone is watching us.

"Come on. How are we going to know if this is the right bed for us if you don't get in it with me?"

"I don't think that's how it works," I say. He bounces up and down on the bed and I blush.

"You should climb on top of me." His eyes tell a story of sex in his truck, or on the beach, or in this bed and I'm about to climb out of my skin.

"You're insane."

"This is a big purchase. We could have this bed for twenty years. We need to make sure it can handle us."

"Noble Sinclair, you are no gentleman. All these years of holding the door for me…"

He holds out his hand for me. I take it and sit on the bed next to him.

"How are we going to know if it bangs the wall unless you ride me?" He pulls me toward him and I kiss him, forgetting I am in the middle of a furniture store in Delaware.

"Ahem." I look up to the scornful eyes of a saleswoman.

"We'll take this one," Noble says, never taking his eyes off me.

"In a queen," I add, and peck Noble on the lips. We should not be allowed in public.

* * *

Our new bed is delivered three weeks later, as promised. The deliverymen, and everyone else in town, can only talk about one thing—the early snowstorm that is bearing down on the East Coast. They recite the latest weather reports as they carefully climb the staircase. The early predictions were all correct. As much as I'd hoped the direction of the storm would change, this time we won't be lucky. The storm is going to wipe out the corn crops of Salem County and all those in the surrounding counties of South Jersey. Noble has custom work scheduled for the next three weeks, harvesting smaller farmers' crops for them and his own, of course, but the storm has wreaked havoc on his schedule and left him at the mercy of the hours in the day.

He and his crew are working from the minute they wake up until the middle of the night. He's come home the last three nights after midnight and crawled into bed. Today is Sunday and it will be more of the same.

"How much more do you have to do?" I am missing him. This house is lonely without him. I've been working late as well, trying to keep myself busy, but BJ and I want him home.

"Everyone's pooling our resources now. No farmer wants another to fail. We'll harvest as many acres as we can before the storm hits."

"Don't they have insurance for the crop?"

"They do, but it's not the same as an actual crop. It might cover their debt, but it's months of work for zero profit if we don't get it out of the ground. The storm, the rain and the wind they're calling for, will bend the stalks and lay them on the ground. The longer they lie there wet, the less likely we are to salvage them. Our best bet is to combine before it hits."

I nod as if I understand everything he's talking about. He's hunched over from exhaustion. He looks ten years older.

"I miss you, Noble Sinclair." I wrap my arms around his waist. I lay my head on his chest and hide my selfish face from him.

"I'm sorry I keep leaving you here all alone." His voice is quiet, weighed by exhaustion. He strokes my hair and I lean into him, not

caring how tired he is. I need him. "I'm also very sorry you're missing homecoming. If it weren't for the storm, I'd have taken you up
there."

"I don't mind." I close my eyes and inhale my husband. "We can
go next year. I'll miss seeing Julia and Sydney." I pause, considering
all the people I only see once a year now. "And a few others, but Violet wasn't going anyway. I guess homecoming's not as fun with a
baby on board." I sigh. There's only one person I need. "I just miss
you."

"I feel the same way, Mrs. Sinclair." Noble lifts my face to his and
kisses me, reminding me of why I miss him, and the guilt melts away.
"We'll make up for lost time during the storm."

He kisses me again and I consider not letting him out of the
house.

"I want to talk to you about something when we have some time."

"What?" What could he possibly have to talk to me about?

"Something good. Later, though. I've got to get into some clothes
to combine in."

* * *

I go to church alone. Noble came with me again last week, and again
it was a cross between a prayerful sermon and my playful husband
entertaining me. What does Noble confess? Does he pray for a way
out of this marriage? I bow my head and stare at the pages of the Bible. I know that's not true. Noble is always so sure of us, of me. He
makes me believe this is where I belong, even when I have no idea
sometimes.

I sit with Butch and Marie and marvel at how far we've come.

Two years ago, I could barely look at Butch and now he's absolutely a part of my family. He witnessed my marriage to Noble and he was there as my loved one, not as Jason's father. It's more evidence that life is indeed crazy, the passage of time cosmic.

Pastor Johnson concludes the service and I hurry out the front door ahead of the crowd. I'm not in the mood to socialize. Let Butch and Marie answer all the lingering questions about the wedding. Noble's mom will be in town in a few months; she can fill in the rest of the details. For now I want to be home, even if Noble's not there with me.

* * *

I park the Volvo in the L-shed and walk to the house. A weighty, almost balmy breeze brushes the hair from my shoulders and then whips it up and around my face. I tilt my face to the sky and the October sun covers me in warmth. The haphazard clouds decorate the bright blue, making it impossible to believe a debilitating storm is on its way. Nothing seems organized, only glorious.

I swing open the door to the kitchen and lean down to hug BJ hello. It's always the same enamored greeting, whether I've left for the weekend or an hour. The last few boxes from my parents' house are stacked in the dining room. There wasn't much to move: boxes in the attic from high school, a few from college, some decorations and other personal belongings. The furniture I left for Clint to use. My clothes filled my car in one trip. It's hard to accept I'm never going back.

I change my clothes and begin unpacking the last few boxes. BJ lies at my feet, snoring. He is the most content living being on this planet. I abandon the boxes for the window. The fields, the lawn, the trees, everything will be different tomorrow. There's no stopping a storm; you can only hope to survive it.

The sun dips to the west, but the temperature's still warm. BJ and I walk barefoot over the lawn and settle into the hammock on the side yard. I lie down and look out over the fields. They're completely empty. The grain has been harvested; the equipment's moved on. It's just BJ and me waiting for Noble to come home from someone else's field. I close my eyes and breathe in the warm air, thankful for one last summery day.

***

"We're going to tell him," Noble says as we pass Frederick, Maryland, and head toward West Virginia.

"Where are we going?" I ask.

"To Oklahoma. We have to tell Jason we're married."

"I already told him," I say, and stare out the truck window. The road is familiar. How many times did Jason and I drive it?

"When?" Noble interrupts my thoughts, but I don't bother to look at him.

"He was at the wedding," I say, but Noble ignores me.

"I want to be there when you tell him."

"Why? This is cruel." He's been through enough. A chill runs through me.

"Annie, I want you to tell him you've always been in love with me and you'll never leave me," he says.

"Annie?" I turn away from the window. Jason is now driving Noble's truck and we're still headed toward Oklahoma.

* * *

I shiver as my eyes open to the darkening sky. It takes less than a minute to realize he's not here. Neither of them is here. Anger wells up inside of me and I clench my teeth. The wind whips around me, commemorating his presence, and I move my arms to cover myself. A piece of paper under my hand falls off the hammock and I grab it. I open it, already knowing what it says.

nice bed

I sit up and look for him, but there's no sign of life. My phone falls to the ground. I pick it up and climb out of the hammock. BJ runs around the house, following the wind's trajectory. There are no lights on at Butch's, no truck parked nearby. Jason was here, though. I fold the paper and slip it into my back pocket and call BJ in for dinner. As I fill his bowl with food, I realize my hands are shaking. I have to settle down. Noble will be home soon.

Noble arrives at 8:30 and promises to come down and eat after a shower. When there's no sign of him by ten, I go upstairs and find him asleep in our bed, the covers at his feet as if he didn't have the strength to move them.

"Here you are trying to help the whole town, and what is the other one doing?" I say to my sleeping beauty. "He's causing trouble. As usual." I pull the covers up to Noble's neck and climb in next to him. I curl up against him and pull his arm around me. Even if he's not awake, I want him to hold me. I need him to.

~9~

Knocked Up

I'm staring out the window as the first flakes of snow begin to fall. It's unusual to have snow this early, before the leaves have fallen. Apparently, the presence of the leaves and the weight of the snow are the two factors leading to the widespread power outage predictions. I've filled the tub with water, knowing that once we lose power we'll have no pump for the well, no water, and I've taken what I'm sure will be my last shower for a few days.

Noble's still asleep. I don't even know what time he came home last night. Sean stopped by earlier to see if I needed anything before the storm. It's a good thing I didn't, because he said every store in the county had empty shelves. No more milk, bread, or eggs. The hardware store was out of shovels and salt, and the big chain stores in Delaware had lines out the doors for days for generators. The Eastern Seaboard is battening down the hatches together.

Sean said Noble and the rest of the county's farmers finished the entire harvest. When I told him I've barely seen Noble in a week, he reiterated what a great guy he is. Apparently, the whole town's singing Noble's praises as their grain rests in the dryers, waiting for transport.

I pull the brownies out of the oven and immediately place a piece of masking tape on the side of the dish with "special" written on it. It took me forty-five minutes to ground and cook the weed in the oil. I don't want to confuse the two pans. It's hard to imagine, especially among the guests at Clint's Halloween party, but there might be someone out there who doesn't want to eat pot brownies. Thus the reason for two trays.

This will be my first visit to my parents' house for a party hosted by Clint. I'll be a guest. I stuff the extra-large pantyhose I bought with towels until I'm satisfied I appear at least eight months pregnant. I pull my mother's wedding dress over my head. It's has an empire waist and a full skirt. Perfect for hiding a pregnancy. I mentally attempt to count the months between their anniversary and Sean's birthday until BJ jumps on my pristine gown and I lose track of my calculations.

The dress hangs in that perfectly inappropriate way that's only acceptable on Halloween. It stretches over my fake belly, practically bursting at the seams. The tiny pearls and sequins reek of the eighties and I kind of love it. I pull the front of my hair back and secure the beaded headpiece as Noble walks into the room.

"Aaah, my lovely bride," he says, and kisses my neck, threatening to keep us here all night.

I put a foot between us, hoping to give us a chance of leaving the house. "I want to at least make it to the party for a little while. Clint's put a lot of work into it."

"Such a prude, my bride is," Noble says, and slips into the denim overalls he's wearing tonight. "It's obvious you put out." He takes a shotgun out of the gun case and slings the strap over his shoulder.

"Oh no you don't. You're not taking a real gun to this party," I say, and Noble eyes me, questioning if I've lost my mind. "I cannot stand one more tragedy. I bought you this one from the Dollar Store." I hand him a toy shotgun with a cheap strap to hang over his shoulder.

"You're kidding, right? This is a disgrace. I am a hunter," he says, completely not agreeing with my safety precautions.

"Please. I know it's stupid, but I'll worry all night you are going to shoot someone and be in prison for the rest of our lives."

"You worry too much," Noble says, and kisses me again.

"That's what happens when you have something you can't bear to lose. You worry about it."

Noble puts a straw hat on his head and takes my eyeliner to black out his front teeth. I can barely stop laughing long enough to take a picture with my phone.

"What? Don't you find me attractive?" he asks, flaunting his new and improved smile.

"Always." I hand him a tray of brownies to carry. I grab the other and we walk through the snow to Noble's truck. He opens the door for me and helps me climb into the passenger side before placing both trays of brownies on my lap.

"Why two trays?" he asks.

"One is brownies. The other is pot brownies."

Noble shakes his head as he closes the truck door and walks to the driver's side. "You're such a criminal," he says, and starts the engine.

"Pot is still illegal?" I ask as if it's the craziest thing I've ever heard.

"What a waste." I search the gray sky for something other than falling snowflakes. There is nothing.

* * *

Several cars line the driveway and the yard at my parents'—Clint's—house. Noble drops me off at the garage and helps me out with my two pans of brownies. He pulls off the driveway and parks on the lawn, the truck pointing toward the road. Noble takes care of everything.

We walk in and are met by the hilarious costumes of our childhood friends. Clint is a hammer. He's wearing all black with a silver hammerhead made out of aluminum foil anchored to a hat on his head. Jocelyn, who he is unbelievably still dating, is of course dressed as a nail. Nadine and Derrick are salt and pepper shakers. Chris Black is a lifeguard with one of those fake muscle chests. He has pierced both nipples and has a chandelier earring hanging from each one. There's plenty to find funny and we do. Noble and I laugh ourselves silly before the brownies even begin to take effect, and when they do, we can barely control ourselves. We spend the party catching up with everyone we've missed the past few months. Sam abandoned Philly to be at his parents' house for the storm, providing us with the pleasure of his company for a few days. He's brought his new girlfriend home with him. She's a police officer, Sam happily her prisoner.

When the clock strikes midnight, I wander through the hallway of my childhood home. The fresh paint on the walls and new flooring and trim solidify its new owner. I marvel at Clint's library in what used to be Sean's room. It used to be decorated with posters and football jerseys, and now the walls are covered with bookcases that stretch from the floor to the ceiling. Dark mahogany, rich with interest, hold books Clint has collected from yard sales. He built a bench into the wall below the windows and it's now a cozy nook for reading. Sean has to come see this. He won't believe it.

"Do you miss this house?" Noble asks, startling me as he wraps his arms around my waist from behind.

"No." The word lingers on my lips. It's not this place I miss.

Noble turns me around and kisses me. "No?" he asks, gauging my honesty.

"I clung to it for a while because if felt like my last tie to a family, but you're my family now." I take Noble's face in my hands. *My beautiful Noble.* "My home is wherever you are," I say, and kiss him with every need I've kept quiet since Noble began harvesting ahead of the storm.

Noble lifts me toward him, perfectly fitting my body to his. His hunger replaces his caress, his hands searching for my skin under my voluminous gown. He finds the hundred buttons in the back and, with a hand on each side of the fabric, rips the gown open. The tearing sound halts his probe.

"I'm sorry, Charlotte," he says, concerned with my mother's gown.

"I'm not." I lock the door before I lead him back to the chair in the corner of the room. "I want it off me more than you do." Noble pulls my dress over my head and I tear off my panty hose and fake bump. I land on top of Noble just as he lowers his overalls to the floor, and I devour his mouth with my own as we fall backward into the chair. When I'm out of breath, I rise up and Noble takes my nipple in his mouth. His tongue swirls it, leaving it hard and protruding and my other one cries out for attention. His mouth quiets it and I moan. I let my head fall back, the falling snow my only view from the window.

Noble lifts me up and guides himself into me. He takes my hands from his chest and weaves his fingers through each of mine. I use our interlocked hands as leverage to rise and fall and when I come down the second time, Noble pulls our hands toward him and I collapse on his chest.

"I love you, Charlotte," he says, and kisses me, not waiting for a response. Noble pulls out and climbs behind me, still leaning me over the chair. He enters me from behind and pulls my hair to the side to kiss my neck as he does. Noble in me, the touch of his body, spreads through me and the warmth takes over. My body has missed him. I've missed him. He holds the side of my head with one hand and kisses the other with lips that lavish every inch of me. They travel down my neck as Noble continues his rhythm in and out and I try and breathe with every inch of him exactly where he belongs. He kisses my neck, my shoulder and runs his lips halfway down my back. He is love, and desire, and everything in between.

I want Noble to make love to me for the rest of my life.

"Don't stop, Noble." I plead for more than right now. Noble doesn't respond; he takes his finger to me as he rams into me from behind. I bite my lip to keep from screaming something that can be heard over the music and come as Noble slows and enters me one final time. He rests in me as I hang my head onto the chair and try to recover.

Noble's lips are on my neck again and I shiver under their attention. He wraps his arms around me and climbs onto the chair beneath me, pulling me toward him. We sit, me on top of him, my face toward the door, and when I shiver, Noble pulls my dress on top of us and warms me with his lips. He holds both my hands and I lean back on his solid shoulder and close my eyes.

"I want you to go off the pill," he says, and my eyes fly open. "I want you to have my baby."

"Why?" But that's not what I'm asking. "Why now?" Noble turns me around and I straddle him. He is happy, completely content with me naked on top of him. I take his chin in my hand and kiss him. My tongue gets away from me, taking what it wants and forgetting the conversation.

"You're not going to change the subject." He pulls back an inch. "You were twenty when your parents died," he says, and I look down at his belly button. He lifts my head and my eyes find his again. "None of us knows what is meant to be, but I'm not going to wait around for any of it."

"You should have married Violet. She's the trailblazer."

"I'm exactly where I should be." He kisses me again and holds my face in his hands. "What's there to wait for, Charlotte?"

"I'll be twenty-five next month. Doesn't that seem young? We just got married."

"You were too young to lose your parents. Too young for so many things." His voice trails off and I hate the other things. Before I can drown in my memories Noble kisses me. His lips, soft and gentle on mine. I'm going to cry. "This is perfect, Charlotte. There's nothing to fix, nothing to conquer, nothing to settle, nothing to wait for." There's *nothing* but truth in his words. "Let's have a baby."

"Can I think about it? I might just want to enjoy you, without sharing you, for a little while."

"There's plenty of me to go around," Noble says. "But you can take as long as you need. I'll just keep trying to get you pregnant whether you're on the pill or not." Noble kisses me again and I rest my head on his shoulder.

Am I really going to be twenty-five next month? Time marches on. It slips through my grasp. My parents are gone…forever. Lily is eighteen months now and it's as if she's been with us our entire lives. People die, others are born, life keeps moving on. Noble seems fine with the forward progress. I'm always lagging behind him. He pulls me into life, forces me to live it. It must be exhausting for him. I stand and watch him pull up his overalls. He is as light as air, not weighed down in the least.

"What?" he asks, and walks over to me. "Did I upset you?" His face is full of concern.

"No." I shake my head. "You couldn't upset me. I'll stop taking the pill and we'll see what happens. Whatever is in God's plan." Now that I am safely with Noble, I'm willing to accept there is a plan without becoming totally pissed off.

Noble pulls me to him and holds me tightly. I bury my head in his chest, thankful to have him. So thankful he's here, in this life, with me.

~10~

Love Hurts

Noble goes out to the Volvo and starts it to let it warm up. The temperature hasn't gone above freezing in weeks. This is the worst winter I can remember, and it's barely begun. I bend over and give BJ a kiss good-bye on the head.

"We won't be late. Just a birthday dinner," I say, and BJ tilts his head, listening. I lock the door behind me and walk to the car Noble has pulled up to the house so I don't have to walk all the way to the L-shed. The wind pierces my scarf and whips across my neck. Noble's waiting to open the door for me.

"Happy birthday, Charlotte." He flashes his signature naughty grin at me.

"Are you sure you want to go out?" I ask. From the expression on his face, I'm surprised we've made it this far.

"For a little while. Part of your gift we need to be home for." My heart begins to race. "We'll get arrested if I put my tongue there in public," he says, and the heat rises in my chest. I lean into Noble and kiss him. I close my eyes and forget it's cold outside as his warmth fills me. "Get in the car," he commands. "Or we'll never leave."

I climb into the Volvo and reach for the button to heat my seat, but Noble already has it on. He is going to be a great dad. Julia is going to kill me when I tell her we're trying to have a baby. I can't even predict Jenn's reaction. She's already annoyed I'm married this young. The only thing appeasing her is our delayed honeymoon to Hawaii in January. We're planning on spending at least a week with her. Maybe I'll ask Noble to wait until after Christmas for a baby.

Noble takes my hand as he drives over the river. The water is the color of steel and the sky a dark charcoal. It reminds me of Jason's eyes, like the water when he was placated, like the sky when he was not. Noble squeezes my hand and I forget Jason. Just because the northeast is gray this time of year doesn't mean I'm going to spend every day reminiscing about Jason. I can't. I'll go insane.

"You know, I don't think I realized when we got married that you're not only rich, but also an older woman." Noble keeps a straight face as we glide through the EZ Pass lane.

"Is this supposed to make me feel better about my birthday?" I ask, not amused.

"Do you see the way I look at you?" He's practically licking his lips.

"Yes. You are a very naughty boy, Noble Sinclair."

"I am going to look at you the exact same way when we are seventy-five and, even if I can't get it up, when we're eighty-five, too."

"There's something to look forward to. Can we talk about something else?"

"What do you want to talk about? What are you looking forward to?" I watch Noble merge, switch lanes, and exit off the highway.

The few people on the streets of Wilmington are bundled up so tight their eyes are barely visible. They're rushing somewhere. At some point during the last five years, I stopped looking forward to things...stopped looking forward at all.

"Charlotte?" he says as he pulls into a parking space next to Miki-motos.

"Mmm, sushi. You're too good to me, Noble."

"I know. You are spoiled rotten. Hard to be around," he says, and jumps out of the car to open my door for me.

The hostess seats us at a table by the window and we watch the Friday rush hour leave the city. It's dark early now, daylight savings time having robbed the afternoon of daylight and paid it to day-break. Noble's days are shorter, too. His work is almost finished for the year. The waitress comes and we order Brooklyn Lagers and three sushi rolls, but save a menu for more. Sushi is one more thing Noble and I have in common.

"I'm going to the bathroom." I dig my phone out of my bag. "Will you keep an eye on this? Sean said Lily is going to call me tonight to wish me a happy birthday and I don't want to talk to her in the bathroom," I say, and wrinkle up my nose.

"No problem. I'll gladly speak with Princess Lily."

"Uncle Nick is her favorite."

I return from the bathroom to Noble is staring out the window, my phone in his hand.

"Did she call?" I'm excited to talk to her. I take a sip of my beer as Noble turns to me with anger in his eyes. His hate-filled gaze makes me sit back in my chair. "What? What's wrong?"

"You got a text," Noble answers with a flat voice.

"From Lily?" *What is going on?*

"No." Noble tosses my phone onto the table in front of me.

I'm still confused as I pick up my phone and press the HOME button. A text lights up the screen.

Happy Birthday, Annie O'Brien

I swallow hard as I read the text. Anger wells up inside of me. He wrote this for Noble as much as for me. Otherwise he would have left off the O'Brien. What an ass.

"I didn't realize Jason was in your contacts," Noble says, still coursing with ice.

"He's not." I stare down at the text on my phone, labeled with Jason Leer as the sender. I'm confused..."I don't...I don't understand," I say as I try to put the pieces together. *He is evil.*

"Is it possible he doesn't know we're married?" Noble asks.

I'm not sure how he can give Jason the benefit of the doubt. I guess it's because Noble doesn't realize that it's not possible for Jason to not know anything. Especially when it comes to me.

"No. He knows," I say, and look Noble in the eye. I don't want him to suspect for one second I'm hiding something from him. That's not how marriage works.

"Have you spoken to him?"

"Not since the wedding," I answer, maybe a little too quickly. "I wrote him a letter to tell him about the wedding." The words lodge in my throat, but Noble's not giving an inch. "And I saw him briefly before the ceremony."

Noble rubs the scruff on his chin and stares at a pointless spot on the table. The waitress places our sushi rolls between us and looks at Noble and then me.

"Can I...uh...get you guys anything else right now?" She takes a step back and waits for our answer. Noble is even scary to strangers.

"We'll take another round, when you have a chance," I say, and down my beer.

"What did he want?" Noble asks, and finally faces me. "Never mind. I know what he wanted…wants." The words sting as they reach my ears. *I could fucking kill you, Jason Leer.* I peer around, half expecting him to be in the restaurant.

"Noble." I grab his hands from his beer glass. "Noble, look at me." Noble turns his angry eyes on me. "He doesn't matter. None of this matters. I don't know why his contact is in my phone, but I don't plan on using it. He's hanging on to the past." I squeeze his hands. "I'm Charlotte Sinclair now."

Noble swallows hard. I rub his hands reassuringly. He has to believe me because there's not much else I can say. I can't keep telling Jason *and* Noble the same thing. At some point I'll exhaust myself.

"Is that my birthday present?" I point to the box Noble placed on the windowsill after we sat down.

"Yes," he says, his demeanor relaxing.

He hands me the box. It's about the size of his palm and wrapped in aluminum foil. I'm careful with the wrapping, not sure what I'm saving it for. Treating this entire meal as delicate now. I lift the lid and fabric pops out of the box. It's small triangles and strings, all a beautiful mix of turquoise and deep blue. As I hold a piece in front of my face, I realize it's a bathing suit, a very tiny string bikini. I raise my eyebrows at it.

"For Hawaii," Noble says, his self fully restored.

"I'll try it on as soon as we get home," I say, and dig into our sushi.

* * *

It's as if Thanksgiving is the day after my birthday. But in fact, it's been over two weeks since I turned twenty-five. The weeks flash on their way past, and I still can't keep up. Michelle and I are busy in the kitchen when the phone rings. Noble walks in and grabs the receiver.

"Oh hey, Happy Thanksgiving," he says. Who would call here on Thanksgiving? "Oh. I'm sorry to hear that," he continues. "I'll bring some leftovers in a little while." With this I can tell he's talking to Butch or Marie. Probably Marie since Butch talks on the phone as little as possible. Noble hangs up and I look at him, my hands covered with potato peels as I try and gather them up from the bottom of the sink.

"They're not coming?"

"No. Marie said Butch isn't feeling well. They're going to hang back," Noble says, and pulls a bottle of wine off the shelf in the mudroom.

"Oh. Maybe it's his knee. I'll check on him after dinner," I say as Lily toddles into the room. She's pulling BJ by the collar and stops every few steps to kiss and hug him. He loves her, but she's tough on him. I always tell him some people's love hurts, and Lily is one of those people. Noble pulls her off the poor dog.

"How about you and Uncle Nick make a list of all the things we're thankful for?" he suggests. Lily delights in anything that begins with her and Uncle Nick. I hear him searching for paper and a crayon in the Lily Art Box we keep in the dining room. I lose track as Michelle pours herself a glass of wine and plops down at the kitchen table for the first time in the last few hours. Thank God she's here. I wouldn't know what the heck I was doing alone in the kitchen with a roasting pan.

"Butch didn't have any family come to town?" Michelle asks, and takes a sip of her wine.

"No. Not this year." I pour myself a glass.

"That's nice." She tips her head, acknowledging our secret conversation.

"It is. Especially for our first Thanksgiving together. I wouldn't mind if he stayed away forever," I say, and can hear Lily laughing at something Noble is saying.

"I think Noble and Sean agree."

"Not you?" I ask, half joking with her.

"I don't know. I guess I always thought you two would be together," Michelle says, shocking me. I'm pretty sure Sean would kill her if he heard this. "Don't get me wrong. I love how things are right now. I'm just a masochist, I guess."

"You would have to be." I nod and gulp some more wine.

* * *

Besides that crazy nonsense about Jason, Michelle was a huge help. Dinner was delicious and I couldn't have done it without her. I took careful mental notes in case I ever have to pull it off alone. While Noble washes the cookware, I pack up the leftovers—one set for Sean and Michelle, one for our house, and a little of everything for Butch and Marie. Butch's knee must be acting up again. He loves a meal hot out of the oven.

I bag the food and invite BJ to come with me while I deliver it to Butch's. Seeing BJ might improve Butch's mood. Somehow the sweetest dog in the entire world and the crustiest old man are perfect companions. Opposites really do attract. BJ and I cross Butch's yard with my bag of leftovers. I pull my coat up around my ears. The wind makes the temperature feel much colder than the forty-three degrees it's supposed to be. I fumble with my bag of food and the keys to the multiple locks on Butch's door as BJ stands ready to pounce into the house, his nose at the doorjamb, his tail wagging furiously.

Once inside I watch Butch hurriedly exit the kitchen and his knee seems fine. Marie, on the other hand, is more worried than I've ever seen her and she was with me when my grandmother died. The air of dismay angers me immediately.

"What's going on?" I ask, leaving no question that I'm not leaving without the answer. Whatever *this* is, it will not be sugarcoated.

Marie takes a deep breath and stops cleaning the countertop. "Butch found blood in his stool this morning," she says, and stares silently at me, but I don't know what any of that means.

"Jesus Christ! For the love of God can a man have an ounce of dignity in this house?" Butch bellows as he hustles from the family room into his bedroom.

"Where are you going?" I yell into the hallway.

"To get my gun, goddammit!"

"To kill me or yourself?" I yell back, and take a deep breath and blow it out my cheeks.

"What do you think it means?" I ask Marie.

"I don't know. It could mean a lot of things, but this isn't the first time." I scrutinize Marie, angry it's the first I'm hearing about it. "I didn't know either. He just told me, which makes me think it's serious. Butch isn't a big sharer."

Empathy replaces my anger. Butch isn't one to make it easy to love and care for him. I grab my cell phone and scroll through the contacts. I stop at Jason Leer, realizing I've gone too far, and scroll back up to Dr. Grubb's phone number. I dial it, expecting to get an answering service of some kind, but Dr. Grubb himself answers.

"Dr. Grubb, hi. It's Charlotte Sinclair," I say, and realize I could have thought this through a little more before dialing. "Happy Thanksgiving."

"Happy Thanksgiving to you, too, Charlotte. What can I do for you? Is everyone all right?"

"Actually, Butch has blood in his stool—"

"Jesus, Annie!" Butch interrupts.

"I don't have very much information, but we're very worried over here."

"Have him at my office first thing tomorrow morning. I'll be waiting for you at eight."

"Thanks, Dr. Grubb." I hang up the phone and turn to Marie. "Eight o'clock tomorrow morning," I say, and notice Butch standing in the doorway, his head hanging low and defeat oozing from him. *Buck up, Butch. If the war didn't kill you...and I haven't killed you...*

* * *

It's been a long week since we saw Dr. Grubb. Marie and I wait for Butch in the waiting room of the building where colonoscopies are done. As far as I know, they're going to put Butch completely out and run a scope of some kind through his colon. I'm trying hard not to figure out the details of how it works.

Butch and Marie were silent the entire way here. For a man as proud as Butch, a tube up the ass is probably a bit degrading. His doctor told us the entire procedure will only take a few minutes, but the anesthesia might keep us here for two hours.

"Are you going to tell Jason?" Marie asks. Her voice is quiet so as to not disturb the other people waiting.

"You don't think Butch will?" I ask, hating to be in the middle of this.

"I'm still grateful he told me. I don't think he'll call his son."

"I'll wait until we know. How much can one person take?" I ask to no one sitting in this room. I've Googled blood in the stool. I know one of the causes is cancer. "How many parents can you watch die?" Marie rubs her hands together. *Why are you not saying he's not going to die, Marie?*

The doctor comes out and takes us back to Butch. He's loopy and the sight of him in his gown frightens me. There's something weak about a man in one of these. It reminds me of the days I spent by Jason's hospital bed in Kansas.

"It won't be long and he'll be ready to go. Keep an eye on him the rest of the day. No driving," he says, and I wait for information I actually care about. "We did find some things that are concerning. We did a biopsy and the samples are already on their way to the lab. We'll be in contact as soon as we receive the results." *Biopsy?*

"Do you do biopsies for anything other than cancer?" I ask, the hot bile rising in my throat.

"Not in this case," he says, and I swallow the bile back.

Butch has cancer.

~11~

O Holy Fight

W e need to get a tree," Noble says, and I know he's right. We do need to get a tree, but I haven't really been thinking of Christmas, of anything, since Butch was diagnosed with colon cancer. *What the fuck?*

Last year was our first Christmas engaged. We had a big tree at my house and an eighteen-inch blue plastic one at the farm. It was festive in a "the seventies was a perfect era" kind of way.

"This will be our first tree as an officially married couple. I know there's a lot on your mind, but we only get one first Christmas together."

I smile at Noble because there is so often no other choice than to smile at him. "You're right. We need to get a tree. Life is full of firsts. Some of which should be commemorated," I say, and kiss him.

The sky is gray. The woods are gray, and the fields are empty. We take the truck to the tree farm down the road and the sight of the evergreens warms me. The owner tells us the largest trees were tagged in October and I'm in shock. Is everyone in the world operating at a much higher function than I? I could barely think about Halloween in October. He assures us there's plenty left that will make a nice tree, especially for a farmhouse.

Noble and I wander through the rows holding hands and I glance up at the gray sky, acknowledging my mother, who is surely looking down on us smugly.

"Is it supposed to snow?" I ask. I haven't seen the weather in weeks.

"Like a foot," Noble says. He raises his eyebrows, suggesting some snow activities we are usually great at. I stop in front of a tree about Noble's height. It's almost as wide as it is tall.

"I like a fat tree," I say, and Noble puts his arms around my neck and admires the tree, too.

"Quiet," he whispers. "You'll hurt its feelings." I turn around in his arms and kiss him, being careful to not offend the rest of the town out tree shopping. "Pick the one that will make you happy."

"I don't need a tree to make me happy." I kiss him completely inappropriately, and Mrs. Heitter walks up behind us and clears her throat.

"What?" Noble asks her. "It's our first Christmas together." He kisses me again, this time lifting me off the ground.

We somehow manage to get the fattest tree on the farm to the side porch of our house. We leave it there to drop as I make us hot cocoa, and together we watch as the snow begins to fall. I hold the mug in both my hands to warm them and watch my husband marvel at the snow falling on his fields. The snow is almost as beautiful as him.

Once the ground is covered, I take BJ outside to run around like a crazy dog in it. I take him next door. Butch hasn't been himself since the diagnosis. He's usually predictably gruff and difficult. Now he's pliable and at times almost pleasant. It's disturbing. I know he likes to sit with BJ. He's warm, a welcome cuddle partner this time of year. I'm also bringing him the blue plastic Christmas tree. Although absurd, it's hard to be sad around it.

BJ bolts to Butch, his tail wagging behind him as if he's the most loved man on the planet. Butch leans over and scratches BJ behind the ears and under his chin as BJ points his head to the ceiling and leans back to enjoy his attention.

"Annie," Butch says, startling me. He rarely says my name, almost never in a kind way, and his voice sounds like Jason's. I stop setting up the tree in the center of the kitchen table. He's worried. Why can't he just be angry? This whole thing is pissing me off.

"When you talk like this, it sounds like you think you're going to die," I say as if I'm discussing a character in a book. "And I don't know why that is, because you're going to live a very long time." BJ jumps up, placing his front paws on Butch's thigh and wagging his tail. "So just keep being the miserable ass you usually are, and I'm sure whatever you were just about to say won't seem so important after we win this fight." Butch's face hardens to its usual scowl and he continues to pet our dog.

"I was just going to say you remind me a lot of Joanie," he says, ending the conversation.

"You remind me of no one." I rearrange some plastic branches on the absurd tree. "Thank God, you're a one of a kind."

* * *

The snow covers the corners of all the windows and drifts at least eighteen inches against the back door. It is the perfect day to decorate our first tree. Noble and I carry the behemoth in and attempt to get it straight in the stand. It's not exactly straight, but I convince myself it's part of its charm. My mother would make us keep doing it until it was straight, but a crooked tree is what she gets for checking out early.

We decorate Fatty with ornaments from both our childhoods and the antique ones from my grandmother. We bought new lights, big round colored ones that shine through and are almost balls in their own right. When we're finished, Noble and I step back and admire our first tree together.

It's beautiful. We did an outstanding job.

As if taking a bow, the tree crashes to the floor. Ornaments break and others roll across the room as Fatty's branches bounce from the collision with the old wooden planks. It's a far cry from the majesty of it standing.

"It looks great," Noble deadpans.

"Perfect." I nod. "I'm going to get my camera. We should get a picture." I walk into the kitchen to find my camera. When I come back, Noble is leaning against the arm of the couch still admiring our first Christmas tree.

Once upright, Fatty becomes my favorite decoration. It welcomes me every time I return to the house. It makes it a holiday. And although holidays are dicey for me since the death of my parents, Fatty forces the happy memories of Christmas back to me. The memories of all the loved ones I've lost.

There are moments when the house is bursting with people and others when it's quiet and peaceful. Today it's bursting. The Sinclairs are in town for the holiday and the party hasn't stopped since they arrived. Their RV is parked out back, but they've been staying at Jackie's house to let Noble and I enjoy our first Christmas together without houseguests. I tried to tell Noble it wasn't necessary, but he assured me it was. He loves his family but also seems happy with them leaving every day.

Noble, his brothers-in-law, and the rest of the men under forty hanging around here finish their drinks and bundle up for the cold. They're hitting the Corner Bar and leaving the women here to finish baking cookies. Noble's sisters, Jackie and Tracy, are already a few bottles in and feeling no pain.

I grab Noble's scarf off the hook and wrap it around his neck and kiss him on the lips.

"Are you sure you're going to be okay here?" Noble says, and peeks over my shoulder at his sisters cackling joyfully. Jackie opens another bottle.

"I'll be fine. Drunk maybe, but fine. Be careful."

***

The last remnants of flour stick to the kitchen table like plaster. I'm scrubbing it and listening to Jackie and Tracy's childhood stories when the guys return. The headlights shine through the back door and highlight a commotion as they get out of the truck and walk to the house.

Travis stumbles in first. He holds the back door open as Walt half carries Noble through the door. They lean too far to the left and end up hitting the wall as they attempt to walk into the kitchen. Travis grabs the other side of Noble and they lead him straight up the stairs.

I've known Noble my entire life and have never seen him this drunk. I follow the stumbling parade up the steps and watch as they let Noble fall face-first onto the bed.

"He's all yours," Travis says.

"Thanks."

"Merry Christmas," he says, and kisses my cheek. "Just what you always wanted."

Travis and Walt leave me to figure out how to undress Noble. I roll him over and unbutton his pants. *This is usually much easier,* I think. Maybe Noble's family being in town is harder on him than I thought.

"Yeah, we almost got in a fight," I hear Travis say downstairs, and I stop what I'm doing and lean toward the doorway to hear better. "There seems to be some unfinished business between Nick and Leer."

My heart stops. I hate the idea of Jason and Noble even speaking, let alone fighting.

"What do you mean? What happened?" Jackie asks, sounding pissed. No one is allowed to mess with her baby brother.

"I don't know what was going on. Leer came up and said something to him that set him off. I've never seen Nick that pissed. They started bumping each other and you know—"

"No. I don't know. And what?" Jackie's not letting it go.

"I don't know, Jack. Guy stuff. They didn't fight—"

"It was real close, though," Walt interrupts.

"What is the big deal?" Travis sounds like he's sorry he ever brought it up.

"Whatever. You're an idiot," Jackie says, having no patience for her husband.

"Why am I an idiot? All I did was carry him home."

"Charlotte, you need any help?" Tracy yells up the stairs, and I realize I've been eavesdropping the whole time.

"No. We'll be fine. Thanks for bringing him home," I yell down, and lean over and kiss Noble's cheek. I finally get his clothes off and the covers on him. I leave a large glass of water with two ibuprofens on his nightstand, and turn off the lights.

* * *

"Charlotte, wake up." I hide my eyes. I'm not ready to wake up. "It's our first Christmas together…and I love you," Noble says, and kisses the back of my neck. I roll over and bury my face in his chest, unwilling to face the day. "You act like you were the one out last night." Noble pushes my hair off my face. The memory of his homecoming last night creeps back in. Noble holds me tight as he kisses the top of my head.

He releases me and slides out from under the covers to rummage through his dresser drawer. I can tell he's messing up every item of clothing I've folded the past week, but his look of satisfaction when he finds what he's searching for is worth it. Noble dives back into bed and under the covers. He hands me a cube-shaped box.

"Merry Christmas, Charlotte," he says, and I wish no one was coming over today. I could stay in bed with Noble all day and not miss a thing. "Open it."

I roll to my back and examine the box. I untie the bow and rip off the paper. Inside, under a thick blanket of tissue, is a round Christmas ornament. I pull it out of the box and hold it at eye level. It's painted with an ocean and a moon, the moonlight shining on the water. In the face of the moon, painted in the shadows, is our wedding date.

"It reminds me of the night before the wedding," Noble says, watching me examine the ball. "When I found you risking your life in the ocean." I rest the ball in the box and carefully place it on my nightstand. I climb on top of him.

"Thank you. I love it," I say, and kiss him. "I have something for you, too." I sit up and jump out of our warm bed. I glance back at Noble, unsure. "If you don't like it, please tell me."

"Wow," he says sarcastically. "It must be a great gift."

"It's unusual." The cold air on my naked skin chills me. I hurry to my closet to finish the task at hand as fast as possible so I can get back under the covers. I move things around and find the back wall with BJ at my feet, nosily looking in as well. I stop what I'm doing to kiss his head and pet him.

"Merry Christmas, cutie," I say. I pull a wrapped package out of the closet and struggle to lift it onto the end of the bed. It's large, two feet by four feet, and it's flat, obviously a picture of some kind. Noble leans forward and takes the package from me. I happily let it go and climb back under the covers.

He unwraps the paper and stares at the sign. In the center is an insignia of sorts. It's two shotguns crossed in an X with a script capital letter *S* in the center. Above it is written SINCLAIR FARMS and below it, A NOBLE VENTURE.

"I love it," he says joyfully as he continues to admire the sign.

"Are you sure? You won't hurt my feelings—"

"Charlotte, I love it." Noble easily lifts the sign and places it on the floor, leaning it against his nightstand. "I absolutely love it and I'm going to put it up by the mailbox for the whole town to see. Thank you." He pins me beneath him as he kisses me.

It is a Merry Christmas.

~12~

Going to War

Michelle's family is coming for dinner, too. In all we'll have over twenty people here. Noble is deep-frying a turkey outside, Michelle is bringing a ham, and I have a duck roasting in the oven. Actually, Mrs. Sinclair has a duck roasting because I wouldn't even know that thing was a duck if she hadn't told me. I'm sure it's going to be delicious. I wash the measuring cups for the eighteenth time and place them on a dish towel to dry for their next use as I look out the window at Butch's house. Jason's truck is parked between the two houses. It's a line in the sand he's daring me to cross. God, I hope this is all in my head.

"Mrs. Sinclair?" I say, and Noble's mother ponders me lovingly.

"Charlotte, why don't you call me Mom?" The request makes me uncomfortable. You only get one mom in this world. "Or Larissa," she says, putting me at ease. "Or better yet, why don't you get pregnant and you can call me MomMom." Mrs. Sinclair raises her eyebrows as if this is the best idea ever.

"I'll work on it," I say, nodding.

"That's the spirit. These things don't happen by accident, you know? They're planned. Whether you think you're planning it or not."

"Yes. Yes, I remember from seventh grade health class with Mr. Huck." I look back out the window and ask, "Mrs.—I mean Larissa—how did the Leers end up on the farm?" I can't believe I've never asked before. Before Jason and me, it never even seemed strange. There are lots of houses on farms that are not occupied by the actual farmer. They're almost always family, though. Land is everything in Salem County. It's not risked on strangers.

"Joanie was a Sinclair. Let's see." Larissa gets it straight in her head. "Her mother, Jason's grandmother, and Mr. Sinclair's father, Noble's grandfather, were brother and sister."

"Oh. I had no idea they're related."

"Well not Butch, but Jason is a cousin of some degree. I never understand past the first generation. Originally, that house was built for Jason's grandmother, Joanie's mother. When she died, it went to Joanie and she and Butch moved onto the farm."

"And if Butch passes?" I can barely get the words out. Butch's medical situation has to have a happy ending. I'm not ready to lose anyone else, especially not Butch.

"It will go to Jason, but it will never leave the family." *How is that possible?* "It reverts back to the Sinclairs upon death to ensure we can control who moves onto the farm."

"Could you keep Jason off?"

"Not us, it's you and Noble's decision now, but I think you'd have a hard time since he's Joanie's son. If Jason dies, though, it won't pass to his minor son; the house comes back to you and Noble."

I begin to pull apart the rolls and place them on the tray for warming. I watch as my hands move slowly over the bread, not caring if they're ever warm.

"You still love him, don't you?"

Larissa's question startles me. When I look up, it's obvious she's been watching me since we stopped talking. I freeze in her knowing stare and swallow hard.

She moves closer to me and takes the bread from my hands. She holds each hand in her own. "Oh, it's okay, darlin'. The tragedy of a woman's heart is its capacity to love more than one man."

A throbbing sounds right behind my left ear; it's almost a pounding and my lip begins to quiver. I'm not admitting to myself, let alone Noble's mother, the capacity of my heart.

"Anyone can see you're devoted to Noble, but when I just mentioned Jason dying, you looked like you were in pain."

"I just don't want anything bad to happen to him," I say with a small smile aimed at ending this conversation.

"I suspect it already has," she says, and raises her eyebrows as she drops my hands. Larissa pours more wine into our glasses and hands mine to me. She offers me a toast and when our glasses clink, I wonder if my mother ever loved more than one man. If she were here, what would she say?

* * *

It's still dark out as I pour coffee into a to-go cup for Noble. The sun is just peeking over the horizon as Noble ties his boots. They are camo, like the rest of him. I could see him a hundred times in his hunting gear and every single time laugh out loud. I giggle quietly as I fit the lid on the cup.

"What? Are you making fun of my wardrobe? I'm going to war out there, baby," Noble says, and turns me around to attack my neck.

"War, huh? Those poor deer frolicking along by the creek, about to be shot with an arrow."

"No. Bow season's over for now. Today we use muzzleloaders," Noble proclaims, and pulls the sides of my robe up around my neck.

"Muzzleloaders?"

"It's a tradition in the Sinclair family. No matter what the weather, we go hunting the day after Christmas."

"Praise Jesus," I say, shaking my head at him.

"What are you doing today?"

"I think I'm going to download a bunch of stuff on my iPad and watch Lifetime movies all day with BJ."

"I'm sure he's ready to come home."

"I know. The smell of all this game roasting was too much for him. I'll walk over and get him in a little while." Noble's arms clench around me. I kiss him, wanting my Noble intact. He holds me tight as we hear the truck horn from the driveway. All the Sinclair men are piled in the cab, ready to go kill something. I don't get it.

* * *

I'm cleaning out the coffeepot when the door opens and BJ runs in, immediately jumping up on my thighs as if he's had no training at all.

"Get down! No jumping," I say, and rub behind his ears. BJ sits nicely as I kiss him on the head.

"Lucky dog," he says, and I look up to the admiring stare of Jason Leer. I should be angry. Angry at him for walking in like he was invited. Angry at him for my birthday message. Angry at him for knocking up Stephanie Harding.

Geez, Charlotte, let it go already.

"I want to talk to you…about Butch, if you have a minute," he says, and the thought of discussing Butch simmers my anger. I tighten the belt on my robe.

"I'll be right back. Help yourself to something to drink. If you're thirsty," I say, not sure if I'm making sense.

I run up the stairs, suddenly full of energy. Invigorated really. I find my favorite jeans in my drawer and throw them on. I stand in front of my closet searching for something comfortable, but not too sloppy. *Why, Charlotte?* I pull the sweater Michelle gave me for Christmas out of the box on the chair and rip off the tags. It's soft, and oversized, and a beautiful turquoise blue. Perfect.

"Heeey!" My body stiffens. "What are you doing?" I yell at Jason, who's leaning in my bedroom doorway with a hungry look in his eyes. "How long have you been standing there?" I ask, suddenly conscious of the last five minutes.

"Long enough," he says, totally unaffected, and I'm certain I could kill him.

"Make no mistake, Jason Leer. You are not welcome in this room, or this house," I say as cold as I can commit to and walk past him. Relief flows through me as I hear his footsteps on the stairs behind me. When I reach the living room, Jason grabs my arm and swings me around.

"You should go to church," I blurt out, surprising myself.

"Jesus can't save me now. I'm already in hell," he says calmly, and lets go of my arm. He wanders around the room scrutinizing pictures, pausing on Noble's and my wedding picture.

"I'll say a prayer for you, then." I leave him in the living room and force my legs to carry me into the kitchen. It's bright and cheery, and if I can get him out here, maybe I can get him out of the house.

Jason finally arrives in the kitchen and stares at me. He doesn't sit at the table. He doesn't walk toward me. He doesn't speak. He doesn't do any of the things normal people would do in this situation. Oh wait, normal people wouldn't be in this situation. The intensity of his stare makes me want to cry even though it's not sad. It's capturing.

"Missed you the other night." He's looking for a fight. "When I saw Sinclair come in." It sounds like the words hurt his tongue. "I was actually hoping you'd be with him."

"What are you doing?" I ask him. The sound of my fractured voice scares me.

"What are you doing, Annie? Playing house with Sinclair? You gonna get pregnant soon?" he asks, and his questions piss me off. "You living the life Sinclair's planned for you?"

"What should I be doing instead? Living the life you planned?"

"I don't even recognize you. Running around here, cooking and cleaning, that's not the Annie I used to know."

I could spit on him. "You don't recognize me because I am happy. I am so *fucking* happy I can't stand it," I say with such hatred I wait for the walls to collapse around us. Jason watches me, giving nothing away. "Is it that impossible for you to accept I'm happy? Like every day, I'm happy." I blush under his stare and fight to hold back the tears, but the sight of him makes me cry. I put my head in my hands, muzzling myself. 'Tis the season.

Jason walks over and pulls me into his arms. My head hits his chest and it's just the slap in the face I need.

"You need to go. Noble will kill you if he finds you here."

"God, how I'd love him to try. The last time we *talked*, I was hoping someone would kill me. Today's different."

"Yeah, well, the conversation's over. Noble and I are married now. You live in Oklahoma with your son."

"Annie, this is never going to be over. As long as I can breathe, I'm going to want you."

"Get out," I say, and pull away from him. Jason lets me go and laughs, pretty much in my face.

"I'm staying home until after Pop's surgery."

I calculate in my head. Five more days in December, three in January, another week of this. *Please, God, save me.*

"I'm sure he's happy you're going to be here."

"I don't know about that. He's pretty dependent on you and Marie. You guys are good to him."

"He's a good man," I say, and then, just to be a bitch, I add, "You should try to emulate that."

Jason's shoulders bounce as he chuckles and walks out the back door. I watch him walk to his truck and drive down the lane. He's probably headed back to Stephanie's parents'. Back to his son, his family now.

~13~

The West Wind Blows

Sorry I'm late. It took forever to haul that truck out. I don't know how he managed to get so far down in the ditch," Noble says as he kisses me on the cheek.

"It's fine."

"It looks like you're ready to go." Noble appraises my long parka and crocheted scarf wrapped around my neck.

"I just walked BJ over to Butch's. How long do you need?"

"Give me five minutes," Noble calls back, running up the stairs.

"I'll go warm up the car." I grab my overnight bag before heading out the side door to the L-shed.

I start the engine and pull the car up to the side door of the house and get out to climb in the passenger side. Odds are Noble's not going to let me drive.

He runs out and yells, "Did you bring my toothbrush?"

I nod. I am now the girl who packs her husband's toothbrush.

Noble climbs in the car and leans over to kiss me. "Happy New

Year," he says, and pecks me again. "I know going out tonight is a lot to ask with everything that's going on with Butch, but I'm glad we are." Noble's smile warms me. "I'd rather be taking you to a hotel all by ourselves, but a party at Sam's will have to do."

"How many people are going to be there?" All I saw was an e-mail with cocktail attire as the dress code. It's nice to dress up once in a while. Although I'm not sure if I'm exactly dressed up.

"I think a lot. Maybe eighty. That's why we need to get there early. Sam's giving us the guest room, but it's smart to stake it out." Eighty is a lot for Sam's small apartment. It's basically a two-story loft with a small guest bedroom off the living room. It's on a pier on the Delaware River and the perfect location to watch the Philly fireworks at midnight.

Sam is talking to the doorman when we arrive and he tells us to go on back, that the door's unlocked. Noble and I walk through the center courtyard and I shiver from the cold.

"You are going to freeze when we watch the fireworks," Noble says, and puts his arm around my shoulder.

"I brought clothes to change into for it." I tap my overnight bag hanging off his other shoulder.

"What dress did you wear?"

"I actually bought something new. I think you're going to like it." I flash Noble a naughty grin, and hope he does. It's a bit of a departure for me and it's absolutely in his honor. We slide the glass door to Sam's condo open and step into the heat. It's going to be a hundred degrees in here by the time everyone arrives. Noble opens the door to the guest room and I follow him in. I take off my parka and straighten my dress. It's extremely short, black, and leather on top. There are sleeves, but they're sheer black with wide leather cuffs at the wrists. It's also tight, fitted and very body conscious.

I roll my coat up and store it on the floor next to the bed. When I turn to Noble, he's staring at me with his mouth hanging open. He likes the dress. He's easy to please. Simple, really.

"Do you like it?" I ask.

"My dick is so hard it almost broke off," he says without taking his eyes off me.

"Heaven forbid."

"Where...when...did you get that dress?"

"I ordered it online. I think it's the shortest thing I've ever worn." I walk to Noble and lean against the front of him. He's right; his dick is hard. I grab it and pull his bottom lip with my teeth. "What are we going to do with this?" I ask, and kiss his neck. Noble's head falls back and he moans as I find his balls with my hand. I reach over and lock the door to the guest room and turn back to Noble.

His pants are hard to unbutton, he's filling them so. As I work, Noble pulls my hair back from my shoulders and runs the back of his fingers across my cheek. He's hungry, yet gentle. It's hard to understand what Noble is capable of. As if answering my silent question, he turns my back to the wall, pulls off my thong, and lifts my left knee to his chest. He crashes into me and then pauses. I swallow, breathe, and look up into the possessive eyes of my husband.

I don't say a word. Not because there is nothing to say but because there's nothing left to say. Noble has taught me the difference between love and need. You can have both with the same person. It's a form of sanity I forgot existed before we got together. What was my life like, when sanity became a lesson?

Noble plunges into me again, holding me up against the wall as he watches me take him in each time. *You like to watch, too.*

I block the thought from my mind and take Noble's hair in my hands and fist my fingers. Noble doesn't stop. I unbutton his shirt, hungry for the sight of his shoulders, and pull it down to his elbows. As Noble still thrusts into me, I lean over and kiss his shoulder as he speeds up.

I dig my fingernails into him and lean my head back. Noble raises my right knee, too, and renders me completely at his mercy. I'm floating above the ground with only Noble's rhythm anchoring me down. I tense, fighting for every breath.

"Noble," I breathe, and he looks me straight in the eye, his warm blue pools loving me. He continues and watches me come. Noble holds me against the wall and I wrap my arms around his neck, holding on for dear life. He finishes and I squeeze myself around him. Noble lays his head on my chest, still supporting me with an arm under each thigh.

"Charlotte, I love you." Noble releases my legs and moves a lock of hair behind my ear. "More than anything else." He's warm and rich with his love, and he blankets me with it every minute I am with him.

"I know." I consider the last five years of my life. How different they would have been without him. Noble lowers my other leg and I stretch them, making sure my hips still work. I pull on my underwear and pull down my tiny black dress. I smooth out the front and, with raised eyebrows, ask Noble if I look okay. He kisses me as he buttons his shirt.

I take the buttons from his hands and work on them myself. I sigh as I work, hating to cover his shoulders. Noble leans down and kisses my cheek.

"What am I going to do with you, Noble?" I ask, believing he's too perfect. Too sure of everything; certainly this, too, is going to come crashing down on us.

"Love me," he says, and kisses me again. "And feed me, and wear that dress more often," he adds, returning to his playful normal.

We exit the room to find about ten more people have arrived. Sam walks over and hands us each a beer.

"You know, you guys are married now. You can have sex at your house, anytime you want," he says, completely unannoyed.

"We're newlyweds," I remind him. *How long?* About four months. I glance down at my ring. It's as if it's been on my finger forever.

Sam's party is compact and eventually spills out onto the shared patio of the condos. There are plenty of drinks, food, and people to talk to, but I only want to be with Noble. Without Julia, Jenn, and Sydney here to yell at me for turning into one of "those girls" who ignore their friends once they're married, I can bask in him.

There are zero decorations in Sam's house except for a large poster board with the wind superstition for New Year's written on it in marker. It reads:

AULD LANG SYNE

It's time to remember those from our past
and not let them be forgotten.
Check wind direction tomorrow
South—$$ & happiness
North—Year of foul weather
East—Famine and bad luck
West—Someone important will die

As I'm reading them, Noble grabs my hand to lead me out the door. He stops and reads the sign, too. When he gets to the west wind, he turns to me and pulls me toward him.

"He's going to be okay, Charlotte."

"I know," I say as Noble wraps his arms around me and holds me close to him. I don't know a thing, though.

We hear the fireworks on the river and get to the edge of the pier just in time for the finale. Noble lifts me off the ground and kisses me, the sound of the last fireworks pushing any fear from my mind. He places me back on my feet and I am in awe of my gentle giant.

"Happy New Year, Noble." I kiss him again.

* * *

I had opened my eyes to the first day of the new year and immediately thought of Butch. Under any other circumstance I would not have left Philly this morning, but it's the last Sunday before Butch's surgery and I want to go to church with him. Even if I do smell like a day-old bottle of whiskey. I really hope I don't. I smell my arm for alcohol oozing from my skin and notice the Volvo's clock says I'm going to be late if I don't speed the whole way.

* * *

I pull into the church parking lot and take the open spot next to Marie's car. She's probably here for the same reason. Noble offered to come with me but looked like I should just bury him instead. The death reference sours me. I drag myself out of the car and shut the door behind me. The cold wind blows my hair and sneaks down the back of my parka. I pull my hood up and tighten the toggle around my neck. Is it coming from the west? I face west out of the parking lot and the wind slaps my face. I turn quickly and hurry through the front door, not letting myself contemplate the wind.

Once inside the sanctuary, the heat is pumping. God wouldn't want us to be cold. I exchange good mornings with Dr. Grubb, who is the greeter today, and carry my program to my pew. I slide in from the outside and sit next to Butch; Marie is to his left. He is gaunt. Daily milkshakes have done little to combat the effects of the chemotherapy. His emaciated frame anchors the skin that is now hanging off of him. Butch has aged twenty years in the past month. I rest my hands in my lap and lower my head.

Dear Lord, thank you for this new year. Please let this be over this week. Let Butch's cancer be removed and let him heal. Let him eat, and gain weight, and enjoy Marie, and his grandson, and—

"Morning," Jason whispers in my ear as he sits down, inappropriately close to me. I open my eyes and turn toward him. He is the devil.

"Great," I say sarcastically. "Now we're all going to be struck by lightning."

I feel like every pair of eyes in this church, as well as the eyes of the Lord, are on me. Me and Jason, that is. Pastor Johnson welcomes us. As he speaks, he moves up the aisle and pauses for a few seconds, smiling at Butch. To Butch's complete mortification, I put him on the prayer list after the diagnosis. Pastor Johnson's eyes skip over to me...and Jason...and return to me filled with concern. He doesn't miss a beat, though, and continues on with his announcements. I twist my engagement ring on my finger and remember Pastor Johnson welcoming me to the ritual of marriage...with Noble.

What will Noble think of this? I have to tell him. Jason's been popping up too much without Noble being aware. Keeping it a secret turns this into something it's not. Jason slips his hand between our thighs and a chill runs across my breastbone. I look down at his hand and up into the eyes of my past.

"It's chilly in here," he whispers in my ear. How long has torturing me been his hobby? He's a bored child entertaining himself with my demise.

Pastor Johnson is obviously clairvoyant because his sermon focuses on temptation. Mr. Chambers, one of the few attorneys in town, stands from his pew and walks to the podium on the side of the altar. Maybe Noble and I should talk to him about our money and our land. Mr. Chambers reads this week's scripture to us.

"There hath no temptation taken you but such as is common to man: but God is faithful, who will not suffer you to be tempted above that ye are able; but will with the temptation also make a way to escape, that ye may be able to bear it."

Mr. Chambers pauses and the pastor nods to him.

"This is the word of the Lord," he says.

"Thanks be to God," we respond, and Pastor Johnson explains that we will never be given a test by God that is more than we can bear. Turn to the word of God instead of our own hearts, our lusts. At this point I actually start to sweat. Jason shifts in his seat until the weight of his immense chest is resting on my side. I lean forward and look past him at several feet of pew uninhabited. Jason is silently laughing, his eyes down, his shoulders shaking.

I think I decipher some talk about the temptation being a

divine test and God's purpose, and finally, in hope of self-preservation, I completely stop listening at the mention of the lusts of my flesh. Instead I begin to pray for Butch and his surgery. Only my life could include the irony of a sermon about temptation creating temptation.

~14~

It's the Fear that Scares Me

They are going to remove it. They're going to operate on Butch and remove all the cancer and we'll all go back to our normal lives...with Butch. I'm driving the Volvo with Butch in the passenger seat. Jason and Marie are in the back and no one says a word. I want to hold Butch's hand, but I've never held it before. I want to cry, but it will only repulse him.

I want this day to be over.

A month of chemotherapy almost killed him. I glance past him at the side mirror and even his posture sings the song of fear. I look in the rearview mirror and Jason is staring out his window, lost in his own horrific thoughts. Thank God for Marie. There's too much fear in this vehicle to manage alone.

We get Butch settled and plant ourselves in the waiting room. Butch is assigned a number we can use to track his progress throughout the day. I find it on the monitor hanging on the wall above the information desk. Marie sits in the corner knitting, or crocheting, I don't know the difference. Jason stands staring out the window, his arm above his head, his forehead resting on it. He is beautiful. I shut my eyes and chastise myself for thinking like this, for thinking at all. His father is about to be operated on. *What's wrong with you?*

Seconds form minutes; minutes crawl to hours. Jason sits across from me and takes out his phone. He stares down at it and I can't imagine anything there brings him comfort. I pull out my own and text him:

HE'S GOING TO BE OKAY.

Jason never looks up from his phone. He texts back:

How did you get this number?
The universe is conspiring against me.

I write back and toss my phone into my bag on the floor by my feet.

I pull out the notebook I've been carrying to all of Butch's doctors' appointments. He has stage 4 cancer. It has metastasized to his liver, which seems to be the greatest concern. There are several lesions, cancer tissue that has a moth-eaten appearance, which will be removed today. Two surgeons will perform resections of his colon and liver. It will take seven to eight hours. My eyes find Jason again. *When was the last time we spent eight hours together?*

While they're in there, intraoperatory ultrasound will confirm placement of the lesions and look for small tumors. Anything they couldn't see. Hopefully the chemotherapy has worked and most have shrunk. I wring my hands as I read everything I've written and try to imagine how Butch must feel. I'm a complete wreck and it's not me, or my dad. I look up at Jason again. He's now just staring at me and for some reason I don't mind.

The doctor walks in and I pull my eyes and the rest of me from Jason. *You're early.* I stand up and face the doctor, who, without saying a word, tells me things are not the way they are supposed to be.

"He's in recovery. We'll move him to a room in about an hour. He tolerated the surgery well," he says, but there's no relief on his face. "Unfortunately, when we got in there, we found small lesions that were not visible on the scan. Their positions make them inoperable. I'm sorry."

I can hear Marie crying behind me. She knew all along.

"What do you mean you're sorry? What else can we do? There has to be something else," I say, ready to storm over to Butch and operate myself.

"If Butch chooses, he can do chemotherapy. There are also targeted drugs we can discuss. These will slow the cancer, possibly alleviate some symptoms for a while."

Jason walks past us and out the door of the hospital.

"But there's no cure? No stopping it?"

"I'm sorry. It's already gone too far," the doctor says, and I want to follow Jason right out of this building.

"How long?" Marie asks through her sniffles.

"Six to nine months with treatment. We can discuss all the options when Butch is up to it."

Up to it? Is anyone ever up to it?

"I'll come back and get you in a little while to see him."

I turn to Marie as she backs into a chair by the window. I find some more tissues in my purse and place them in her hand.

"I know you love him, Marie." She nods, still crying. "I'm going to find Jason. Are you all right?" I lean down to her eye level as she nods and cries again. Butch is lucky to be loved by her. *Lucky*. I roll my eyes.

* * *

I exit the elevator into the freezing parking deck and search for signs of Jason. I walk to the far end where the Volvo is parked and see him leaning on the front fender, staring out over the concrete wall of the garage.

My feet are moving, but I don't know how. I reach Jason and wrap my arms around his neck and pull his head to my shoulder. He melts there and puts his arms around my waist, his whole body touching mine, shielding me from the truth of our lives—everything is lost at some point. I run my hands through his familiar curly hair and inhale the kiwi right before I close my eyes, still clinging to Jason for survival.

He leaves his head on my shoulder until the weight of it causes a dull pain. I keep smoothing his hair, unable to give him anything more. I turn my head and my lips are close to his ear, too close. The chill runs from the back of my throat down my chest and I pull back from him.

Jason's eyes are almost black, but there's no sign of anger. Some version of surrender, an alien in his body, inhabits them.

"I can't do it, Annie," he says, without an ounce of strength in his voice. There's nothing that has scared me more in my life than the sound of fear coming from him. "I can't watch him die." No one should have to live through this...twice.

"I'll do it," I say, and pull him to me again. "I'll take care of him. I love him." Tears fill my eyes and one streaks down my face as I add, "And I love you."

~15~

Two Step

It's an odd routine Noble and I have established. I drive to Delaware every morning and swim. I'm home in time to have breakfast with Noble and then he works on paperwork, our taxes, or has meetings in preparation for the upcoming planting season. Running a farm is a business and his degree from the Rutgers Business School is an advantage. I think many people thought it was a waste of money at the time, but Noble is intelligent and he's got the degree to prove it. Whether he's negotiating contracts or securing a credit line, he's as knowledgeable as the other side.

I've been swimming every day. At first a half mile was almost impossible, but now I'm able to bang out 5,000 yards and still make it home in time for breakfast. My old swimming buddy has been e-mailing me workouts and Noble bought me a waterproof iPod that makes the time fly by. It's been the only way I can keep my sanity in the absence of work to focus on and having to watch Butch deteriorate a little every day.

There are lots of doctor's appointments and phone calls, everyone trying to keep Butch as comfortable as possible for the rest of his life. When I asked Noble what he thought about me taking a leave of absence from work to help care for Butch, he hesitated. He said he didn't want that for me, caring for someone to their death—that I'd been through too much already with the loss of my parents. I didn't tell him I already promised Jason or that I owe it to Butch. I just hugged him and he said he would help me in any way he could. That's Noble.

Today is different, though. It's the beginning of March and Noble is out plowing the fields already. The weather is warmer today, at least sixty. This winter was cold, but we haven't had snow since December. It's actually felt a little boring. Noble had a truckload of mulch delivered for me and now it sits in a four-foot-high pile near the flower beds. I put on my old sneakers, my dirty shoes, with my old jeans and old shirt to match. Noble might make a farmer out of me yet. He was also kind enough to bring the wheelbarrow and shovel from the barn. When I get close to the wheelbarrow, I see a pair of work gloves in it with a note.

Protect your hands and call me if you want help.
It's too much to do alone.

I shake my head. He's really going to spend the rest of his life taking care of me. I rip the tags off the gloves and put the trash in my back pocket. They fit perfectly.

"Figures," I say as I fill my wheelbarrow with the first load of mulch and head toward the flower beds behind the house.

The March sun is still cool, and once in the shade it's almost chilly, until I'm on my tenth load; then I'm plenty hot. I crouch down on my hands and knees and push the mulch into the back corners, creating a rich bed of mulch to welcome spring.

"Helwo," I hear, and my head jerks up to see a toddler, no bigger than Lily, looking me right in the eye. His are a light gray, and I instantly know who this little boy is. He's beautiful, like his father, as if he spit him right out of his mouth. *No question of paternity.*

"Hi there," I say, with the voice I reserve for Lily. He takes two steps and plops in the mulch next to where I'm working.

"Pop Pop scary," he says, and shakes his head.

"You know what?" I ask, and lie in the mulch next to him. "He scares me a little, too." I nod my head exaggeratedly. His eyes bulge with disbelief. "Yes, he does," I say, and add, "but I think he's really a nice guy." I sit up and watch him as he runs his fingers through the mulch. When I stand, his eyes follow me to the wheelbarrow.

"Do you want to help me?" I ask, and offer him one arm of the wheelbarrow. He gets his footing under him and walks to me. He grabs one handle of the wheelbarrow and I grab the other and we sort of get the empty barrow back to the mulch pile.

"Do you know how to count?" I ask, and he proudly nods.

"One, two, five, one."

"Exactly, that's very good. Why don't you help me count how many shovels of mulch I get?" His eyes take in the huge mountain of mulch and I begin. "One," I say, and he repeats it as I empty the shovel into the barrow. We continue for fourteen shovels. When we take the mulch back, I have to help him with his side, but we finally make it, counting our steps the whole way.

"One, two, three, four, five... seventeen, eighteen," he repeats as I say them.

"What's your name?" I ask.

"Jay," he says, and I'm happy he wasn't born with three heads as I had cursed him years ago.

"What name?" He breaks into my thoughts with a gentle pull of my hair.

"You can call me Annie." Jay smiles at me and I think everything in the world is going to be just fine. How could it not be for this little boy?

"Jay! Jason Jr!" I hear Jason yell from the other side of the house.

"You better get going." I point Jay in the direction of his father. He "runs" around the side of the house and after a few minutes I hear the sound of Jason's old truck driving away.

I lie back and look at the sky dotted with small clouds throughout its deep blue background. Life is amazingly crazy. How could so much change in two years? Jay is here, Lily's here, Butch will be gone soon, and through it all, life will go on. The clouds blow out and are replaced by an almost identical group, and I hear Noble whistling as he walks around the corner of the house.

"Wow, you got a lot done."

"I had some help," I say, and sit up as Noble sits down next to me.

"Oh yeah? Did Sean stop by?"

"Jason's son was just here," I say, and the joy drains from Noble's face. "He said his name is Jay," I add. "He also said Butch is scary, so we know he has a good instinct for people." Noble's jaw is clenching and his neck is red. "What's wrong?"

"What's wrong? You and Jason are now going to spend your days hanging out with his son?" he asks, and the sound of bitterness turns my lip.

"Jason wasn't here. Jay wandered up by himself. I never saw Jason." I stand, brush the dirt off the back of me, and hold out my hand for Noble. He takes it and I help him up. "He's just a little boy. Almost the same age as Lily. Can you imagine someone hating her?"

"I don't hate *him*, Charlotte." Noble walks away.

***

I woke up this morning knowing I had dreamed of Jason and Jay, but I couldn't remember the details. Instead of being curious, I was happy with the unknown. I remember dreaming of the little blue bird again, too. *That freaking bird.* How many years has it been? That dream used to haunt me and I'm sure it's because I was working outside yesterday that the bird nightmare returned. I left the wounded bird to be killed by a cat in Butch's yard when I first moved home, before I was able to care for myself, let alone anything else.

Noble sleeps beside me, lying with his arm stretched out across me. Any other girl in the world wouldn't be able to dream of another man with Noble sleeping next to her. I am a very special ass.

***

I drive to Delaware and swim harder than I have since high school. Every stroke punishes me and washes away the dreams of Jason. The woman in the lane next to me stops swimming and watches me. She asks what's gotten into me today. But it's what got into me years ago—Jason Leer. There's got to be a way to get him out.

Noble's gone by the time I get home, but my swim has cured the guilt from this morning. I text him.

I MISS YOU

I put my phone down and change to finish the flower beds. I collect the wheelbarrow and shovels from the shed and head back toward the mulch pile, which is considerably smaller than when I started this project. By the time I'm on my third trip for mulch, the sun is shining brightly above me. Jay runs out of Butch's house and barrels toward me. The sight of him warms me until I notice Jason following him. I swallow hard and focus on Jay.

"Annie," Jay says, and I search my mind for memories of Jason from our childhood. Was he ever this sweet? This child before me has known no darkness; he's pure light. Was Jason this way before the death of his mother?

I hand Jay a small shovel I found in a bin of outdoor items we keep for Lily's visits.

"Can you help me today?" I ask, and he nods, practically jumping up and down. Jay takes the shovel and examines it from every angle, happy to have his own tool. Jason's now standing over us, watching our familiarity with disbelief covering his beautiful face.

"I was shocked when he counted to eleven," he says, and I beam proudly at Jay. "But I almost fell over when he told me Annie taught him." The smile on Jason's face could start a war. I look at him without an ounce of guilt on my face. "You still got a little fight left in ya."

"You've got the wrong girl. I'm tired of fighting," I say, and take a shovelful of mulch from the wheelbarrow. "I'm happy now, remember? Stop working so hard to ruin it." I throw the mulch in the bed and turn back for another shovelful.

"I'm moving back," he says, and I stop shoveling. I stop moving, and thinking, and breathing.

"Back where?" I ask, unable to comprehend.

"Back here. I'm taking the season off to be with Pops. I want Jason Jr. to know him and I want Pops to spend his final days with his son and grandson." I follow Jason's gaze across the field. Noble's tractor turns and heads away from us.

"Where are you going to stay?" I ask, the ability to formulate concern returning.

"We'll stay at the Hardings'," Jason says, and I close my eyes, angry, sad, and relieved at the same time. "But I plan on being here a lot. Is that going to be a problem?" he asks with an evil grin.

"For who?"

"For your husband." He takes a step closer to me and my barrow of mulch.

"Does my husband have a reason to care where you live?"

"If he's smart he does."

I roll my eyes. "Noble will be happy Butch's family will be with him." I move a step toward the flower bed.

"And you? Are you gonna be happy?"

"More like annoyed, I'm sure," I say, and offer my hand to Jay. We leave Jason standing by the flower bed as we awkwardly push the wheelbarrow to the other side of the house, counting our steps the whole way.

~16~

The New Normal

Jason's return is much less disruptive than I thought it would be. I keep up my routine of swimming and having breakfast with Noble every morning and spending time with Butch throughout the day. I stop by after breakfast and wait with him until Marie comes. He often comments he doesn't need to be babysat, but the one day I skipped he asked me where I was when I finally arrived in the afternoon.

I usually leave Marie and Butch alone around lunch and try to catch up with Noble, but now that the weather's broke, he's not home for lunch often. I come back and have a cup of tea with Butch and help Marie make dinner. She doesn't need the help, but it gives us a chance to exchange information on how he's doing and brainstorm what more we can do. In between I pick up groceries and medicines, and cook and clean. Mostly I try to figure out how to make every single day Butch has left worthy of him.

Jason comes and goes randomly at first. He seems to be trying to figure out how he best fits in. He brings Jay most days and I try to facilitate a relationship between him and Butch, reminding Butch that sometimes his voice sounds a bit gruff and he may not be coming off as sweet as he sounds in his head.

"Annie!" Jay yells as he comes running into Butch's kitchen.

"Stop the goddamned yelling," Butch says, and I silence him with an angry sneer.

"Keep it up, Jay," I say, and kneel down to Jay, who's holding a mason jar up to the sunlight shining through the kitchen window. "Is that what I think it is?" I ask, showering Jay with amazement. "A cricket?"

Jay proudly nods, peering into the jar with me. He is utterly scrumptious.

"Go show Pops," I say, and Jay hesitates.

"Butch, you have to see what Jason Jr. found," I say exaggeratedly, and nudge Jay toward the old dragon. "I think he's an excellent bug hunter." Jason is satisfied in the corner of the kitchen. He likes Butch to be annoyed, especially because it's me and his son doing the annoying. Jay takes the jar to Butch, who holds it up to the light and nods his head approvingly at Jay.

"You should let it go," Butch says, and hands the jar back to a wary Jay.

"Yes. If you love something, set it free," Jason says from the corner, and I roll my eyes at him. Jay looks like he might cry.

"How about this?" I kneel down to Jay and his cricket again. "How about if you keep him in the jar today and when the moon comes out tonight, you set him free to play with the other bugs?" Jay doesn't give away whether he likes the idea. "You would want to play with your friends, wouldn't you?" I ask, and realize Jay should be spending more time with children.

"He name Chomp," he says.

"Chomp? I love that name. I'm going to change the sheets on the bed. Do you and Chomp want to help me?" Jay nods and follows me to Butch's bedroom, carrying Chomp in his jar with two hands.

* * *

I change the sheets on my own bed when I get home and think of Jay and how much life he injects into Butch's house. I shower and wrap a towel around my hair. The moonlight catches my eye and I look out the bathroom window. Jason and Jay are staring up at the sky, at the rising moon, and I let my eyes linger on it as well. It's a half-moon, always twice as interesting as a full. So much is left to the imagination.

Jay screams and jumps around. He let Chomp go and is now chasing him. Jason's laughing as his son runs in circles and I can't take my eyes off them. Two Leer boys playing in the moonlight that called them home to say good-bye to their father. They are beautiful. Jason looks up at the moon again and I turn from the window and brush my hair.

"Do you want ice cream for dessert?" Noble asks as he walks in.

"No. I'm not hungry," I say, and he watches me the same way I watch Jason. "Thank you, though." Noble walks over and throws me over his shoulder and onto the bed, me laughing the entire time.

"You have no idea how beautiful the sound of your laughter is. I could listen to it all day."

"You usually do when I'm with you," I say, and roll on top of

Noble. My wet hair sends a chill down my back and Noble covers us with a blanket to keep me warm, wrapped in his arms. "I think I'm spending my days with the wrong man," I say, meaning Butch, but it's true for Jason, too. Rather than try to clear up the statement, I kiss Noble and he makes me forget what we were even talking about.

* * *

After tossing and turning, I finally abandon my bed and leave for the pool early. I couldn't sleep, the image of Jason in the moonlight haunting me. All the horrible thoughts I had of his baby have been erased by a friendship with a two-year-old who is impossible not to love. Somehow this pisses me off, too. It's one more thing Jason has control over.

As I pull onto Woodstown Road, I pass Jason. He waves, but I am frozen by the sight of him. As usual, his reaction time is light speeds ahead of my own. I grab my phone from my bag and text him.

IS BUTCH OK?

I smile knowing how much texts annoy him. And then I stop smiling when my phone rings. I answer but don't say hello.

"Where are you going?" he asks, not bothering to say hello either.

"Is Butch okay?" I ask again. Apparently we are either naked or fighting…sometimes even those two intermingle.

"He's fine. I couldn't sleep," Jason uncharacteristically gives in.

"Good," I say to both. "I'll see you later."

"You didn't answer my question." He doesn't sound the least bit offended.

"I know," I say, and hang up. I merge onto the Delaware Memorial Bridge and cross the river to the pool.

* * *

The first five hundred yards are the worst. They're always the worst. I add in long sets of thousands and let my mind wander as I listen to the music on my iPod. By the time I finish my last lap, my face is purple and I am out of breath. I float on my back and let my body recover. It's time for some short sets. Something to take my mind off things.

I clean my goggles and look at the pace clock at the far wall. My breath catches and I swallow hard. Jason Leer is sitting in the observation deck next to the clock. I don't have to take off my goggles to confirm. I know it's him. He is unbelievable…in every way.

I do forty fifties in individual medley order and when I finish I'm not sure if I can pull myself out of the water. I love these workouts. They renew me. I take off my cap and goggles and go underwater. I shoot up, locking my arms on the side of the pool and shifting to sit on the side. I stare up at the balcony. Jason is leaning over in his chair, his elbows on his knees. *Don't you have anything better to do?* That's the problem.

I half expect him to be in the women's locker room by the time I get in there. I shower and change. I have yoga pants and a hoodie to wear home, never expecting to be anything but alone, not seeing a need for underwear.

"See you, Sue," I say on the way out the door.

"Bye, Charlotte. See you tomorrow," she says, and winks as if we're in on a secret.

I walk out the door and Jason is leaning on my car. I roll my eyes and shake my head in disgust.

"Are you training for something?" he asks. I stare blankly at him, not trusting myself with emotions. "Because some guys were talking about you in there. About how you come every day and swim your ass off. They wanted to know why. What you're training for."

"How did you even get in there? You're like a creep."

"I told them I was your husband," he says, and I can't keep my mouth from flying open.

"Have you lost your mind?"

"Are you competing in something?"

"No. I lost a long time ago," I say, and walk toward my car. "Now get off my car." Jason doesn't move, but instead studies me and I would love to hear his thoughts on what's going on because I have no idea.

"Come to breakfast with me."

"No."

"Annie, you need to eat. I just watched you burn a couple thousand calories."

"Oh, I'll eat. Just not with you."

He turns to me and leans on the driver's door. Why does he have to be so comfortable all the time? He really does piss me off.

"It's strange to see you with Pops. Do you remember when you used to think he hated you?"

"He still hates me." Nothing has changed with the way Butch treats me. I just choose to believe he loves me when he yells.

"You're impossible to hate."

I nod and purse my lips. "Yeah, well, you're not. So get off my car."

Jason laughs as if my anger is the most amusing thing to him. Just hilarious, I am.

I pull the door open and Jason moves over, shutting it behind me. I put the key in the ignition and turn the wheel with my sore arms.

I wish I could go out to breakfast with him.

I slap myself inside my head. *Never, ever, Charlotte.* I watch as he pulls out of the parking lot behind me and follows me back to Jersey. Maybe I should go back to work.

~17~

I Didn't Know What I Wanted

Butch is having a bad day. The first of many, I suppose. He's not sweet or angry, which makes me worry he's defeated. The doctor said six to nine months. We still have a lot of time with him. Months.

He can barely walk. Jason helps him to the kitchen table where Jay and I are making a picture with glue and glitter. It's everywhere and the old Butch would have bitched a fit about it, but the man in front of me barely seems to notice.

"What hurts?" I ask.

"I don't know." Butch's voice is weak. "And my goddamned knee," he adds. This is the beginning of the downhill portion of our trip together. Butch coughs. It goes on and on and the mere sound of it rattles my own insides.

"That's new," I say.

"Nice, huh?" Butch seems broken.

I get up from the table to find the dustpan and brush. Jay yawns and rubs his eyes and Jason takes him into the spare room and tucks him in for a nap. I silently clean up the glitter, although I kind of like it strewn all over. Maybe the colorful dust can hold off death. Butch coughs again, reminding me death makes its own schedule.

I finish collecting the glitter and make Butch lunch. I'm tiptoeing around him until Marie arrives and relief is injected into me. My escape…

"I'm going to go make lasagna for dinner," I announce, and grab my bag, practically running out of the house.

"Do you mind if I come with you?" Jason asks, and I shake my head without really understanding the question. He's going to come to my house. The one Noble and I share.

"Pastor Johnson is going to come by later," I say, still ignoring the fact that Jason is coming with me. *What month is it? March. What did Noble say he's doing today? Plowing…yes, plowing. Noble is plowing a field right now.*

I walk out the door and Jason follows me. Once we exit the shed, he steps next to me. I don't know if it's being out of that house, away from death, or because I just love him being next to me, but I'm suddenly lighter and genuinely happy. A misbehaving smile occupies Jason's lips, like he's infiltrated enemy territory by entering Noble's house. He can be such an ass.

"Don't be so proud of yourself. No one ever said you can't come in our house."

"Oh, Annie, I'm not proud, and I think you did tell me once I'm not welcome." He takes the screen door handle from my hand and holds it open for me. I walk into the house, my house.

"Do you want a beer?" I say, walking toward the refrigerator.

"It's two o'clock."

"Is that a no?" I open one for myself and take a long sip of it.

"I'll take one," Jason says, still smiling. He's escaping Butch with me and it feels like home. It's our history. Jason and Annie running from the darkness, together the whole way. Well, maybe not the whole way.

Jason twists the cap off his beer and looks around.

"Under the sink," I say, and watch him open the cabinet door and throw his cap away. I hold mine in my hand, running the ridges of the circle around my fingertips. Anything to keep my hands to myself.

"Do you still smoke?" I ask, and shake my head, a little surprised by the question. I love these times when I speak completely without thinking. They usually work out great for me.

"Why? You want a cigarette?"

I could punch him and the smug look on his face. "Do you want to sit down?" I motion toward the kitchen table. Jason shakes his head. His face turns serious and I should run. This was a mistake. I'll add this to the list of horrible mistakes Jason and Annie have made. Two complete assholes.

We stand facing each other in silence for what seems like six hours. I want to look away, let my eyes escape him, but they're as much a hostage as the rest of me.

"How about a tour?" Jason asks, pissing me off.

"How about no?"

"What's wrong, Annie? Can't you show an old friend around your new house? Seems completely normal."

"Things are always so normal with us. I used to be bored to tears when we were together," I say, and Jason crosses the kitchen to stand in front of me, his gray eyes dancing just above mine. His lips part and I swallow hard as a chill runs from the tops of my shoulders down to both nipples. I lower my eyes to the buttons on his shirt and rest my hands on the counter behind me to keep from moving them to his chest. The chill dances across my thighs and down the sides of my calves. *This is not normal.*

Jason leans into me and I stop. I stop breathing as he covers me. I close my eyes and he whispers in my ear, "Look at me, Annie."

I try to breathe. *Why? What good is it going to do now?*

I open my eyes and defiantly look at Jason. Nothing's going to change. Not for the better. I'll look at him all day if he wants. I'm sure I deserve the torture of it for something I've done, or will do.

I hear the truck pull into the side yard and Jason and I turn to the window over the kitchen sink. Noble's coming home.

"I should go," he says, and steps back, allowing me to breathe.

"No. Stay. I want him to know you were here."

"Why?" Jason's confused by my motives.

"Because I don't want to lie to him and I don't want to figure out how to tell him you were in here."

Jason walks to the door as Noble hops out of the truck. "You'll figure it out," he says, and steps through the back door.

Noble watches Jason walk back to Butch's. I consider throwing Jason's beer bottle in the recyclables can, but that's lying, too. Noble and I are only going to make it through this if we stick together.

I can't tell if Noble is pissed or terrified when he enters the kitchen. He seems quelled by the sight of me. He stops, noticing the two beer bottles, and turns to me for answers. But really, what is the question?

"Jason was just here," I say without any apology.

"I saw him leave." Noble's voice houses his own defiance.

"Butch is getting worse." Noble stays still, not satisfied in the least. "He's not himself. Not angry. Not fighting." Noble grabs Jason's beer bottle and reads nothing on the label. "He's coughing terrible, too. I wanted a shot, but I thought it was too early, so we each had a beer." *There, that's it, the whole truth.*

"Why didn't you text me? I would have come home and had a beer with you."

"I didn't know what I wanted until it was in my hand. I'm sorry." *What am I apologizing for? This is why people lie.*

Noble turns and walks upstairs. I'm losing him. I follow him into our bedroom. He's looking in his dresser for something. Searching the top drawer. I stand next to it and look down into the drawer, too.

"What are you looking for?"

"I don't know," he says, and bows his head, defeated. I turn Noble toward me and press my body against his. I run my hands through his hair and pull his face to mine. He kisses me, but it's a guarded, frustrated kiss.

"I'm sorry, Noble," I whisper onto his neck as I kiss him there, and behind his ear, and on his cheek, and on his lips. Noble takes a deep breath and lets it out slowly. This is what we have to work with. He has to work with it.

Noble kisses me violently, reminding me of who I'm married to. He lays me on the bed and admires me with his sad eyes. Noble's my husband and I love him. *I love him!* I scream the words inside my head. What must be screaming inside his? I reach out my hand and when Noble touches it, I pull him on top of me. He shakes the bed as he lands on me hard.

"Attacking me again?" he asks, my playful Noble intact.

"If I have to," I say, and roll on top of him. "If you weren't such a prude—" Noble's lips silence me as he reminds me once again of the many joys that come with being Mrs. Noble Sinclair.

I roll off Noble and onto my side of the bed.

"Come to the Harvest Dance with me," Noble says as I lay my head on the pillow beside him. A million reasons not to go to the dance furrow my brow. Noble reaches over me and grabs the frame on my nightstand. It's a picture of him with the red sky behind him taken at the first dance we went to. The first night we became a couple.

"I'm not sure I'm in the right place to celebrate the harvest, or wish it luck."

"It's not about the harvest." He holds the picture up. "It's about us. It's the first night I knew we would be together forever."

I take the picture and put it back on my nightstand. I roll on top of Noble and kiss him. He is *so* good.

"How can I say no to an invitation like that?"

"You can't."

~18~

Old Scars

I couldn't bring myself to ask if he's going. As it turns out, it wasn't necessary; Nadine said he and Stephanie are going with a big group of people. I have no idea what that means, but I'm certain it was Nadine trying to soften the blow. She finishes adding the highlights to my hair as Jocelyn finishes my toes. It's a proper end to the winter months.

"What are you wearing tomorrow night?" Nadine asks, and I brace myself for her scorn.

"I don't know yet. I'm heading to the mall from here. Clint's coming with me." Nadine raises her eyebrows as she sweeps up the area around me.

"Do you and Clint realize the dance is tomorrow?"

"I've heard that, yes. We're confident we'll find something. What are you wearing?"

Nadine smiles ruefully. "Think bright lights, big city." She sweeps her hand through the air in front of her face. "It's metallic," she says, and I know it's going to be over the top and wholly fabulous.

"I love it already."

* * *

I check out of Salon Nadine with her wishes of luck for finding a dress. As I pull into my driveway, my parents' driveway—Clint's driveway—I am again reminded of the inevitability of life. It keeps moving whether I'm ready or not. Clint hops in the car and lights a roach as I pull onto I-95.

"You know, Charlotte, I am really beginning to love this tradition. It's like our day," he says, totally high.

"It is. I couldn't do it without you. Did Jocelyn get a dress yet?"

"She did. She seemed a little worried we're just going today to find something."

"In a million years I didn't think we'd go to the dance this year, but Noble really wants to. It's significant," I say, and remember Noble's sweet request.

* * *

Clint practically skips from the car to the mall. He's just the person to keep me from obsessing all day. I could spend the next six hours trying to figure out how I feel about Jason and Stephanie going to the dance. I've never seen them together. What if they dance? They are obviously going to dance. *It's a dance.* Maybe Clint has a Valium I can take tomorrow night. A normal person would be upset, or maybe not care at all. I can't even figure out how I feel, let alone a normal person.

I rummage through the dresses as Clint eyes the other shoppers. There's red, green, blue, off-white, and black. Red is out. It's Jason's favorite color and he'll read too much into it. White and off-white are also out; I just got done with the whole wedding thing. I didn't think I wanted black, but when I pass the mermaid gown on the mannequin, I know it's the one. It's simple. A crew neck and cap sleeves top off the long black gown with a slit up to the thigh. The back is the money shot. Rachel Zoe cut out an almost diamond shape. The cap sleeves are joined by a tiny button at the top and the entire back is open. The mermaid hemline pools on the floor. It's dramatic and unexpected. Most importantly, Noble will love it.

"How's Butch doing?" Clint asks as we sit at "our" table in the Nordstrom Café.

"He's holding his own, I guess."

"It's kind of crazy out there on the farm these days," he says, half laughing.

God, I wish it were funny. "Yes it is." I sigh deeply.

"Is it weird having Leer home?"

"It's nice for Butch. In fact, he's the happiest I've ever seen him since Jason moved back. He's probably missed him for years."

"How's it for you? And Nick?"

"Noble tolerates him. I try not to think about him. He's where he belongs, with his dad, who just happens to live within a hundred yards of me. It's only temporary," I say, and the thought of Butch dying, of Jason leaving, spoils my mood.

"Hey, what's wrong?"

"I'm just thinking about Butch," I lie. "It's not fair."

"Very few things are in life," Clint says, ending the conversation. I'm thankful for the silence as our food's delivered. Thankful until I become lost in the thoughts that torture me.

*　*　*

I visit Butch early, hoping to avoid Jason. I'll see enough of him tonight; no need to start the morning off with a dose of the cowboy. Butch is lying in his recliner. He's covered with a blanket and I realize the house has a chill. It's warming outside, but the night air is still cool. Winter still has custody of spring.

Butch lurches forward as a cough erupts in his chest. It goes on too long, warning he'll never truly kick it. I pour him a glass of water from the pitcher in the refrigerator and grab another cough drop on my way into the family room.

"Here," I say, and Butch sits up to take the glass from me. "Did you get any sleep last night?"

"Some," he says.

Does he even attempt to sleep in his bed these days? I grab his finger and squeeze it. Butch coughs again, making me think I should call the doctor for something to suppress it.

"Thank you," he whispers, and I think he's talking about more than the cough drop.

"You're not going anywhere yet, old man," I say. Marie comes through the kitchen door. I'm thankful she loves Butch, too.

"Well, I'm going to get out of here. I have a dance to get ready for."

"Harvest Dance?" Marie asks, and I nod. But the sight of Butch under his blanket makes the idea of a dance seem absurd.

"Enjoy it. Life is meant to be enjoyed," Butch says, and I raise both eyebrows at him.

"Well said, old friend." I wave as I walk out the back door and cross the yard to my house.

The emptiness of the house, the quiet peace, makes me realize how drained I am. Just a few minutes with Butch sucks the energy from me. His kindness is more taxing than his gruffness. I lie down on the couch and cover myself with Noble's coat that's lying on the back of it. It's warm, just like Noble. I drift off to sleep and don't dream at all.

* * *

I wake up to Noble's lips on mine. He's sitting on the edge of the couch, smiling down at me as I focus on him.

"Why are you so tired, beautiful?" he asks.

"It might have something to do with you keeping me up until all hours of the night," I say, and kiss him again.

"I warned you I'll never get enough. Would you like to shower with me?"

"I would love to." Noble lifts me over his shoulder and carries me up the stairs to the bathroom. He places me on my feet and I watch him turn on the water and pull the curtain to the wall. He turns to me without a care in the world.

"The water's heating up," he says, and his eyes heat me up.

"I can't wait to see you in your suit."

"Funny because I can't wait to see you in nothing." Noble pulls my shirt over my head. He tosses it over his shoulder and grabs me, pulling me toward him. He buries his lips in my neck, tickling me there.

He leans over and takes my breast in his hand, my nipple in his mouth, and I stop breathing. I watch as Noble swirls my nipple with his tongue and then stands before me with hunger in his eyes.

"Get in the shower," he directs, and I happily oblige. There's no place I'd rather be.

* * *

I'm finishing my makeup when Noble comes in elegantly dressed. His charcoal suit stretches perfectly from one corner of his body to the next. Even without the suit, it's his untrimmed hair, his deep blue eyes, and his constant smile that make him insanely hot. His tie is a deep gray with white stripes and I realize why as he hands me a large white lily on a wristlet.

"It's beautiful."

I watch in the mirror as Noble adjusts his tie behind me and checks his watch. "When do I get to see you in your dress?"

"I showed it to you yesterday," I say.

"I want to see you *in* it. Big difference." Noble kisses my cheek and turns and walks out of our bedroom.

I pull the dress over my head. It fits beautifully. I turn to see my back in the mirror, fully exposed. I'm not used to being completely bare, but I know it's the most dramatic part and worth any chill I catch tonight. I put in my grandmother's turquoise chandelier earrings and grab an evening bag out of the basket in my closet. It's a silver sequined clutch I haven't used in as long as I can remember. I unzip it and a Polaroid of me, Violet, Jenn, and Sydney completely naked and covered in body paint rests along the side of the purse. I lift it out slightly and frown. The only evidence of the night Violet chose to throw perfect away. *Why do we create it only to destroy it?*

The squawking of birds calls me to the window and I watch as thousands of black birds fly through the sky. They're moving from one field to the next, floating atop an invisible ocean as they search for something to eat. They confound me. The way they perch in the trees and look like leaves. How they swoop down around my car as I'm driving the empty roads.

I look up into Noble's admiring eyes staring down at me. He turns to the window to see what's captured my attention.

"The black birds," I say. "They amaze me how they fly like that." As if on cue, the birds swoop up and balloon to the sky and gracefully fall back to a new section of the field.

"Predator confusion," Noble says. I can't take my eyes off the birds. I love Noble and his insane breadth of knowledge. Noble wraps his arm around my shoulders and leans against my back, studying the birds as well. "The odds are better they won't be killed in a large group. Plus, the way they fly causes predator confusion, like an optical illusion."

"There's safety in numbers," I say, and commit it to heart as I embark on a night that will surely include Jason Leer.

Noble pulls me away from the window and twirls me around as he whistles at the sight of me finally finished.

"You know, I'm not going to be able to wear dresses like this once you knock me up."

"I'm thinking about knocking you up right now." He holds my arms out to the side and turns me around, landing me with my back to him. Noble kisses my lower back and the heat rises up me and settles in my cheeks. He runs his hand over my backside and faces me. "You're beautiful, Charlotte."

"You're biased. I'm your old lady." He runs the back of his fingers up the side of my face and with his thumb traces the scar on my cheek. I pull his hand down and kiss it, hoping he'll forget about the scar, about Jason.

"Thanks, Noble."

"You're welcome." He kisses me. "But for what?"

"For asking me to the dance," I say, and kiss him again.

* * *

Noble hands the keys to the valet and takes my hand as we walk in the front door of the Reed estate. I used the drive over to consider every possible circumstance of talking to or seeing Jason and Stephanie. I covered dancing, food, across the room, nearby, and pretty much every other scenario or social situation I could come up with—that is, everything but walking through the front door and right into him.

I literally walk into him and almost fall backward because of course that ox doesn't budge at all.

He turns around and catches me before I knock Noble over. Jason pulls me toward him, away from Noble, and holds my elbow as I steady myself on my heels. His smug face manages to send a chill over my skin at the same time anger burns inside me. He always did have a way of igniting every emotion in me at the same time. I pull my arm back and know I should say hello, but I'm not sure what that sounds like.

"Hello, Jason," Noble says, and reaches over my shoulders to take my coat off for me. I switch my purse from one hand to the next and slip my arms out of each sleeve. Noble steps to the side and hands it to the coat check as I face Jason's gray eyes traveling from the bottom of my dress to the tops of my shoulders and settling on my glare. Again he smirks, knowing I will kill him if he ruins tonight. He should go back to Oklahoma. His departure will coincide with Butch's, though, and I can't hope for that.

"Jason!" Stephanie yells over the crowd. She never makes eye contact, but I'm certain she knows I'm right here. "I need you," she shouts, and I have to consciously keep my top lip from curling. I will not give her the satisfaction.

"You better get back," Noble says to Jason, practically gloating. I stand between the two of them as Jason just glares back at Noble. I look from one to the other, and, thank you God, Jason turns and walks away. He touches his open hand to my bare back and whispers, "Nice dress," into my ear on his way by. My back arches at his touch. When he's fifteen feet in front of me, the air releases from my lungs.

"Maybe this was a bad idea," Noble says.

"Any excuse to get you in a suit is a great idea," I say, and try to pull myself together without detection.

We find Sean and Michelle and take pictures with them and every other person standing around us. This is the first Harvest Dance Sean and I have both attended. Michelle was pregnant with Lily for the first one we went to, and last year Lily was so young Michelle didn't want to leave her.

"Did Lily love your dress?"

"She did. I told Sean we're in big trouble with that little diva."

"She'll have Sean wrapped around her finger by the time things get really bad."

"I'm sure," Michelle agrees as we watch the crowd begin to fill the dance floor. I don't see Jason anywhere. Stephanie is on the other side of the floor talking with some girls from high school.

"Do you think Lily can come over next week?"

"Name the time. She'd come to your house every day if I let her." Michelle turns to me. "Anything special planned?"

"I've been spending some time with Butch's grandson and I was thinking he might like to play with someone his own age."

"Butch's grandson, as in Jason's son?" Michelle asks, and to her credit doesn't sound shocked.

"That's the one." I tilt my head to Michelle. "It's one cozy commune on the Sinclair farm these days."

Noble comes up behind me and wraps his arms around my waist. With his chin on my shoulder, his lips near my ear, he says, "Dance with me," and I can't think of a reason to say no. Well maybe one.

Noble leads me onto the dance floor, holding my hand as we walk through the crowd. He finds a spot in the middle and turns around. Noble pulls me to him and I rest my head on his gorgeous shoulder as the orchestra plays something familiar. Or maybe it's holding on to Noble at a dance that's familiar.

Stephanie stares at me from the side of the dance floor and Noble holds me tighter. What is she thinking? Surely she doesn't hate me, because I've done nothing wrong. She does look like she hates me, though.

The song ends. Jason emerges from the crowd and stands at the edge of the dance floor. A male vocalist begins the one song Jason used to sing to me. It's about being wanted, and if there was one thing I never questioned with Jason, it was how much he wanted me. I could sense it every time I was within fifty yards of him. Tonight it makes me sick. I could throw up if given a bucket. I lean into Noble and let him hold me up as Jason downs a shot, his eyes never leaving mine.

Yes, it was a horrible idea to come here. Jason and I shouldn't be together in private, let alone at this dance. Noble kisses my cheek and I lean back to see him. My lovely Noble. I push the sight of Jason, the thought of his truck, of the loft, of Cedar Creek Lake out of my head. If I could, I would erase every second of it from my memory.

I lower my head to Noble's shoulder and admit I would never choose to forget if given the chance.

The song ends and a fast dance begins as Sam emerges from the crowd. I hug him, and we all step off the dance floor. For me, it's an escape. I'll hide in the crowd the rest of the night. Noble and Sam fall into the familiar dialogue of best friends who don't get to see each other often enough, and I stand there, still picturing Jason in my head. Noble looks at me apologetically, not wanting to abandon me. I release him from any husbandly duties with a wink. I want him to enjoy himself.

"I'm going to run to the bathroom," I say, and peck Noble. "Take good care of him," I direct to Sam over my shoulder as I make my way through the crowd.

I finish drying my hands at the sink and reapply my lip gloss. I forgive the universe for its song choices because it's kept Stephanie Harding out of the bathroom while I've been in here. I considered holding it the entire night, but that seemed cowardly. Although I am terrified of what I might say to her... or do to her. *Whore*.

I take one last look in the mirror on my way out. I do love this dress, and I love being at this dance with Noble. It's like I've stepped back in time, but I mourned the possibility of that long ago. I open the door and look into the almost-black eyes of Jason Leer, who is leaning on the wall opposite the bathroom door. I pause for a second. The sight of him disarms me and I realize it's because he's drunk. He's sloppy. It's a weakness I'm not accustomed to with Jason. *How drunk were you the first night with Stephanie? Does he drink every night he's with her?* The concept sparks a bitter joy as I walk through the door.

"Annie, we need to talk."

I turn to walk back to the dance floor, back to my husband, and Jason roughly grabs my arm. His paw around it fills my mind with the heady memories of a life with Jason Leer. I glare at his hand touching me and raise my eyebrows to him. I hope he hasn't noticed the goose bumps now covering me.

"Save your breath," I say, and steady my voice.

"You're running as fast as you can, Annie, but you'll never get away."

I square my jaw and inhale the smell of whiskey on the powerful Jason Leer. I open my eyes and Noble is fifteen feet away from us, his eyes fixed on Jason's hand on my arm. His jaw is clenched, his body taut, and I'm reminded of the one time I thought Noble was capable of killing someone, when Jack Reynolds manhandled me two years ago.

I yank my arm from Jason's grasp, and he glares at Noble, silently challenging him to say something. I walk to Noble without turning back. I'm sure Jason's still there because Noble hasn't taken his raging eyes off him.

"I'll meet you back at the table," Noble says. I place myself squarely in Noble's view and his eyes finally focus on me.

"That's what he wants," I say, willing him to hear me. "Don't let him separate us," I add, and take his hand. Noble looks down at his hand in mine. He runs his thumb across my skin. He returns his eyes to mine and silently studies me, deciding his next move.

"Lead the way," he says, and relief flows through me.

I don't leave Noble's side for the rest of the dance. I watch Stephanie try to help Jason to his truck at the end of the night. Ollie and Possum help her, the weight of the great Jason Leer anchored by alcohol. The thought of tomorrow's hangover brings me joy. *Who's reckless now?* If I behaved this way, he'd have me checked into rehab tomorrow.

Noble tips the valet and we drive home in silence. It's a wordless acceptance of the predicament of death. Butch's life binds Jason and I together, his death the only escape. I won't hope for that. I watch Noble in the dim light of the car and wonder what he hopes for.

Noble parks the car in the L-shed and takes the key out of the ignition. We sit silently, me staring at him, him staring at the back wall of the barn.

"Did you have fun tonight?" I ask, and he still doesn't look at me. "Are you disappointed we aren't going to the Barnyard Saloon?"

"No. I'm glad we came home," he says, and gets out of the car. He comes around to my side, opens my door, and practically lifts me out of the car.

"Noble—"

"I don't want to talk about it, okay?" His words are slow. He's wounded.

"I'm not sure," I say, searching his eyes for some sign of comfort.

"Not sure about what?"

"If it's okay not to talk."

Noble shuts the car door and walks to the house, leaving me alone and in the dark, and I don't know why.

When I walk into the kitchen, Noble already has his jacket off and an open beer in his hand. He's huge, his anger filling the room. His suit pants and dress shirt adorn his perfect body as his mind steals his smile.

"I'm going up," I say, and should kiss him, but he wants to be alone with his fury.

"I'll be up in a little while."

I change out of my beautiful black dress. It promised a fairy tale but delivered me alone to unbutton it. I put my grandmother's earrings back in my mother's jewelry box, and I take off my rings. My engagement ring sparkles in the moonlight. It's perfect…and he's perfect. I take a deep breath and close my eyes. *Don't make this harder than it needs to be.*

The old steps creak under my feet as I descend. Noble's sitting on the couch, the TV tuned to the Weather Channel, a beer in his hand. I stand to the side and even though he knows I'm here, completely naked, he never takes his eyes off the weather. I watch him take a sip of his beer and still he never looks my way. What awful thoughts are running through his head?

I straddle him on the couch. I lean my forearms on his shoulders and run my fingers through his hair, and his hands never come near me. His eyes are distant. His love for me trapped in some horrific reflection. His silence is killing me.

"I need you to tell me," I plead with him.

"I'm afraid of what I might say." His eyes are dead; his warmth has hardened.

"I'm not."

Noble leans over and places his beer on the side table. He sits back up and takes my face in his hand. He runs his thumb over my scar, his eyes deep pools of disgust. He pulls me to him and kisses me. His kiss saying he's leaving tomorrow, never coming back, and this will have to last us a lifetime. I move closer to him, my naked body a shroud around him. Noble's eyes follow his hands to my breasts and his touch radiates through me. I watch as he caresses me, claiming what's his.

"I don't want him to ever touch you," he says, his voice low but unmistakably resolute. He returns his eyes to mine and I'm ready to promise him anything.

"Noble—"

He halts me with a raised hand and shakes his head. "I won't lose you," he says, and a chill runs through me. My sweet Noble is gone, replaced by a man pushed too far. "Not to him or anyone else."

"You won't. I'm yours," I promise. I kiss him. I let my lips convey how much I want him, how much I need him, as I take him. Noble responds, forgetting his demand, and pulls me to him, his lips forcing every other thought from my mind.

"Come to bed," I say, and Noble doesn't respond. "Come make love to me in our bed," I plead. Noble moves my hair back and kisses my shoulder. His lips move to my neck, and to my ear, and then he leans back, leaving me cold.

"You're so beautiful, Charlotte. So incredibly beautiful."

His compliment frightens me. He's serious, his playfulness fractured, damaged beyond the point of wanting me.

"Noble, don't do this." I hate even thinking of Jason, in our house, naked with my husband, but Noble's letting him come between us.

I can't tell if it's fear or anger or both but it can't stay here. Not tonight, not ever. "You're scaring me."

Noble studies me. He rubs his hands over my thighs and up my back. Where has my Noble gone? I didn't know there was this much distance inside his head. That may be what scares me the most.

"How can I frighten you?" he whispers. "I'm incapable of hurting you."

"I'm not afraid of you hurting me. I'm terrified of living without you," I say, and lower my eyes.

"You don't ever have to worry about that," Noble says, and raises my chin. His smile, his warmth intact, melts me on top of him and I realize I was on the verge of tears. Noble kisses me, and when he leans forward, I wrap my arms and legs tightly around his body. He stands and walks upstairs to our bed with me attached to the front of him.

~19~

Resurrection

It's been two weeks since the Harvest Dance. I switched my routine the day after and now spend most mornings with Butch and swim in the afternoon to limit the time I see Jason. Noble noted the change but seemed unwilling to discuss the reasoning. Marie seems to understand without saying a word.

Today is different, though. Jason, Jay, Butch, and Marie are coming over to dye Easter eggs with Lily and me. She's so excited you might think she's expecting her prom date. She colored a picture of an Easter basket full of eggs for Jay and had me help her write the letter *J* above it. I try to recall if Jay knows his ABCs. Maybe we'll work on those next.

At one o'clock I pull my car close to Butch's back door. As I enter the kitchen, Jay runs over to me.

"Annie!" he yells, and Jason and Butch look up at me. I've missed seeing Jason. More than I should ever admit. Even though I should be pissed at him for causing trouble at the Harvest Dance, his beautiful face and gray eyes practically disable me in the doorway. He hasn't shaved in a while and a light beard is beginning to form and…and…yeah, that.

I kneel down and Jay wraps his arms around my neck. He is such a little love bug.

"Hi, Jay. I missed you," I say, giving him my full attention. "Are you ready to dye eggs?"

"I don't know how," he says, his words filled with worry.

"Ah, it's easy. I'll show you." I pat his back and stand up with his arms still around my neck. I lift him, too, and the shock lingers on Jason's face. Utter amazement settles on his ridiculously hot, unshaven face.

"Where's Butch?" I ask.

Jason nods to the living room. "Says he's not coming."

"Bad day?" I ask, and Jason shrugs. It's difficult to tell a bad day from a good one now. I put Jay back on his feet and walk into the next room. Butch is in the recliner with his feet up. It reminds me of the times when his knee was our biggest problem. I miss those days.

"You ready to go, Butch?" I ask with a soft voice. I hate being gentle with him. He rolls his eyes at me. He must not feel that bad. The worse he feels the sweeter he gets, preparing to meet his maker. "Do you have something better to do today?" I say, and Butch grumbles as he attempts to get out of the chair. I leap to his side and support him until Jason takes the other side with ease. With an arm around Butch's waist, he takes the weight off me and I'm glad he's here.

"Be careful," I warn him, noting his detachment from the entire term careful. Jason smiles at me and I turn my eyes away as a chill runs across my nipples. *Why, God?* Jason and Butch follow me out. I open my car door and wait for Butch to bitch that driving across the lawn is ridiculous. When he doesn't, I glance back at Marie, who's frowning. Butch, Jay, and I ride to my house, following Marie and Jason on foot, and I pull up close to the door with Butch's side of the car. Instead of dying eggs, I want to rest my head on my steering wheel and cry.

Jason opens Butch's door and helps him out while I carry Jay. For only being a few months older than Lily, he's a lot heavier. He's probably going to be an ox. Jay plays with the ruffles adorning my black, V-neck wrap dress. He follows them to my waist and leans over to see they cascade down to the hemline at my knees. It's a carefree dress I wore to church and now to dye Easter eggs with this cute little boy in my arms. I'm going to miss him, too, when they leave. All the Leer boys will leave at the same time.

"Aunt Shar, Uncle Nick wuz here but he don't want make eggs."

"No?" I ask.

Jason has that smirk on his face I always want to slap off. BJ runs over, excited to have everyone in his house. He's almost as tall as Jay and loves being able to lick his face without having to jump on him. Jay giggles and hugs BJ, which has the dog practically rolling on the floor with joy.

Joy… let it in, Charlotte.

We dye eggs and I'm not sure if the kids or the adults enjoy it more. I show Jay and Lily how to use a white crayon to draw on their eggs, and Marie draws intricate lace and geometrical patterns on hers before dipping them in the cups. Butch draws a cross on his, which renders us all speechless.

Jay and Lily only spill two bowls of dye and by the time we're done, we've created five dozen glorious eggs. I make Butch comfortable in the recliner in my living room and get him a cup of tea. Marie takes the kids in to play and leaves Jason and me to clean up. I move the egg trays to the counter and place them on newspaper to catch any lingering drips.

"I'm sorry," Jason says as he carries cups to the sink to empty the dye.

"For what?" *I cannot talk about this.*

"All the trouble I caused you at the dance." Jason doesn't look sorry.

"What trouble? There was no trouble," I blurt out too fast, sounding like the inept liar that I am. Jason smiles sincerely as he appears to fight back laughter.

"Why haven't you been around the past few weeks?"

The familiar need to punch him returns. "I've gone to Butch's every day," I say, and roll up the newspaper covering the table.

"What time do you go?" he asks, but he's not challenging my answer. He's collecting information.

I hear Jay giggling in the other room and from the sound of it I can tell BJ is smothering him with his beagle love again.

"Your son loves dogs."

"He loves this one for sure. He's the happiest I've ever seen him here," he says, and follows me to the mudroom, where I crush the newspaper into the paper bin.

"That's great. He should know about New Jersey." Jason is standing too close, or the room is too small. I stand up straight and he's practically touching me. I'm surprised my heartbeat doesn't push him away.

"Not New Jersey. He loves it here...with you."

"Don't." My voice is thick with regret. Jason puts his hand on my back and pulls me to him. He leans back and runs his fingers across my collarbone and I realize I'm sweating as the chill skips across my skin. I should punch him in the face and throw him out of my house, but instead I drop my head back, exposing my neck for his rediscovery. A deep ache growls from my groin as every muscle tightens, praying for his touch. My body is electrified with the memories of Jason coursing through it. I take a deep breath and let it all rise from the dead.

The back door opens and Michelle walks in as I stand with my head hanging back, my body at the mercy of Jason Leer.

"Hey," she says, trying to take it all in. "I was just coming to pick up Lily." She looks from Jason to me and says nonchalantly, "Noble's right behind me, pulling the tractor in now."

"I'll be right back," I say, and turn to go upstairs as I hear Jason tell Butch it's time to go.

The commotion of Butch's departure and Lily leaving are in the background as I pull myself together on the second floor. When I come back down, the house is empty except for BJ wagging his tail in the kitchen. I see Noble through the kitchen window. He's walking away from the house, punishing the ground with each angry step. I lean over the sink to see him better. An egg catches my eye, cracked and abandoned in the bottom of the sink. It's bright turquoise and as I turn the shell over in my hand, I realize it had an A on it. I close my eyes and the chill stings me again as I watch my pissed-off husband storm across his field.

~20~

In Every Way

Just pulling out of the farm lane spreads relief through my body. I gaze through the Jeep's window at the blue sky above and crack it to inhale the spring air. There's a lot to be thankful for…not much of it resides on the Sinclair farm, though.

We've neglected Violet and her new baby and that's not going to fly. She has summoned us all for a barbeque and some baby time. I've always loved how Violet takes what she needs when she needs it, except for the one night in Key West when it threatened to ruin her life.

I've seen the baby and he's beautiful, and Violet is beautiful with him in her arms, but with everything that's going on with Butch, the joy of a baby seems artificial, contrived somehow. I have to force myself to remember it's Violet and Blake's baby, forever. It's an incredible bond I can't seem to connect with the two of them. For some reason, though, I can't imagine Jay without Jason. They are forever connected in my mind.

Violet and Blake are staying at her parents' while their new home is being built. It's going to be massive, but I wouldn't expect anything less. Noble parks on the street in front of Violet's parents' and cuts the engine.

"Being here reminds me of their engagement party," he says, and ponders me. "A lot's happened since then."

I think back to the night when Noble kissed me on their back patio. I'm not sure what would have happened between the two of us if Jason hadn't shown up. I hold Noble's hand and run my fingers over the back of it and the length of each finger.

"If you had told me that night we would be sitting here right now, married, I wouldn't have believed it," I say.

"I would." Noble pulls me to him and kisses me gently and tenderly, and wholly nobly.

* * *

Everyone's already here. Julia is solo since her new boyfriend couldn't make the trip to South Jersey to see the baby. Something tells me he really didn't have to work. South Jersey and a baby not enticing? Sydney, though, easily convinced her new man, a shipbuilder from Maine who she met on the island of Capri, to make the trip.

Noble settles in with Blake and the ship maker and a beer on the patio, and I go inside with the girls for our baby time.

"Can we call him Bob?" Julia asks, and I laugh behind Violet's back. Robert does seem a bit formal.

"Absolutely not," Violet dismisses.

"Dick?" Julia jibes.

"That's short for Richard," Violet corrects.

"I know," Julia says.

"Violet, can I ask you a question you probably don't want to talk about?" I ask gingerly, interrupting.

"Less than I want Julia to call my baby a dick?"

"Maybe. How did Blake ever move past the Key West guy?"

Sydney and Julia brace for the apocalypse. We're all silent as Robert coos on Violet's lap, his presence a testament of life's ability to move on.

"I don't think he did. He wants me enough to live with the horrific knowledge of what I've done." Violet examines me closer, unaffected by her own words. That must be how she deals with it. "He said the only thing that would bring him peace would be to kill him, or to know he died."

"Oh God," I say without realizing I'm speaking.

"I know. I try to imagine knowing a girl he fucked is walking around and is then invited to our wedding—"

"Let me guess. It's too ridiculous to imagine?" Julia chimes in with her well-known take on the issue.

"Can we talk about something else?" Sydney begs, her limited patience for all things depressing having been depleted.

"I saw Renee twice this week. She misses you, and I miss you," Julia says, switching to her kind voice. She asks, "How's Butch doing?"

"Maybe something happier than the dying guy?" Sydney suggests.

"He's hanging on."

"And you?" Julia looks like she might hug me, if she was the type to hug me, which she is not.

"I'm coming apart at the seams. When Jason's near me, like within one hundred yards of me, I'm totally confused, consumed by him and what I want him to do to me." All six of their eyeballs bulge in their heads and I swear I think the baby's even listening. "But when I can get some distance, when I can breathe and think, I know it will ruin my life," I say, and add too loudly, "I know I want to be with Noble."

"Are you trying to convince us or yourself?" Julia asks, and I sigh.

"His son, the baby he conceived with someone else while we were together, is two years old now. How long is it going to take?"

"How long is what going to take?" Violet asks with extreme worry covering her face.

"How long to get over him?"

"I'm not sure you'll ever be over him. If the baby didn't do it," Violet says, and she's right. What more could he possibly do to make me stay away forever?

"How's the kid?" Julia asks, and I frown.

"Adorable," I say, and add, "I love him, too." I need a shovel to bury myself in Violet's parents' backyard.

"Do you ever see his whore mother?" Julia asks, and I wish she lived closer. I could use this type of conversation on a daily basis.

"Thankfully, no. They were at a dance together in March but she never comes to Butch's." I look at Julia, searching for answers to a question I can't even ask myself.

"You do realize yours is the only town in New Jersey that has a dance for adults?" Julia asks. Robert stretches his precious arms and arches his back, causing us all to move in closer in awe of him. Are all babies this enchanting? What was Jay like as a baby? Was he as cute as Robert? What was Jason like holding his son in his arms?

"Be careful, Charlotte." Violet's words cut through my concentration. She's the only one among us qualified to give the warning. I withdraw my eyes from the baby and force them to meet Violet's. "There are some things in this world that last forever."

"Hold up. What are we even talking about here?" Sydney sounds a little frantic. "You are not seriously considering leaving Nick?"

"No!" I yell.

"She's not considering anything. It's not about thinking," Violet says, and my stomach cramps.

"Well what? Are you now the cheating type?" Sydney's not letting it go.

"No. I'm not doing anything with him. I'm just having trouble spending so much time with him. He affects me."

"Not in a good way?" Sydney asks, still confused.

"In every way," I say, barely above a whisper, and a chill runs across my chest.

Noble opens the patio door and walks into the room. We all gawk the baby as if this is how we've been fixed the past half hour.

"Did Charlotte tell you guys she's going to be knocked up soon?" Noble teases them.

"Yes, she was just telling us all about it," Julia says, and we each look in a different direction.

"Nick, do you want to hold the baby?"

"Little Robbo, Bobbly Fly, Big Rob?" Noble asks.

"Please don't do that," Violet says, and loosens up to a smile as she hands the baby to Noble. He sits down and lays the baby on his lap lengthwise and talks to Robert as he holds his tiny hands in his own. The four of us watch in awe as Noble tells the baby how much everyone loves him and that he knows he's going to be big and strong someday.

"Which is good. You'll need to run fast, too, if Mommy doesn't loosen up on the name," he whispers.

"Why do I hang out with you people?" Violet asks as Sydney puts her arm around her and kisses her cheek.

I realize how much I miss these girls when I can barely let go of them at the end of the day. I don't want to go home. I don't want to go back to Butch, but I also miss him and I'm worried about him. I need to know how his day was and if he felt okay. What did he eat? Did he get up and walk around? It's time to go home.

Noble holds my hand in the car and pulls it to his lips as we merge onto the highway.

"I never thought I'd say this, but it was nice to get off the farm for the day." The guilt of what I'm putting him through swallows me.

"I'm sorry for all of this, Noble."

"You can't help any of it. It's not your fault. You didn't want Butch to get sick," he says, always trying to comfort me.

"I know, but you didn't want me to take care of him, and it takes so much of my time and emotions, and it's not fair to you...and Jason's there." Noble squeezes my hand slightly, as if he changed his mind.

"If I could change it, I would. I hate you being around him. I hate the way he looks at you, and the way you look when he's anywhere near you." I turn to Noble, confused. *How do I look?* "He affects you in a way that scares me. It did even before we were together. You two weren't normal. I don't really understand it and I don't like it."

His words startle me. All this time I've been lying to myself about my ability to cover my feelings for Jason, but Noble knows me too well.

Noble rests his eyes on my cheek and I know he's staring at my scar. His eyes return to mine and they are filled with hatred. "And quite frankly, I will never get over what happened to you the last time you guys fought. I can't imagine he would hurt you like that, but I can't erase the sight of your face from my mind, and I will always connect that image to Jason Leer."

I reach up and touch my scar, the only one visible from our two years together. The end of a board hitting my face and finally convincing me we could never be together. Noble and I have been over the details of the injury a hundred times. He's looking for a reason to hate Jason and this scar on my face is as good as any.

"But I can't change Butch's situation, and I love you for taking care of him. He's lucky to have you in his life."

The mention of Butch pulls me from the horrible memories and I turn back to Noble and stop touching my face. How deep are Noble's scars?

"Noble, you wanting a baby is only about us, right?" I ask because I have to, not because any part of me wants to know the truth. Noble takes my hand again and kisses it slowly, with all the meaning of his love.

"Completely. A baby is not a weapon or a guarantee. Anyone who saw Stephanie Harding at the Harvest Dance knows that."

I search my mind for images of Stephanie at the dance. Was she suffering? How did I not see that?

~21~

Regrets

Marie asked if I would come over this evening so she can have dinner with her sister. We could all use a break from this house. Poor Butch, he wouldn't want us here if we needed a break. She almost didn't go. She was frantic because Butch has been sick all day. Something made him throw up several times and has left him even more frail than usual. I finally convinced her he was stable, and I would call her if he even woke up. That settled her enough to drive off the farm and live her own life for a few hours.

I watch Butch sleep as the wind howls. It drives through the roof, under the shingles, and I swear blows past me as I sit near the edge of his bed. We pulled the rocker into his bedroom to make it easier for Marie, and now I'm perched in it, my feet resting on the wooden bed frame. BJ snores quietly at Butch's feet. Today Butch lies almost completely flat and his breathing is deep. I'm sure that means something. If I Googled what happens to the body in the last few weeks, all of this would mean something, but it won't change anything. A chill runs through me and I pull my sweater up around my neck as I turn my head and see Jason watching me from the hallway. Jay is at his knee, pulling his pant leg and asking him for something. When Jay sees me, he runs to my side. I lift him into my lap and we rock together.

I lean my head on Jay's and inhale the kiwi scent; the desperate need of the scent has been replaced by the innocence of the child on my lap. We sway under the watchful eye of his father, as his grandfather sleeps beside us. Jay's eyes droop and he falls asleep in my arms. I am ensconced in the Leer boys.

"What would the Leers do without you?" Jason asks, and it reminds me of an old dream.

"I've dreamed of your mother," I whisper like a crazy person. "It was when we weren't together, your senior year," I say, and Jason just continues to watch me. Probably trying to figure out when I lost my mind.

"I knew you used to dream about your mother, but not mine."

"The dreams of my mother slowed down considerably after we…" *We what?* "Ended. But for some reason I had several dreams about your mother." I realize for the first time. "Maybe it's because I was spending time with Butch."

"Or maybe it's because you missed me."

I hold Jay in my arms and keep rocking. "She asked me to take care of all of you for her. She wanted me to promise," I say as Jason hangs on every word. "And she was beautiful," I add, and he lowers his head. How much can one human being lose?

Jason walks to the foot of the bed and stares at his father. His closeness sends my stomach into flips and I curse my body for having not one ounce of control. *He's just a man, practically a boy.*

You're married.

We are silent as we watch Butch breathe. What are Butch's regrets about this life? A day he would give anything to take back. If Jason had never had sex with Stephanie, he'd be holding me right now, not standing next to me making me want him in paralyzed silence.

"Why?" I say, barely audible over the labored breathing coming from the bed. Jason looks down at me and even though he knows exactly what I'm asking, I say, "Why did you let her in? Why did you ruin us?"

Jason moves a chair next to mine and sits down. I turn to face him and his sadness chokes me. I am so selfish with him. How can I ask him this while we sit by his dying father, his son in my arms? Noble really does have the best of me.

"Annie, I'm sorry." I shake my head at him and at this ridiculous sentence he has said over and over again. "Not just for what I did, and what I lost because of it, but for what it did to you," he says, arguing with my dismissal. "The thought of you hurt like that makes me sick and I'm sorry for it every day."

"I might be lying to us both, but I forgave you." Jason's face relaxes but I can't relent. "Why?"

"You didn't belong with me."

"That's not true," I argue immediately, barely letting the words clear his lips. We've been over this a hundred times. I did belong to him and with him. "I loved you more than anything else on this earth and you knew it. You had to have known it."

Jason exhales shortly. "I know, Annie." His eyes seep into my soul, and I surrender to them. "I know you loved me. You're so stubborn you probably would have stayed with me forever, too, but I thought you belonged in a different place...with a different person," he says, and the mention of Noble cuts me. "You loved Rutgers and New York City. You were alive there. A person in my world who found her world...and what you found was never going to accommodate me."

The bitterness rises in my throat. The tired conversation of where I belong and what I need from the one person who could've given me everything and stole it all in one night.

"I would have given it all up for you." I will him to finally believe what he never trusted when we were together.

"Do you remember our spring break at the cabin in Texas?" he asks, and the memories stab me. "You wanted me to give up bulldogging." I nod without saying a word. "I asked you why you never said anything and you told me I shouldn't have to give up something I love as much as bulldogging for someone who loves you as much as I do."

I remember the conversation precisely. I still think that. I hated him at the rodeo, but he wasn't him without it.

"But you are what I wanted," I say, and close my eyes to keep the tears from coming.

"I know, Annie. But I wasn't where you belonged. When you chose to go to that dance, you realized it, too." I take a deep breath and face Jason. He's not angry; he's just my Jason sitting before me, completely oblivious to who I am.

"You're wrong. When you told me about Jay, it was as if I died." Jason looks as if I might break him. "New York, Rutgers, work, none of it mattered. The first day I woke up without you in my life I stopped caring about any of it," I say, and shake my head at him. "About anything." Jay stirs, my disgust infiltrating our coziness, and I lean over and hand him to Jason. I stand up and walk out of Butch's house. The sun has set and the rain has started. The wind drives it sideways into my face, and I run back to my house and Noble. It took me months to find something to care about again. Or did Noble find me?

Noble is sitting on the couch watching TV, alone. I lie down, my head in his lap, and cry. Noble rubs my back and covers me with the throw lying on the back of the couch.

* * *

When I open my eyes, I'm in my bed, next to my husband. He carried me up here last night. I lean up on my elbows and watch him sleep. Noble is a beautiful man. He deserves better than what he has, but then again, don't we all. I raise his arm and crawl in between it and his chest and wrap my arm across his body. *My lovely Noble*, I think as I close my eyes rightfully in his arms.

He pulls me close to him without opening his eyes and kisses the top of my head, and the warmth of Noble Sinclair spreads through me. His kindness always welcoming me back. His patience, endless.

"Good morning," he says as if this is the first morning we've ever woken up next to each other. I lean up and kiss him and watch his beautiful blue eyes adjust to the morning light. Satisfied that Noble is still wonderful, I lay my head back on his chest.

"Is there anything I should know?" he asks. Jason thinks he knows everything and Noble knows nothing, and I'm as lost as the two of them.

"Why?" I ask, not really paying attention to the conversation.

"You're distant. I'm planting and you're taking care of Butch, and the moments we're together are a bit unsettling. I just need to know how you are."

"I'm exhausted. It's the saddest thing I've ever witnessed and this is the second time Jason's seen this show. It's horrible." Noble's muscles tighten at the mention of Jason.

I roll on top of Noble and bury my face in his chest. His arms circle me. If I could find a way to spend the rest of my life right here, I know I could be happy. We could be happy together.

"Noble, are you planting today?"

"Yes, why?"

"Can I come with you? Would that be a bother? I think I could use a break from Butch's and…and I want to be with you."

Noble holds me tighter. "You can come. I would love to have you."

* * *

Noble pulls down the jump seat in the tractor and I climb in. He reaches across my lap and pulls the door shut. I admire my farmer husband as we take off on our bumpy ride. His faded Pink Floyd shirt has a rip at the neck but is still magnificent as it stretches across his chest. We ride through our field shoulder to shoulder as we plant corn and I question if this could possibly all be part of a plan for me.

Noble enters information into the touch screen to his right as I stare at the picture of us from our wedding night. I should have known it found its way into this tractor. He said it would be his favorite and here it is, riding along with him most days.

"What are you doing?" I ask, completely oblivious to how any of this works.

"Getting my rows straight," Noble says, and presses some buttons. "The tractor has GPS I use for planting and spraying. It's more cost-efficient for fuel and keeps my rows straight." He finishes with three more buttons and turns to me. "Everything is software driven now. This tractor knows as much about the soil as I do. All the engines are hooked to software."

"How did farmers keep them straight before GPS?" I ask, imagining all sorts of archaic strategies.

"They didn't. At least my dad's rows were never straight."

They always appear straight from the road. Of course, I'm usually going by too fast to notice.

Noble and I start down the field and the peace of the earth fills me. As we move over the ground, a family of rabbits scurries and a lone deer runs toward the woods. It stops, looks into the cab of the tractor, and turns and disappears into the trees. We're high above the action, like watching a movie.

"When you see animals, do you always think of hunting them?" I don't understand it. How can he kill something? Take a life?

"I've never thought of killing BJ," he says, and I punch him in the arm.

"Thank God! You watch them differently, though. But then again, you view most things differently." Noble grabs my hand as he turns the tractor with his right one. "What do you like about hunting?" I ask, and attempt to seem unaffected by the act of it.

"Are you considering joining me there, too?"

"No. I just can't make sense of it," I admit, and lose my battle with my face as my nose scrunches up in mild disgust.

"It's not easy to explain, especially since you've never been. You have no point of reference."

"Try." I hold his hand in both of mine. Noble leans over and kisses the top of my head, completely uninsulted. The tractor steers itself down the row.

"I usually go out early, when the uncivilized world is waking up. Daybreak is their clock. It's quiet…and crisp, and my senses are never more acute. I listen to the leaves beneath my feet and the birds above my head. I can hear the air and the light and the silence, and it all has something to say. There's none of life's useless chatter and it's mentally freeing."

I slip my hand between Noble's thighs. His passion moves me. He takes a deep breath and looks at my hand and at me. I smile, asking him to continue.

"It awakens an instinct we all share; it's just honed and cultivated in a person who begins hunting in their youth. Like one's survival instinct that lies dormant until their life is threatened. It's the same for protection. Now that I have you, I'm very protective of you, more so than I ever felt before I had something I was unwilling to lose."

I watch Noble turn the tractor again and know I need to protect him, protect us. I take a deep breath and slowly let it out, not wanting Noble to notice my new burden.

"It's all exhilarating. I'm not doing it justice."

"You haven't said a word that involves an animal," I say, grasping my miniscule concept of hunting.

"That's the thing. The animal part is only a few seconds, a few heart-stopping, primal seconds," Noble says, and I sense he's through explaining hunting.

I turn my attention to the field in front of us. For as far as I can see, there's dirt ready to be planted. It's an endless line of tranquility, ready to be grown.

"Are you lonely out here? I mean, when you don't let me come with you." It's just him and his thoughts all day, surrounded by acres and acres of land.

"I have the radio and the Internet and my awesome picture." Noble nods at the picture from our wedding night.

"It's unbelievable you run this whole farm with just a few other people." It's amazing, actually. This industry has surrounded me my entire life and I barely know a thing about how it runs.

"Impressive, huh?" Noble winks at me and I squeeze his thigh. What an incredibly hot farmer.

"Some farms have one hundred laborers helping with crops. We have three combines. They're just different business models."

"It's a lot of ground," I challenge.

"It's a lot of equipment. We can harvest a hundred acres a day with the combine. More with a grain cart, and some of our crops we don't harvest. The processors come in for the spinach. It leaves me time to do the custom work for the smaller farms," Noble says, as if this makes running the farm any less impressive.

We dip down suddenly and I brace myself to keep from hitting the windshield, forgetting my other questions.

"What's that?" I point to a small pool of water in the middle of the upcoming row.

"Field tile," Noble says, frustrated by the sight of the water.

"Huh?" My complete lack of knowledge of Noble's daily activities is astounding.

"Around the turn of the century, immigrants hand dug trenches in all the fields around here and installed a network of pipes. The originals were terra-cotta tiles, field tiles," Noble explains as if this is common knowledge in town. "They're three to seven feet below the ground and when one becomes plugged, it creates a wet spot. We have to find the clog and replace the tile." Noble looks down. "Can you put your hand back?" I oblige, and study the water again.

"They're everywhere? Even in the fields around my parents'?" Noble nods, smiling at my hand between his legs.

"They created more tillable ground. Without them, certain fields would be filled with water." Noble rubs his chin as he shakes his head. "I should have replaced it in March."

"Anything else you regret not doing?" I ask, and Noble turns his attention from the ground to me. The tractor drives itself as Noble's eyes drive into mine.

"Some days I regret not taking you out of your parents' luncheon." Noble watches me, gauging my reaction, but it's all dead inside of me. There's nothing left of that day. Jason took the fragments with him. "I could have saved you a lot of heartache."

How different would my life have been if I had leaned on Noble instead of Jason in the wake of my parents' death? There's a quiet joy in Noble as he says this. Reminding me of the damaging effects of my relationship with Jason generates some power for him. It's weak, though, and I don't like it.

"But I honestly have no regrets. It's impossible to sit here with you and question anything."

~22~

The Tide Is Turning

May third.

Four months since we were told six to nine months with treatment. Someone should have asked how long without treatment. Although, what difference would it make?

There are days when I think he won't make it another minute and then there are better ones. It's finally hot, going up to eighty-four today, and I wish Noble and I could escape to the shore. He took me last May and asked me when we were going to get married. It's been a year but feels like a lifetime. What a terrible newlywed I am. I sneak downstairs and make Noble breakfast and bring it up to our bedroom. He opens his eyes when the aroma of French toast fills the room.

"What's all this?" he asks, rolling onto his side and filling me with his warmth just from the look in his eyes.

"Breakfast, for my husband, who I love," I say, and lean over to kiss him. "I've been a terrible wife the last few months, neglected you really. We're supposed to be newlyweds."

"I am horribly neglected. You should be having sex with me six times per day," he says matter-of-factly, and takes a bite of the toast.

"Six times a day is a lofty goal. I might have to come out to the fields."

"Then you should. What are you doing today? After me, that is?"

"I don't know. It's going to be beautiful..."

"And you want to go to the shore?" he says, and I marvel at how obvious I am to him. "I can't go today, but if you give me a few days I might be able to sneak in a quick trip. I'm sorry." Noble's regret reminds me to feel guilty. I shouldn't be at the shore anyway. "I have some jobs lined up I can't put off."

"It's okay. I know you're busy." *I'm busy, too. I have to watch Butch die some more.* "Maybe I'll lay out here. I wish Jenn were home. I would escape to her lake house."

* * *

After lunch I put on my bathing suit and sunscreen. I am absolutely bright white and should not be in public. Maybe it's better Noble can't go to the shore. I head to the backyard on the other side of the barns, far from the view of Butch's house, and spread out my blanket. I lie on my stomach, up on my forearms, and read the newspaper as if I care about one word written in it. Eventually, I roll to my side and close my eyes, and the sun takes my consciousness away.

* * *

The little blue bird is in her hands. Mrs. Leer holds it in both her palms and it squawks and squawks as if it's trying to tell us something.

"Annie, defend the poor and fatherless: do justice to the afflicted and needy. Deliver the poor and needy: rid them out of the hand of the wicked."

"Huh? Mrs. Leer, what more could you want from me? Did you hear about Butch? He'll be there soon."

"Annie, it's up to you," she says again, and looks down at the little bird. I bow my head and cry.

"I feel terrible about that bird. I swear I do. I don't know why I didn't help it. I could barely help myself back then. Forgive me," I say to the bird, and to Mrs. Leer holding it.

* * *

I wake to the weight of my dog jumping on my chest and him licking my face. I'm startled and disoriented, and tears are streaming down my cheeks.

"What's wrong?" Jason says, and is immediately on the blanket with me. I see his mother in his face and it makes me cry harder. "What's wrong, Annie?" Jason pulls me up. I lay my head on his shoulder and try to figure out what more I can do for Butch. What does she want me to do?

"Is Butch all right?" I ask, lifting my head off his chest and wiping the tears from my face.

"He's the same. I let BJ out and he ran around your house like a bat out of hell. I wondered what he was after, but it was you. He knew you were back here." I rub behind BJ's ears. Such a sweet little guy. "That dog sure does love you."

BJ snuggles in next to me. His fur feels strange on my hot, bare legs and I'm suddenly aware I'm in Jason's arms in a bikini. I scoot back on the blanket.

"Jason Jr. loves you," he says, and I sit up straight. This is danger-ous, a low blow even for Jason.

"He barely knows me."

"He knows everything he needs to know."

I ignore him. It's too much to listen to. "When you guys go home…" I choke on the words. "You should enroll Jay in nursery school. He's ready. He's very smart." I gather the newspapers the breeze has spread across the blanket. Jason moves closer, his body parallel with mine, his legs behind me. His closeness triggers the vi-tal memories I fight to ignore and I shiver.

"What if this is our home? What if we stay?"

I close my eyes and let the internal war take over. The majority of me wants him to disappear, while a small fraction will disintegrate in his absence. The breeze stops, the papers stop blowing, and the trees silence. It's as if Jason has stopped the Earth.

"The tide is changing," I think out loud.

"What?" he asks, never taking his eyes off me.

"My grandmother used to say when the wind stopped it's because the tide changed directions. What time is it?"

"Almost one thirty," he says, checking his watch.

"Probably going out. The tide is turning."

"Thank God," he says.

"Thankful now, are you?" It's as if we've never lost a thing in our lives because we have everything, right here on this blanket.

Without permission, my hand rises to the fresh scruff on Jason's face. I rub my thumb across it as a tingling electrifies my body. The current silences the sarcasm and relaxes my resolve. My eyes find his, deep charcoal now as he covers my hand with his own.

"You're making this impossible." I swallow hard. "You make everything impossible." I squeeze my eyes shut as tears run down my face.

Jason holds my face in both his hands and wipes my tears with his thumbs. "When I see you and Jay together, I know anything is possible." This makes me cry harder. I'm approaching a sob and I want to run and hide. "With you, Annie. You can do anything. You can make this work," he says. But he's wrong. I can't save him or me, or Jay, or Butch. My God, poor Butch, and Marie who he'll leave behind. All of us will be left behind…again.

Nothing is possible.

"Why didn't you come back when I first told you about the wedding? Why are you doing all of this now? Now that I'm married?"

"I underestimated you."

"Again," I say, and Jason never takes his eyes from mine. "You underestimated me again."

I let go of Jason and stand up next to the blanket, waiting for him to get up, too. He just sits there, staring at me in my bathing suit. His eyes swallow every inch of me, leaving nothing left to force my body to move, and I want to lie down with him forever. I swallow hard and lean over to grab the corner of the blanket. He pulls me down and under him.

His lips are on my neck before I realize where I am and I'm climbing out of my skin at the touch of him. How long has it been? He is ruining me with every breath from his lungs.

"Get off of me!" I yell, and push him, but he doesn't budge. I pull his ear until he lifts his head from my neck and he pulls both my hands above my head, pinning them. I am throbbing everywhere. "Let me go," I say, and the look in his eyes sends a chill down the entire front of my body.

"I'm never going to let you go."

"You have to stop," I say, barely above a whimper, and Jason releases my hands.

"Stop what?" He backs off a few inches. We haven't fallen to rape.

"All of it. The birthday text, the egg, the talk of possibilities. I'm married. And it's to a guy I never want to hurt."

"He brought this on himself. I have not an ounce of guilt." Jason sits up, disgusted with the topic of Noble. I stand and walk into the house while BJ trots along behind me, and Jason sits alone on my blanket in my yard. *God, please help me.*

* * *

Noble and I sit in our pew at church and I miss Butch. His absence is one more reminder of his declining health. He hasn't been out of the house since we dyed Easter eggs. He wasn't up to church today—he never is anymore—and Marie stayed home with him. I'm not up to it either, but if I stop doing everything I don't feel up to, there'll be nothing left.

It was sweet of Noble to bring me. As I think of it, I hook my arm around his elbow and rest my hand in his. He turns and kisses my head. One moment of peace. His body tenses as Jason sits down inappropriately close to me. I take a deep breath and try to let it out slowly, not sharing with Noble how Jason affects me. Jason only smiles at us the way he would have in high school before any of us were together.

If there was ever a day to be forgiven for being unfocused, today is the day. Pastor Johnson rolls through the morning announcements and before I know it I'm standing between Noble and Jason, silently confessing my sins.

Dear God, I wanted him more than anything on this earth, and standing here beside him even with Noble right here, I know I'm going to want him again. Please forgive me and give me strength.

We sing and we sit, very close again. What were Noble's confessions? His are between him and God. Mine are squarely between Noble and me. Jason leans over my lap to pull a hymnal from the pew holder and I could kill him. It's unthinkable I ever found him the least bit entertaining. Him and his ridiculous antics.

Mrs. DuBois is called to the pulpit to read this week's scripture. Noble opens a Bible next to me to follow along, and I search for a hole to crawl into. Jason leans forward and I quickly hand him a Bible before he has a chance to drape himself across me again. *Ass.* He silently laughs beside me.

Mrs. DuBois begins. "Let every man have his own wife, and let every woman have her own husband. Let the husband render unto the wife due benevolence: and likewise also the wife unto the husband. The wife hath not power of her own body, but the husband." Noble raises his eyebrows playfully at me and my stomach clenches. "And likewise also the husband hath not power of his own body, but the wife. Defraud ye not one the other, except it be with consent for a time, that ye may give yourselves to fasting and prayer; and come together again, that Satan tempt you not for your incontinency. This is the word of the Lord," she finishes.

"Thanks be to God," we respond, and I'm beginning to question why every single sermon Pastor Johnson creates is specifically for me. Don't the other parishioners feel neglected?

Pastor Johnson goes on to point out the importance of prayer. It's such a priority that giving your body to your spouse should only be interrupted for fasting or prayer. You should not abstain from sexual

relations with your husband except to more deeply immerse yourself in prayer, or else Satan might be able to tempt you because of
your lack of self-control. The congregation howls with laughter as
the pastor's connection is reached, the only thing more important
than sex with your spouse is prayer. I want to ask Noble if he'll just
hit me with the truck. Jason appears to have wiped the shit-eating
grin off his face. Apparently, the sermon hit home for him as well.

"I am really beginning to like this church thing," Noble says, and
takes my hand as we walk to the truck. "Even the Bible says I should
have power over your body and we should be doing it all the time."

I squeeze his hand and refuse to look back, or in any other direction. If Jason wants to come to church just to torture me, then he
should be tortured, too.

"How about breakfast?" Noble asks, almost giddy now that God
is on his side.

"Whatever you want," I say.

"That's the spirit. Exactly what the scripture is teaching us." He is
a fool, a happy, hot one, but a fool.

"I think you missed some big parts of the message."

"Bigger than what I got out of it? We'll have to go back next
week," Noble says, and holds the passenger door open for me. When
I climb into the truck, he leans in and kisses me on the lips. I raise
my hands to the sides of his face and let my lips linger on his. When
I open my eyes, his are filled with delight.

"Maybe we can go to the earlier service, though?" he says, and I
realize he's still the underdog in this screwed-up situation. A ring, a
wedding, a house, some pointed scripture, and yet still fighting for
equal in the wake of Annie and Jason's love affair. The tragedy of it is
palpable.

~23~

Away

The delivery of the hospital bed is what did it. The mere sight of it a realization that death will soon come. More death. How much can one person withstand?

Jason holds the door open for the men to carry it into the house and they set it up in the family room. It's now the death room. Is this where Jason's mother spent the last of her days? As I think of how cruel life's been to Jason, his eyes meet mine. A tiny chill fights through the sadness and I turn away to go help fit the bed with the special sheets we rented. The fact these are rarely purchased is just another sign of death. Hospice will come today. They will spend the last of Butch's days with him. Hospice, Marie, Jason, BJ, and I will halt our lives to witness the end of Butch's. I shove the pillow in the case and violently shake it in, not sure it's the right size, but eventually it conforms. Marie comes into the room and spreads the blanket on the bed. Even with the warmer weather, Butch is cold all the time. He's thin now, frail. Why does death have to be so debilitating?

My parents were probably happy until the very end. I only remember them as wholly alive, and watching Jason carry his father to his deathbed, I am thankful. He doesn't deserve this. None of us deserves this.

More prescriptions are given, a cream for a red rash Butch tears at when he has the strength and some other pills and liquids I didn't listen carefully about. Hopefully Marie could stand the conversation, because I'm at the end of what I can endure.

Jason moves the recliner next to the bed and Marie sits in it, watching Butch as I watch her. Butch turns to me and is taken over by a coughing fit before it can completely surface. That cough. It's been death's greeting for months, unwilling to leave us until it takes Butch with it.

I hate it.

I hate all of this.

I lean over and find the button to elevate the bed and raise his head a few inches, hoping the incline will help him breathe better. What the hell do I know, though? Butch falls back to sleep and my eyes meet Marie's, mine filled with disgust, hers consumed by sadness. Marie touches my hand and when the tears fill my eyes, she stands and puts her arm around my shoulders.

"I know, Charlotte. I know."

Marie loves Butch as much as I do. It's Butch, and my parents, and the look on Jason's face, and the knowledge that I am completely neglecting Noble, and BJ lying next to Butch every minute of the day. What will be left of all of us when this is finally over?

The home health care aide arrives and we leave her to tend to Butch.

"Do either of you want a cup of tea?" Marie asks, her death watch skills kicking into gear.

"No," I say, and Jason shakes his head.

"Being with someone when they pass is an honor," Marie says, and Jason and I just stare at each other. The feelings churning inside of me are far from honor. They verge on hatred, and anger, and utter hopelessness. I swallow hard and look down at the floor.

I'm not sure if I'm capable of doing this. There should be some qualifications for being with someone as they die.

I need to get out of here.

Away from death.

"I'm going to pick up the prescriptions," I say, and hurry to the kitchen. It's not until I'm halfway to my car in the L-shed that I realize Jason is with me. I stop walking, confused by his company and still angry about Butch.

"I'm going with you," he says, and even though it's not his decision, I really don't care at this point where anyone is because soon Butch will not be here. We drive the eight miles to the pharmacy in silence. The image of Jason carrying Butch to his deathbed is choking me and I'm on the verge of tears when we pull up to the drive-through window. We're told it's going to be at least an hour and my shoulders drop. Time is of the essence. This isn't an allergy pill. There's a man dying, ripping his skin off his arm because something is making it itch there. *Give me the fucking medicine*, I scream in my head.

"Okay. We'll be back," is what I actually say. I pull out of line and onto the road toward Swedesboro.

"Where do you want to go?" I ask, knowing neither of us is going back there.

"Oklahoma," he says, and my heart breaks for him. "Or anywhere else with you."

Jason being home with his father is fucking with his head. He hasn't ridden in too long; he hasn't competed. His passion is shriveling and he's holding on to us to keep himself from disappearing, but I can't help him.

"How about lunch? Maybe someplace on the water," I say, knowing it will piss him off.

"Or McDonald's. I've had some great meals there," he says, and I realize I will always be more pissed off than him.

The sight of Butch lying in that bed steals my thoughts. What is BJ going to do when he dies? How will he understand? He's never seen anything die. Maybe that's why he was a terrible hunting dog. Maybe he hates death. Noble seems okay with it. He kills things all the time.

I head into Swedesboro and turn right onto Lake Road. We ride in silence as we pass Lake Narraticon and follow the back roads into Mullica Hill. From the street, Blue Plate seems quiet, but the parking lot in the back is almost full. I haven't been here since my parents were alive, and I've never been with Jason or Noble and for some reason that makes it safe. I consider Jason sitting in my passenger seat, scruff covering his gorgeous face, his chest barely contained in his T-shirt and I'm certain there's no safe place. I swallow hard, open my door, and hop out.

We get a small corner booth for two. I wanted to ask for a large table for eight, but there's no hope. We could be at a ten-top and have some condition that renders us unable to swallow, and we'd still want each other. It's a large part of our fuckedupedness.

We order hurriedly and sit in silence, staring at each other. I'm glad I don't know what he's thinking because my thoughts are morally wrong and I can't handle it for both of us.

"The days are getting harder," Jason says.

I take a sip of my tea, wishing there was vodka in it but knowing intoxication is a bad idea. "And shorter," I say. Every minute is precious and yet I want Butch to be out of this misery, but I don't want him to be away from me.

"Charlotte…," he says, and I just stare at him. He will try anything at this point.

"You're kidding, right?"

"If you were ever afraid you would lose yourself, if calling you Annie has some meaning other than I love you, then I'll call you whatever you want."

I shake my head and lower my eyes.

"This is going to end soon and I don't want to be without you. I can't be." This cannot be happening. "You don't love him."

"Why is it so hard for you to believe that I do? I do love him," I snap at him. *I don't know how I'm capable of loving anyone after a tour with you, but I love him.*

"Because with every cell of my body I know you belong to me. Next to me, on top of me." I swallow hard at the thought of him beneath me. "With me inside of you."

"I get the picture."

"And because I know that. Because it's true. You can't be in love with him."

"You didn't want to pull me away from New York City? You so selflessly fucked Stephanie Harding to make sure I ended up where I belong, but now you'll have me leave my marriage? You are fucked up," I spit at him.

"If you give us a chance, I will never let you go again. I promise. Annie, you've got to give us another chance. You've got to know it's not a life unless we're together."

The waitress brings our food and Jason and I just stare at each other. I am baffled. I hate him. I love him. I want him…to leave.

"I want you to go away with me when this is over."

"What will be left of me? You think it will be enough for you. If I hurt Noble like that, I won't be the same person. You wouldn't want me."

"Impossible," he scoffs. We sit in silence until he finally takes a bite of his sandwich. I eat a little and stare at my glass of tea. I wish I could be drunk, unconscious actually. I'm no longer capable of living my life. Not this one, at least.

"You're always sure of everything. Even when you're wrong you're sure," I say, watching him finish his meal, completely unaffected by his plot to ruin my life, and Noble's, and probably my brother's because why should he be exempt from this torture. "I'm never sure of anything. Do you know why?"

Jason looks at me, bracing himself for what's coming.

"Because the last person I was sure of, I was completely wrong about. I never thought you would be capable of doing what you did. How could you?"

Jason just stares at me, taking every word he deserves.

"How could you put your hands on her? Put your *dick* in her?" I lower my voice. There's no need to yell; it's grotesque without the dramatics.

"I guess you were lying when you said you forgave me," he says.

"This is what you're asking me to turn Noble into. A person who no longer believes in anything he's ever known."

"What I'm asking has nothing to do with Sinclair. He put himself between us. That's his problem. He knew I wanted you back the entire time," Jason says, taking money out and putting it on the table for lunch. "I'm asking you to let yourself be happy. Let yourself believe in me again because I sure as hell know you want to."

I stand up from the table and start walking. I don't stop until I get to my car, but as usual Jason is there one step before me, blocking my door.

"You're making every single day of this nightmare even harder," I say.

"I think the exact same thing about you. Going home to that *house* every night." The cruelty of today continues as Jason leans into me and places his lips on mine and some internal sob caves my chest in and steals my breath. He puts his hands above my head, leaning on the Volvo behind me, and separates my lips with his tongue. And I let him. I let him in, in every way. My blood courses through me and throbs everywhere as I give in to what my hands and my mouth and lips have wanted for months. I wrap my arms around his neck and he pulls me to him. I pull his hair and my tongue takes over my thoughts.

I pull away from him. His eyes are ravenous. He will take me right here in this parking lot if I let him.

"It doesn't change a thing," I croak out. "You knew all of that before my body told you."

"I did, but now you know it, too," he says, and takes the keys from me to drive us home.

Home…

* * *

The ride is long and silent. Betrayal sits between us and contemplates how many lives Jason and Charlotte can ruin, their own apparently not enough for them. I lean my head on the cool window and focus on the sky as the almost full moon rises. It's not even four o'clock yet. The supermoon will be here in a few days. What lunacy will it bestow upon us?

"I love you, Annie," Jason says, and I never take my eyes off the moon. I never turn to him or acknowledge he spoke. Through with the talking, done with the truth. Let him know everything. Now I want to know nothing.

~24~

Hold On

The banging on the screen door startles me. The sight of Margo on the other side of it elates me. I run over and open it for her and hug her until she can't breathe.

"What are you doing here?" I ask, not really caring, just thankful she's with me. "Please tell me you're moving home today."

"No." Margo shakes her head. She and Jenn have made it painfully clear they are not moving home. "It's my grandmother's birthday tonight. Eighty years. Any of this sounding familiar?" There's a vague recollection forming in my mind. "I texted you weeks ago and told you the date."

"Yes. I kind of remember." I turn and walk into the kitchen with Margo following me. "Eighty, huh? God bless her."

"Oh, he has. She's a treat," Margo says, and I remember the time her grandmother snuck us liquor in high school at her brother's graduation party. "Remember, we're supposed to have a little reunion tomorrow? Sam's coming down from Philly. Does any of this ring a bell?"

"It does. I'm sorry. I've been..." What have I been? *Fucked up.* "I've been really overwhelmed with Butch and—"

"Margo! What are you doing here?" Noble walks over and hugs Margo.

"We're having a party tomorrow," Margo says as she stands on tiptoes to hug Noble.

"Is that what Shabo's coming to town for?"

"Yes. I guess Charlotte forgot to tell you. I'm here for my grand-mother's eightieth tonight, and tomorrow is all about us."

"She did forget, but who can blame her?" Noble kisses my cheek, knowing I forgot because my brain doesn't function anymore. "Let's party here," he offers, and I immediately cramp up.

Why not? Of course we can party here. It just seems like such an unhappy place these days. Why would anyone want to party here? This is probably exactly what Noble needs, some joy filling the house. I hope it's exactly what I need, too.

"I have to go. I just wanted to check in with you," Margo says to me, and turns to Noble. "What time do you want us tomorrow?"

"Come around three. We'll start early."

"Oh geez. It's going to be one of those nights," I say. "We can't disturb Butch."

"We won't bother a soul in that house," Noble says, and I hope that's true.

Margo slips out the back door and I latch it behind her. I watch her walk to her car and stare in silence as Jason approaches her. It should be normal. They've known each other since kindergarten. His father is dying. It feels utterly sinister, though.

"Charlotte, do you hear me?" Noble says, half laughing, and I turn and rush away from the door.

"Sorry."

"That's okay. Are you excited Margo's home?"

"She and Jenn always make things better," I say. My mind is still on Jason talking to Margo.

"They'll be better soon. Just hold on," Noble says, and I love him. "Hold on to me if you have to." I wrap my arms around his waist and hold him tight.

"Are you going to Butch's this afternoon?"

"I think I'm going to wait a while. Maybe after dinner. When are you going to be done?"

"Another couple of hours. Why don't you let me take you out to dinner tonight? I feel like sushi."

"Hmm. Me too." Guilt washes over me. How dare I go out to dinner while death keeps performing next door?

Noble leaves, returns to his work, and I vacuum the downstairs. I used to work. I used to function every day without considering imminent death. New York is a lifetime away.

When I finish, I pick up my phone to check the weather for tomorrow. There's a text from Margo:

> **We need to talk.**
> **I'm heading to the party.**
> **I'll come by early tomorrow.**

I could write back and ask her what about, but I already know. We need to talk about Jason, about Charlotte and Jason. Really it's about how Jason is trying to ruin Charlotte's life, or is it how Charlotte's trying to ruin her own life? I can't even figure out whose fault this is anymore. I'm lost, as usual, and I'm starting to hate us both.

I delete the text and put the phone in my bag hanging on the back of the kitchen chair. I finish cleaning the house and when I notice Jason's truck is gone, I walk over to Butch's. Marie and Jay are coloring at the kitchen table; Butch is lying in the hospital bed in the family room. Any joy I felt with Margo's arrival drains from my body, leaving an empty shell moving around Butch's house.

I stand over Butch's bed and squeeze his hand. I wish he would wake up and be an asshole for a little while. Say something nasty. I glance back over my shoulder at Marie. She's here practically twenty-four hours a day. How does she do it?

"Marie, would you like to get out of here for a while? Maybe go see your sister?" I ask as I return to the kitchen. Marie looks at me as if the idea is absurd. "It might do you some good. It's refreshing to get out," I say, and Jay studies me, trying to figure out what's happening.

"I do have a few errands to run. Can you and Jason Jr. take care of Butch for a little while?" she asks.

"What do you think, Jay? Can you help me take care of Pops?"

Jay nods his head proudly. Marie hugs me before grabbing her purse from the counter.

"We're having a barbeque tomorrow night at our house," I say, and Marie looks at me kindly. "I'm afraid it's going to be too loud. That it might disturb you guys."

"Nothing is going to disturb Butch and I'll be fine. It will do me good to hear someone having fun. And I'm sure it will do Nick good to have some fun with you," she says, and adds, "Don't worry about things over here. You've got a lot on your plate, taking care of all these boys."

"I'm only in charge of BJ."

"The rest just need to be near you," Marie says as Jay walks over and climbs up into my arms.

"What color?" he asks, holding a crayon too close to my face.

"Blue," I answer. "Today we'll learn a lot of colors. How's that sound?"

Jay nods and climbs down to get the box of crayons. I watch him as Marie touches my elbow and disappears out the door.

Jay and I sort all the crayons by color and master the different color names. By the time we're done, he knows yellow, green, blue, black, and red by heart, and we have created several beautiful pictures. I started to make a beach scene on mine but recognized I was only immaturely taunting his father. I changed it to a flower. We hang all the pictures on the fridge and step back, appraising our work together. The collection is a sign of life. Jay is a sign of life.

"I think it's time for you to take a nap," I say, realizing it's after two. "Do you want to lie down on the couch? Annie will put the TV on something you like." Jay shakes his head. I'll bet this house is a very scary place. "How about if we rock in the recliner? You, Pops, and Annie can all take a nap together."

We cuddle in the recliner and I cover us with a throw. It's warm and cozy, and Jay is still small enough to fit perfectly in my arms.

"Annie?"

"Yes." For some reason him calling me Annie is more right than anyone else.

"Where Pops goin'?"

I take a deep breath and let it out slow. What has Jason told him? What do you tell a two-year-old about death? What do you tell a twenty-five-year-old about death?

"He's going home. He's going to be with God in heaven," I say, and Jay just stares at me. "He'll be happy there, and even though we're really going to miss him, we'll be happy he's there, too."

I think of my mother and my father and of Mrs. Leer, and I look at the ceiling to keep from crying. I rock Jay until he's almost asleep. I turn the chair and raise the footrest. After a few minutes I close my eyes and join Jay and Butch, asleep in the death house.

* * *

The hacking wakes me. It goes on until I think some organ has dislodged and then it stops and Butch's eyes close again. My eyes wander from the corners of the ceiling down, along the bookcase, and down to the hospital bed in front of me. Jay's face is on my chest, his hand in my hair, and he's hot on me. I uncover us and lean up a little.

I can feel Jason in the room and when I turn the recliner, he's watching us from a chair by the bedroom. He doesn't look evil, or devious, or treacherous, only beautiful sitting quietly on the edge of the room. We stare at each other without speaking, or smiling, or thinking. I'm sure I could spend the rest of my life in this position. I will spend the rest of Butch's here.

"What time is it?" I whisper.

"It's five," he says. The expression on his face never changes. He's lost in his thoughts and that's more terrifying than telling me everything. "Your phone's been dinging. Someone's looking for you."

"I should get back…" *Home. I should get back home.* Jason doesn't move, and Jay doesn't move. Watching him lying in my arms, I question how he could be the result of anything but love. The thought makes me sadder, but I'm already at the bottom so I can't tell the difference. "He should wake up, too, or else you'll never get him to sleep tonight," I say, and behold Jay's sweet face one more time.

I sit up, straightening the chair with me, and I pull the hair off Jay's sweaty face. I kiss his forehead to stir him and when he does, I lean forward and he sits up, too. Jay slumps over and lays his head back on me, wrapping his arms around my neck and grabbing my hair. Apparently he's as good at letting go as his father. I rub his back roughly to wake him.

"Mommy," he says, and I'm a little repulsed.

"No, Jay. You've got to go home to Mommy. She's probably wondering where you are. I'll bet she misses you," I say, and stand up and walk to Jason. He stands and takes Jay from me, never releasing me from his stare. He's a ticking time bomb, ready to explode at any minute. Stupid Charlotte wants to ask him what's wrong, but smart, sane Charlotte just grabs her bag on the way out of the house. It's empowering to have actually made a good decision for once. I'm proud of myself as I walk across the yard and into the kitchen.

My pride disappears at the sight of a pissed-off Noble. He's pacing in the kitchen and stops to share his distaste in a horrendous glare when he sees me.

"What?"

"I was worried. I didn't know where you were."

"I was at Butch's. Where else would I be?"

"You said you were going to go after dinner."

"Why didn't you just come over there?"

"I saw the truck…" Noble's words trail off, and I close my eyes as a pain stabs behind my left one. I can't keep ahead of all their emotions, all their needs. Butch dying has screwed up the obvious line created by my wedding, and now some people are jumping ahead. I feel like screaming, but I know I owe Noble more than that. If only there was something left.

"Let me just freshen up and we'll go, okay? We'll get out of here for a little while," I say, and walk upstairs without waiting for an answer from Noble. Something's got to give on the Sinclair farm.

* * *

After dinner, I make Noble take me to the driving range where I quickly display every reason I was never on the golf team.

"Wow, you're terrible," he says, laughing the entire time.

"I know. Absolutely horrible." I watch Noble power the ball farther out than any other golfer. "You, on the other hand, are fantastic," I say, and bounce my eyebrows at him.

"I had no idea golf turns you on."

"Let's see…you plowing a field, you painting a room, you in a suit, you playing golf…there seems to be a common denominator." Noble leans over the divider and kisses me, inviting me to love him.

I take another shot and it almost hits the man three stalls down.

"Sorry," I yell down with an innocent wave. The man is not appeased. "Isn't this the part where you are supposed to come over and wrap your arms around me and 'show me how it's done'?" I ask Noble dramatically.

"Hell no. I don't want anyone to even know I'm here with you and God knows there's no helping that swing." He continues to hit his balls with his back to me. I slip my club between his legs and when he's set to swing, I raise it slightly, grazing his balls and making him jump.

"Charlotte Sinclair! Have you no civility?" Noble is smiling his amazing smile and if it weren't for BJ—okay, and Butch—I would never go back to the farm again.

"I'm not going to behave. We should just go," I say, completely serious. I'm done with the driving range.

"Where do you want to go? Because I'm not taking you back there. Not yet anyway."

"Let's get some ice cream and have sex in the truck somewhere," I offer.

"Or maybe just skip the ice cream," Noble says, and picks up our buckets and clubs. I follow him.

*　*　*

I wake up to Margo jumping in my bed.

"Hey," I say, still overwhelmingly thankful for her arrival. "How's Granny?"

"She's eighty and still raising hell."

"As it should be." Margo climbs under the covers with me. It reminds me of a million years ago when we would lie in bed talking for hours. We had so much to talk about back then. It all seems like nothing now.

"Where's Noble?"

"He just went out to the grocery store to buy food for today."

"How did he seem?" I ask, grateful for help in figuring this whole thing out.

"Better than Jason," she says, and I realize there's no help. "I talked to him yesterday. It sounds like you two have been through hell."

"We're still going through it. That's the thing—it's hell with him. That's not how life should be."

"To be fair, you're both living under some horrible circumstances," Margo says, but I don't want to be fair. "He loves you, Charlotte. I've never been surer of anything in my life. He loves you."

I sigh. "I know he does."

"And he wants you back."

"I know he does." I stare at the freshly painted ceiling of Noble's and my bedroom.

"Look, I'm the queen of holding a grudge, but he moved me. He's going to spend the rest of his life trying to get you back. He made me believe that you should give him a second chance."

"Do you realize what you're saying? Where you're saying it?" I ask, disgusted this conversation is taking place at all, let alone in Noble's bed.

"I'm not saying you should give him a second chance. I'm just saying he made me think you should."

"What?" I am losing everything, including my patience.

"When in doubt, do nothing. Just hold on. Don't make any big decisions when things are really good or really bad."

"I already made a big decision. I married Noble. The decisions portion of this is over. Now we're on to the happily-ever-after part."

"Just get through this with Butch and in a few months things will be completely different."

"Yeah, it's cosmic. I know," I say.

It is divine.

Does Margo give this kind of fucked-up advice to other people or just reserve it for me, her most screwed-up friend?

Truce

I hear Sam arrive as I'm getting out of the shower. He and Noble are joking around and the sound of it fills me with relief. *Please, someone, make Noble happy because I've got nothing left in the tank.* I put on short black shorts and a loose white tank and find my flip-flops under the bed. I rummage through my jewelry box and find a beaded necklace with a turquoise cross pendant and put it over my head. I center the cross on my chest and consider myself in the mirror. How can I look like this while Butch is dying next door? He barely even sits up anymore.

Sean and Michelle, and Lily of course, come over for dinner, too. Once Margo and Clint and Jocelyn arrive, Noble heats up the grill. We've set up chairs and a table by the hammock on the side yard. I wanted it way in the back, but Noble thought we should be near the grill. I hope that's really why because the sight of Butch's house, and Jason's truck at Butch's, is enough to ruin the party for me.

Butch's door opens and Jay comes barreling out. He runs over, tumbling halfway to us and rolling back to his feet. He finds Lily and the two of them fall easily into a familiar playtime.

"Holy shit," Margo says, leaning into me but still loud enough for anyone to hear. "He's Jason's?" she asks as Jay brings over a bug to show me and climbs into my lap. Margo's eyes almost fall out of her head and I am amazed at her inability to take it all in. Jay has become such a staple here the last few months. He's impossible to not accept. "Of course...he loves you, too."

I look up to the watchful eyes of Noble from behind the grill. He's not angry or surprised. He's pleased with my relationship with Jay as long as Jason's not a part of it, and oddly, he isn't. Jay stays for the barbeque and even eats some chicken I cut for him. He gobbles down watermelon and of course has two servings of strawberry shortcake.

Jason comes out at dusk and calls for Jay; his voice and his eyes quickly land on our small gathering. Sam's easygoing demeanor is replaced by sheer shock as he puts the pieces together of Jay's obvious family lineage.

"Can't believe I missed that," Sam says, and Jay turns toward his dad. "What's he doing back?" he asks, sounding annoyed.

"He's taking care of his father."

"I thought you stopped working to do that because he wasn't coming home," Sam says, and I realize how quickly things have changed here. It feels like Jason and I have been in this awful situation forever, but it's only been a few months.

"Yeah. Now we're doing it together," I say, and sigh.

"How's Nick with that?" Sam looks straight at Jason, who's staring back at us.

"How's Nick with what?" Noble asks as he joins our conversation.

Jay runs over and pulls on my shorts. "Bye-bye, Annie," he says, and Noble's face hardens.

"It's temporary," Noble says as I lean down to Jay's height.

"Bye, Jay. I'll see you tomorrow." He hugs me. Stephanie Harding may be a whore, but she is doing a great job with this child. He is undeniable. Maybe he just inherited that from his father.

Michelle and Sean take Lily home and a joint is lit. I pass. I can't function with all my faculties at this point, let alone high. When the mosquitoes begin to bite, the party moves inside and a second joint is lit. My party is mellowing and my dog hates the smoke, so I go outside with him.

Dr. Grubb's car pulls in front of Butch's and I run over.

"Dr. Grubb?"

"Hi, Charlotte."

"What's wrong?"

"I'm going to see. Marie called and said Butch is having trouble breathing." *Oh God, no.* He grabs a bag out of his backseat and follows me into Butch's.

I walk straight to Butch and his eyes are filled with fear. I hold his hand and lower my voice to calm us both.

"Dr. Grubb is here. He's going to take care of everything," I say, and hope there's something the doctor can actually do. He listens to Butch's heart as Jason storms in, always so gentle. Dr. Grubb moves to his lungs and then takes his pulse. Butch's hand shakes and when I release, it he clenches his chest. How could I be sitting with my friends next door when Butch is lying here terrified? I should have been here.

Dr. Grubb asks for Jason's help in turning Butch and I leave the room as usual, Butch's dignity a priority for all of us.

"Why didn't you call me?" I demand too harshly of Marie once I reach the kitchen.

"You need some time, Charlotte. This is too much for a young girl. You should be enjoying life."

"I'll have time when he's gone. I want to help him," I say, and hear my voice crack on the last words.

"I know you do. Jason had just taken Jay home. I felt bad calling him."

I take out my phone and text Noble.

BUTCH IS HAVING TROUBLE BREATHING.

DR. GRUBB IS HERE.

BJ IS WITH ME.

I'M SORRY.

So am I.

I love you.

"I just gave him a sedative. It's dyspnea," Dr. Grubb says as he walks into the kitchen, and washes his hands in the kitchen sink. I stare at him, waiting for more information. "Shortness of breath," he offers. "It's scaring him. Hospice will get him something to help with it but once he falls asleep, he should be out for the night."

"I should have known," Marie says, and I realize why.

"It's common," I say, again hating the process of death. Marie nods at me and turns to Dr. Grubb for more discussion on dyspnea. I take a corn bag off the counter and warm it in the microwave. I watch it turn and listen for any sounds from the family room.

When I go in there, Butch's eyes are open and staring at the ceiling. I hold his hand and lay the corn bag against his side. His hand is bony and knobby, his skin rough, yet soft. It reminds me of Butch. This has to be close to the end. How long? *How long goddammit?*

My turquoise cross catches my eye and I take it in my free hand and close my eyes and lower my head.

Dear God,

Thank you for Dr. Grubb, and Marie, and Jason, and BJ. I don't know what to say but I don't want Butch, or anyone else, to suffer any longer. Please have mercy on us.

I don't want him to go either. I want him to say something.

I want, I want, I want. I don't even know what I'm saying, but I know it's all wrong. What am I even praying for…

Butch's eyes close and he slips into the deep sleep I recognize from the last few days. He's calm. Marie goes to bed in Butch's room where she stays now, and Jason and I stand by his side.

Jason touches my cross. He holds it in his hand and turns it toward him to examine. An evil little grin crosses his face.

"What do you pray for, Annie?" he asks, and I want him to be out of this. Out of this house and out of this hell.

"Are you okay?" It is the stupidest question ever.

Jason runs his thumb over the cross. "No. I'm not okay." His eyes meet mine and I'm sure I would sell my soul to leave with him right now. The knowledge of what I'm capable of, the frank understanding of my depravity scares me. Not for myself, but for Noble. I knew he should never have wanted me, should never have taken a chance on me.

Butch's hand is cold. His fingers are like icicles in my own. I let go to bury his hand under the blanket. I tuck Butch in, one of the few minor things I can do here.

"Would you like a cup of tea?" I whisper to Jason.

"No. A cup of tea is not what I need," Jason answers, his mood switching from caring for his father to torturing me. The look in his dark eyes is one of hunger. He follows me into the kitchen and I turn on the stove and move the kettle to the lit burner.

"I don't want to fight," I say, and turn toward him. "But have you considered the fact that you only want me because you're here, being tortured by your father's health, and you need something else to focus on? Something that, in your head, you can cure?"

Jason just stares at me from a few feet down the counter. I find a cup in the cabinet and a tea bag from a basket Marie has left out.

"Your life is suspended in death. You haven't been able to rodeo; you're in a place that's housed nothing but bad memories for years. I'm sure you would focus on just about anything to escape it in your mind."

Jason stays silent as the kettle whistles. I pull it from the burner before it wakes anyone. The house is deathly quiet, Butch's heavy breathing audible in the kitchen. An outside light shines through the window, but otherwise it is dark and silent throughout. Death's perfect party.

"Because I think this is a lot, a lot to handle. I don't even realize how much until I get out of here for a few hours. And even though I love Butch, he's not my dad and that's got to make this a completely different kind of hell." Jason stares out the back window at my house and guilt stabs at me. *Shut up, Charlotte. What do you know about his hell?* But I think I know plenty.

I hold the cup in both hands and blow on the tea to cool it. My eyes never leave Jason. They roam around his chest and his neck and finally settle on his hair and the side of his face that is visible in the dim light.

"When I decided to move home, I wasn't sure exactly why I was coming," he says, and I stop drinking. "I'm still not sure, but I'm where I should be." Jason's eyes find mine in the dim light.

"Marie says it's an honor," I offer. It's what I hold on to when I curse the fact that I ever met Butch, ever found myself here every day.

"I can't begin to consider what this would be like without you, and without Marie," he says, his words hinting at his gratitude. "Your presence makes every moan, every cough, every sigh bearable." My heart breaks for him. "But you leave and your absence, your return to that house, makes me sick."

I swallow hard. There's nothing I can do about where I return to. It's where I live…with my husband.

"I think you're creating a competition to somehow protect any shred of sanity still left in your mind. You're avoiding the present by jeopardizing our futures."

I listen to Jason's breath, and I watch his chest rise in his shirt, and I think he's considering what I've said. Surely if he steps back, if he can actually listen, he'll find some truth in my words.

Jason stands in front of me and looks at me with silence in his eyes. There's no sign of misbehavior, or defiance, or anger, and the quiet scares me.

"Annie, don't fight me," he says, and I don't understand. "For the next few minutes don't fight me, don't think, don't remember, don't be angry," he pleads, and I nod in agreement, needing to know what he's thinking.

Jason leans down and places his lips on mine. My eyes are open and I watch without moving as he moves back and assesses my reaction. Certain I'm listening and not going to stab him, he returns his lips to mine and I do as I'm told and let him. They are soft and round, and so incredibly a part of my existence. I part my lips to breathe and he moves his over mine, caressing them with his own.

Jason kisses me, torturously slow, making me want to rip off my own clothes. His tongue in my mouth, my nipples rising to rub against him, my hands weaving in his hair, and my mind empty of every last thought except how he feels against me.

He takes a breath and opens his eyes. He takes my bottom lip in his teeth and licks it. He raises my head up with his chin and grazes my neck with his lips and the chill caves my chest in and weakens my knees. Jason's arm wraps around my back and holds me to him, wherever he wants me.

Jason's body presses against mine and I begin to throb, everywhere. His lips find my ear and he whispers, "Does that feel like a competition?"

I shiver and his hand on the center of my back pulls me toward him. The guilt retaliates and I lower my head, my eyes. *How can I do this?*

"Don't feel guilty," Jason says as he leans down and picks up my eyes with his own.

"You wouldn't love me if this didn't make me feel guilty," I say, and move him back with both hands on his stomach. I walk back to my perch by Butch, shaking.

* * *

"She's been sitting like that all night," Marie says, but I can't open my eyes.

"My God. She's not going to be able to walk." It's Noble. In Butch's house?

"I know. I'm worried about her. She has the weight of the world on her shoulders. It's too much."

"I'm taking her home," Noble says right before lifting me into his arms and walking out into the fresh morning air. He carries me all the way across the yard and I raise my arm to rest around his shoulder and lean into his chest. I should walk, but I can't. I can't even find the strength to tell him I should walk. Noble lays me on the bed, and my pillow under my head immediately sedates me. Sleeping sitting up, leaning over a hospital bed railing, has left me exhausted and enthralled with my bed.

* * *

I open my eyes and Noble is reading in the leather chair in the corner of our room. He looks up at me, but his face is wrought with concern.

"It won't be long," I say. "This is all coming to an end soon." I roll over and fall back to sleep, unable to face consciousness yet.

When I do open my eyes, it's to the sound of Jay playing below my bedroom window. He yells, "Daddy" over and over again, calling to his dad to throw him a ball. The only pause in his cheers must signify Jason finally throwing it. I pull myself out of bed and walk toward the window, hoping to watch them undetected, but when I pull back the sheers, Jason is staring right at me.

There's little left in me that knows the right thing to do. Actually, that's not fair. I know exactly the right thing; there's little left in me that cares what is right.

Noble deserves better than this.

I stare out the window, wishing I could fly through it. Away from here.

~26~

The Final Bout

The burst of energy came yesterday. Butch actually spoke to us. He told us to stop goddamn staring at him, but he spoke. I let my mind linger on the lie this might actually turn around. He might live. Jason had no hope, rightfully so since the hospice nurse explained a final burst of energy is not uncommon. Why must the act of death be so common?

I pull the heated corn bag out of the microwave and take it into the family room. BJ is asleep next to Butch, cuddled on his bed. Jason is standing at the foot of the bed and Marie is curled up in the recliner, asleep. I curl Butch's hand and fingers around the bag. His fingers are still cold. He would be bitching about it if he could speak. I hold my hand over his and try to warm them.

Butch begins to mumble something. Something I can't understand and no one else in the room cares about.

"Butch. Butch, it's okay. Whatever it is will be okay. We love you," I say, and remember what a glorious place my mother is in.

Another person leaving us here to carry on as they are granted eternal grace. This time, the memory doesn't make me angry. I want Butch to be there. Anywhere but here, in this bed, at the mercy of morphine.

The mumbling stops and the world pauses. Butch is no longer breathing, no longer fighting. His eyes are open and his lips are parted slightly, but he is gone.

"Marie," I say quietly, not wanting to scare her or disturb death in its work. "Marie." Marie stirs in her chair. She sits up and finally focuses on me. "He's gone," I say, and the tears flood my eyes as Jason walks out of the house. "He's gone." Marie caresses Butch's face. She closes his eyes and takes my hand from Butch's.

"It's an honor, Charlotte," she says, and I begin to understand. "You're a good girl. Butch adored you," Marie says, and it's more than I can handle. "But you know that."

I need to find Jason.

"I have to go," I say, and take one step back from Butch's body.

"Be careful, dear," Marie says, but the sound of her voice makes me sick.

* * *

His truck is gone. He's left the farm. I take the Volvo and drive through town. I pass the Corner Bar and the two others in town, but there's no sign of him. I drive past the church and Cowtown and Ollie's house. He could be anywhere.

The orange barrel blocking the entry to Stoners Lane has been crushed and thrown to the side, and without pulling in, I know Jason is down there. I pause on the shoulder, trying to explain to myself what I'm about to do, how I think I can help. Because there's nothing that can help this.

I pull onto Stoners Lane and sink into every hole in the path. Jason's truck sits alone in the clearing with him in it. I park the Volvo next to his truck and watch him through my window. He stares straight ahead and I think I should leave. I can talk to him later, at the house. Maybe Noble will come with me. I shouldn't disturb him. Everyone mourns differently. And then he looks at me and I burst into tears. *A lot of help I'm going to be.*

I wipe the tears from my face and climb out of the Volvo and into Jason's truck. He watches me silently as the door closes with a familiar groan. This old truck, Jason behind the steering wheel and me next to him…I turn my attention to the sky. The rain moved out this morning and a blanket of bright white clouds has filled in behind it. They are blowing past, rolling, with random slivers of blue sky sliced through the fabric. The sky is heavenly today.

So here we sit. For over two hours we sit three feet apart in silence. It's always Jason that knows what to do, how to comfort me, but today he needs me to know and I know nothing. He and Butch were complicated. They lost each other when they lost Mrs. Leer and the tiny shreds of a relationship they were hanging on to weren't enough to support a complete severance.

"Are you hungry?" I ask. *I am an idiot.*

"No. I'm not hungry," he says, and his voice floats through the car and lands in the center of my chest, caving it in a little.

There's nothing I can do here.

"I'm going to go back. See if Marie needs any help." I reach for the door handle and Jason roughly grabs my arm. He startles me. He hasn't moved in hours. I look down at his grip as he loosens it slightly. Jason pulls me toward him but I pull my arm back.

"I can't do this," I say, and open the truck door. Before my feet are on the ground, Jason's already standing in front of me. His dark eyes burning holes through me.

"Do what, Annie?"

"I can't help you mourn your father and mourn him myself. I can't love you and love Noble," I say, gradually gaining the strength in my voice. "I can't say good-bye or ask you to stay."

"You can do anything."

"I can't do any of it!" My anger ignites. I try to walk around Jason, but he moves, barricading me here with him. "What do you want from me?" I yell. "You want me to fuck you? Here? Is that why you came here?" I am sickened and I don't know what part of today is killing me. Jason leans into me and if I didn't know better, I would think he hates me from the anger in his eyes.

"Isn't that why you came here?" he asks.

"I don't know why I'm here."

"Yes, you do, Annie. You know. You've gotta know." He pushes me back to the truck with a hand on each shoulder. I tilt my face to the sky and Jason buries his lips on my neck and drags them up to my ear, my skin electrified everywhere they touch. "You know."

"Know what?" I ask, fighting for air. "I know everyone dies." I run my hands through Jason's thick hair and hold on for dear life. "I know I want you," I say, and a sob catches in my throat.

Jason kisses me. He is rough and greedy and plotting to abscond with me and I can do nothing but savor the taste of him. I can't pull him close enough to my body. He'll never be inside of me the way I want him. He leans back, mere centimeters from my face. My past will destroy my future.

"I know my husband deserves better than this."

Jason steps back, letting me go if I choose, but I left him once before and I almost died because of it. There has never been a way for Jason, Noble, and me to exist together. Not since I told Noble I love him. I inhale deeply, trying to center myself in a world rarely on its axis.

"After the funeral, I want you to leave Salem County," I say, and Jason looks like he doesn't believe a word I'm saying. "I mean it. You can't stay here. We had our chance. Now I belong with Noble."

"That's not what you want." His words are written across my heart.

"Forever." He looks at me, gauging my honesty, my commitment to what's right. "I want you to leave forever." He glares at me, ready to rip my soul right out of my chest. To Jason I'm denying it and no longer deserve it. I let my eyes fall to the ground between us, unable to face him or what we have become.

***

My arm hurts where he grabbed me and my lip is cut a little. Both remind me of Jason and I never want them to heal. When I get home, I turn on the shower, as hot as the water will go, and I undress. I'll never see Jason Leer naked again. He'll never touch my skin, I think as I run my hand across my stomach. Jason will be gone soon, per my request; one more loved one vanished from my life. What kind of a life is this?

The water burns me as I step into the shower and I turn it back to cold a little. I stand with my back to the nozzle, questioning how Noble can even love me. How can I let him love me? And how can

I let Jason go? Butch is with Mrs. Leer now. The thought of Butch starts the tears and I sob until I can no longer breathe. I cry as the water continues to pelt me. I crouch down in the shower and cry into my hands.

Noble opens the shower curtain slowly and the kindness in his eyes makes me sick. He turns off the water and wraps me in a towel. He carries me to our room and dries me off. All the while I cry. I whimper like a child facing her first punishment. Noble raises each arm to put my robe on me and sits me on the bed. He brushes my matted hair, without saying a word. What needs to be said?

"Noble, I don't deserve you."

"No one is deserving of someone else, Charlotte," he says, and puts the brush back on my dresser. "Do you love me?"

His question makes me cry harder. "I do. I love you, Noble, and I don't ever want to be without you."

Noble sits next to me on the bed and takes me in his arms. "Then you won't be. I promise." He lays me down and covers me with our quilt. "I'm sorry about Butch," I hear him say as I close my eyes and breathe in the strength that is Noble.

~27~

Burial

It wasn't supposed to rain today, but it's good. It will bring Jason some comfort. Everyone knows, "Happy is the dead the rain rains upon."

"It's a shame about the weather," Noble says. *Maybe not everyone.* Noble hasn't lost anyone yet.

Noble and I walk into the church and I pause. How many of these will I go to throughout my entire life? I step through the doorway of the sanctuary and my stomach churns with bitterness. I would give anything not to be here. Another father gone. Jason, Marie, and Jay are all sitting in the first row. Well, Jay is standing on his father's lap, but they're up there together.

"Do you want to sit with them? I'll walk up there with you," Noble offers. He holds me up in every way.

"No." *We're finished together. I can't help him now.* "Where's Stephanie Harding, though?"

"She's not coming."

I turn to Noble, shocked. I wasn't expecting an answer.

"I saw her the other day. She seemed a bit pissed she wasn't involved in Butch's care."

I shake my head in disgust. "Pissed off enough to leave Jason and Jay here alone?" As if on cue, Jay runs back and into my arms. I lift him up and he puts his head on my shoulder. I bury my nose in his hair. I'm going to miss this little boy when he goes back to Oklahoma. Noble and I walk Jay back to the front of the church, past the Hardings. Mr. Harding is overweight. He rests his crossed arms on his stomach and almost smiles as I pass. Mrs. Harding is an eighth the size of mister. She is small and thin, with short hair that's curled in sections surrounding her head. Her face needs some sort of beak to complete it. She turns her eyes toward Jay and me and a scowl settles on her face. If you could shoot hatred across the room, I'd be dead. I think Mrs. Harding has impeccable aim. On the other side of Mrs. Harding is Stephanie's sister, Janice. She has a baby in her arms and a small child by her side. All the babysitters are here. It seems as if the whole town is here, everyone except Stephanie. I put Jay down on the pew next to Jason and hug and kiss Marie. Jason stands and I hug him, too.

"I'm sorry," I say, and we both know I'm apologizing for more than his father's death. I turn to Noble and Jay pulls on the hem of my dress to sit by him. Noble sits down, leaving room for me between him and Jay. Noble is studying me with the strangest look. He has been for days. He's watching me, probably waiting for me to have some critical breakdown. It's as if he's evaluating or analyzing me, or this situation. *It's over. All of it. What's left to figure out?*

The service is a blur. I can't believe Butch will never sit in this church again. Noble puts me in the car and drives me to the cemetery. I throw a rose on Butch's casket with Jason and Marie, and I hope Butch is happy in heaven.

We drive back to the farm in silence, my hand unable to let go of Noble's. I'm clinging to him more than ever before and it's probably scaring him. Maybe that's what he's picking up. The sun comes out as we drive down the lane toward the tent on the side of the farmhouse. When Marie asked about having the luncheon on the farm, I wanted to offer to pay to have it anywhere but here. Now that we're home, I'm glad I gave in. I can hide in my house if I have to.

Cars follow us down the lane, the death march of vehicles, and park on the side lawn. The sight of Butch's house lodges in the back of my throat and I swallow hard to keep from crying. I walk directly to the tent. There are tables and chairs for one hundred people. I hope that's enough. Sean has the firemen helping the elderly across the wet grass. Butch was young. Barely sixty. *What the fuck?*

I peruse the food. Satisfied everything is where it should be, I look up to find Noble. He's watching me. Even while speaking to other people, he never takes his eyes off me. The worry I put that guy through. It's a miracle he hasn't run away screaming. I owe him a honeymoon. As soon as I'm able to be awake all day, I'll talk to him about it. I signal I'm going to the house to change my shoes. Noble nods and I escape to the house.

As soon as I'm safely in the kitchen, I take them off. I hold them in my hands and examine the black stitching around the opening. My funeral shoes, too conservative to wear anyplace with life. I hurl one against the refrigerator and pull back with the second, gunning for the oven.

"Nice aim." Knowing it's Jason behind me, I hang my head and lower my shoulders. "Don't let me stop you. I wouldn't want to wear them either."

"Second worst day of your life?" I ask, turning to him.

"It's hard to say. They're adding up quick. But I got the impression you don't care anymore, or at least you don't want to care anymore."

"I'll never stop caring."

"Will you stop loving me? Stop wanting me?"

"Probably not. We've been over this, though," I say, unable to have this conversation again.

"Jay and I are going back to Oklahoma next week," he says, and it's a knife to the heart. "Unless you give me a reason to stay."

"There's no reason to give you." I walk to the sink and stare out the window at the tent full of people in my backyard.

"It's my understanding that if I want, I can live in Pop's house."

He can't be serious. "Yes, that's true, but you wouldn't do that to me," I say, and turn back to him.

"We've been here for months," he says as if we've been one big cozy family.

"But your son's mother has been absent. There's too much history for one farm."

"What if we lived here without her?" he asks, his eyes begging me for something I will not give.

"What good would that do? What are you thinking? My husband is not going to share me with you." I think Jason is losing his mind.

"Jay is going to miss you, Annie."

"I'm going to miss him, too."

"And me, will you miss me?"

"I've become an expert at missing you. I can do it on one foot." I smile at Jason because there's nothing left but the memories of how it was when it wasn't this. Jason moves closer to me and I put my hand out to stop him, to stop this. He holds it and runs his hands over mine softly. He closes his eyes as if in pain, and I can barely hold the space between us.

"Annie, you should be with me. I know I've said it a hundred times. When this moves to our past, you'll see it." I shake my head and try to pull my hand back, but he tightens his grasp. "Call me before I leave. Come see me. Go somewhere with me. Anything. Please, Annie, change your mind. Don't do this to me...and to you."

"If I was able to leave you at Stoners the other day, do you really think there's another moment in time that will change my mind?" What we had is buried six feet underground, too.

"You have to believe." Jason doesn't listen. He never listens. "You have to change your mind."

"Charlotte?" Noble's voice breaks Jason's hold on me and I take back my hand. Jason looks at me one last time before turning and walking out of my kitchen without so much as a glance in Noble's direction.

"Change your mind about what?" Noble asks, but it doesn't sound like his voice.

Noble is a stranger standing before me. I can't begin to understand what's going on in his head, and his wonderfully happy eyes are replaced with accusations and hatred.

"Change my mind about spending time with Jay before they leave," I say, and turn back to the window, hoping my lying is improving.

I take the bottle of Jack from the cabinet and find a small glass. I pour a shot and down it.

"Would you like a drink?" I ask Noble.

Noble looks at me with dead eyes. I miss his happy ones. Noble is always happy, but not today. Did he love Butch as much as I did?

Noble picks up the bottle and grabs a glass. He pours himself a shot and another one for me.

"Together forever, Charlotte," he says, and clinks my glass before swallowing the whiskey. I lay my head on his shoulder and wrap my arm around his back. *Together forever.*

I avoid the rest of the luncheon and hide in my kitchen doing shots with Noble. No one bothers us. The sun hasn't even set when Noble carries me upstairs and helps me take off my dress. Even after a bottle of Jack I don't recognize him. I want him, though. I want my old Noble back and I want the old Charlotte back. I want so many things time has taken from me.

I kiss Noble and the intensity of him rattles me. It shakes something free in my core and I need him to know that it's him. It's always going to be him.

"Noble."

"Not now, Charlotte. I just need you now," he says, and takes me like an animal on our bed. Will anything ever be the same again?

~28~

Everybody Dies

I stay busy. It's been five days since Butch's funeral and in two more days Jason will be on his way back to Oklahoma. Once he can bulldog again he'll be fine, and once he's gone, Noble and I will be fine. He's been preoccupied since Butch died, but I think he's back to his normal self. He dropped me off at Sean and Michelle's for Michelle's sister's baby shower, and he took my car to get a new battery put in it. I've been in such a fog I didn't even notice it needed changing.

Every day I promise myself a new beginning, and every day I step outside to Butch's house and it kicks me in the back of the knees. Noble is cutting peppers for a salad when Sean opens the back door at the same time he knocks on it. He walks into the kitchen and surveys the room. He's cagey and it's weird.

"Steve Largent just called," he says, and I can't imagine why I would care about Sean's high school friend calling him. "Jason Leer was found shot in the woods."

My insides curl up and die.

I've had the feeling once before, standing on a fence in Kansas. Noble is staring at me, but I don't care. I don't care about anything.

"He's dead," I hear Sean say.

I take a step back, trying to get away from the inside of my head. It's closing down on me and if I can just get out from under it, I'll be able to understand what Sean is saying.

"They're still investigating, but it doesn't sound like an accident." Sean and Noble lock eyes. A hollow weep emanates from my throat and Sean looks around the kitchen. He pauses, staring at Noble's work boots by the back door. "Sorry. I'm sorry," Sean says, and moves to stand in front of me. "Charlotte, do you hear me?" *There must be some mistake.*

The vise around my mind is closing. I see Sean's eyes. They're the same color as mine, but his don't look like they hurt sitting there inside his head. They're fine. "Charlotte," he snaps, and I see his lips moving. I nod, not wanting to anger him.

"I also wanted to know if I could borrow your work boots, Nick? You don't mind, do you?" Sean grabs a bag out from under the sink and looks around as if he's scanning the room for something else. He puts the boots in the bag and turns back to me. He grabs me with both arms as Noble's boots swing in the bag hanging off his elbow.

"Charlotte, I'm sorry. Sorry to be the one to tell you and sorry he's dead." Sean's voice reminds me of the days following my parents' death, when he took care of me. "I'll come back in a little while," he says, and turns his attention to Noble. "Do you need me to do anything?" Noble shakes his head without saying a word and Sean hurriedly walks out the back door. Noble watches Sean leave and bows his head.

There are seconds…minutes…maybe hours.

I don't know.

"I'm going to go upstairs," I say as if I just learned English and I'm not sure of the wording. The pain in my head is protecting me from thinking. I walk up the stairs alone. Forever alone now.

I find the rowel necklace in my jewelry box. The one Jason gave me with the red stones surrounding the blue one. Jason surrounding me. I hold it up to the light and Noble walks in. He stands watching me, waiting for me to throw myself out the window.

"I knew we were never going to be together again, but as long as he was out there somewhere, that was enough," I say, and look down at the necklace in my hand. "It would have been enough."

Noble comes to me and puts his arms around me, but there's something wrong with his face. He's not warm. He's not happy. Maybe I just can't recognize it anymore.

"Something about us didn't work. I understood that, but I always knew he was out there. How could he die? He was so strong. I saw a steer stomp on his head once," I say, and the images from Kansas fill my mind and connect with the sick growl inside my head. "You saw that, too. Do you remember?"

Noble nods and secures a few stray hairs behind my ear. I shake my head in disgust. "How could he survive that and be dead in the woods?"

"I don't know, Charlotte," Noble says. How could he know?

"I wished he would die before," I admit to the air. "Isn't that awful? I hoped horrific things would happen to him. The day his father died, I told him to leave Salem County forever." Noble holds my arms and is suddenly listening closely. "I told him to leave and never come back. That I belong with you."

Noble moves us both to the bed and holds me in his arms, but it doesn't matter. Nothing matters.

"Isn't that horrible? On the day his father died. We were awful to each other. And now he's gone forever and I am dead inside," I say without an ounce of concern for Noble or anyone else. *Fuck everybody*.

* * *

I just want to touch him one more time. I hate him for leaving me and I hate myself for many things, but mostly I just want to crawl into the earth with him when he's buried tomorrow.

The emptiness fills me. The idea that he's gone overwhelms me. I walk around in a fog every minute of the day and then stop to acknowledge he's gone and slip back into my unconsciousness. The fear of losing him never felt this way in my nightmares. He took my emotions with him, vanished with them to the life after this one, and abandoned me to live in a world without him.

Kevin was uncomfortable with my call. I hadn't spoken to him since my parents' funeral and I wasn't very nice back then. I keep telling myself he's an undertaker, that he sees people at their worst every day, but it doesn't seem to be helping. I'm certain if he wasn't friends with Sean I wouldn't be walking into the funeral home today.

"Hi, Charlotte. I'm sorry about Jason," Kevin says. He sounds scared. I am a scary person.

"Hi, Kevin. I can't thank you enough for this. I know it's asking a lot," I say, and try to inflect some actual gratitude into the statement. Kevin nods, probably afraid to speak.

"He's downstairs, in the embalming room. Have you ever been to the working area of the funeral home?" Kevin asks, but he already knows I have not. "Charlotte, are you sure you want to do this?"

"Better today than tomorrow in front of the whole town."

I follow Kevin to the basement of the funeral home. He opens a door that leads into a cold, softly lit room. There are small windows at the tops of the walls, all covered with frosted glass to keep out wandering eyes. Wouldn't want to scare the children. A silver showerhead hangs above Jason and a drain opens below. A wall of cabinets lines the wall behind the gurney he is lying on, and a sour vinegary smell fills my nose. I curl my lip at it. He is covered with a sheet.

"We're waiting for the family to bring his clothes." *The family.* How sickening. *Take your sweet-ass time, Stephanie.*

"May I?" I ask, motioning toward him.

"You can't hurt him now," Kevin says gently. "I'll be upstairs if you need anything."

"Thank you, Kevin," I say, this time easily finding the gratitude. Kevin has been taking care of Jason, and now he's allowing me to say good-bye, far from the eyes of this town. Far from Stephanie and Noble, too.

Kevin shuts the door behind him and I look at Jason in disbelief. He can't really be gone. His hair is still jet black, his mouth sutured shut, his hands crossed at his waist, and I force my eyes over every inch of him. He is dead. Not in there. No longer a part of this life.

The world is silent.

The color of his skin is all wrong, and his gray eyes are muted. Thank God.

"I love you," I say, and cry. "I can't believe you're gone. I won't accept it." The sobs form in my throat and I squeeze my eyes shut and lower my head. If he were here, I would be in his arms. He wouldn't let me cry like this, but he's not here. Only this hardened, off-color corpse is left for me.

I touch his hand and it's cold and hard, and it doesn't give me the chill I long for. I sob again, this time forgetting where I am. "When I find out who did this, I am going to make sure they feel as awful as I do right now." How could anyone have done this? Who could have looked him in the eye and killed him? Who had the *honor* of being with him when he died?

"Or maybe I'll just ask them to take me, too," I say, and lean over Jason's body, crying, too dead inside to care. My chest heaves as I cry a thousand painful moments with every breath.

I'm lying with him in Bryant Park, and driving west to Oklahoma in his truck, and decorating a Christmas tree, and sitting next to him at Cowtown...How will I ever let these memories fade enough to care about anything else in this world? I cry until my throat hurts, but I don't give in. There is no physical pain that will ever interfere with this derelict's departure.

"Charlotte." Sean's voice barely reaches my ears through the torrent. He lifts me up and I disintegrate in his arms. Sean holds my head on his shoulder, tight to him, as he rocks back and forth and I sob. I won't stop until he comes back. I won't stop until my body finally gives up and lets me follow him. "Charlotte. Please stop crying, Charlotte."

I run out of tears and air. I can no longer sob. I can only look around the cold room and wait to throw up or pass out. What will become of me? Sean leans me back and looks in my eyes.

"You're going to kill your husband," he says.

Everybody dies.

"Charlotte, I know you've lost a lot, but you've got to keep living."
My chest trembles as a new sob forms. Sean holds me tightly by the
shoulders. "I don't know why you're still here. Why they're all gone
and you're here," he says, and I don't know either because I know
I should be with them. "But we're both here for a reason. I'm sure
of it. And you've got to keep living. Lily needs you…and I need
you…and BJ needs you…and your husband—"

"Noble would be better off without me. He's too good for me.
For Jason and me."

"Don't say that. Don't ever say that." I try and listen to Sean. He
has never wanted anything but the best for me. I'm almost certain
he's still here to take care of me because I can't take care of myself.

"Do you remember your wedding day?" Sean says, and breaks
through my horrid thoughts. "Charlotte, do you remember me walking you down that staircase?" He shakes my shoulders, trying to force
the images into my head. "Do you remember the look on Nick's face
when he first saw you? Charlotte, it wasn't even a year ago."

"Sean, too much has happened. I am not a good person," I say, remembering all the times I wanted Jason, would have forsaken Noble
over the past few months, and the times when I gave myself to him
without a thought of Noble. My actions confirming I never deserved
Noble's love.

"You are a good person. My God, Charlotte, you are one of the
best people I know. You're kind to people, you've given your own
life for others. It's time to take it back, though. Before there's nothing left." I try to hear him, to listen to my brother. "You're still here.
So make it for a reason. Be good from this day forward. Find your
strength, Charlotte. We need you."

~29~

Even the Fucking Rain Left Me

I pull out of the cell phone waiting area of the Philadelphia International Airport the second Harlan calls. He and three other teammates of Jason's flew in for the funeral. They're staying at Butch's, which is weird but hopefully more so for me than them.

I'm lonely in the car, lonely in my house, lonely because I'm alone. A powerful force I could never quite explain is absent from the Earth. The breeze doesn't blow, the clouds don't roll in, the atmosphere has changed, and not for the better. It's weak and timid, missing its strength, and I suffer his absence to the core of my being. My mind won't accept he's gone, but my body knows without a doubt he's no longer a part of this world.

They're standing on the curb and look like absolute aliens in their huge hats and bigger belt buckles in Philly. I stop the car and jump out into the waiting arms of Harlan Wilder. God, this should be under different circumstances. I greet the others. They are familiar and kind, but I have nothing really to say to them. They climb in the back, Harlan up front with me, and it reminds me of the times he picked me up from the airport in Oklahoma.

"What time's the funeral?" Harlan asks, sadness suffocating his playful demeanor.

"Eleven is the service."

"Do you folks in Jersey have some kind of lunch or party afterward?" Jersey is as foreign to Harlan as he is to it.

"It's customary to have a luncheon, or in some cases a wake, which is more of a party, but I don't know what Stephanie has planned." Harlan watches me kindly. "She didn't call for my opinion on the arrangements."

Harlan smiles for the first time since I picked him up. "I missed you, Jersey."

"I missed you, too, Harlan." I don't say anything else, afraid I'll sob the last ten miles of the trip.

*　*　*

Butch's house is completely different than the death cave it had become. The hospital bed is gone, the medicines have been disposed of, and Marie and Jason had sorted his clothes and belongings after the funeral. It's as if the last five horrible months never happened.

"There are sandwiches and beer, some soda, and a few other things in the refrigerator for you guys. Help yourselves."

Harlan lays his bag on the kitchen table and rummages through it. "I stopped by his place and picked up a few things I thought he'd want you to have," he says, and I can't imagine what he thought should come to me. Everything should go to Jay now.

He pulls out two stacks of letters bound in rubber bands, my handwriting on the front of each envelope, and I cry at the sight of them.

"I thought these should come back to you," he says, and hands them to me. "Jason showed them to me once. I knew where they were." I can't take my eyes off them. "I found this, too, and figured it belonged to you." Harlan holds up a gold heart on a chain with the letter *A* engraved on it and I completely lose it. I hung it on his bed in Oklahoma and told him I was leaving my heart with him, and now he's taken it to his grave. It will never beat again.

Harlan walks over and holds me tight to him. He rubs my back and shushes me as I sob into his shirt. I've been avoiding how utterly sad I am, letting my anger usher in the numbness, but faced with these letters and my heart, I can't hide from Jason anymore. This is exactly how he would want it.

"Hey, hey, Charlotte…are you sure you're okay?"

"I'm nothing. My brain won't accept it. It's not possible," I say, and wipe the tears from my face and step back to face Harlan. "You were with me in Hayes. How is this possible?"

Harlan hugs me again. "I don't know. Someone hated him enough to want him dead."

"I'm the only person who's ever wanted him dead," I say, barely able to remember hating him that much. "And I didn't kill him."

"You did when you left. He told me it wasn't a life without you. Said he was dead inside."

"That's how I feel now. Like I don't care if the sun rises or the ocean dries up. If he's not on this Earth, what's the point?"

Harlan rubs my back, then holds me at arm's length to look me in the eyes. "One foot in front of the other, darlin'. Keep walkin' until you figure out something to live for. You got it?" I nod my head, half-assed. "Oh no you don't. You're the most hardheaded person I've ever met; now put it to some good. He wouldn't want you weak," Harlan says, and I swear I told him the same thing once.

I leave the cowboys to settle in and walk home as Steve Largent pulls down the lane in his police car. I'm carrying my letters and the *A* necklace and I don't want to talk to Steve, or anyone else for that matter. He parks by the tree and meets me by the house.

"Charlotte," he says, and something feels wrong about this visit.

"Hi, Steve, something I can do for you?"

"I was hoping to talk to you and Nick. Sorry about the timing. I know it's a busy day. I have some routine questions, some things to note for my file."

"Your file on Jason?" I ask, and swallow hard, my stomach knotted into a ball of disgust.

"Yes. Unfortunately, yes. It's pretty shocking. Do you have any idea who'd want to kill him?"

"I wanted to for a while," I say. Good thing Sean's not here. "But that was a long time ago...you probably know that. Everyone in this town knows our history."

"I think I know the highlights of the story," Steve says kindly, and I open the door for us to walk into the house. Noble's pouring a glass of water when we walk in.

"Hi, Nick," Steve says, and Noble walks over and shakes his hand without smiling. It's strange to see Noble's face without a smile on it. How long has this been the case? When did he stop smiling?

"I'm sorry to bother you guys, especially without calling first. I just have a few questions for you." Noble's eyebrows rise, but he stays quiet. Also not like him. "How long has Jason been back home?"

I think in my head. January and February were peaceful.

"As far as I know, he came back for good in March."

"For good?" Steve asks.

"He was here in October, right before the storm." Noble glares at me. "I didn't speak with him. He was also here over Christmas and for Butch's operation in the beginning of January."

"So the last three months?"

"Yes," Noble says, and seems less likely to kill someone. Did something happen while I was out? Is he pissed Harlan's here? And why would that piss anyone off?

"Where were you on June fifth?" Steve turns his question back to me.

"When he was killed?" I ask, and try to remember anything that happened before Sean came here and told me Jason died. For the first time since that day, I remember that he also took Noble's boots. I look at Noble.

"You had the baby shower," Noble says.

"That's right. Jill, Michelle's sister, had her baby shower that day." Steve nods and makes a note of it. *Am I a suspect?*

"How about you, Nick? Where were you that day?"

"I took Charlotte's car in for some repairs. Minor stuff, but it took a while."

"Do you have a receipt?"

My eyes dart from Noble to Steve, and my heart races in my chest. *Do you have a receipt?* I want to scream.

"I'm sure I do somewhere. Do you need it right now?"

"No. In fact, just tell me the service center and I'll follow up on my end."

There's a pause, or at least in my head there's a pause.

"It was Al Hanz's Body Shop."

I exhale and realize I'd been holding my breath. This is crazy. Noble would never hurt Jason or anybody else.

He takes a sip of his water. "Would you like something to drink, Steve?"

Where are my manners?

"No. I'm going to head out. If I need anything further, I'll give you a call or stop by." Steve walks to the back door and I follow him. I look past him and the absence of Jason's truck stabs me. "Sorry to just stop by like this."

"It's no problem," I say, and latch the door behind him.

I walk back into the kitchen and Noble is nowhere to be found. This was all in my head, I tell myself, and open a beer and chug it down. It's a surprise I haven't tried alcoholism yet. This life is an addiction waiting to happen. How appropriate to begin some sort of abuse after Jason dies. He'll probably haunt me for it.

* * *

I drive the cowboys and Noble drives Marie. We park outside the church and linger in our cars, none of us rushing to go inside. When Noble walks Marie to the front door, I open my own and step out of the Volvo. I raise my eyes to the sky and the bright sunshine pisses me off. He deserves better than this. This god-awful sunshine should be reserved for the miserable and the hopeless; the sky should be raging to commemorate the loss of our greatest storm. I pick up a rock and throw it toward the sky. I turn to the cowboys, all watching the crazy person who drove them here. I sigh and continue walking. *Fucking sky…*

We take our prayer cards from Mrs. Battaglia and move into the sanctuary. Noble's instantly at my side and supports my elbow. He walks me to the front without a word and when we reach the casket, he leaves me there and turns to speak with Jay and Stephanie, who are sitting in the front row.

Jason is wearing jeans, his red plaid button-down, and his championship buckle. I'm not surprised it's not the one I gave to him with our initials engraved on the back. I slip the *A* necklace from my hand and place it under his and a tear runs down my face. *I guess I do have a little fight still left in me.* I let my mind absorb what's left of my beast lying here.

Jay pulls at my skirt and I look up to see Noble occupying Stephanie. She's smiling. How can she smile? She appears to be basking in the attention. It would be impossible to hate her more. I bend down to speak with Jay.

"I'm sorry about your daddy."

"Me too," he says, and buries his head on my shoulder.

"My daddy died too."

"He did?" he asks, leaning back to see me.

"Yes and I miss him very much. But I know he'd want me to be happy. That's what your daddy wants for you, too. He wants you to be happy," I say, and rub Jay's back. "He's with Pops and God now. I know it hurts, but you'll be happy again."

"When?"

"Someday soon, I promise."

Harlan walks up and hugs Stephanie as I hold Jay in my arms and squeeze him.

All of them gone at the same time.

The service is beyond my comprehension. I'm sure it was lovely, but I didn't hear a second of it. Just more words to not comfort me, only serving to make me sicker. Noble holds my hand, either out of habit or unbelievably he still harbors some love for me after everything I've put him through.

The cowboys take Marie and my car and I ride with Noble to the cemetery. We park in the line of cars and I grab Noble's arm as he reaches to open the driver's door.

"Can we just stay here? It's too much." Noble nods and closes his door. "The whole thing makes me sick. Butch, Jason, his son at two funerals in a month...it's too much death."

Noble takes my hand, kisses it, and holds it in his own. "You're so pale, Charlotte. You've got to eat something."

"I'm not hungry. June is a horrible month," I say, and watch Stephanie toss a rose on Jason's casket.

Noble puts the truck in drive and takes me home. No luncheon, no fellowship, no heart.

~30~

Surrender

It's been a horrible month. I can barely look at Noble. Most nights I go to bed first and cover my face with the blankets. I act like I'm asleep and silently cry and hope Noble doesn't notice. A part of me wants to talk to him, to reach out to him, but I don't. Night after night, I deny us both. I can't remember why he loves me, why he ever would've loved me. I can't remember anything but Jason. He's in heaven, with his mother and father, and I'm here.

The rain is heavy on the window. It beats furiously, trying to pull me out of unconsciousness, but even awake I am benumbed. It slows to a light tap, giving up on me, as BJ snores in his bed on the floor beside me.

I hate you...and I love you, and I miss you, and I'll never, ever forget you.

I hear Noble on the phone, but I don't care what he's saying. When he looks at me, I try to smile. He deserves a smile, doesn't he? I don't think he even looks at me that often anymore. It's as if we died, too.

"Charlotte, I'm going out for a while," he says.

"Okay."

Noble just stares at me as if he doesn't know me. I'm not sure there's anything left of the girl he used to know. "Why don't you go for a swim?"

Because I'll drown myself.

"Maybe," I say.

Noble turns and walks out of our bedroom. I hear the door shut and the screen door slap behind it. I take the bundles of letters Jason saved out of my top drawer and lay them out on my bed, our bed. I swallow hard and turn and find my rowel necklace. It's a miracle it's stayed with me longer than Jason. There were so many times it should have been destroyed.

I open each letter and read them to myself. My words, in my handwriting, calling out every minute of my last two years of college. They are angry, and funny, and full of love delivered in a stamped envelope to Stillwater, Oklahoma. In some I thank him for coming to me, for reminding me to survive, for caring for me when I cared little for myself. They are signed *Charlotte*, and *Annie*, and *Your Obsession*, and I cry as I read them, the image of him holding them too much to bear.

At the bottom of the pile, I find the last letter I wrote. The last one before he told me Stephanie was pregnant.

August 3, 2009

Dear Jason,

We did it.

Really, I did most of the work. You were pretty much a giant pain in the ass the whole time. In fact, if you weren't so unbelievable in bed, I would have unloaded you a long time ago.

We counted in years, then months, then weeks, and now we're down to a mere matter of days to be apart. I wouldn't have changed a minute of it. I'm not sure you'd agree, but every minute of the last two years have brought me to you. In a little over a week, I'll be with you forever—and I'll never look back.

I am who I am because of you. Remember that when I drive you crazy. I love you. When you look up at the moon tonight, know that soon we'll be seeing it together.

Love,
Annie

I bow my head and a tear falls onto the letter. I wipe it off, careful with the precious artifact Jason saved all these years.

You pulled me out of hell when my mom and dad died and now you expect me to pull myself out of this one. You would want me to fight. I swallow hard and sniff as tears streak down my face at the thought of him. *You said I was the strongest person you'd ever met.*

You made me invincible, like you.

I run my fingers over the letters on the paper and remember New York City and Rutgers and how strong I was. How strong I had to be to stand up to the great Jason Leer. I pull the letter to my chest and sob into my pillow.

BJ surprises me as he jumps on the bed and lies right in front of me, his head on Noble's pillow as if it's his own. I pet his head.

"You liked Jason, didn't you?" I ask BJ. I sit up and pull him into my lap as I survey the scattered letters on the bed and the necklace next to them. I gather them and put the rubber band around the stack, slipping the necklace in with them.

I cry with the letters in my arms, but it's not the dead sobs of the soulless; it's a good-bye.

* * *

I shower, aware of the shampoo in my hair and the razor on my leg. I acknowledge the difference between existing and living. Jason used to call it dead among the living.

I love you, Jason. I'm going to make it if it kills me, I think to myself. My stubbornness always amused him. Again, I cry in the shower. I am going to make it; it's just not going to be pretty. I laugh at myself and try to remember the last time I laughed. I can't recall, but I'm sure it was with Noble.

I wrap myself in my robe and feel the fabric around my neck. I watch in the mirror as I brush my hair. My presence, awareness of life, my only distraction. I brush my teeth and put lotion on my legs and elbows and check my watch. It's 4:30 p.m., July 9. Today is Noble's birthday.

I walk into our bedroom, in our house. What he must be thinking today, his birthday? When he left, his zombie wife didn't even know what day it was. He must be in misery. The navy blue walls of the room engulf me and the painting of the farm warms me. It's our home, my home.

I kneel next to my bed and rest my head on my hands, folded together. I take a deep breath and silence my mind. The power of prayer.

Dear Lord,

I surrender.

I give up control.

I don't know what I'm doing down here. If it's not about my mother and father, or about Jason, or Butch, or my husband... it must be about you. Please...

The silence lingers in my mind. I let the peace take over.

I am not alone. I am at peace.

* * *

I take a deep breath and open my eyes to Noble kneeling beside me, his eyes on me. He still loves me. Even after everything I've put him through, I can see by the look in his eyes my lovely Noble still cherishes me. I let the gratitude spread across my lips and smile at Noble in a way I haven't in weeks, maybe months.

I turn to him and take his face in my hands. Folded in prayer and now supporting Noble's beautiful face as I pull him to me and kiss him.

"Noble, I love you." Noble sits back and I climb on top of him, my legs wrapped around his waist. "And I know you're going to think I'm crazy, but I think God sent you to me. I'm supposed to spend my life with you." Noble leans in and kisses me gently. His lips remind me of joy, and the ocean, and sunshine, and for the first time in weeks I want something other than to die. I want my husband and I tell him with my body. I tighten my legs around Noble's waist. His hands pull my hair back and pull me toward him. They run down my legs and up my arms. Noble is touching me as if for the first time and I want him to.

I take off my robe and pull Noble's shirt over his head. I kiss his shoulder, his arm, and his neck. They intoxicate me. I pull Noble up and onto the bed. I undo his pants and pull them off. He lies before me, naked on our bed. My lovely Noble.

I lean down and kiss his ankle and his calf. I run my tongue up his thigh and take him in my mouth. Noble threads his fingers through my hair and I forget we've ever not belonged to each other.

I kiss his belly and his side. I take each of his nipples in my mouth and swirl them with my tongue until they're hard and alive, awakened with me. I listen to the sound of Noble's moan and feel the wetness between my legs.

When I find Noble's neck again, I climb on top of him and take him in. As I rise, Noble grabs my arms and holds me at eye level. He deep blue eyes overflow with desire and love.

"I love you, Charlotte," he says, and it's the first time I've heard it. The very first time there's no other noise to drown it out. I hold Noble's hands for leverage and ride him, watching him the whole time. I can't take my eyes off his face. My beautiful Noble, always with me.

I lean over him, never breaking my rhythm, and open my mouth to tell him I'm about to come, but the wicked look on his face tells me he already knows. He moves his hands to my bottom and pushes me down to a rhythm that sends us both over the edge, and…I breathe. I breathe in my husband and this new day.

I am thankful.

I lay my head on Noble's chest and listen to his racing heart. I'm sure it's different than all the other hearts in the world.

"Happy birthday, Noble." I kiss his chest.

"It's a great one," he says, and plays with my hair.

"I'm sorry I didn't get you a gift."

"You just did. You're all I'll ever want, Charlotte."

* * *

"Charlotte. Charlotte, wake up. You're having a bad dream," Noble says as he shakes me. I open my eyes and try to remember the dream before it seeps away. It disintegrates quickly.

"It was about that little bird that I left behind. That little blue bird," I say, but can't remember anymore. Noble wraps his arm around me and pulls me so my back is against his chest; he's encircling me, making me forget anything that could be wrong, at least while I'm awake. BJ's snoring on the floor, reminding me there's still good in this world. I kiss Noble's arm. He is the best of this world. I roll over and lay my head on my pillow as Noble opens his eyes in concern.

"Noble."

"Yes," he says, bracing himself.

"Thank you."

"For what?"

"For protecting what we are when I couldn't, when I didn't." Noble leans over me and kisses my forehead. "I'm still going to be sad, still fucked up for a long time," I say, not wanting Noble to think this whole nightmare is over in one prayer.

"I know, Charlotte. You may never be the same, but you'll always be mine. I never loved you because you were perfect. I loved you because you are you, your strong, hilarious, brilliant, beautiful self. You'll fight for us. You'll always fight for the ones you love," he says, and I promise myself to fight for Noble. "Never give up," he says, and it reminds me of a time Jason begged me to give in.

The moonlight shines just enough to make out the silhouette of Noble's head on his pillow. I kiss him one more time and close my eyes. I peacefully drift off to sleep. Is there anything better in this world than peace?

* * *

Noble and I make breakfast together. French toast. We wallow in our newfound light and quietly eat, stealing glances of each other to confirm last night really happened, that we might actually survive this nightmare.

Sean knocks on the back door as he walks in. He pulls Noble's boots out of a bag and sets them in the mudroom where Noble used to leave them whenever he came in.

"Hey," he says, and then freezes, confused by our breakfast spread. It's so normal, which is so abnormal for this farmhouse recently.

"Morning. Do you want some coffee? Hungry?" I ask, and Sean smiles sincerely.

"No." His face turns back to discomfort. "They arrested Stephanie Harding yesterday. She confessed to shooting Jason."

I try to understand his words. I am in shock. "How? When? I don't understand. I thought she loved him."

"Who knows? She's crazy, I guess. I heard she said he ruined her life."

Ruined her life. That's rich coming from her. Noble doesn't seem shocked at all. He sips his coffee almost pleased. He always sees things differently, better than I do.

"What about Jay, Jason Jr.?" I ask. Where is he if his father's dead and his mother's in prison?

"I guess he's with her family. I haven't heard anything about him." Sean's worry is lifted by the sight of Noble and me together, more together than we are apart. "Thanks for letting me borrow the boots," he says, and walks out the back door.

I examine Noble. Sean thought there was a chance Noble killed Jason. Did I think that, too? Could he? Would he? I never thought Stephanie could. I never thought anyone could kill him. It's impossible to know what a person is capable of.

"You okay?" Noble interrupts my thoughts.

"I will be."

"We're going to church tomorrow. Set your alarm because we're going to the early service. Too many ghosts at the late one."

"I don't know…" That church only reminds me of funerals. People taken too early.

"I do. It's as much for me as it is for you," he says, conjuring thoughts of what Noble's capable of again.

"What are your plans for today?" he asks.

"I'm going to the cemetery," I say before I realize I'm going. Noble's fear rains inside our kitchen. Our delicate beginning threatened by a visit to death's door. "I've got some good-byes to say."

"Do you want me to come with you?" he asks, and if there

was ever a doubt in my mind of his capacity to love me, it's erased.

"No. I'm going to be okay."

* * *

I filled my bag with blooms from the rose and hydrangea bushes in the yard. I also found a small American flag in the shed. BJ sneezes on the way to the cemetery and I apologize for all the crazy smells. I open the windows and we ride the rest of the way with them down.

"When was the last time I took you for a ride?" I ask BJ as I rub his ears with my right hand. He leans into it and looks at me with those sad eyes. "You've had a rough few months, too. We're going to make it," I say, and he tilts his head, listening.

I scatter the roses on my grandmother's grave. She lived a long life, especially compared to the others I'm here to visit. My parents' graves are next to each other and I pull the hydrangeas out of my bag and place them neatly at my mother's headstone. She wouldn't want them scattered. That's more my grandmother and me. My mother liked a little more order in things. I didn't bring anything for my father. I couldn't think of a thing he would want except for his family to be happy.

Butch's grave has the remnants of a patriotic flower arrangement in a holder near the headstone. I pull off the dead flowers and leave the greens. Marie's been here. I need to call her this week, make sure she's okay. I stick the flag into the dirt near the flowerpot. *Such a miserable bastard.*

"I hope you're giving 'em hell up there, Butch." I choke up a little on his name and glance back at BJ in the car. He's watching me from the passenger seat.

I move down the row to Jason's grave. It's next to his mother's and still unsettled next to the established graves surrounding it. I stare at the stone, reading every letter, every number engraved on it.

"Of all the things you have done to piss me off, this is the kicker." I kneel down in front of the headstone and run my fingers over the top of it. "You are so going to get it the next time I see you. I think I might tie you up." My eyes fill with tears. I might not be as ready for this as I thought. I pause and again study the stone.

"That Stephanie is something else. Really, great job picking that one." I take the garden shovel from my bag and search for a suitable spot to dig. "And you thought I would be the death of you," I add, and fight back the sorrow. I break through the ground and watch as the breeze bends the blades of grass surrounding me. I pause, realizing he's beneath me. *You're not, though.*

"I'm going to build a life with Noble. I tried to tell you I'm happy, that I love him. You never did listen." I take several shovelfuls of dirt and pour them to the side, leaving a hole about eight inches deep between me and his headstone. *There was a day when I would have used this little shovel to dig all the way to you and climbed in.*

"Are you with your mother? Did she pull some strings to get you in?" I ask, longing for him. I toss the shovel to the side. "Stupid cowboy. Why do you have to be so far away?"

The folded paper is tucked away in the side pocket of my bag. My eyes linger over the words one last time. The only note I read from him while we were apart.

nice bed

I refold it and place it in the hole. I force back the tears and cover it with dirt.

"You wouldn't want me weak…so I'm going to be strong." I stop crying and stare at Jason's headstone again. "Until I see you again." I kiss my fingers and run them across the letters of his name, knowing I can never stand and walk away.

BJ howls in the car.

"One foot in front of the other until you figure out something to live for," I remember Harlan saying. BJ howls again and I stand up. I turn and walk back to our car. When I get in the car, he jumps in my lap and smothers me with kisses. It reminds me of Jay giggling as BJ attacked him with his love.

I put the car in drive and head toward home.

When I get there, Noble is sorting through papers on the kitchen table. Relief covers his face as I walk through the back door.

"It's going to be okay," I say as BJ runs over and wags his tail at Noble's feet. That dog always did have great taste. He loved Butch when no one else would.

"What do you want to do about the house?" Noble asks, and I know he's talking about Butch's. I want to say, "Burn it down," but that seems a bit dramatic.

"It doesn't matter to me," I say instead, and Noble studies me. "Actually, would you mind if I asked Marie if she'd like to move in there?" The last I heard, she was staying at her sister's since Butch passed.

"Not at all. I love Marie," Noble says, and walks over to hug me.

"If she declines, we can turn it into a giant dog house for BJ."

"Yes, we must continue to spoil this dog," he says, and we both look at BJ wagging his tail at our feet. I bury my face in Noble's chest and inhale him. *Thank you, God.*

~31~

A Tiny Spectacle

It's strange to walk to Fellowship Hall from our car instead of the sanctuary. This is Noble's deal, though. He wants to try the contemporary service. I want to try living. So here we are.

I slip my hand in Noble's and let him lead me past the greeters to seats on the aisle, in the back where Noble likes to be. We settle in about three rows from the last and stand as the hall fills with people. Extra chairs are brought in as contemporary music is played. Parishioners come in jeans, and shorts, and flip-flops, and carry their coffee with them. It's all bizarre, but I go with it. I'm overdressed in my sundress and wedges, but it felt good to dress up this morning, to care about something. I should have eaten, though. My stomach is churning. I lean onto Noble, my hand still in his, as the congregation sings the words projected from a PowerPoint slide onto a large screen at the front of the room.

The lyrics are about guilt and sin and looking to God to take them all away. I squeeze Noble's hand. It's hot in the hall and I shift from one foot to the other, seeking comfort. When the song ends, another begins and a new slide is flashed on the screen. There are two guitarists, a keyboardist, a full drum set, someone with a tambourine, and a few vocalists on the stage. This is very different from the 10:30, and I can immediately identify all the things my mother liked better about the traditional service.

My head hurts by the time the song ends. I just want to sit down. I think if I could sit, I would feel better, maybe less hot.

"Lord, we come to you with humble hearts, seeking forgiveness," the male vocalist prays into the microphone, and I lower my head, not quite prepared for prayer. I sway and grab the chair in front of me for support.

"Lord, we as—

The sound dies out.

My vision is closed by darkness.

"Charlotte…Charlotte, are you okay?" I open my eyes to Noble kneeling above me, my face in his hands. Beyond him is nothing but faces. Every person in this town looking down as I am lying on the church floor looking up. *Oh God, no.* "Charlotte, look at me," Noble says, and I focus on him again. He's terrified.

"Please tell me this is not really happening," I say, and Noble smiles, relieved I can hear him.

"I wish I could," he says, and sits me up. He pulls me in front of him to support my back with his body and I'm able to see all the concerned faces examining me. *Who the hell passes out in church?* Mrs. Johnson pushes through the crowd with a glass of water. Noble takes it and hands it to me. I just stare at it, not sure if my arm still works.

"Let's give her some space. Everybody move back, please," I hear

Pastor Johnson say, and I might try standing to kiss him. I roll my
eyes because I am inappropriate…in every way. Mrs. Johnson puts
her hand on Noble's shoulder.

"Take her back to the visiting room, Nick," she says, and Noble
stands and picks me up next to him.

"I can walk." I raise my hand to my head. It's pounding. It's probably going to explode from embarrassment.

I drink my water in the visiting room and Mrs. Johnson brings
me a donut from the kitchen. Noble's eyes never leave me as he takes
the cup from my hand and hands the donut to me.

"Are you feeling any better?" Mrs. Johnson asks as Dr. Grubb
walks in.

"I heard you took a spill," he says kindly. Yet another person I've
been through hell with. "Why don't you both come to my office and
I'll check you out," Dr. Grubb says to Noble.

"I don't want you to miss church." I take a bite of the donut. "I'm
a lot better already. It was hot in there." Noble's face turns to utter
concern again. I'm guessing it wasn't that hot.

Noble drives me to Dr. Grubb's office and runs around the car to
open the door for me.

"Do you want me to go in with you?"

"Of course. You're my husband. I'm sure this is nothing."

Dr. Grubb has me pee in a cup before escorting me to an exami-
nation room where Noble's waiting. When he comes in, he motions
for me to hop up on the bed. I do as I'm told and dutifully open my
mouth when asked, follow the light with my eyes, take deep breaths,
and sit still while Dr. Grubb calculates my heart rate. He is calm and
kind as he works, and Noble never, not once, takes his eyes off me.
Dr. Grubb wraps my arm in the blood pressure cuff and I feel ridicu-

lous. This really is nothing. There is not another bad thing that can happen to me. I've lived my share already.

"Tell me how you've been. How have you been feeling?" Dr. Grubb asks, and makes some notes on a piece of paper. He puts his fingers on my neck, massaging my glands, as I try to recall how I am.

"I'm tired a lot. At least I want to sleep a lot," I amend. "For a while I thought I was depressed. Actually, I was depressed." I look at Noble apologetically. He smiles, absolving me. "During that time, I wasn't interested in food. The thought of it made me sick, but I'm pretty hungry now."

I remember how out of breath I was yesterday carrying BJ up the stairs to bed and add, "I think my allergies are acting up, too, because I'm out of breath a lot and have a slight headache most days."

"Are you on any medications? An allergy pill?"

"No. No pills."

"Well, we won't know for sure until you get a blood test tomorrow, but I think you're pregnant."

Noble and I look at each other in shock.

"When was your last period?" Dr. Grubb asks, but I couldn't tell you what today is.

"You had it May twelfth," Noble says, surprising Dr. Grubb and me. "We had a picnic and Margo was in town. We went to the driving range the night before." I smile at the memory. He's right. I got my period the day of the picnic.

"And I haven't gotten it since," I say, still not comprehending.

"Well, then, you are about nine weeks along. Congratulations! You two are going to have a baby."

A baby...

~32~

It's Cosmic

The light blares of holiness behind them. My mother and Mrs. Leer are standing together, but I can't see their faces because of the light.

"Where's Butch?" I ask, but neither of them answers me. They keep walking toward me. Mrs. Leer's hands outstretched, the little blue bird resting in her palms. "Have you seen him?" I ask again, and both of them completely ignore me.

"Mom!" I yell. She looks from the bird to me. They lean over and I realize a little girl is standing next to me. She holds out her hands and Mrs. Leer puts the little bird in her hands. The girl stares up at me and the blue bird matches the color of her eyes.

"Mom," I say, ready to cry. I want her to speak. "Stop haunting me with this fucking bird."

***

I open my eyes and she's gone. I take a deep breath and look around my room. Noble is asleep next to me with the baby in his arms. Her face is turned to me and both of their mouths are curled into tiny smiles. *Thank you.*

I have so much to be grateful for.

They have made me stronger than I've ever been before. Every day she was in me was like having a powerful force growing inside of me, pulling me into the future. And finally, on February 11, 2013, Noble drove me through the snow to the hospital. My carefree Noble was a bit of a wreck. He didn't relax until Kathryn Grace Sinclair arrived and then he was completely captivated. She was the perfect Valentine's gift, pure love, for both of us to share.

Kate was a ball of fire the minute she took a breath of her own. We should have named her Patience so she'd at least have some. She's happy, and stubborn, and demanding, and beautiful, and Noble says she's exactly like her mother. She was born with light brown hair, which has darkened as it filled in. She has blue eyes the size of quarters that shine every minute she's awake. Some days they are ice blue and others they are deep, like the color of the ocean.

My mother and father departed too soon. They'll have to wait to meet Lily and Kate. Their absence was the only damper on Kate's arrival. No one should have to bring their baby home without their own mother there. Before Kate, I missed my mom, but now I long for her. For every doubt, every question reserved for my mother, I now depend on Michelle or Marie for answers. They're both good to me, but I still want my mom.

I couldn't have made it through the first few months without Marie. She's patient and kind and seems to know exactly what to say and when to say it. A few years with Butch would sharpen anyone's people skills. She moved into Butch's house and became one of the few people Noble and I trust with Kate.

The thought of Butch saddens me. I don't let myself think of the other one. Still. I wish Butch could have met Kate. He would be as enchanted as the rest of us. This little baby pulled so many of us from the darkness. She demanded us and we all happily surrendered to her. She wasn't a sweet, innocent child; she was a lifeline to the living and we all held on tight.

At three months, Kate rolled over. She rolled over and kept going until she was on the other side of the room. Noble videoed her as she did it. Once she discovered movement, she never stayed still. Noble didn't mind, though. Everything Kate did amazed him. He is totally and completely enchanted by his little girl.

I take one last look at the miracles lying next to me and thank God before falling asleep again.

* * *

Noble's off today and wants to spend every second of it with his two girls. Without plans, I revert back to my old self and suggest we head to the shore. It's beautiful out. I joke with Noble that he won't be able to drive and film Kate's first trip to the shore at the same time so maybe I should, but he only holds the door for me. I sit in the back with Kate, but since I can't keep my hands off Noble, I lean forward and play with his hair as he takes us to the ocean.

Kate falls asleep just as we cross the bridge over the back bay. She fought it the whole way. I think she sensed we were headed somewhere fun and refused to miss a second of it. I expect her to wake up when I unhook her car seat belt and lift her into my arms, but she just slumps down and continues to sleep. I follow Noble over the dune and stop at the first sight of water. I inhale the salt air deeply. It settles into the tiny corners of my being. It's been too long.

Noble passes me, carrying more gear than we've ever taken anywhere before. He opens a chair for me and helps me into it so as not to disturb Sleeping Beauty. I silently watch Noble work the umbrella pole into the ground. His shirt's off, his arms are flexed, and I feel like trying for another baby.

Noble catches me practically drooling and lowers his sunglasses at me. He opens the top and fits the umbrella into the pole and even that seems dirty in all the right ways. He unfolds his own chair, pulls the beach bag next to him, and puts the cooler under the umbrella. I pull Kate's hat out of the beach bag and place it over her head.

Aaah, we're settled.

"When did we start traveling with this much stuff?" I ask, remembering how we used to come to the shore with barely a towel.

"I wouldn't want it any other way," Noble says, and turns to me.

"Me neither."

"Do you miss work?" he asks, and I'm surprised it hasn't come up before. I look down at Kate in my arms. She makes it hard to miss anything. Her sweet face rests on my chest.

"No," I say, shaking my head.

"I'm glad you didn't go back."

"You are?" I was lost after Butch and Jason died; I thought I'd never do anything again. The weeks passed, and just when I was about to talk to Noble about going back, we found out about Kate. I just wanted to enjoy it, take a few months off to feel life again. Now that she's here, I can't imagine leaving her every day.

"Yes. But I'm selfish when it comes to you."

"Someday maybe." I'm finally coming to terms with the complete unpredictability of the future. Time is cosmic, I think, and Kate stirs in my arms and wakes up smiling.

Marie says it's unusual for babies to wake up as happy as Kate, that most are hungry, or wet, or not really ready to be awake. I think Kate is just happy to be up. I have this sense that she only sleeps to allow her to conquer the world when she's awake.

Kate leans her head back and pushes her body away from my chest. She's strong. She sees Noble next to us and screeches. Noble screeches back and I shake my head at both of them.

"Hey, Screechy Pants," he says, and leans in to kiss her. Kate screeches again. She is delighted with her daddy.

Noble takes her from my arms and turns her toward the ocean. Kate stops moving and just stares at the horizon. Noble and I watch her as she gazes into the distance.

"She loves the ocean, too," he says.

"Or she's terrified of it," I say, and watch her. "I don't even think she can see that far." Kate does seem affected by it, though. I hope she loves the water.

~33~

Raising Hell

At six months, Kate is already pulling herself up. Marie says she's going to walk early, possibly skip crawling altogether. Kate's impatient with her limited mobility. She's also impatient with smushed banana and pureed vegetables. She watches my sandwich as if she wants a bite. She nods toward it and I swear she could charm anyone out of anything. I pull off a tiny piece of the roll and hand it to her. Kate grabs it and shoves it in her mouth.

"You are a baby, right?" I ask, and Kate kicks her legs and bangs her cup on the tray of her high chair. I finish eating and glance out the window, waiting for Noble. It's 12:30. Now that Kate's with us, he tries to get home for lunch every day before her nap and I want her to finish lunch before he comes.

Kate grabs the last of her bananas and shoves them in her mouth as I wipe off the tray. She looks up at me with an ornery look in her eyes…her gray eyes.

Her gray eyes.

I drop the sponge and grab her chin, tilting her head toward the light. Her eyes sparkle defiantly at me. The same way her father's always did.

"No," I whisper, the words choking me. "No." Kate reaches out and touches me as the tears run down my face. *You are the devil like your father.* I shake my head at Kate smiling up at me. I love her as much as her father...more.

What have we done?

The depravity of Jason and me, of what we were together, is looking me straight in the eye and I love her. Maybe even more because she's my last link to him, but I can't reconcile what Noble will now forever know I'm capable of. I rest my head on the side of the high chair and sob.

"Charlotte? Charlotte, what's wrong?" Noble's voice cuts me. How can I face him? How can I expect him to ever look at me again?

"I have to tell you something," I say, and raise my head to face Noble, but his eyes are fixed on Kate's. Marie walks in and freezes, the deep tension like quicksand around her legs. I stare at Noble, staring at Kate, who plays with her cup, oblivious to any drama. She tires of it and throws it over the side of her high chair as she leans over to watch it bounce.

"Marie, can you take Kate to your house?" I ask, still not taking my eyes off Noble. Marie unbuckles the baby and carries her out the back door without ever saying a word to any of us.

"Noble, I have to tell you something."

"No," he says, and I shake my head. He's not going to let me off easy. I owe him the truth, from my mouth. "No. I have something to tell *you*," he says, and I'm confused. Noble walks toward me and takes my face in his hands. He kisses me softly and wipes the tears from my face with his thumbs, and he lowers his arms to the counter behind me.

"Charlotte, after Butch died, Stephanie came to see me." Her name, the thought of her near Noble, paralyzes me. "She told me she saw you and Jason at Stoners Lane the day Butch died."

My breath catches as I review every image of Stoners Lane from that day, none of them containing a hint of anyone's presence but Jason's and my own.

"She said you fucked him." Noble's words are harsh. I remain completely still, unable to react to what he has known for months. Noble leans into me, his arms at my sides barricading me. "But in my head I heard that Jason attacked you because, like Stephanie, I couldn't believe it was your choice, too."

How could Noble have known this whole time? How could he still love me?

The ominous stab of guilt rises in my chest and lands in my throat. I swallow hard, but the ugliness won't subside. My God, what has he been going through all this time? He knew at Butch's funeral. He knew when he walked in on me and Jason in our kitchen. He knew the day Kate was born. I am atrocious. I steady myself, preparing to hear he is leaving me. How could he not? I've lost them both.

"I texted him from your phone," Noble says, and my stomach begins to churn. Noble studies me as I try and keep up. He doesn't look like my lovely Noble; he's conflicted.

He takes a deep breath and fixes his eyes to mine. "I signed the text *Annie*," Noble says, and I realize I've never grasped my husband's duplicity. Noble can lie and keep secrets and still make love to me.

"Jason was ecstatic. He was hoping you would change your mind. He was surprised to hear from you."

For once he listened. He believed me when I told him we were through. I close my eyes, shut them tightly to hold back the tears. Noble was toying with him. It's cruel.

"I let him believe it was you, and I arranged to meet him in the woods behind the back field."

My glare freezes on Noble.

"What were you going to do?" I whisper. Noble stands six inches from me, but he's somewhere far away. Gone inside his own mind, searching for answers. "Noble?"

"I don't know." He shakes his head; his eyes are dim with doubt. "I thought I was going to tell him to leave. I wanted him to know exactly what he did to you that August. The way your collarbones jutted from your chest, how you wouldn't eat, wouldn't talk to anyone. I wanted him to hear how your laughter was silenced and know what the world was like without your smile."

"Oh, Noble," I say, and lift my hands to his face. He takes both in his and kisses my fingertips.

"But I think I was going to kill him." He's stone-faced before me. Frozen in guilt and horror. I shake my head, denying his own accusation. "I do, Charlotte. I wanted him to die. Stephanie just got there first."

I freeze, now realizing the source of his guilt. "She thought the text was from me," I say, and Noble nods, admitting to the events he set in motion.

"Oh, Noble," I say again, shaking my head. "You weren't going to kill Jason."

Noble's arms drop to his sides and he hides his eyes from me.

My tortured husband stands before me confessing a crime his heart would never allow him to commit. He's everything good in this world. Only Jason and I could come close to destroying that.

"Noble, look at me." His eyes are fixed on the ground. I take his face in my hands and raise them up. "Look at me." I brush my lips across his, willing him to hear my next words. "A crazy person killed Jason. A hundred texts wouldn't have caused his death. Stephanie killed him…not you." There's a slight shake of his head, still denying his innocence.

"When Butch was dying, I know you thought I was busy, that I didn't notice what was going on. But I watched the two of you together, I listened to you cry, and I heard the love in your voice when you spoke of him." Noble has spent months convincing himself he's a murderer.

"I loved Jason. I still love him." Noble lowers his eyes again and my heart practically breaks in two. I hold his face in my hands and force him to hear me. "But Jason and I were careening through life together trying to make sense without any faith outside of each other." The sight of Noble is almost too much. He has to believe me. He has to know.

"With Jason, I was lost. With you, I am found. I'm meant to be with you now. I'm supposed to spend the rest of my life with you. You are my best friend, and I love you more than anything in this world." The tears stream down my face.

Noble wipes the tears from my cheeks and grabs my hand. He holds it against his chest, and I feel his heartbeat through his shirt. He is my gentle giant, incapable of the hatred he suggests.

"You could *never* do that."

"I love you, Charlotte. I won't ever lose you." He says it as an argument. It's his defense.

"Noble, you know who you are, and you know me. Better than I know myself, I think. We belong together." He's silent, searching his mind for absolution. When he looks at me, his eyes are deep pools of love, and my own guilt returns.

"About Kate…"

"I don't need you to tell me anything. I love you. And I love Kate. I may not be her father, but she's my daughter," he says, and I wrap my arms around his back and pull him to me.

"You are her father," I whisper in his ear and kiss his neck, and Noble holds me close. I rest my head against his shoulder and take a deep breath. There is nothing between us. Nothing will ever be between us again.

I could stay like this forever.

"I'm going to get her. It's time for her nap and I want her home with us." Noble kisses my lips and it reminds me of our wedding day. He steps back and a cool air surrounds me, replacing his warmth with the cruelty of Jason and I together. Noble walks out the door and I lower my face into my hands and sob.

I shouldn't have taken care of Butch.

I should have let Butch fall on the church lawn when I saw him struggling there years ago.

I should have taken Jason back when he begged me to. I should have forgiven him.

I should have listened to my mother and never loved him in the first place.

I walk out the back door, avoiding Noble and Kate's return. I walk away from the house and to the fields. The heavy August wind blows my hair off my face as the sun's strength bears down on me and the soybeans waiting to be harvested. The plants sway, brushing against my legs, as the wind dances across the tops of them. I stand on the edge of God's grace, a perfect crop growing at my feet, and the melody of "In the Garden" fills my ears. I want my mother. She would never have allowed any of this to happen if she was with us. I never knew sadness until I was forced into a world without her.

The song's words pierce my thoughts and I remember standing next to my mother in the sanctuary as we sang this hymn, her voice more audible than my own. I listen as the entire hymn plays in my mind.

If He walks with me, how can He stand this trek? Is someone going to try and tell me this was part of a master plan? I take a deep breath, lost again. I close my eyes and pray.

Dear Lord,

I know it's not for me to understand, but why in a million years would this happen? Why? Thank you for Kate, and Marie, and Sean, and Michelle, and Lily, and BJ . . . and thank you for Noble, but why?

What the fuck are you doing up there?

I open my eyes and search for the wind. The plants are still. The air is resting; the tide is turning.

What have we done? Noble is one of the finest people I know and we had him thinking about killing someone. Is there a person alive immune to the destruction of Annie and Jason?

My God, Noble. Jason and I deserved each other. Noble didn't deserve any of this.

"Charlotte," Noble says as he wraps his arms around my shoulders and supports me from behind. I lean against him, always so sure he's there. "Sometimes, when I see you praying, I pray for this conversation. It's too much to be kept between us." He holds me tight, my arms wrapped around his.

"I love you, Noble."

"I know you do."

~34~

Counting My Blessings

So you were right about Noble," I say, and sit down on the grass next to Jason's headstone. "He is apparently not perfect." I sigh and look up at the sky. It's completely gray, with black clouds rolling in from the west. It's probably already raining over the river.

"Or maybe you were wrong. You were wrong about so many things." The silence is draining. I always wished he was more agreeable... "Or maybe Noble was perfect, and we ruined him. After all, I've never known two bigger assholes than us. What do you think?" I ask the grave stone, wishing it could answer. "It's kind of crazy, in your short life, I know of three people who wanted to kill you." Apparently one of them was capable of it.

"Kate's yours."

I hear the thunder in the distance and the wind picks up.

"But you already know that. You know everything, at least everything there is about me. You really are an ass, you know? A fertile one"—I shrug—"but still an ass." I lay the flowers down by the headstone. "Two illegitimate children. No wonder my mother wanted me to stay away from you," I say, and warm at the mention of my mother and Jason in the same sentence. "You're a Lothario. A total hussy." Lightning strikes. I get up and run to my car, not wanting to be struck dead near Jason's grave. Oh how fitting for the two of us, but not for Noble. I close the door as the rain comes and BJ climbs into my lap.

"I need you to sit in your seat," I say, and move him over. We drive home through the rain and park in the L-shed. We wait until the worst of it has passed, and BJ and I go to Marie's to get Kate. I hold her a little tighter as we all walk home to Noble.

He smiles when we walk in and it's the same smile I remember from third grade, and high school graduation, and the formals at Rutgers, and our wedding day. Thank you, God, for Noble Sinclair.

He takes Kate from my arms and showers her with the overflowing warmth of Noble. How will she ever leave this house if he keeps this up? We are the luckiest girls in the entire world. How did we ever end up with the love of Noble Sinclair?

* * *

Noble and I take Kate to the county fair. Instead of using the stroller, Noble insists on carrying her the entire time. I'm fine with it. I could watch his arms flex for the rest of my life, but she's going to be the most spoiled child in the entire county. Noble and Marie don't seem concerned at all.

We stop at the pig races and watch as one named SpongeBob comes in first place. I hold Kate while Noble wins the skillet-throwing contest, and we get her a balloon to celebrate. As we walk past the pony rides, Kate leans toward them and screeches. Noble and I stop walking and just look at each other. Kate is not appeased as Noble talks to her and tries to keep walking. In the end, he takes her on a pony. He walks next to her, holding her as she rides. She beams as if she was born to be on top of it. Noble and I make eye contact and he shakes his head kindly.

God help me, I cannot raise Jason Leer. I barely survived loving him.

Kate is delighted with the ponies and screams until Noble takes her one more time. As they go around in a circle, Mrs. Battaglia stands next to me at the fence.

"She's a beautiful little girl, Charlotte."

"Thank you." I beam proudly at Kate and Noble.

"It's her eyes. They're so unique, almost gray."

"I know. They're atmospheric," I say, and we both wave at Kate and Noble as they go by.

"You're a lucky girl."

"Yes, incredibly blessed." I leave to meet Noble and Kate at the entrance of the pony rides. Kate is sad to leave, but abides. We walk to the front lawn and lay out our blanket. I sit between Noble's legs, leaning back on him, Kate asleep on my chest. She sleeps right through the fireworks, undisturbed by the world. It is, after all, her world; we're just living in it.

As we're walking to the car, Stephanie's sister and her two sons cross the parking and I need to know where Jay is. I've tried not to wonder. It's none of my business, but not a day goes by that I don't hope he's well. I would love for him to meet Kate someday. They are, after all, brother and sister, but something tells me the Hardings are not going to be as excited about the idea.

* * *

Noble reads to Kate and puts her to bed. I take a shower and collapse on my pillow. Apparently the fair wore out both the Sinclair girls because I do not hear a peep from Kate. When Noble comes in, I cuddle in his arms and drift off to sleep.

* * *

My mother and Mrs. Leer are on Kate's sides as they sit in the yard. Their blanket is the one we took to the fair, and the three of them are looking at something. When I get closer, I can see them. Kate has to be six or seven. She's such a big girl, sitting here with her grandmothers.

The little bird catches my eye and ruins my mood. I want to pick Kate up and carry her home. I'm tired of this conversation, or lack of conversation, about the bird. It's tragic. Life goes on, though. No one knows that better than me and I don't want Kate bothered by this.

I glare at my mother as Kate picks up the bird. She holds it to her face and kisses the side of the bird. This is cruel.

My mother takes it from Kate and stands up in front of me. She is beautiful, smiling at me. The sight of her makes me want to cry.

"Say something, Mom," I say, my voice cracking a little. "Say something." My mother takes my hand and opens my palm. She places the blue bird in my hand and wraps the other around it.

"Charlotte, it's a blue jay," she says, and nods. It's a blue jay…

* * *

It's Jay.

My eyes fly open and I turn to Noble. I shake him awake.

"Noble. Noble, wake up."

"What's wrong?" he asks before his eyes fully open. "Are you okay? Kate?"

"We're fine. Noble, the little blue bird in my dream, it's Jay." Noble sits up and looks at me. He doesn't say a word, and his silence solidifies my thoughts. "I need to find Jay. I need to make sure he's all right."

My God, I'm sure of it. The little bird in my dreams is Jay. Where is he? My mind is chasing every thought I've had of him. Every piece of information I have about the Hardings. Why is he never at church? Where is he spending his days? He's…how old is he now? He's three years older than Kate. He must be three and a half. He should be in nursery school, going to music class, something. Kate has every adult within a fifty-foot radius of her making her life a fairy tale. What does Jay have?

Noble pulls me toward him and we lie back down.

"I'll help you however I can," he says, and falls back to sleep.

I can't sleep, though. I have to find Jason Jr.

~35~

Bird Watching

I have no clue where to start. I thought about hiring a private investigator, but nonlocals stick out around here. I may as well knock on the door myself, which I haven't ruled out yet. Even a car parked along the road where it shouldn't be will be noticed. No matter where I'm driving, I go past the Hardings. I could be headed ten miles in the opposite direction and I still circle back, hoping to catch a glimpse of Jay outside. He should be running around, catching bugs. He loves it outside.

I never see him, though. I've gone by at every hour of the day and I've never seen a soul outside the Hardings' house. How can they stay inside all day? Mr. Harding is on disability. Mrs. Harding retired from the school board office last year. I've never thought of them as horrible people but their daughter is clearly crazy. The apple doesn't fall far.

I wish Jason were here. Of course, if he were here, Jay wouldn't be left in there in the first place.

I pick up the phone and dial the church office. If I remember correctly, Mrs. Johnson works there every morning until noon.

"Good morning, Salem County Presbyterian."

"Hi. Mrs. Johnson?"

"Yes."

"This is Charlotte Sinclair."

"Oh, hello, Charlotte. How are you? And how's that little blessing Kate doing?"

"We're all fine. I was hoping you could help me with some information."

"Really," she says. Mrs. Johnson must have almost as much information as Ms. Cioffi, the lady who owns the town's flower shop.

"Do you know if the Hardings bring Jason Jr., Stephanie's son"—I choke a little bit on the words—"to church or Sunday school?" I pause, worried I'm overstepping my bounds, actually knowing I'm overstepping.

"No. As a matter of fact, we haven't seen any of the Hardings in a long time. Does the baby still live with them?"

"He's not a baby anymore. He's about the same age as Lily. I think he's about three and a half now." I pause, not sure which direction to turn in next. "Well, thanks for the information."

"No. Thank you. We're just about to send out our Fall Kickoff information and I am going to make sure the Hardings receive the mailing, including information on Sunday school."

"Great," I say, and hang up with Mrs. Johnson.

* * *

Michelle brings Lily over to see Kate and I use the time to pump her for any information she's heard.

"It's weird, but I haven't heard a word about him since the arrest," she says as I clean up toys in the wake of the girls.

"Weird or sinister?" Michelle raises her eyebrows at my question. "Do you ever see him at any three-year-old parties? Any play dates? Anywhere?" I ask, sure I'm sounding a little hysterical.

"No, Charlotte." She peers at me, trying to decipher the extent of my craziness. "Are you sure you're keeping a proper distance from this?"

"Oh yes. Improper would be when I pretended to enroll Kate in day care last week and visited the two day cares in town looking for him." Michelle's mouth drops open. "What? I need to know where he is and that he's healthy and happy. A little boy shouldn't just disappear off the face of the Earth." I stop cleaning up the toys and sit down, exhausted by my failure in finding one ounce of information about Jason Jr.

Michelle leaves and I throw Kate in the car to go see Clint. He's cleaning the air ducts at my parents' house. He was a great choice to live here.

"Hey, Mama, and hey, my little Katie Q. How's it going?" Clint asks as he gets up to his feet and takes Kate out of my arms. He makes all kinds of strange faces at her and she rewards him with her signature giggle. Clint switches her to his hip and gives her a few nails to play with. I shake my head no and he takes them back and replaces them with the box of tissues from the counter.

"Clint, have you heard about or seen Jason's son since Stephanie was arrested?" I get right to the point. I'm desperate.

"As a matter of fact, I haven't. I completely forgot about him. Where's he livin' now?"

"The last I heard he was at the Hardings', but there's been no sign of him. At least not one I can find." Clint swings Kate through his legs and brings her up to eye level again to her absolute delight. "Are you working now?"

"No. I've been off a week and I'm going absolutely bananas. Thank God I have such a great landlord."

"Do you want to pick up some extra money?" I ask as an idea begins to form in my head.

"Always looking to pick up extra money. Are you soliciting me?" Clint bounces his eyebrows. "What? You and Sinclair have been married a while now. Things are probably getting stale. I'll give you a discount," Clint says, chuckling through the whole last sentence.

"That's very generous of you, but we're not stale. I want you to watch the Harding house for any signs of life."

"What do you mean *watch*?"

"There's a deer stand in the woods behind the house. I want you to sit in it all day and see if Jay ever comes out of the house."

"You want me to spend an entire day in a deer stand?" Clint seems to be less enthused about the plan.

"I want you to spend several days."

"Right. Sure. Several days," Clint says as he walks around shrugging and making crazy faces at Kate. "I'll just camp out in a deer stand for a week."

"I'll pay you two hundred dollars a day."

"Just to sit there?" Clint yells at me.

"Yes. Will you do it?"

"Hell yeah, I'll do it."

"I'll pick you up at eight thirty tomorrow and drop you off on the side of the road. You can walk through the woods and watch the house. I'll pick you back up at the end of the day."

"What am I supposed to do for lunch?"

"Pack it. I would come eat with you, but if they see a car on the side of the road, they'll get suspicious."

"I think you're crazy."

"I know. I'll pick you up tomorrow morning," I say, and scoop up Kate.

* * *

Marie comes over for dinner and plays with Kate while I make a salad. Noble hustles in late from the fields and runs upstairs to shower. The hours are getting longer. Soon he'll be around much less than he is now and I'm going to miss him, but it's nothing compared to how much Kate is going to. She always beams the minute he walks through the door. He sneaks by her, knowing he'll never make it to the shower if she catches a glimpse of him.

We eat with Kate at the center of our attention. Marie sits next to her because the hours she spends with her almost every day are apparently not enough. I just watch how she captivates her audience and remember watching Jason walk through a crowd. You couldn't take your eyes off him either.

Marie begrudgingly leaves us after dinner. Noble walks her back to her house and carries her leftovers for her. When he comes back, he settles into a block-building extravaganza with Kate as I finish cleaning up the kitchen. *Cooking and cleaning*...Jason wouldn't recognize me now. I wouldn't trade this for anything or anyone in this world.

I dry my hands and return to the family room. Noble and Kate have taken over the floor in front of the hearth with their block village. Kate is banging two together, enjoying the cracking sound when they collide. She accidently hits Noble's tower and the blocks fall. Noble makes an exaggerated face at her and Kate's nose scrunches up in anger. She picks up a block and throws it at the wall. I close my eyes and shake my head. *Please God, let her soften.*

Noble lifts Kate over his head and zerberts her belly until she giggles and I can't take my eyes off them. Noble turns and studies me.

"What?" he asks me, lifting Kate again. I shake my head in silence. "Tell me right now or your belly is next."

"How is it so easy for you to love us? Kate and I?" I ask. To watch Noble, you'd never believe Jason was ever a part of our lives, that he is the father to this little girl in Noble's arms.

"I had a great teacher in the art of forgiveness."

I look at him, puzzled, as he puts Kate back on the floor to grab more blocks.

"I used to watch you with Jay—the living, breathing evidence of betrayal—and you showed me love. You didn't love that little boy because of Jason. You loved him in spite of Jason, in spite of what he'd done." Noble walks over, raises my chin with a finger, and kisses me. "You could love anything. I'm just following you, and I must say, it's glorious. Much better than bitterness." He kisses me again and Kate throws another block at the wall.

* * *

Clint's first day is uneventful. I drop him off before nine and he climbs into the deer stand with his cell phone, headphones, my camera with a zoom lens, and his lunch. I pick him back up at four and he reports there was no sign of Jay. Mrs. Harding apparently went to the grocery store, but no one else came or left the house. Clint seems completely bored until I hand him two hundred dollars in cash. Then he's excited to get to work tomorrow.

The next three days are some of the most beautiful of September and yet Clint still reports he's not seen Jay once. How is it even possible to keep a child indoors that long? He must not be there. They must have shipped him off to an aunt's house in Tennessee or something. There is no way he could still be in there. The sight of the house makes me sad. It's an old two-story farmhouse close to the road. There's a shed hooked to the back of it with a window boarded up. It's a dingy color, not quite white, not quite gray. A perfect shade of yuck and I need to know that Jay is not in there. The house is at the intersection of two roads with a large woods behind it. I park on the side road and have Clint walk through the trees to get to the car.

On the fourth day, I've all but given up hope. I wait with the car running, but Clint doesn't come out of the woods when he's supposed to. I text him, but he doesn't walk out and meet me at my car a few seconds after I stop, like usual. I don't like parking the car here. I dial Clint's number, but he doesn't answer.

I exit my car and close the door softly. It's quiet out here; every noise will echo. I walk through the woods with my bright pink tank top calling all attention to me. When I get to the deer stand, I climb the ladder and find Clint sleeping like a baby.

"Clint," I whisper. "Clint, wake up." I shake his arm and he finally stirs. "Come on. We gotta go," I say, and finally rouse him. He lifts his head and realizes where he is. "Be careful coming down. I don't want you to break your neck."

I climb down with Clint following me. He's groggy. How long has he been asleep up there? We get about halfway through the woods when I notice Clint has stopped.

"I forgot my bag," he says, and I look at his lunch bag in his hand. He gives me the "you know" face and I realize it's his bag of weed. Clint turns and walks back to the deer stand. When he's on his way back to me, I hear someone yell from the other side of the woods.

"Who's there?" The voice is gruff and loud and reserved to scare all intruders. Clint hauls it and I turn to run as well. I hear a shot fired and don't turn back around until I get to my car. Clint's running out of the woods when I climb in and start the Volvo. He barely has the door shut before I'm speeding away. We sit in silence and pant as we drive toward Clint's.

"It doesn't seem like that great of a plan anymore," I say.

"No?" Clint asks, his voice bloated with exaggeration. "What gave it away? The gunshot?"

"I'm sure it was just a warning shot."

"Is there any such thing in Salem County?" Clint asks, and I sigh. *Where the fuck is Jay Leer?*

* * *

I go to bed and resign myself to knocking on the Hardings' door in the morning. Apparently, there is no other way to find out what is going on. Maybe it won't be awful…horrendous…catastrophic. Maybe Jay is safe and sound and the Hardings are actually much kinder than they appear. This is yet another shitty plan.

* * *

I wake up and remember the one person who always knows what's going on.

I check the clock and ignore the fact that it's 7:30 a.m. I dial Margo and pray she answers.

"What's wrong?" she asks after answering on the second ring. My poor friends. Something is always wrong with Charlotte.

"I need a favor."

"Anything. But why do you need it before sunrise?"

"I need you to find out where Jason's son is," I say, and there's nothing but silence on the other end of the line.

"Oh." Margo says. She must think I'm as crazy as the rest of my support group. "Where is he living?"

"I thought with Stephanie's parents, but I haven't seen or heard a word of him. I asked Nadine and she has no idea. She said Janice doesn't like to discuss anything that has to do with Stephanie whenever she's in for her hair. I've asked at church. I've watched the house. He's not in any of the day cares, he never goes outside, and I don't think he has any friends—"

"Okay, okay, I'll see what I can find out. Does Nick know about this quest?"

"He knows. He knows everything now," I say, and Margo promises to get back to me as soon as she finds something.

It's a long day and a half before I hear from her, but Margo finally calls. I'm carrying Kate upstairs to bed when I hear Noble answer my cell phone. He follows me up and trades me my phone for Kate. The two of them seem happy with the new arrangement. I take my phone into the bedroom, hoping for good news.

"It's bad," she says, and my heart drops. I stay silent, unable to figure out what to say. "I had to promise my cousin I wouldn't tell anyone this, especially you. I don't know what you plan on doing with the information but try and keep my name out of it."

"I will and thank you. I know it's hard to go against family."

"Yeah, well, you're my family, too."

I warm at Margo's words, but I'm still half sick.

"They're very angry about Stephanie's arrest and conviction." No surprise there. "They absolutely hate Jason and blame him for her current situation. His son is a constant reminder of him. It doesn't help that he looks just like him," Margo says apologetically.

I swallow hard. Why can't he be at an aunt's in Tennessee?

"They never take him out, never play with him; he's barely bathed. Janice told my cousin that he doesn't even talk anymore. It's like he's not even there when she goes to the house. He's timid and jumpy around everyone."

"Have they ever hurt him?" I don't want to know. Utter rage creeps up my neck.

"I didn't have the heart to ask and my cousin didn't say."

"I've heard enough," I say, ready to drive to the Hardings' tonight.

"What are you going to do? It's not like you can call in the A-Team."

"I'm going to have to figure out a way they'll give him to me."

"Uhh…"

"What?" I ask, afraid of the answer.

"They hate you, too. I think the word *whore* might have come up. The Hardings think if it weren't for you, Stephanie and Jason would still be together."

"I didn't kill him," I spout.

"I know. Of course this is not your fault. Stephanie's their kid, though. Try and see it from their point of view."

"There is no point of view that justifies treating a little boy the way they are." I am completely disgusted and done with these people. They can rot in hell for all I care; I am getting Jay out of there. "Thanks for the information. I'll figure something out."

"I know you will. You always protect the ones you love."

Margo and I hang up and I remember the one time I didn't protect the one I love. I should have been protecting him from Jason and I didn't always do it. That's all different now.

I find Noble reading by the fire downstairs. I drop my phone on the coffee table and climb into his lap.

"I need to talk to you," I say.

"Great," he says, making fun of my ominous tone.

"If you want me to stop trying to help Jay, I will. You deserve a say in this. If there's a reason that I'm not seeing, something that could hurt you or our marriage, please tell me."

Noble kisses me and laughs, his lips still on mine.

"That's so cute," he says, mocking me.

"What?"

"The idea of you backing down or giving up. Really, Charlotte, it's adorable."

"I would," I say, and kiss him so he'll believe me.

"Well, in that case, no. There's no reason Jay should spend the rest of his life in hell. What has you so worried?" Noble asks, searching my face for answers. I look up into his beautifully warm, blue eyes and feel strength oozing from him.

"I'm about to open up the seventh circle of hell on the Hardings." Noble's eyebrows rise. "I suspect it's going to leave a mark."

"Give 'em hell, Charlotte." Noble pulls me to him and holds me tight.

They're going to wish hell is the worst of it if they've hurt that little boy.

~36~

I'm Really Not a Whore

I try on four dresses before I find one that might do the trick. It needs to say, "I'm really not a whore…obviously." It's embarrassing it took three to get here.

I settle on a black dress with three-quarter-length sleeves, a wide and high neckline, and a slight flare to the skirt that comes to my knees. It says, "What? This girl? Obviously not a whore." I find my grandmother's coral cameo in my mother's jewelry box and carefully pull it over my head. If she were alive, she'd want me to get Jay. She was generous. I straighten my dress in the mirror.

What do you think, Grandmom?

* * *

I park on Main Street and walk by Ms. Cioffi, Mrs. DuBois, and Mrs. Heitter. I flash them each my "I'm really not a whore" wave but keep walking, not wanting to talk or explain. The door to the office sticks and I practically fall into Mr. Chambers's familiar office. It consists of two rooms, the waiting room with a woman whose job description includes receptionist, assistant, and paralegal and his office behind a door to the left.

"Good morning, Charlotte," Mrs. Rogers says, obviously not thinking I'm a whore.

"Hi, Mrs. Rogers. How's it going?"

"Fine, and yourself? What brings you in today? Was everything all right with the wills and powers of attorney we did for you and Nick?"

"Oh yes. They're perfect. I have a new matter to discuss with Mr. Chambers." *As in, not with you.* I glue the smile on my face and Mrs. Rogers just stares at me, waiting for more information.

"Charlotte, good to see you," Mr. Chambers says as he takes my hand in both of his while he shakes it. "Come on back." He motions to the office.

"Mary, hold my calls."

I wave to Mrs. Rogers and walk into the room to the left of the reception. I sit in the same chair I sat in when Noble and I came to discuss setting up a trust for Kate in the event something happens to us. Sadly, it didn't seem that implausible, considering I have no parents. I hope I live forever with Kate.

Mr. Chambers sits behind his desk and pulls a legal-sized notepad out of the holder on the side of his desk. He searches his blotter for a pen and finally opens the drawer to his desk and takes one out. He's set.

"I need your help," I begin. "I'm concerned with the care Jay Leer, Jason and Stephanie Harding's son, is receiving."

"Wow. I haven't heard that name in over a year. To be honest, I forgot they had a son."

"Exactly, no one has heard a word about him. It's as if he's fallen off the face of the Earth."

"What kind of help are you looking for?" Mr. Chambers asks, still completely confused.

"I want custody of him." Now that I'm saying this out loud to someone other than Noble or Margo, it sounds ridiculous.

"Why?" Mr. Chambers is slow on the uptake.

"He's being mistreated by Stephanie's family. They blame Jason for Stephanie's incarceration and they're taking it out on that little boy."

"You have no standing as a family member."

"What if I'm raising the child's half sister? Would the courts want blood siblings to live together?" I ask, and recognize the detonation of my statement.

Mr. Chambers stares at me in silence. He turns his head a millimeter to the side, never releasing my eyes.

"Is that the case?" Mr. Chambers's words laboriously fight from his lips.

"Yes. Kate's father is Jason Leer." My heart pounds under my prim-and-proper dress. I clutch the cameo in my hand. I haven't spoken those words to another living soul. The only time I've admitted it was at the site of Jason's grave.

"Oh, Charlotte, does Nick know?"

"I wouldn't be here if Noble didn't know," I say as if I'm honorable.

"You know, there are limits to the name Noble?" Mr. Chambers says, and I know his comments are born of concern, not judgment.

"Yes. His limitations have recently become quite clear."

"Well. It seems like you two are making it work just fine." Mr.

Chambers takes some notes and focuses on the painting of George Washington's crossing of the Delaware River on the side wall. "I'll need to do some research, but I think the easiest thing to do is have Stephanie voluntarily surrender her parental rights followed by your immediate adoption of the child."

The thought of any woman signing over her parental rights makes me sick, even Stephanie. How did we all end up here?

"Do you believe it is Stephanie's wishes to have you and Nick raise the child?"

"I doubt it. Stephanie and I haven't spoken in years. I do think that if she knew what her son's life was like, she'd want something very different for him." I squeeze the cameo and take a deep breath. Maybe I should have let Noble come with me. "I'd like you to arrange a meeting so I can speak to her about it."

"You want to visit Stephanie Harding in prison?"

"If there's another way, I'll take it, but I don't think a letter or phone call will convince her." I'm guessing Mr. Chambers is wishing I never walked through the door today. "Will you help me?"

He sighs. "I'll contact her attorney to schedule a meeting and create the necessary documents. There's not much more I can do."

"I appreciate it. How long do you think it will take? The child is in misery."

"I'll call this afternoon and get back to you." I stand up to leave him to his work. "Charlotte, have you considered what you're going to do if she refuses?"

I lie awake every night thinking about it.

"I want the Hardings to feel as hellish as that little boy. I want you to bury them in legal proceedings. Children's Services, the tax office, disability, any and all legal remedies that I can seek for Jay Leer

I want explored. Bankrupt them if necessary. That child deserves a life." The wretched resolve in my voice wipes the warmth from Mr. Chambers's face. It's best he knows now what he's dealing with.

* * *

Some of the graves have mums, but most of them still have flags left over from the summer holidays. I sit down facing Jason's headstone and crisscross my legs. It's as if I'm sitting right on his chest, or as I like to call it, the sofa cushion.

"Kate is the absolute worst combination of the two of us," I start, and smile as I admit I might be raising a monster. I close my eyes and envision Jason with her. If he were alive, he and Kate would make me completely insane. Noble's influence might be the only thing that saves her.

"Jay's sweetness must have come from the Hardings," I say, and the memory stings. Of all the things Margo told me about Jay, the fact that he's no longer speaking is the most painful. I try to sugarcoat every other piece of information, but he was always saying something adorable.

"She opened the door and walked out of the house this morning. I was watching her when she reached up for the knob. She had to stand on her tiptoes. She's not even a year yet," I say, appalled. "You'll love this part. She turned and saw me, and I said, 'Don't you dare, Kathryn Grace!' She laughed and walked right out the door." *God help me.* This has to be payback from my mother.

"She's beautiful, though. Just like you." The words catch in my throat and I fight back the tears that always accompany me on these visits.

"And she's going to run this town." I know he wouldn't want her any other way. "I've never seen a child more alive and aware of her place on Earth. She's not even a year and she's completely unstoppable."

I look down at my legs and pull the grass from the ground around them. I throw the grass at the gravestone in disgust and fight back the anger as I cry. *Just love him.*

"I wish you were here. I don't know how that would work. Actually, I'm sure it wouldn't work at all, but I still want you here with us. I think Jason Jr. is going to be good for her. She'll love him and he'll show her how to be sweet. Maybe. Until I see you again…"

~37~

Common Ground

I would go and talk to her for you," Noble says, and rescues me from trying to figure out what to wear for my first trip to a women's penitentiary. Hopefully my last.

"But?" I ask, turning toward him. Noble climbs off the bed, taking both of my hands in his own and examining them as he runs his thumbs across my skin.

"But I suspect it's you Stephanie needs to make peace with. Giving Jay to *you* will be nearly impossible for her."

"Even if it's what's best for him?" I ask, hanging on to some shred of false hope I've been carrying around since I met with Mr. Chambers.

"She isn't exactly known for making good decisions," Noble says, and pulls me to him. He hugs me and I squeeze him tight.

I try and hug him this way at least once a day, terrified of the day when he'll no longer be here.

"Why aren't you dressed? It's getting late."

"I don't know what to wear." Noble looks at me, confused. "For women," I begin, not really knowing how to explain it. "What we wear makes a statement even if it's the wrong one. I don't want to appear too happy. I'm afraid Stephanie will hate me more. I also don't want to look like a wreck. I am asking her to give me her son." Noble ponders me, trying to decipher the unspoken code of accessories. "I want my outfit to say, 'I'm stable. I'm the best choice' without pissing her off."

"I suspect you lost out on not pissing her off a long time ago."

"Why, though? I didn't do a thing to that girl," I spout, letting anger from years ago spill out. "At least not until..." My words trail off. I guess the day of Butch's death is something to be angry about, but I wasn't doing it to her. Maybe the things she did were never about me.

"I know," Noble says, and hugs me again. "But for Stephanie to justify all the things she's done, she probably needs a reason and I think it's you. Everyone has to find a way to sleep at night, Charlotte." I lean my head on his chest. Going to see Stephanie is a stupid idea. "Just don't expect a warm welcome. I'm sure in her head you're the reason she's in there."

"She's never going to sign over custody, is she?" I ask, defeat weighing on my words.

Noble lifts my eyes to his with a finger under my chin. "You can do anything. Figure out a way to talk to her so she hears you."

"I hate her," I admit.

"Try something a little lighter," Noble says, and I drop my head to his chest again. "I'll be right here when you get home. If she won't sign, we'll figure something else out. Today is not the end."

"I love you," I say, and hold him tight.

"How could you not?"

Noble makes me laugh, even today.

* * *

Mr. Chambers picks me up at exactly nine. His Audi is dark blue, the color of a moonless midnight. The interior is sleek with tan leather seats, and as I place my bag on the floor by my feet, I realize Kate and BJ are destroying the Volvo. I'm glad he offered to drive. We head out of town and take the on-ramp to 295 North. The prison is in Clinton, about a two-hour drive from Salem County.

"What's it like? The prison, I mean. What is the Edna Mahan Correctional Facility like?" I swallow hard as I ask and realize I'm going to have to toughen up. I can't spend the entire visit crying or biting my lip.

"It's like a campus. There's grass and separate buildings. Some are housing and some are supporting structures. The buildings and grounds are picturesque; the entire campus, though, is surrounded by a high fence and barbed wire."

"Oh," I say, and realize in all of my preparation for this meeting I probably should have researched the actual facility.

"It's two compounds, one for minimum security and one for maximum and medium. Because of Stephanie's conviction, she is housed in the maximum side. There's also a compound for inmates with specific mental health needs."

That's where Stephanie belongs. Crazy bitch.

When we pass Trenton, I pull my folders out of my bag and begin reviewing all the documents I have printed out and labeled with my notes. A clean set for Stephanie to keep rests in my bag.

"What are you reading?" Mr. Chambers asks me kindly.

"I created a presentation of sorts for Stephanie. I researched all relevant information regarding children of the incarcerated and the pros and cons of kinship guardianship. It's a statistical-based account of why Jay is not being given the best opportunity." Mr. Chamber raises his eyebrows at me, impressed. "I also brought some pictures of Jay from the last summer I saw him. I thought she might like to have them." I stare at the pictures in my lap and it's Jason looking back at me, smiling that I'm on my way.

"I hate to be the one to tell you this, but since you are not Stephanie's attorney, your entry into the facility will be treated the same as every other visitor." I watch Mr. Chambers as he exits onto 31 North. I stay quiet, unclear on what his statement means. "You won't be able to take any of that in," he says, and my chest caves.

"What?"

How will I show her? "You'll need a photo ID to gain entry. Other than that, you may take one key into the facility. No purse, no cell phone, no money, no sunglasses, no pictures."

"Oh my God. Prison is horrible."

"And you're only going to be there an hour," Mr. Chambers says, and the pang of empathy I feel for Stephanie surprises me. I try to fit the emotion somewhere next to the bitter hatred I've shelved in her honor.

"How will I show her?" I say, desperately trying to organize the presentation in my head.

"You'll have to speak from the heart."

"There's nothing in there for her," I say, and realize she killed any chance when she killed Jason.

"Try and remember this is not about her," he says, and looks down at his directions. "Hopefully she'll realize the same."

Mr. Chambers is a good man. I watch the trees go by as we ride in silence. The leaves are beginning to turn the farther north we go. The holidays will be here soon. Who will they be worse for, Jay or his mother?

"What does she do all day?"

"Stephanie?"

"Yes. How does she spend her time?" I ask as we take the 78 West exit.

"Her attorney said she's involved in the Puppies Behind Bars program." I look at Mr. Chambers quizzically. "They raise service dogs."

"Oh. That's nice. I'll bet Stephanie likes dogs." I remember the sound of Jay's giggle when BJ used to lick his face.

"The inmates of Edna Mahan also sew the uniforms for the entire state prison system. She probably participates in that work as well."

Mr. Chambers takes Exit 15 and I miss the highway. We'll be there soon. Too soon. What if she says no? He turns right on Freedom Road. How poetic. We park outside the visitors' entrance. I pack all my belongings into my tote and place it in the trunk of the Audi. I brush some stray hairs off my face and straighten the buttons on my black hooded cardigan. It's long and I'm wearing it over a white tank top. No jewelry except my wedding band. I even asked Noble if he minded if I left my engagement ring at home. It's too beautiful. My hair is pulled back into a loose ponytail and the only makeup I have on is ChapStick.

Mr. Chambers looks at me encouragingly as we maneuver through the intake procedures. The guards are not pleasant or nasty; they are just doing their job, which is apparently to maintain security rather than put me at ease because the whole thing, from the color of the walls to the guns on their waist, is scaring the hell out of me.

We take our seats in a small room. My chair is uncomfortable, or maybe it's just me that's uncomfortable. Mr. Chambers hops up at the arrival of Stephanie's attorney. He shakes his hand warmly and they exchange pleasantries. They are peers.

"Charlotte, this is Craig Simmons. He's Stephanie's attorney."

Mr. Simmons takes my hand and smiles at me as he shakes it.

"Pleased to meet you," I eek out. Shouldn't he hate me, too? This is just a job to him as well. What a strange way to make a living. He turns his attention back to Mr. Chambers.

"I set the attorney meeting up and told Stephanie that Charlotte wants to discuss Jason Jr. with her, but I haven't had a chance to speak with her again since you and I talked. She doesn't know the details. I did at least have a chance to do some research on the surrendering of parental rights. If she considers it an option, I can explain everything to her in detail."

"What are your thoughts on her openness to the idea?" Mr. Chambers asks as we hear footsteps in the hallway.

Stephanie is escorted into the room and I can't take my eyes off of her. She is wearing her prison-issued khaki V-neck shirt and pants. They are both the exact same color—the color of nothing. She has a neon-green hair tie holding her ponytail back and I wonder if she likes neon green or if that was the only option.

Stephanie looks straight at me and I can't decipher her emotions. There's no hatred, which is what I expected to ooze from her, or maybe disgust. Either way, none of it's evident. Her attorney motions for us all to take a seat. I pull out my chair and wish Noble were here. He'd be better at this than me. He'd make her understand.

"Stephanie, do you know Paul Chambers?" her attorney asks.

"Yes. From church," she says, and Mr. Chambers shakes her hand.

"How are you, Stephanie? We miss you and your family at church," Mr. Chambers says.

Stephanie looks concerned and I suspect this is the first she's heard her family no longer attends church.

"And of course you know Charlotte," her attorney says, and I wish I could be as removed from this situation as he is. To him this is an introduction; to Stephanie and me it's an historic battle. One whose history sentenced Stephanie's future, and my own.

Stephanie nods and purses her lips. She folds her hands and sets them on top of the table in front of her. I see her unpainted nails and my eyes travel up her long khaki sleeve to her face. Everyone in the room seems to be waiting for me to say something and I lower my eyes in fear. *Don't look away*, I hear Jason say in my head, and I close my eyes and fight back tears. I can't do this.

My mind searches and lands on Jay and Jason playing in the moonlight when he released his cricket. Regret lies in my stomach like concrete, settling me to face Stephanie.

"I want to talk to you about Jay, Jason Jr." The words somehow come out of my mouth and I watch them register with Stephanie as if they were spoken by someone else.

"You have no right to talk to me about him," she says as if she barely cares about the topic. I take a deep breath. I am failing…everyone.

"Then let's talk about Jason." The men in the room simultaneously shift in their seats, the two women threatening the civility of their Tuesday. "Why did you kill him?"

The room is completely absent of sound as all eyes focus on Stephanie Harding. She is unmoved by the attention.

"I wanted to kill you," she says, and her attorney opens his mouth to interrupt. Stephanie rolls her eyes and silences him with her hand. "Do you have any idea what it's like?" She pauses, deciding how much to share. She leans onto the table and it's as if we are alone. "Spending every day of your life watching someone you love, love someone else?"

"Why didn't you kill me, then? Why him?" I ask, and the pain in my voice cracks it on the last word.

"Because the thought of him moping around, mourning you every single moment for the rest of our lives was too repulsive to consider."

"We weren't going to be together," I say, willing her to believe me. Why, though? Who the fuck cares at this point?

"Why did you text him? I saw your text asking to meet you in the woods, and I saw the way he skipped around after he read it. He was going to leave me forever."

"I didn't send the text," I say, and my chest releases its air. "Noble did," I add, and the attorneys swing their heads at me.

Stephanie is shocked.

He was skipping around because we both knew we would never be together. We had accepted it and were through talking about it. Until Noble sent that text from my phone.

"Why?" she asks, shaking her head, trying to fit together the pieces Noble and I never speak of.

"Because he couldn't stand to watch it any more than you could," I say, and it's as if the shocked attorneys are no longer with us. Stephanie lowers her eyes. "What did you expect would happen when you told him about Stoners Lane?"

I watch Stephanie rummage through her own head and for the first time since she entered the room her face displays an emotion, but I'm not sure which one it is.

"I wanted him for years. I loved him. At least I thought I loved him. Everything was him," she says, and I realize neither of us can say his name. There's more common ground here than should be. "I had no idea what I was getting into. I knew he still loved you the first night we were together, but he was so pissed off at you; I thought it might be the end."

"It was," I say, and stare at her.

"I tried everything to make him happy. I would have done anything for him, but it always came back to him gazing out the window, or up at the moon, or only half smiling at Jason Jr., and I always knew he was thinking about you."

Guilt swallows me for something I never did. I wish Stephanie and Noble had never met Jason and me. We could destroy anything. Noble and I nurture things; Jason and I demolish them.

"It drove me crazy. Like everybody else in here," she says, and I feel awful.

"I'm sorry all of this happened," I say, and mean it. All of it, starting with the death of my parents.

"Do you think he was a bad man?" she asks.

"I don't know," I say, realizing the jury is still out for me some days.

"All of this," she says, looking around the room, "was because of him."

Because of us, I think.

"I think he was a man without a mother, and at one time he was a boy without a mother," I say, and tears fill Stephanie's eyes, knowing history is alive. "And I think that's a painful existence."

Stephanie looks away and wipes a tear from her face.

"What about Jason Jr.?" she asks, and relief spreads through me.

"I think he's in the wrong place." I start out slow, searching for every word and not wanting to destroy the tiny momentum we have. "He's not in school and he's smart."

"My parents have him." My jaw clenches as I try to not roll my eyes.

"He never goes outside." Confusion settles on Stephanie's face. "Never. You know how much he loves it outside. Bug hunting, digging, running...never."

"What?"

"I'm sure there's an explanation, but for whatever reason Jay doesn't have much of a childhood with your parents. He doesn't talk anymore. Not a word. No friends, no pets, no play, no church. He's just existing there," I say, and watch Stephanie try to absorb my words. "No Daddy, no Mommy," I add, and she breaks into a sob.

"Call someone, call your sister if you don't believe me, but I wouldn't be here if it wasn't true."

"Why are you here? What do you want?" she asks through tears.

"I want you to give me custody of him," I say too fast. It flies from my mouth, having been solidified in my mind weeks ago.

Stephanie's head shakes back and forth slightly. If I wasn't completely fixated on her, I might not have even seen it.

"Noble and I can give him a life. He'll have a farm, and a dog, and parents who are there to help with his homework, and coach his baseball team, and bake cupcakes for his birthday at school. He is the sweetest child and he's trapped in a nightmare he didn't create." I pause, knowing it's a lot to consider. "I love him," I add carefully. "And he'd be with his sister."

Boom.

Stephanie's eyes dart to my own and I nod, admitting Kate is Jason's daughter. Mr. Chambers shifts in his chair and raises his hand to his mouth. He rubs his face, contemplating stepping into the conversation.

"I can send you pictures and letters. You could watch him grow up. Will you receive a picture of him in his Halloween costume? Will he even have one? Do you get a lot of information from your parents?" I ask, and by the expression on Stephanie's face, I already know the answers are no. What is there to take a picture of in his current life?

"I know what I'm asking is insane, but our past doesn't have to dictate his future. I know you love him more than anything, and when he was with you, he was the sweetest child I'd ever met."

Stephanie cries and I fear I've gone too far.

We've all gone too far.

"I have some information to review with Stephanie that she'll need to make a decision of this magnitude," her attorney says, and I swallow hard, never taking my eyes off her. "Leave the paperwork here and I'll call you after we've had a chance to talk."

I want her to interrupt, to say she'll sign right now, but she doesn't. Mr. Chambers stands and it's my cue to leave, but I can't take my eyes off Stephanie. All these years of hatred left in this room at the Edna Mahan Correctional Facility in Clinton, New Jersey.

My mouth forms into a small smile without my permission and Stephanie looks at me with understanding. I silently stand and turn my back on her and the attorneys as they wrap up their conversation. Mr. Chambers follows me out to the car and I collect my things out of the trunk. I take my seat next to him in the Audi.

We turn back onto Freedom Road and head home as I call Noble and tell him she's considering the proposal and we'll be back in about two hours.

"I'll be right here waiting," he says, and it reminds me of his pleas for me to get over Jason and move on after I first found out about Stephanie. Life keeps moving forward. I hang up with Noble and watch Mr. Chambers pull onto 295 South. He merges into the left lane and settles in for the longest part of the ride.

"How do you think that went?" I ask, not really wanting to know the answer.

"I don't know, Charlotte. It's a lot to ask," he says, and I realize it's crazy to have ever thought Stephanie would give Jay to me. "If nothing else, I think she realized what the child's life is like and hopefully she'll make some changes even if they don't involve you."

I'm not appeased. I should be. I should only want what's best for Jay, but I want him to be with me. Always. So. Selfish.

I look up at the clouds dotting the crystal-blue sky and think of Jason.

He loved me.

~38~

God's Grace

W hat was it like?" Noble asks as I sit on our bed and take off my boots. He's leaning on the dresser watching me, the look in his eyes pure love, just like every other day.

"It was dismal," I say, and just stare at him. It is a miracle he's still here with me. That our love wasn't part of the Jason and Annie carnage.

"What? Why are you looking at me like that?" Noble asks, and I walk to him. I lift my hands to his face and run my fingers through his hair. I lean up on my tiptoes and close my eyes and kiss him. I kiss him as if the police are coming to get him and my love is the only thing that's going to keep him here.

"I don't want you to ever leave me," I say, breathless.

I watch Noble's face as the truth in my words sinks in. I love him and I am right where I should be, and it is solely by the grace of God.

I turn Noble around and walk him backward to the bed. I pull his shirt over his head and pause to admire the view; his shoulders have always been my favorite part of him. I run my hands up his arms, pausing on his biceps, and brush across each shoulder before pulling his face to me again. This time the desperation is replaced by hunger and a heat rising inside of me as I unbutton my husband's jeans and lower his zipper.

Noble drops his pants, steps out of them, and sits on the bed in front of me. He's still almost at eye level with me and I lean into him and kiss his lips again. The sweetest, most adoring lips on the planet. He unbuttons my sweater and pulls my tank top over my head. I unhook my bra and let it fall to my wrists and to the floor.

"I love you," I say. "It doesn't seem like enough."

"It is." Noble returns his gaze to my chest. "Especially when you say it topless." He grabs my breast and pulls me to his mouth, sucking on my nipple.

"Aaah," I say as a searing pain shoots through me. Noble immediately lets go, concern overwhelming his desire. He examines both my breasts and holds them in his hands, as if he is measuring or comparing them.

"Charlotte, I think you're pregnant."

I hold my breath and repeat Noble's words in my head. *Pregnant?* As Noble lifts my breasts and caresses them, I realize, besides a rough night with Jason, they've never felt this sore before—that is, except when I was pregnant with Kate. He's right. I rack my brain, trying to remember my last period.

"When was your last period?" Noble asks, thinking the same thing.

"It was during the summer. I haven't had my period since August," I say, still going back through September, confirming to myself it's true.

Noble kisses me again, my breasts still in his hands.

"You're going to have my baby," he says, and beams from ear to ear. "We're going to have another baby."

* * *

BJ and I drive past the Hardings' on our way to Jason's grave. There's no sign of Jay and it makes my stomach churn. Or maybe that's the baby, Noble's baby. I keep trying to gauge whether he's more excited about this baby than he was when we found out about Kate, but that was a different time. Everything was different in the wake of Butch's and Jason's deaths.

As time keeps moving forward, so do we and we are in a stronger place than ever before. The perfect place for a baby, and Jason Jr., to join us. I stop the Volvo on the path closest to Jason's grave and give BJ a kiss. He cries and wags his tail, begging to come with me, and I search for signs prohibiting dogs in the cemetery.

"I don't think you're allowed to come," I say, and keep searching for a sign. I'm sure he's not allowed. BJ just looks at me, pleading with those big, round beagle eyes. "Okay, but do not dig anywhere," I say sternly, and BJ gets up and climbs into my lap. I hook his leash on his collar and we head out for a visit.

We stop at Butch's grave first and BJ tilts his head at me when I say, "Hey, Butch," to his headstone. I pet BJ behind the ears to put him at ease. At Jason's grave, I sit in the grass in front of his headstone and collect my thoughts. BJ sits next to me as if he has his own thoughts to collect.

I sigh.

"I'm pregnant." I know he already knows. "I'm going to have

Noble's baby. We're happy, and it's his, and that's how it is for normal people. I'm sorry you missed out on that."

I miss him.

"If you weren't such a whore…," I add, the tears welling up in my eyes. I pull my knees to my chest and rest my head in my arms on them.

When I look up, BJ has his leg cocked and is peeing on the corner of Jason's headstone.

"Okay, it's probably time to go," I say, and smile at the cutest little dog in the entire world that has always had great instincts about people. I run my hand across the letters on the headstone, willing myself to stand.

"I'll love you forever. Or at least until we're together. Then you'll probably make me hate you." I stand and BJ stands next to me, ready to return to the car.

"Until I see you again," I whisper, and walk away.

***

It's January. The holidays dragged by. It was as if time wouldn't pass. It's been months since Noble and I were fingerprinted for the adoption…twice. We filled out an endless amount of forms and we waited.

It was Kate's first Christmas and she approached it like she does everything else—ready to conquer. The Sinclairs were in town and they were completely enchanted with their newest grandchild. She grew more beautiful, more intelligent, and more stubborn each day. Noble was fast becoming the only person who could reason with her. She seemed to bend for me and Marie out of love, never born of defeat. Is it normal to enter the terrible twos at age one…month?

I continued to pray for her and for myself. Surely her teenage years will kill us both. I can hear Jason laughing from above and I hope my mother is in heaven making him as miserable as possible. He fucked with the wrong O'Brien with that one.

The clicking of the turn signal seems louder than usual as Noble turns onto our road. It's a drum roll announcing our arrival. I've never felt more blessed than on this drive home from the courthouse. Stephanie is a better person than I ever gave her credit for. It's my understanding that her parents practically cut her off when they found out she had relinquished her parental rights in order for us to adopt Jay.

I'm determined to fulfill my end of the agreement. I've already sent Stephanie letters describing his room and included a few pictures. One of which was BJ asleep on Jay's new bed. I'm not sure if she'll be allowed to keep the pictures, though.

We stop at the farm lane and wait for the train to pass.

"Look, Jay, the train. Do you remember it from when you used to help me take care of Pops?" Jay leans up in his seat and looks out the window at the passing train, but still doesn't say a word. I catch Noble's eyes in the rearview mirror. He's scared. Terrified of what we've taken on. The engineer waves and I wave back, as usual. Jay and Noble both watch me like I'm crazy, but I'm used to that.

Jay's feet dangle off the seat, his booster seat keeping them far from reaching the floor. His hair is too long, his face is dirty, and his pants are too short, but he's home now. I want to reach over and hold his hand, but everything I've read tells me to move slowly, not to bombard him. He's just a little boy and he's been through so much. His story makes my past sound like a carousel ride.

We pass Butch's house and Jay's eyes never leave the window.

"Do you remember Pop's house? It was a long time ago, but we used to play there. You helped Annie and your daddy take care of him. And Marie, do you remember Marie?"

Jay looks at me as if he does but still says nothing. I wait, holding my breath, for the words that never leave his mouth. Hatred for the Hardings wells up and I force it back down. I don't want Jay to sense anything but love.

Noble stops the Volvo near the house and BJ comes barreling out of the back door and hauls it to the car.

"Do you remember BJ?" I ask as BJ barks for us to open the door. "He definitely remembers you. He missed you." I open the door and let BJ jump in the backseat with us. He steps over me to get to Jay and licks his face. Jay giggles, and for an instant I think everything is going to be okay.

Noble pulls BJ out of the car and unbuckles Jay, smiling at him the whole time. Noble's smile could stop a war. He is warmth and home embodied and as unsure as I am of what I'm doing with this little boy, I know his life is going to be wonderful because he's lucky enough to live it with Noble Sinclair.

Noble sets Jay on the ground and BJ tries to knock him over with love again. Marie calls BJ into the house from the side door and we follow him in. Marie beams at Jason Jr. She missed him, too.

"Hi, Jay," she says, sounding every bit the grandmother. The thought of grandparents pushes the useless Hardings into my head again and I force them back out. "I sure did miss you."

Jay still says nothing. BJ is at his side and as Jay kneels down to pet him, I relax the slightest bit. Kate comes tumbling into the room, screeching her approval at our arrival, and runs to Noble. She climbs into his arms and is rewarded with a giant kiss and a toss into the air. She adores him until she sees Jay on the floor with BJ. Kate's eyes bulge and she demands to be put down.

She runs over to Jay and stands in front of him, appraising him from head to toe. Jay stands still, not sure what to make of her. Kate pulls her hands to her chest and smiles gleefully at him and in that moment, she reminds me of myself. Sometimes I forget she's half me. She wraps her arms around Jay's neck and hugs him and Noble takes a picture with his phone. Brother and sister united. Life is cosmic as Margo would say.

Kate leads the way as we take Jay up to his room. On the wall we had a mural painted of the woods with bugs, and birds, and small animals all throughout it. In the space next to the bed, BJ is painted on the wall and Jay walks over to that first. BJ joins him in gazing at the wall and Noble takes another picture. I motion at him to put his phone away and he takes my picture. I roll my eyes.

"This is your room, Jay. It will always be your room," I say, and sit on the bed. The quilt has a cowboy on a horse swinging a rope above his head. There's a plush blanket and flannel sheets on the bed. I hope he's as tactile as his sister because Kate loves to *feel* things.

Jay walks to the other side of the room, followed closely by BJ and Kate, and looks at all the pictures I printed out and hung on his bulletin board. There are two of him dying Easter eggs. One of which is him and his prized egg that has a *J* on it. There's one of him and Jason with a football, and one of him and Lily lying on the hammock out back.

"Do you remember Lily? She's your cousin and she's coming over tomorrow because she can't wait to play with you." Jay doesn't say a word. How long has it been since he's said something?

The adults swell, all crowded in this little boy's new bedroom, all hoping he'll love it here as much as we love him. It's too much to put on him. He should be carefree and searching for bugs. A year and a half since his father died, almost half his life. Out of all the tragedies associated with Jason Leer, the sight of this little boy right now is the worst.

"Who's hungry? I was just about to make lunch," Marie says, and Kate takes Jay's hand and pulls him out of his room.

"Be careful, Kate. Don't play on the steps," I say as I watch Marie lead both of them downstairs for lunch.

Noble puts his arms around me and I bury my face in his chest. *How are we going to do this?*

"It's going to be all right, Charlotte. He's going to be fine," he says, and raises my face to his. "You can do this. You can love him enough to make this work." He kisses me and I'm overflowing with doubt. "I've been amazed by you in the past. Today I'm sure of you and what you're capable of. Now go work your magic on him."

There is no magic, though. If there were, I would use it, but this is just going to take time. I've been seeing a child psychologist since we were told Jay would live with us. Jay will meet with her, too, now that he's here, but with only my account of what's happening, her primary concern was reactive attachment disorder, or an inability to establish healthy bonds with caregivers. If not treated, it could develop into a lifelong, debilitating condition that may affect all future relationships.

Regardless of any diagnosis or theories, the psychologist confirmed what I already knew. This child is in desperate need of a loving, stable, safe, and permanent home.

~39~

Karma

Jay's birthday is February first. It's been four years since I was standing in Butch's kitchen when he received the call announcing his birth. As I watch him lick the syrup off his fork, it's impossible to believe the news ever made me sick.

I fold the letter to Stephanie and finish addressing the envelope to the Edna Mahan Facility. In the body of the letter are two pictures: one of Jay sleeping in his bed with BJ curled up next to him and one of him bundled up in his snowsuit making a snow angel. I lick the tacky strip and sense some type of discord within me. I realize I'm jealous of Stephanie. She is a witness to the sweetness of Jay, pictures sent every few weeks depicting his happy existence. She doesn't have to hear his sobs in the middle of the night or his deafening silence throughout every waking hour. *Get a hold of yourself, Charlotte. You're now jealous of the incarcerated?*

BJ sits at the base of Jay's chair and it reminds me of the way he used to always be at Butch's feet. At the time, I thought it was to catch any morsels Butch was willing to share, but now I think he was protecting him, too. Protecting him from loneliness. What is he protecting Jay from? There's nothing here that could hurt him.

Kate throws her sippy cup and it hits Jay. This is her favorite mealtime entertainment. When Jay picks it up, his eyes dance with playful revenge. I shake my head, knowing he has a lot more of his father in him than just his appearance. That's okay. He's going to need it. Jay throws the cup back at Kate and it hits her in the eye. She rubs it and surveys her tray for something else to throw at him.

"Okay, you two. That's enough. We don't throw things at each other."

Noble comes into the room on the tail end of my latest pearl of wisdom I'm sharing with the two of them. He picks Kate's cup off the ground and I know he's considering throwing it at me.

"Noble," I say, accusing him. "You need to be a good example."

Both kids watch Noble with anticipation as he carries the cup to the sink. He buries his face in my neck, kissing me until I giggle. Jay and Kate laugh, too, and Kate bangs her tray, signifying she is through with her imprisonment. Noble ignores us all and continues to kiss me until I push him away. My neck still tingles from the touch of his lips and I peck him while I rub it.

I wipe off Kate's face and hands and release her. Jay walks to the sink and Noble helps him wash his sticky fingers. We bought a step stool to help him reach, but I'm still afraid he's going to mix up hot and cold. What he's learned in a few short weeks amazes me. We've been counting and doing our ABCs. Well, I've been counting and doing my ABCs; Jay has been watching me, but I think it's sinking in. I read him and Kate at least three stories every night, and when I'm tucking him in and we are lying in his comfy bed with BJ next to us, I read him one all his own. Jay loves books. If I'm able to step out of the sadness, I realize he loves just about everything.

I've been racking my brain on what to do for their birthdays. Kate would like an actual circus to pull up on the train and set up out back, I'm sure. Since Jay won't talk, I have little to go on for what he'd like. I wish Kate's had been first so Jay could see a birthday in action. I'm not sure if he's ever been to a party or had one in his honor. At least not one since he could remember.

I hate the Hardings.

After lunch, Kate goes down for a nap and Noble takes Jay out to run errands with him. He loves to travel with Noble because he likes to sit up front in his truck. I watch as they pull out of the L-shed and onto the lane. There goes Jason Leer's son with Noble Sinclair.

I finish wrapping Jay's presents and leave them in a pile on the dining room table. The enormous stuffed horse looks absurd wrapped in red plaid paper with a giant red bow on it. We also got him a battery-operated lantern for his room, a set of binoculars, and a fleece-lined hoodie with a big J on the back. It'll be interesting to see how Kate handles not being the center of attention tonight. I think having a sibling is imperative for her. Jay might save her from herself.

* * *

Michelle and Sean bring Lily over, and once Marie arrives it's time to start the party. Jay seems shy until Lily forces him to play with her. I'm thankful to have her. Next to BJ and me, she seems to be the person Jay wants to be with the most. She holds his hand as they walk to her art table and begin drawing. Where Kate drags him by the hand, he and Lily are peers, first friends. Noble catches my eye as he places Kate's pigtails in funny positions and makes her giggle. He was one of my first friends.

Noble looks up and warms me with his smile. Could he possibly know what I'm thinking? Noble has surprised me in the past, knowing and seeing more than I thought he did. He's a wise man. He reminds me of my father, who never seemed to be bogged down by the details but always knew what was going on with us.

We turn off the lights as Jay stands on his chair in front of his cupcake. My arm is around his waist as I count *one, two, three*, nodding each time for Jay. He nods along with me, and we all sing to him as he beams in the spotlight. When we're done singing, he's unsure of what's next.

"Close your eyes and make a wish, Jay. Something you want to come true," I say, and swallow hard, pushing tears from my eyes. I hold Jay tight as he closes his eyes. He opens them and looks directly at me. "Now blow out the candle."

Jay looks at his cupcake. I demonstrate blowing it out into the air and Jay turns and blows out his candle. Everyone claps and cheers and I catch Michelle's eye in the group. She is as repulsed as I am by a four-year-old's lack of experience with birthday wishes. She shakes her head.

"I don't know how you're doing this," Michelle says as she helps me clean the table. Sean, Noble, and Marie are manning the living room and putting together Jay's new toys as the kids furiously play with each one.

"I just wish he would talk to me," I say, and cry. *Why is it so important?*

"He will, but he doesn't need to. You and he know what the other needs. You two don't need to talk," she says, and I cry for the loss of the one person this was always true of.

"Oh great. Who made the pregnant girl cry?" Noble asks as he walks into the room and right to me. I'm in his arms before either of us has a chance to answer.

Michelle comes over and rubs my back. "He's going to be okay. He's come so far already."

I lean back and peer into the living room. Jay is sitting on the floor looking at Lily through his binoculars. BJ puts his nose right in front of the lens and Jay jumps in surprise. He giggles as BJ licks his face, finally absent of his new toy.

*　*　*

When I pull into the cemetery, BJ stands in the passenger seat and wags his tail.

"Why do you like coming here? You'd like going anywhere. It must be nice to be a dog," I say, and BJ just stares at me, tail still wagging.

I park on the side of the path and grab the shamrock flags from the backseat. As I open my door, BJ whimpers and jumps on my lap.

"You're not allowed," I say, and he keeps his snout pointed toward the door, not breaking eye contact with his breakaway.

"Okay, but you have to stay on a leash." Reaching down to the floor, I grab BJ's leash. I find the ring on his collar and hook it to him. I take one last look around, not wanting to run into anyone in charge of the cemetery's administration.

BJ and I place the flags on each of my parents' graves. They always made St. Patty's Day fun. *God, I wish you were here. Both of you. You would not believe what this life is turning out to be.*

I mosey past Butch's grave, and Mrs. Leer's. I stop at Jason's. I sit on the freezing ground; the cold seeps through the denim of my jeans. I stare mindlessly at his headstone. I've memorized it a hundred times over.

"Well, Jay is four and Kate is one…and you're gone." I will never accept it. Each day, his children's age marks another he's not here, but it will never sink in because he will always be with me.

BJ sniffs around the headstone. "BJ," I caution, and he eyes me as he cocks his leg and pees on the corner of the stone.

"BJ says hi." I roll my eyes and pull his leash. BJ cuddles in my lap. His work here is done.

"Jay won't speak to me. He won't speak to anyone. He's happy, though. At least during the day he's very happy. The nights are not quite as peaceful. He dreams a lot." If Jason were alive, he would blame this on me, but in Jay's case it has nothing to do with me. Maybe it's karma.

"I usually spend at least part of each night sleeping with him, and then I dream a lot," I say, and lower my head. "I dream of you." I fight back the tears. "But you're an asshole, so I usually wake up pissed off." I run my hand across the grass, wishing this asshole were here with me.

"I want you here with me…with us. Jay would talk to you. He would love you even more than I did. If that's possible." I close my eyes and swallow, and a chill runs down the front of my chest.

I sit in silence, staring at the memorized words of the headstone, until BJ stands on my lap and licks my face. It's time to go back. BJ knows it's time to go home.

Until I see you again.

* * *

We go to church every week and I pray, beg really, for Jay to be okay. I want him to be whole again, and I know I'm asking a lot, but I can't help myself. I am always so selfish when it comes to anything Jason Leer. I want him to run over and show me a bug he's found. I want him to giggle. I want him to love life. But more than anything, I want him to speak. His lack of words is a wall he's formed that I can't take down. He'll have to dismantle it himself, and every day I pray he speaks to me.

Jay wants no part of Sunday school. We drop off Kate in the day-care room and she immediately takes over, setting the tone for the party that's now going to be taking place in child care during the service. Jay sits on my lap every Sunday. I hold him and point to the screen with the song lyrics during the service. One Sunday I thought he was going to sing, but he closed his lips without a word.

During confession, I open my eyes and see Jay's eyes squeezed shut. What could he possibly have to confess? I shift in my seat. My eight-month-pregnant belly is difficult to sit with, especially with a four-year-old trying to cuddle there, too. Noble holds out both hands and Jay reaches up, wrapping his arms around Noble's neck as Noble pulls him onto his lap. He pulls Jay back to his chest and holds him tight.

I revolve the vision of them in my mind. Noble threads his fingers together and places them on Jay's lap, forming a safety belt around him. It may be the hormones, but in this very instant, Noble eclipses my father as the finest man I have ever known. I lower my head, the sight of them too much for me to contain my emotions.

"You are a mess," Noble leans over and whispers in my ear.

I put my arm on the back of his chair and lean over to kiss him. Jay looks down at me and smiles. I pull his face to me and kiss him, too.

* * *

When I tuck Jay in, I lie back in his bed and read him a story. This one is about a little boy who believed he could fly, even though he was afraid to jump. When I finish, I close the book and place it in the book rack next to the bed. I inhale deeply. It's becoming harder and harder to breathe.

Jay rolls toward me and places his hand on my belly. I watch him as he runs his hand over my basketball of a stomach from one side to the other. When he's done, he looks up at me.

"It's a baby in there," I say, and Jay pats his hand. "We don't know if it's going to be a girl like Kate and Lily or a boy like you." Jay's curiosity drains from his face, leaving fear in its place. His hand slinks from my belly and I catch it and hold it there.

"No matter whether it's a boy or a girl, you are going to be its big brother. You and Kate will have to take care of this little one. You'll have to teach it everything you know. He, or she, is going to be the newest member of our—Jay and Annie's—family."

Jay's concern is replaced by peace as BJ squirms up between us, his head in Jay's armpit. I shake my head. This dog is too much.

"I'm going to leave you guys to go to sleep," I say, and with great effort, sit up. I lean over, trying not to crush the two of them, and kiss Jay's forehead.

"I love you, Jay," I say as if my entire existence were designed to place me here at this moment. "I love you, too, BJ," I say, and kiss his forehead as well.

I labor out of the bed and turn off the ceiling light. I turn on Jay's night-light as I hear him switch on his lantern. I close the door all but a slit on my way back to Noble.

He helps me out of my maternity dress, or as I've been calling them lately my muumuus. I am a slow grazing cow, completely unable to do anything quickly. It won't be much longer, though. A few more weeks and Noble's and my child will join this mismatched clan. Life is insane.

Noble rubs my shoulders and kisses the back of my neck and the warmth of Noble spreads through me, quieting all my aches. He lays me down and makes love to me with the tenderness he reserves for me alone.

"Noble, I love you very much."

"I know you do, Charlotte," Noble says, and tightens his arms around me.

* * *

It's not until 3:00 a.m. that we hear Jay crying. I roll over in bed and place my hand to my forehead.

"I'll go," Noble says, and gets out of bed. He pulls on his pajama pants and a T-shirt and leaves me in bed to go lie with Jay.

Thank you for Noble Sinclair.

I wake up again around five and reach out for Noble. He never came back to bed. I pull my muumuu over my head and tiptoe into Kate's room. She is asleep in her crib with her stuffed rabbit in her arms. She's smiling, and she looks like me without those gray eyes shining.

I close her door softly and walk across the hall to Jay's room. I swing the door open a few inches and find the mountain of Noble asleep in Jay's bed. I walk to the bed. Noble, BJ, and Jay are all lying next to each other. Jay is awake and smiling up at me as I sneak in for a closer look at my three favorite guys. I wink at him and kiss his cheek.

"Go back to sleep. It's still early. Too early to be awake." Jay rolls over and slides under Noble's arm, and closes his eyes. *Good night, my loves.*

* * *

The sun is shining brightly as Jay buckles his seat belt and we pull out of the L-shed and down the lane. We wait for the train to pass and both Jay and I wave to the conductor. I have to remember to tell Stephanie about the train in my next letter. Why do I constantly justify him living with me?

The argument's been won. He's here. Home.

"We only have a few things to pick up. Bread, milk, yogurt for your crazy sister." Jay laughs at my depiction of Kate. "Do you want to count?" I ask, and Jay nods.

"One, two, three, four, five…" I say the numbers and Jay nods his head between each one.

We park at the grocery store and I let Jay pick a cart. He decides to push it rather than ride in it and I warn him that we have to be careful about running into people, especially me. He ran it over my heels a few weeks ago and I cursed so loud they could hear me in the meat department.

I show Jay the list as we go down the aisles and we match the words on the food to the words on the list. I know he's very smart. If he would just speak. I save Jay from running into several displays—I will never understand why they're in the middle of the aisles—and slow him down when he goes too fast. He pleasantly switches gears with each reminder. He's young, not mean.

I'm bent over, reading the labels on the milk gallons, when the cart lunges forward.

"Ow! Goddammit! What the hell?"

I look up to the beak face of Mrs. Harding as I straighten and pull Jay back to me, instinctively pushing him behind my thigh but never taking my hand off of him.

"I should have known," she spews.

My complete, infernal hatred for the Hardings that's been a part of my being since I first discovered Jay there wells up to my throat and I fight to not spit it on the matriarch of this hellish family. We stand in silence, glaring at each other as the shoppers around us stop and stare.

"You make me sick," she spits out, and Jay walks around to the front of me, shielding me from her venom. "Walking around town like you're doin' somebody a favor. Like some martyr."

I stay quiet. This is not the time or place. Jay should not hear any of this. What must he have heard living there? If this sets him back, I will kill her myself.

"Goin' to church every weekend." Mrs. Harding says it as if the sight of me in the house of the Lord grates on her every second of the week. "Holding your head high and the hand of that stupid husband of yours."

Don't fuck with Noble! I'm losing my patience with this witch.

"When we all know you're nothin' but a whore." She says each word slowly and practically spits *whore* in my face, and I have had enough.

"Oh yeah?"

She nods, affirming her argument.

"Well I'm the *whore* that's raising your grandson."

Jay and I stand firm, waiting for her to lash out. Mrs. Harding considers her response as the shoppers around us watch us forlornly.

"Hmmph," she moans, and turns to walk away.

Jay pushes our cart and it rips into her heels again. I brace myself for the wrath.

"Disgusting little—"

"You get what you give. It's called karma, lady," I say, and take a deep breath as she leaves her cart by the milk and walks out of the store.

I bend down on one knee and look into the shining gray eyes of Jason Jr.

You've still got a little fight left in you.

"Are you okay, Jay?" I ask, and Jay nods and puts his arms around my neck to hug me. I rub his back, grateful he's not upset, and try to stand. Thirty-five weeks of pregnancy has me a little off center and I struggle to get back to my feet.

Clint comes running from the cereal aisle. "Don't get up, Charlotte," he yells. When he reaches me, he supports my arm as he helps lift my balloon ass to my feet.

"You should have hit her," he says.

I've never hit anyone in my life, I think. But I have. I hit Jason once. A long time ago in Texas. I don't ever want to feel that way again. I smile down at Jay and run my hand through his thick black hair.

"What's up, tough guy? You protecting your mama?" Clint asks Jay, and he looks at me. We haven't talked about my name or my relation to him.

"Thanks, Clint. We need to get home," I say, and sigh. Clint helps us check out and carries our two small bags and Jay to my car. After I climb in, Clint shuts my door and waves as we pull out of the parking lot. This town might be too small for Jason and me, at least for our scandal. The Hardings can't live forever, though. No one else seems to, why should they?

~40~

Defining Moments

This baby won't come out. I swear it's because it hears Kate screeching and running around the house and knows its only hope is to stay safely inside my womb. I'm scheduled to be induced next Tuesday, a full eight days after my due date. It's not soon enough. The summer heat is kicking in and only a few of my maternity clothes still fit. I am orca.

Noble brings home Jersey strawberries to cheer me. Kate, Jay, and I eat them until our fingers are stained red. Their sweet flavor improves my mood slightly. I can't sleep. I can't roll over. I can barely breathe. I'm trying to suffer in silence, but this really just sucks.

When I finally do go to bed, I am hot and wide awake. I listen to Noble as he sleeps next to me. We have made progress in this house. Jay sleeps through the night now with only his lantern and BJ to shelter him. Kate has slept through the night for a year. She has always appreciated a good night's sleep. I hope this new baby is the same. Names run through my head in the darkness. Noble's agreed to Noble if it's a boy. He isn't as big a fan of his name as I am, but I love it and I love him. I want our son to bear his name.

The girl name wasn't as easy. It took us forever to settle on Kate's. We didn't even choose it really; my grandmother did for my mother. Noble doesn't want Larissa after his mother and since Kate and Jay are both namesakes, I think we could use a little originality. In the end we decided to wait until we meet the baby to choose a name.

I have a name picked out, but I'm not telling him. I can tell whatever I suggest at this point he's going to nix. I am strategically waiting until he has the baby in his arms to bring it up. Sneak, I know.

When the rest of the house finally wakes, I get to work and forget about my aching body. We have a big breakfast before sending Noble out to the fields. Kate, Jay, and I play in the yard without our shoes on as we wave good-bye to Noble. We kick some balls back and forth and blow bubbles to Kate's delight as we drink in the warm sunshine. We frolic.

I grab juice boxes for the kids and when I turn around, Jay is facing Butch's house, Marie's now, and staring at it. Silently, as usual. Kate chases a butterfly. She tries to jump to reach it and always ends up on her bottom in the grass. She coos and calls, screeches, and even says the beginnings of a few words. And Jay says nothing.

I stand next to him, afraid I'll never get up if I bend down.

"Do you remember Pops, Jay? Do you remember who used to live there?"

Jay wraps his arms around my thigh and buries his face in my leg. *Say something, Jay.*

* * *

I ask Marie to come over and sit with Kate while she takes a nap. I tell Jay we're going to visit some old friends as he and BJ climb into the car. BJ rides in the back with Jay. I see where I stand with him. We ride, listening to music, the few miles across town to the cemetery. Jay stares out the window and I wonder whether he remembers this place from Butch's and Jason's funerals. Is that possible? It's been almost two years for both of them. He can't remember.

I park in my now-familiar spot on the path of the cemetery and grab the flags off the front seat. I open Jay's door and he climbs into my arms, but my belly is too big. I place him on the ground next to me. BJ wags his tail, waiting for his invitation.

"Not today, big guy." I'm already unsure of this visit. I don't need to test how scarring it is to watch your dog piss on your dad's grave. We'll save that for later. "Next time. You wait here. Protect the car." I close the door on BJ.

"This is a cemetery," I say, turning my attention to Jay as I hold his hand and walk through the graves. "For some people, when they die, their family picks a place to remember them forever. Each of the stones sticking up from the ground marks a loved one's place." Jay looks around the cemetery as we walk. He's not frightened. He's interested.

"When Pops died, there was a place chosen for him," I say, and start to regret this decision. "And when your daddy died, we picked out a spot for him, too. They're near each other." We reach the graves and I let go of Jay's hand.

"Sometimes, people bring things they remember would make their loved one happy. Pops was a soldier, and very patriotic, so we brought him these flags." Jay stays silent, as usual, but I can tell I haven't lost him yet. I hand him a flag to place near Butch's grave and demonstrate how to push it into the earth. Jay takes his from me and does the same.

"And for your daddy, I brought you because nothing ever made him happier than you did. He loved you very much," I say, and walk toward Jason's headstone still holding Jay's hand. We step over Mrs. Leer's grave but I don't introduce her to Jay. We'll save that for another day. I kneel down in front of Jason's and run my hand over the letters engraved in the stone. I say each one as I touch it.

"J-A-S-O-N, spells Jason. That was your daddy's name." Jay places his tiny finger on the etched letters and my stomach clenches with disgust for Stephanie. How could she do this to her son?

"And sometimes we talk to our loved ones at these spots." Jay looks quizzically at me. "They never talk back; we just want them to hear us. But I think your daddy hears us wherever we are, even if we don't speak the words out loud."

I sit back, crisscross apple sauce, and Jay turns and sits exactly the same next to me.

"I just came to say hi," I say, and Jay seems to understand the person I'm speaking to is not with us. "And to tell you that I still love you and I miss you." The words usher in the tears and I let them fall down my cheeks. "I'm glad you're in heaven. I want you to be happy, especially if you're not going to be with us." I squeeze Jay's shoulders and kiss the top of his head.

"I brought Jay. He's big and strong and four years old now. I know you can see him up in heaven and you must be very proud because he's awesome. He's one of my most favorite people in the entire world. He and Kate are going to have a little brother or sister soon. I think it's going to be a brother, but Noble swears it's a girl," I say, and lower my head. My heart aches for him. Jay raises his arm and threads his hand in my hair. When I look up, he is smiling at me.

I run my hands over the letters of his headstone again and say good-bye the same way I always do.

"I'll love you until I see you again," and think to myself, *You are still an asshole, though. I just cleaned it up for Jay.*

I take a deep breath and exhale. For the first time, Jay's confused.

"I loved your daddy. Very much. And I will love him forever." Jay turns his attention to the headstone. "Confusing, huh? Apparently, we're all capable of loving more than one person. Some people say it's a tragedy, but Annie thinks it defines us." Jay reaches up and touches my face, still not completely at ease.

"I love Noble, too," I say, realizing he's worried. "You and I, and Kate, and this new baby are very lucky to have Noble. He's a great man." Jay relaxes and hugs me and for the first time I don't care if he speaks to me.

"Now, how are we going to get Annie back on her feet?" Jay should be worried. I shift to all fours and use Jason's headstone for leverage in standing. *Please, God, do not let me push this over.* Jay pulls my arm and somehow I'm vertical again.

"I want to show you something." I turn Jay away from the car and walk a few rows south. We stop in front of the graves of Kathryn and Jack O'Brien. "These are my parents' graves. Jack is my daddy and Kathryn is my mom." Jay looks up at me and back at the headstones. "You see, we have a lot in common. We both miss our parents." I pull Jay close and kiss his head. "But we have each other." Jay takes my hand and I know our time in the cemetery is done.

We walk hand in hand back to the Volvo, back to BJ. Jay accepts his kisses from BJ with his usual giggles. We weren't even gone a half hour and never left the dog's sight and he still acts as if we were lost for a month. I pull out of the cemetery and onto Route 40. When we get out of town, I peek into the rear seat. Jay stares out the window, thinking hard about something. I hope this visit wasn't a mistake.

"I love you, Jay," I say, the same way I have said it a thousand times since he's come to me. I turn my eyes to the road and settle back in my seat for the last few miles home.

"Love you, Annie."

It takes a few seconds for the words to register. That sweet little voice I haven't heard in years pierces me with love, and instead of thinking straight, I try not to burst. I pull the car over to the shoulder and turn to Jay.

I smile into the backseat and will myself not to cry.

"You and I have lost a lot. But we're together now for a reason, and that's how it's going to be. We're a family…forever," I say, beaming at Jay. He's smiling, too, and I think we might actually be okay. We're going to live. I pull back onto the road and stop at the train in front of our house. Jay unbuckles and moves his seat to be on the same side of the car as the train. He waves out the window to the engineer, who waves back. Jay stands up and leans into the front seat of the car.

"I know," he says, and I can't help myself. I start crying but keep the smile plastered on my face to not scare him.

"I love it when you talk to me, Jay," I say, and he beams proudly. The train moves and we drive down the lane and park in the L-shed.

We're home.

Epilogue

I wave to Jay and Kate as they ride around the arena. Jay gives me a subdued hello and Kate waves furiously, yelling *Mommy* at the top of her lungs. At six and three and a half, they are already more comfortable on a horse than most children twice their age.

"Your children are unbelievable. They were born to ride," a gentleman says as he leans on the fence next to me.

"Yes," I say, and nod at the two of them. "They get it honest. Their father was hell on a horse."

"And what about this little girl?" he says, and turns his attention to the stroller.

"This is Marisol," I say, and Marisol reaches out of the stroller and delivers a warm smile to the stranger. "She's about ready to get out there, too."

"What a pretty name."

"It's a combination of *mar y sol*, sea and sun," I say, remembering how easy it was to convince Noble of the name once he laid eyes on

Marisol. She was blond, with enormous blue eyes, and completely his.

"You're a busy mama," he says, noticing my belly.

"Yes." Instinctively, I hug my stomach. "And this is going to be Noble Jr. As long as I can convince his father of the name."

"I'm sure you can. You ladies have a way of making us see things the right way," he says, before turning to leave. "Keep these kids riding."

"I will. I doubt I'll have a choice."

"Bye," Marisol says, and waves to the stranger as he walks away. Noble pulls into the parking lot and hops out of his truck. Even today, after three children, a house, a farm, and me as a wife, he's still gorgeous. He smiles as he walks toward us, and Marisol and I are filled with the warmth that is Noble Sinclair.

"How are my girls?" he asks, unbuckling Marisol and pulling her up into his arms as he kisses me on the lips.

"Daddy, Daddy," Jay and Kate yell from the arena. Once Jay first spoke, he made up for lost time. He told us everything every day and Kate was thrilled to have someone to talk to. When he called Noble Daddy, we didn't stop him. In my heart, I don't think Jason would mind. He'd want Jay to have a father, especially one as extraordinary as Noble.

"These children are lucky to have you. How come you're so good to us?" I ask Noble.

"My father used to say, the best thing you can do for a child is treat their mother well," he says, and wraps his free arm around me. He pulls me close. "The rest I learned from you. How are you feeling?"

"Blessed."

Noble gazes at the sunset over the arena. He closes his eyes and takes a deep breath. When he exhales, he looks out to the horizon again.

"Life is all about the view," I say, taking it in as well.

"It's perfect."

"Be careful with perfect, Noble," I jibe. "It's brilliant at hiding its flaws."

"I never said flawless. I said perfect."

Please see the next page for an excerpt from the stunning first installment of the Lost Souls series, and find out how Charlotte, Jason, and Noble's story began…

Forgive Me

Available now

~ 1 ~

"My soul is forgotten, veiled by a boring complication"

My foot will bleed soon. Judging by the familiar curve in the road, I'm still at least two miles from home. Of course I end up walking home the night I'm wearing great shoes. The pain shoots through my heel as the clouds flash with lightning in the dark sky.

Maybe I'm bleeding already. I mentally review the last few hours. Anything to distract me from the agony of each step. The texts, the endless stream of drunken texts, run through my mind.

We're soul mates. I roll my eyes. Brian deserves a nicer girlfriend, someone sweet like him. Someone who doesn't roll their eyes at this statement.

We belong together. Bleh.

What does it say about my relationship when the only thing I ever tell people about my boyfriend is, "He's a really nice guy"? And how, after two years of being apart, did I ever take him back? The last three weeks have felt like years, years I was asleep.

We're perfect together. My mother thought we were perfect. Hell, this whole town thought it.

No one is ever going to know you the way I do. He was watching me as I read this one and I had to work hard to keep a straight face. At the time I wasn't sure why, but here on this deserted road, in the middle of a thunderstorm Brian would never walk through, I know it's because he never knew me at all. Or my soul. It's not his fault. I'd nearly forgotten it myself.

I stop to adjust the strap on my sandals and two sets of eyes peer out from the ditch next to the road. They're low to the ground, watching me. I've always hated nocturnal animals.

"Anyone else come out to play in the storm?" I say to the other hidden nightlife. I move to the edge of the shoulder, facing the nonexistent traffic, and give my new friends some room. I wince as I step forward and watch as a set of headlights shines on the road in front of me and the scene around me turns mystical. The steam rises off the pavement at least five feet high before disappearing into the blue-tinted night. The rain lasted only twenty spectacular minutes, not long enough to cool the scorched earth.

I'm lost in it as the truck pulls up beside me, now driving on the wrong side of the road, and Jason Leer rolls down his window. I glance at him and turn to stare straight ahead, trying not to let the excruciating torture of each step show on my face.

"Hi, Annie," he says, and immediately pisses me off. I might look sweet in my new rose-colored shorts romper, but these wedges have me ready to commit murder.

"My name is Charlotte," I say without looking at him, and keep walking. The strap is an ax cutting my heel from my foot. *Why won't he call me Charlotte?* Of course the cowboy would show up. What this night needs is a steer wrestler to confound me further. The same two desires he always evokes in me surface now. Wanting to punch him and wanting to climb on top of him.

"What the hell are you doing out here? Alone—" A guttural moan of thunder interrupts him, and I tilt my head to determine the origin, but it surrounds us. The clouds circle, blanketing us with darkness, but when the moon is visible, it's bright enough to see in this blue-gray night. We're in the eye of the storm and there will never be a night like this again. *God I love a storm.* The crackling of the truck's tires on the road reminds me of my cohort.

"I'm not alone. You're here, irritating me as usual." I will not look at him. I can feel his smartass grin without even seeing him, the same way I can feel a chill slip across my skin. It's hot as hell out and Jason Leer is giving me the chills.

Lightning strikes, reaching the ground in the field just to our left, and I stop walking to watch it. Every minute of today brought me here. The mind-numbing dinner date with Brian Matlin, the conversation on the way to Michelle's party about how we should see other people, the repeated and *annoying* texts declaring his love, and the eleven beers and four shots I watched Brian pour down his throat all brought me here.

"If you're trying to kill yourself by being struck by lightning, I could just hit you with my truck. It'll be faster," he says, stealing my eyes from the field. His arm rests out his truck window and it's enormous. He tilts his body toward the door and the width of his chest holds my gaze for a moment too long.

"Annie!"

I shake my head, freeing myself from him. "What? What do you want? I'm not afraid of a storm." I am, however, exhausted by this conversation.

I finally allow myself to look him in the eyes. They are dark tonight, like the slick, steamy road before me, and I shouldn't have looked.

"I want you." His voice is tranquil, as if he's talking a suicide jumper off a bridge. "I want you to get in the truck and I'll drive you home." Thunder growls in the distance and the lightning strikes to the left and right of the road at the same time. The storm surrounds us, but the rain was gone too soon, leaving us with the suffocating heat that set the road on fire.

I close my eyes as my sandal cuts deeper into my foot, and Jason finally pulls away. My grandmother always said the heat brings out the crazy in people. It was ninety-seven degrees at 7:00 p.m. The humidity was unbearable. Too hot to eat. Too hot to laugh. The only thing you could do was talk about how miserably hot it was outside. By the time Brian and I arrived, most of the party had already been in the lake at some point. Even that didn't look refreshing. The sky unleashed, and Michelle kicked everyone out rather than let them destroy her house.

I stop walking and shift my foot in the shoe. The strap is now sticking; I've probably already shed blood. Jason drives onto the right side of the road and stops the truck on the tiny shoulder. He turns on his hazard lights and gets out of the truck. *He's a hazard.* I plaster a smile on my face and begin walking again. As soon as he leaves, I'm taking off these shoes and throwing them in the pepper field next to me.

Before I endure two steps, he's in front of me. He's as fast as I remember. Like lightning: always picked first for kickball in elementary school. His hair is the same thick, jet-black as back then, too.

The moonlight shines off it and I wonder where his cowboy hat is. He's too beautiful to piss me off as much as he does. He blocks my path, a concrete wall, and I stop just inches from him.

"I'm going to ask you one more time to get in the truck." A lightning strike hits the road near his truck and without flinching he looks back at me, waiting for my answer.

"Or what?" I challenge him with my words and my "I dare you" look on my face. He hoists me over his shoulder and walks back to the truck as if I'm a sweatshirt he grabbed as an afterthought before walking out the door.

"Put me down! I'm not some steer you can toss around," I yell as I fist my hands and pound on his back. He's laughing and pissing me off even more. I pull his shirt up and start to reach for his underwear and Jason runs the last few steps to the truck.

"Do you ever behave?" he asks, and swings the truck door open. He drops me on the seat and leans in the truck between my legs. I push my hair out of my face, my chest still heaving with anger. "Why the hell are you walking alone on a country road, in a goddamned storm, this late at night?"

My stomach knots at his closeness and this angers me, too. Why can't Jason Leer bore me the way Brian Matlin does? Jason raises his eyebrows and tilts his head at the perfect angle to send a chill down my spine.

"Brian and I broke up tonight."

"And he made you walk home?" Shock is written all over his face. Brian would never make me walk home. He is the nicest of guys. Not great at holding his liquor, but nice.

"No." I roll my eyes, calling him an idiot, and he somehow leans in closer, making my stomach flip. "He proceeded to get drunk at

Michelle Farrell's party and I drove him home so he wouldn't die."
I think back to all the parties of the last six years, since Jason and I
entered high school. Besides graduation, we were rarely in the same
place. I've barely hung out with Jason Leer since eighth grade. At the
start of high school, everyone broke into groups, and this cowboy
wasn't in mine.

"Why didn't you call someone for a ride?" He breaks my revelry.

"Because apparently when Brian gets drunk, he texts a lot. My
battery died after the fiftieth message professing his love for me."

"Poor guy."

"Poor guy? What about me? I'm the one who had to delete them
and drive him home. I thought he'd never pass out." I'm still mourning the time I lost with Brian's drunken mess.

"Why didn't you just take his car?"

"Because I left him passed out in it in his parents' driveway. I got
him home safe, but I'm not going to carry him to bed."

At this Jason lowers his head and laughs. My irritation with him
twists into annoyance at myself for telling him anything. For telling
him everything. I want to punch him in his laughing mouth. His
lips are perfect, though.

"It's not easy to love you, Annie."

"Yeah, well, I've got fifty texts that claim otherwise. Judging from
the fact that you can't even get my name right, everything's probably
hard for you." Jason leans on the dash and his jeans scrape against
my maimed foot, causing my face to twist in pain. Before I can re-
gain my composure, his eyes are on me. He moves back and holds
my foot up near his face. He slips the strap off my heel and runs his
thumb across the now broken and purple blister. I close my eyes, the
sight of the wound amplifying the pain.

"My God, you are stubborn," he says, his eyes still on my foot. Thunder groans behind us and he straightens my leg, examining it in the glimmer of moonlight. I'm not angry anymore. One urge has silenced another and has awakened me in the process. He pulls my foot to him and kisses the inside of my ankle, and a chill runs from my leg to both breasts and settles in the back of my throat, stealing my breath.

I swallow hard. "Are all your first kisses on the inside of the ankle?" I ask. His hands grip my ankle harshly, but he's careful with my heel.

His eyes find mine as he drags his lips up my calf and kisses the inside of my knee. I shut up and shudder from a chill. There are no words. Only the beginning of a thought. *What if,* arises in my mind against the sound of the clicking of the hazard lights.

The lightning strikes again and unveils the darkness in his eyes. He lowers my leg and backs up, but I'm not ready to let him go. I grab his belt buckle and pull him toward me. Jason doesn't budge. He is an ox. His eyes bore into me and for a moment I think he hates me. He's holding a raging river behind a dam, and I'm recklessly breaching it.

With a hand gripping each shoulder, he forces me back to the seat and hovers over me. Even in the darkness I can see the emptiness in his eyes and I can't leave it alone. He kisses me. He kisses me as if he's done it a hundred times before, and when his lips touch mine some animalistic need growls inside of me. He's like nothing I've ever known, and my body craves a hundred things all at once, every one of them him. With his tongue in my mouth, I tighten my arms around his thick neck and pull him closer, wanting to climb inside of him.

Jason pulls away, devastating me, until I realize there are flashing lights behind us. His eyes fixed on mine, he takes my hands from behind his head and pulls me upright before the state trooper steps out of his car and walks to our side of the truck.

* * *

"Charlotte, honey, are you going to get up? I heard you come in late last night."

I roll over and put my head under the pillow. I don't want to get up. I don't want to tell my mom that I broke up with Brian...again.

"Is everything okay?"

She's worried. I take a deep breath and sit up in bed. The sheet rubs against my heel and the pain reminds me of Jason Leer.

"I broke up with Brian last night."

"Oh no. I have to see his mother at book club on Wednesday."

"I can't marry him just because you can't face his mother at book club."

"I'm not suggesting you marry him, just that you stop dating him if you're going to keep breaking his heart." My mom leaves my room. Her face is plagued with frustration mixed with disappointment.

I climb out of bed and lumber to the bathroom. My green eyes sparkle in the mirror, hinting at our indelicate secret from last night. I wink at myself as if something exciting is about to happen. My long blond hair barely looks slept on. I think breaking up with Brian was good for me.

* * *

"Jack, she broke up with Brian again." I catch this as I enter the kitchen.

"Through with him, huh?" My father never seems to have an opinion on who I date as long as they treat me well. Brian certainly did that.

"Dad, he just didn't do it for me." Jason's eyes pierce my thoughts again, haunting me. The trooper sent us home and I left him in his truck without a word. There wasn't one to say.

"Do what? What did you expect him to do for you?" my mother spouts. She's not taking the news well.

"When he looks at me a certain way, I want to get chills," I start, surprised by how easily my needs are verbalized. "When he leans into me, I want my stomach to flip, and when he walks away I want to care if he comes back." My parents both watch me silently as if I'm reciting a poem at the second-grade music program. They are pondering me.

"What? Don't your stomachs flip when you're together? Ever?"

"Does your stomach flip when you look at me, Jack?" she asks.

"Only if I eat chili the same day," my dad says, and they both start laughing.

"Charlotte, I remember what it was like to be young. And your father did make my stomach flip, but I think you're too hard on Brian. He's a nice boy."

"Yeah yeah. He's nice." I butter my toast and move to sit next to my father at the table. *He is nice.* For some reason Brian's kindness frustrates me. He's a boring complication. "I ran into Jason Leer last night." *And he kissed the inside of my leg.* I smile ruefully.

My mother's eyebrows rise and I fear I've divulged too much. My father never looks up from the newspaper.

"Butch and Joanie's son?"

"That's the one." I try to sound nonchalant as a tiny chill runs down my neck.

"I haven't seen him since Joanie's funeral. Poor boy. She was lovely. Do you remember her?"

I nod and take a bite of the toast. "From Sunday school."

"Jack, do you remember Joanie Leer? Died of cancer about a year ago."

"I remember," my dad says, and appears to be ignoring us, but I know he's not. He always hears everything.

"If you don't want to be with Brian, that's fine, but please not a rodeo cowboy," my mother pleads, not missing a thing.

"I only said I saw him. What's wrong with a rodeo cowboy?"

"Nothing. For someone else's daughter. I really want you to marry someone with a job. Someone who can take care of you."

"Can't a cowboy do that?" *From what I've seen, he can take very good care of me.*

"Charlotte, please tell me you're not serious. They're always on the road. Their income's not steady. It's a very difficult life." My mother's stern warning is delivered while she fills the dishwasher, as if we're discussing a fairy tale, a situation so absurd it barely warrants a discussion. She's still beautiful, even when she's lecturing me. "I know safe choices aren't attractive to the young, but believe me you do not belong in that world and he'd wither up and die in yours. Do not underestimate the power of safety in this crazy life."

"How do you know so much about rodeo cowboys?" I ask.

"Yeah, how do you know so much?" my dad asks. He stares at her over the newspaper.

"Is your stomach flipping?" she asks, and gives him her beautiful smile she's flashed to quell him my entire life.

"Yes," he says, and winks at her.

~2~

"I run out of the water, swallowed by complete devastation"

Noble?" I stare out the window as we pass field after field and lose my attention to the crops. I follow them to the horizon, the only boundary between the earth and the sky. The perfect blue meets the green fields as if it's watching over them. This is Noble's world.

God's country.

"Yes?" He brings me back to his truck. I turn to him and watch him drive with the ease that's always a part of him.

"Would you say I'm your best friend? That we're best friends?" Noble takes his eyes off the road to meet mine. I've seen this look before. He's not sure whether to laugh.

"Are you going to give me half a BFF necklace or something?" he asks, as if I am the most ridiculous person he's ever known.

"I was just thinking about how things change."

"Charlotte, what's going on?" He's listening closely now. We pass the cornfields, almost knee-height. How many corn crops have I passed in my lifetime?

I shake my head. "I was just thinking."

"About what?"

About what? "You are one of my closest friends. You, Margo, Jenn, and Sam. And at Rutgers I can't survive without Julia, Violet, and Sydney."

"Where are you going with this?" Now he's worried. Noble turns left and a new set of fields draws my attention.

"What happened to the others? Jason, and Ollie, and Possum? Where are Heather Miller and Dana Davino? Why aren't we friends with them anymore? I went to Jason Leer's birthday party every year of my life until we hit high school, and then I never hung out with him."

"Charlotte, things change—the passage of time, circumstances—but people don't. We're still friends, just old friends. Jason was into the rodeo, and we weren't. We just went in different directions."

Noble turns onto the farm lane leading to his house and crosses the railroad tracks that sever it. An acre and a half back, we pass Jason Leer's house on the left. His truck is parked near the barn separating his and Noble's yards. I swallow hard at the thought of my ankle in Jason's hand.

"Wait here," Noble says, and pulls up near the side door of the farmhouse.

"Why?" I ask, knowing my cheeks are probably flushed. Noble notices and seems confused for the second time today. I'm not making any sense.

"Because my mother will interrogate you about my love life at

Rutgers and we'll never make it to Jenn's." Noble's easy smile lights up his face. *He is my best friend.* "Just wait here, okay?"

Noble leaves me, and I can't take my eyes off Jason's truck. I wonder what he's doing today, what Jenn and Margo will say if I invite him to the lake house with us. The door to Jason's house swings open and hits the side of the house. Anyone else exiting a house that way would indicate anger, but Jason smiles as he strides over to his truck. I watch in delight. Everything is so powerful about him, and I can't take my eyes off him. A chill runs down the back of my neck and I tilt my head to thwart it.

Jason reaches for his truck door and glances back. At the sight of me, he stops. The smile drains from his face. It's replaced with something else. Something coercive. I should lean down in the truck. Crouch down and escape his gaze, but that would be cowardly, and something about Jason Leer brings out the best and worst in me, neither of which is anywhere near fear.

He takes one step toward me as Noble practically skips out of his house. He breezes to the truck and climbs in carrying cucumbers, without even noticing Jason. As he pulls away, he waves at Jason, and I sit in awe of him. We drive a few miles, me trying to understand what Jason does to me and Noble singing along to music without a care in the world. He lowers the volume and examines me.

"Charlotte, what?"

I release myself from all things Jason Leer.

"What if the person you're supposed to be with you've known your whole life? What if they're an old friend?"

Noble's gaze is serious, and that's terrifying.

"An old friend or a best friend?"

"Old, either, does it matter?" This line of questioning is not relaxing him.

"Is this about Brian? Are you second-guessing breaking up with him?"

"No. This is absolutely not about Brian."

Noble studies me. "What you're talking about will change everything. I'm not saying it never happens, just that if it ends, it never ends well."

"Have you ever been with someone you know in your heart is the exact right person for you? That everything swirling around you just moves you closer to that person?"

Noble takes his eyes off the road and looks at me as if I have a unicorn horn growing out of the center of my head.

"Did you get high before I picked you up?"

"No," I say, and lower my head. I'm not making any sense today. None of this makes sense.

"You're scaring me a little."

"I know," I say, and drop the subject. It's a stupid one.

* * *

The drive to Jenn's lake house is about a half hour. Noble and I spend it with the windows down and the music playing. We pull down the long gravel-cut lane winding through the woods and park behind Jenn's and Margo's cars.

A day on the lake is the perfect end to June, I think as I jump out of the truck and grab my bag. The cloudless sky agrees with me. This will be the last summer we're all home together. It seems everyone branches out after their junior year. Jenn has already said she'll be on a beach somewhere full-time and Margo wants to stay at school and take summer classes. I'm not sure what I'll do, but it's not going to be in Salem County if these girls don't come home.

I hand the bag of cucumbers to Jenn and she starts washing them. "Compliments of Noble Sinclair." I give credit where credit is due.

"Oh, Mr. Sinclair? You don't say? I love that you still call him Noble after all these years. Can't just commit to Nick like the rest of us," Jenn says.

"She's stubborn," Noble concludes.

"It's nice to know a farmer. I'm going to make you cucumber salad as thanks," she says.

"I was going to bring some tomatoes, too, but they're about a week out."

"Let's meet back here in a week. I'll make a tomato salad then," she adds, and begins cutting the cucumbers.

"Sam should be here any minute," Margo says, and grabs a cucumber. "Why don't you guys take out the canoe? It's covered in spiders. I couldn't get within three feet of it."

I look out the window at the lake. It's completely still, no signs of life.

* * *

Noble and I sweep the interior of the canoe for webs before pulling it to the water's edge and placing the paddles inside. We step into the water and gingerly board the canoe. We almost tip at Noble's entry, but we right ourselves and set off on our sail with Noble at the bow. His neck and shoulders appear enormous from this vantage point. As he pulls the water with his paddle, his biceps bulge. When we exit the shade of the coast, Noble takes off his shirt and I am in awe.

"How come you don't have a girlfriend?" I ask, and Noble keeps paddling.

"What makes you think I don't?"

"You wouldn't keep something like that from me, would you?" I'm wounded at the suggestion. Noble turns around and his warm, inviting smile confuses me all the more. Why is he alone? Or is he?

"I'm just waiting for the right girl," he says, and paddles with deep strokes that push us from shore. "Until she comes along, I'm trying to meet as many wrong girls as possible," he adds with the naughtiest grin.

"Sounds like a great plan to catch something nasty."

"That's very romantic, Charlotte. Just because things aren't swirling around me, or whatever the hell you were saying earlier, doesn't mean I'm a venereal disease waiting to be contracted."

"Says you," I retort, and continue paddling the canoe. The river is completely empty except for Noble and me. We row close to the shore of a tiny island with no beach. The trees hang over into the water and there are sounds of bugs, and birds, and God knows what else inhabiting it. Noble takes his paddle and pushes us away from the island just as I duck under a branch and we row back to the open water.

"How deep do you think it is here?" I ask.

"I can throw you in so you can find out."

"That won't be necessary," I say, and push my paddle straight down. It touches nothing but water. "Deep," I say, nodding. Noble rocks the canoe from side to side, coming within a few inches of taking on water each time. I don't say a word. I will not give him the satisfaction. Instead I tilt my face to the blue sky and let the sun warm me. It is the most beautiful day. Almost too bright to face it even with my eyes closed. The glare is blinding. Noble bores of tormenting me and begins to row back to the house. I match his paddling and between us the canoe is charging toward home.

I stop rowing as I see Jenn, Margo, Sam, and…Sean standing on the dock.

"What's your brother doing here?" Noble asks, his voice filled with the doom I feel.

"I don't know. Keep rowing." Dread settles at the bottom of my stomach.

When we get close to shore, I can see them clearly, each of them staring at me with unspoken sadness. Their faces scream at me to row the other way. Something horrible has happened. I lay my paddle across my lap and listen as the devastation in Sean's eyes cries out to me. Noble rows us to shore and gets out first, immediately turning around to help me. I run out of the water and face my brother's stricken face.

"Mom and Dad were in a car accident. A delivery truck T-boned them on the Swedesboro Road. Mom was airlifted and is being operated on now." *Where's Dad?* "Get your stuff."

"I'll follow you guys," Margo says.

"I'll drive, Margo. We'll follow you, Sean," Noble says to Sean, and I grab my shoes and climb into Sean's truck. We pull onto the lane, the one I rode in on an hour ago, and everything has changed. None of it for the better.

About the Author

Eliza Freed graduated from Rutgers University and returned to her hometown in rural South Jersey. Her mother encouraged her to take some time and find herself. After three months of searching, she began to bounce checks and her neighbors began to talk; her mother told her to find a job.

She settled into Corporate America, learning systems and practices and the bureaucracy that slows them. Eliza quickly discovered her creativity and gift for storytelling as a corporate trainer and spent years perfecting her presentation skills and studying diversity. It was during that time she became an avid observer of the characters we meet and the heartaches we endure. Her years of study have taught her laughter is the key to survival, even when it's completely inappropriate.

She currently lives in New Jersey with her family and a misbehaving beagle named Odin. An avid swimmer, if Eliza is not with her family and friends, she'd rather be underwater. While she enjoys many genres, she has always been a sucker for a love story...the more screwed up the better.

Learn more at:

ElizaFreed.com

Twitter, @ElizaBFreed

Facebook.com/ElizaFreed